WHAT PRICE? AMERICA?

MICHAEL WHEARY

Published by Calypso Concepts

Printed in the United States of America
by CreateSpace, an Amazon.com company

Cover Design: Calypso Concepts

We hold these truths to be self-evident, that all men are created equal, that they are endowed by their Creator with certain inalienable rights, that among these are life, liberty and the pursuit of happiness.

The Declaration of Independence
1776

WEDNESDAY

1

The twin horned moon clawed through the cerulean sky, casting pale light across the seamy streets of Tijuana, Mexico. Along the smog choked Avenida Revolución, merchants bartered with the departing *norteamericanos* for one last sale in the fierce summer heat. Soon, dusk would ripen to darkness, and the *touristas* would be displaced by others seeking more sinful pleasures within the dimly lit cabarets and shuttered bordellos scattered throughout the city.

Beyond the decadent fringe, lanterns twinkled in the fading light as a group of migrants gathered to cross the border to America. Urban *capitalinos* stood shoulder to shoulder with hinterland farmers, each awaiting their turn to enter the Land of Opportunity. Upon their arrival, hard work and perseverance would allow them to rebuild their lives, as it had for the countless generations of immigrants that preceded them.

José Torres took one last swig of his *cerveza* and tossed the empty can into a nearby industrial drum. The can tumbled off the overfilled container and mingled with the growing pile of litter churned out by the anxiously waiting crowd. He stared at the discarded can for a moment and frowned. *We're the trash of the world,* he mused. *The people nobody wants. Or needs.*

A farmer from the outskirts of Jiquilpan, José had found it difficult to turn a profit on his homestead during the current economic downturn. Without a drastic course of action, he would soon lose the land that had been part of his family for generations. Spurred by a cousin's promise of employment at a central California chicken processing plant, he decided to leave his life and family behind and seek his fortune in America.

As he drifted aimlessly through the milling throngs, he wondered how many migrants shared a plight similar to his own. How many had no marketable skills, no real education, and hoped to survive in a world increasingly defined by greed and corruption.

His meanderings soon brought him towards two men loitering near a mound of moldering tires. Standing atop the heap of cast-off rubber, another man surveyed a group of Border Patrol vehicles parked menacingly on the opposite side of the border.

The man to José's left clapped him enthusiastically on the shoulder. "Hola, señor!" he said amicably. "I am Paulo Cervantes." Paulo was a solidly built man, mid-thirties, with a square jaw and short curly hair. His light blue work shirt stretched tightly across his barrel chested frame; a testament to a life filled with hard physical labor. "What brings you to this fair city today, amigo?"

José shot him a crooked grin. *"Desesperación."*

The stranger to José's right barked out a laugh. "Then you've come to the right place, padré."

José looked the other man over. Younger than Paulo, the stranger had dark, brooding eyes framed by an untrimmed moustache and bushy eyebrows. Tattooed arms bulged under his bright red tee.

"I am Enriqué," he declared. "And who might you be, señor?"

"José Torres. From Jiquilpan."

Enriqué took a moment to study José. He looked to be around thirty, with coarse black hair and a broad flattened face. His head looked a bit large on his stocky, well-muscled body. "Ahhh . . . Jiquilpan," he said. "You've come a long way, señor."

"Si," José replied. "And I won't be stopped now." His gaze shifted towards a steel framed fence towering a short distance away.

Enriqué and Paulo followed his gaze. Less than a hundred yards away, a ten-foot high barrier erected by the U.S. Customs and Border Protection agency stood between the migrants and their intended destination. Stretching from the mesas east of Mexicali to the breakers of the Pacific Ocean, *La Frontera* was little more than an annoyance for those determined to cross north.

"I know how you feel," Paulo muttered. "I've come all the way from Zacatecas to provide for my family. A nephew in Fresno has offered to put me up until I can find a job there."

"What kind of work are you hoping to find?" José asked.

Paulo's face tightened. "There's only one kind of *chamba* for those who are *indocumentado,* amigo. The work that no one else wants to do. Hours and hours of backbreaking labor with little pay and an even smaller chance for advancement."

José shot him a puzzled look. "But, isn't America known as the land of opportunity?"

Paulo chuckled. "The opportunities are there–for those who have the skills, and for those that speak the language. But, most of the work is part time–and pays far less than you might expect." He gave a sour smile and shrugged. "But, beggars can't be choosers when you have mouths to feed."

"What about Mexico City?" José asked. "I heard there were jobs there that–"

Paulo waved him off. "No, señor. There's . . . nothing there." He looked up at the man straddling the mound of tires and shouted. "Julio! Have you got time to talk about your *experiencias* in Mexico City?"

A tall, lanky man with slicked black hair and a pencil thin moustache scrambled down the stack of tires to join them. "Time is *all* I have," Julio said curtly. He thrust a cigarette between his lips and regarded José with a wary eye. "What would you like to know, señor?"

"What's the job market like in Mexico City?"

Julio lighted his cigarette and blew a stream of smoke into the hot, dry air. "I was a financial advisor in Mexico City when the economy melted down at the end of the last decade. Virtually overnight, my clients' investments evaporated and so did my career. But it was not just the financial industry that took a hit when the economy collapsed. Within a few years, many others with respectable professions soon found themselves out on the street."

"Now can you see why we must go to America, José?" Paulo said. "If the educated among us can't find jobs in our country, how can someone with limited skills hope to survive?"

José pulled on his chin. "Perhaps our government could–"

"El Govierno!" Julio spat. "El Govierno is the *reason* we are here! They sold our industries to foreign investors and did nothing while our economy crashed and burned. Their inept policies have failed time and again to provide jobs for those that need it most." A look of disgust crossed his face. "Don't count on the government to change things, señor. If we want to bring real change to our society, we're going to have to change it ourselves."

"Don't talk like some big shot *revolucionario*, Julio," Enriqué said. "We still have the freedom to–"

"Let me tell you about your *freedom*, Enriqué. The only freedom we have is to take jobs no Americano will accept, and leave behind our homes, our culture, and our . . . dignity . . . in the process." He gave a bitter laugh. "Is that the price we must pay for your . . . freedom?"

Enrique's eyes dropped. "What choice do we have, Julio? We have families to feed."

"And we *will* feed them, amigo. But, things must change so our children–or their children–aren't forced into making the same sacrifices we face today."

José glanced nervously at several Border Patrol trucks parked across the border. "It's getting dark. Do any of you have a plan to cross the border?"

"Years ago it was easy," Paulo said, "one could simply cross the river and hop on a trolley into San Diego. From there, one could catch a bus or train bound for Los Angeles or points beyond. But now, it is much more difficult. *La Migra's* eyes are everywhere." He pointed towards a group of helicopters probing the mesas north of the city. "There they are . . . waiting to hunt us down. They look at us as we would look at a mosquito–just another pest that needs to be swatted away."

"Is there some way for this *mosquito* to bite back?" José asked.

A smile played across Paulo's face. "There are ways. Come."

The quartet ventured into the night, carrying their meager possessions in nylon knapsacks strung across their backs. They slowly drifted east–past poverty-stricken *barrios*, past graffiti streaked *maquiladoras*–until the last vestiges of the city were left behind. Weed choked fields yielded to pockmarked plateaus and desiccated arroyos tumbling dryly towards the sea. Along the horizon, the border fence cut a ghostly gray scar against the onyx sky as it faded into the wilderness.

As the migrants scurried across a dried out streambed, Paulo pointed towards a gentle slope several hundred yards away. "We'll cross over there–at the top of that hill."

José shot him a puzzled look. "Where? I don't see anything."

Paulo smiled wryly. "Trust me, amigo. Wait here until I signal." Scampering up the slope towards the base of the fence, Paulo scuffed at the ground until a faint rectangular edge was revealed. He waved for the others to join him.

"I'll need your help to move this," Paulo said. "Grab the edges of the panel and move it away from the fence."

Enriqué grunted as he lifted the rectangular slab off the ground. "*Mierda*, this thing is heavy. What the hell is it, Paulo?"

"A part of the fence," Paulo replied. "The Americanos left a few pieces laying around after they built the fence, so we . . . borrowed . . . one to cover the entrance to the tunnel."

Julio's eyebrow rose. *"Tunnel?"* He stepped back and peered anxiously into the abyss. "Is it . . . safe?"

Paulo nodded. "It's not as deep as it looks." To demonstrate, he climbed down the hole and turned on a flashlight, casting a diffused glow throughout the four-foot wide shaft. "I hope none of you are claustrophobic," he said dryly.

Julio stooped down and entered the tunnel, followed by José and Enriqué. The metal plate was dragged back over the entrance, entombing the quartet within. Their journey through the tunnel was less than thirty feet, but it felt like an eternity every time chunks of clay crumbled onto their heads.

"Are we fuckin' there yet?" Enriqué grumbled.

"Quit your bitchin', amigo." Julio said. "We're almost through."

"I can't help it–amigo. I'm staring at José's *asno*, and I don't think he changed his shorts today."

Laughter echoed throughout the dimly lit tunnel, temporarily diffusing their anxiety.

Several uneasy minutes later, Paulo reached the end of the shaft and pushed aside several dried tumbleweeds camouflaging the exit. He peered over the top of the hole and scanned the immediate vicinity for the Border Patrol. At the moment, La Migra appeared to be concentrating their surveillance along the outskirts of the city, but it was not unusual for scouting parties to scour the backcountry in search of migrants avoiding detection.

Bounding from the tunnel, Paulo extended his hand downward. "Hurry!" he whispered. "The coast is clear for the moment."

The other three men scrambled out of the hole and looked expectantly towards Paulo for guidance. He met their gaze and pointed towards the mesas in the distance. "This is where we say goodbye," he said softly. "We'll have a better chance at success if we split up and make our way through the canyons alone."

José clasped Paulo's shoulder. "Gracias, amigo. May your journey– and your life–be successful."

"And yours as well, José." He flashed the group a smile. "Maybe we'll meet again . . . someday."

The others nodded politely; acutely aware the chance of any future reunion was nonexistent.

Julio looked anxiously towards the city. "We'd better get moving. Two of those choppers are headed right this way."

The quartet bid hasty farewells and scattered through the maze of canyons, their chances of success left to the whims of Fate.

José groped his way cautiously down a coarse gravel pathway, using the faint glow from the moon to guide him through the deepening darkness of the canyon. Navigating the steep terrain became increasingly difficult as his exposed skin became the target of every razor sharp plant that made the environment their home.

A loud roar reverberated at the far end of the canyon and José grew alarmed as a helicopter headed his way. He wedged his body into a furrow of the canyon wall, hoping to become as inconspicuous as possible. The chopper moved slowly through the craggy ravine, like an oversized dragonfly searching for its prey. Squeezing his body tighter into the scarred canyon wall, José blinked the sweat from his eyes as he watched the mechanized beast soar directly overhead.

Several seconds later, the helicopter drifted past his location and José let out a sigh of relief. *Mierda, that was close. La Migra almost had me–*

And then, without warning, the night exploded into day.

2

Ryan Rysinski inched cautiously along the battered Ford Expedition's rear fender, a relic from the previous decade when sport utility vehicles were the *transporte du jour*. He leaned out from the hulking truck to catch a glimpse of the driver in the side view mirror, but the darkly tinted windows made any chance of identification impossible.

This driver's window tint is way above the legal limit, he thought to himself as he unclipped the strap on his holster and edged closer towards the driver's door. Behind him, the cruiser's flashing lightbar reflected off the truck's smoked glass like a frenzied disco mirrorball.

Stopping just short of the door, he rapped on the window with his baton. As the driver's side window curled slowly downward, two diametric scenarios dashed through his adrenalin-surged mind. *Who will it be tonight? The harried mom overwhelmed by her kids or the fugitive lying in wait with a shotgun in his hand?*

As soon as the window snugged into the door, Ryan rushed forward, his hand curled tightly around the butt of his firearm. *Who will it be tonight—the lady or the tiger?*

He exhaled audibly as an antsy wisp of a man stared numbly back at him through a pair of thick lensed glasses. "What s-s-seems to be the pr-problem, officer?" he managed to stutter out while weaving a hand through his thinning brown hair.

Ryan directed his flashlight into the truck's cabin. "Your driver's license and registration, please." He suppressed a smile as his gaze drifted over the errant motorist's face. In his eyes, the driver strongly resembled Barney Fife, the bumbling deputy with a heart of gold whose misguided forays caused constant consternation for the fictional town of Mayberry's sheriff.

The motorist passed the documents towards Ryan's waiting hand. "I wasn't sp-speeding, officer," he said meekly. "I'm s-sure of it."

Ryan glanced at the registration and withdrew the citation pad from his belt. He began jotting information into the appropriate sections.

"I said I wasn't sp-speeding, officer," he pleaded a little more firmly.

"I never said you were–sir." He looked the driver over. "Did you know your registration had expired?"

Anxiety touched the driver's face. *"Expired?"*

"Back in April–over two months ago. Didn't you get a renewal notice?"

"I don't r-remember," he mumbled. "You're giving me a t-ticket for that?"

Ryan scribbled several more words and tore the slip from the pad. "Not *this* time," he said. "But, you're getting a warning. Make sure you take care of it–pronto."

The driver took the slip and smiled weakly. "Th-thank you, officer. I'll get it taken care of r-right away."

"There's one more thing you'll need to take care of, while you're at it."

The driver frowned. "What's th-that, officer?"

"Your window tint is darker than the legal limit allowed in California. I'll have to give you an inspection ticket to get it fixed."

"I'll need to re-remove the tint?"

"It's really for your own safety, sir. A less . . . *experienced* officer could feel threatened if they can't see who's behind the wheel during a routine traffic stop."

"But, that will tie up my truck for a day while they st-strip and re-tint the windows." He shot Ryan a sideways glance. "Isn't there s-s-some other solution?"

Ryan's eyebrow twitched. "What did you have in mind, sir?"

The driver pulled a fifty-dollar bill from his wallet and thrust it towards Ryan. "A little s-something for your t-time?"

Ryan's eyes narrowed. *How freakin' pathetic. I better end this charade before Barney winds up in the hoosegow.* "Thanks for the offer, but the department frowns on this kind of–transaction."

The driver met Ryan's gaze and lowered his hand.

Ryan scrawled his signature on the ticket and handed it to the repentant motorist. "Drive carefully, sir," he said curtly. "It's a dangerous world out there."

3

Standing in a dimly lit Arlington Heights parking lot, KNBS reporter Karen Mitchell could barely suppress her anger as she delivered her narrative for the late night news. "According to police, this evening's tragedy occurred when suspected gang members opened fire at a Mexican restaurant on Pico Boulevard, fatally injuring a six-year old boy and wounding two others seated at a nearby table. The motive behind the shooting has not been determined, but the police believe it is gang related. Any witnesses to the crime are urged to contact the LAPD or their local Sheriff's Department. For Channel Six News . . . this is Karen Mitchell."

Kyle Martin snapped off the light and lowered his camera. "That's a wrap, Karen." He watched dispassionately as the ambulance drove out of the parking lot and headed towards the county morgue. "Looks like another one bit the dust."

Karen glared at her cameraman but remained silent. Kyle was a mid-twenties throwback to sixties hippiedom with his long, scraggly hair and goatee that constantly needed trimming. A devoted nonconformist and Karmic enthusiast, the daily travails of life failed to unnerve his chipper soul. "You feel like grabbin' a couple brews after we finish tonight's segments?" he asked amicably.

She gave a sour smile. "Not tonight, Kyle. It's been a really long day."

Kyle shrugged. "No problemo." He glanced at his watch and frowned. "*Shit!* We better get back to the station before Stan rips us a new one."

The ride back to the studio was only remarkable for its silence as Karen brooded over her just wrapped broadcast. *A birthday celebration at the neighborhood restaurant. A hail of bullets fired from a cruising sedan. A six-year old boy whose life ended much too soon.* The image of the crimson streaked sheet shoved unceremoniously into the ambulance would haunt her for a long, long time. She watched with growing exasperation as Kyle hummed to a tune playing on the radio, apparently unaffected by the evening's tragedy. *Doesn't anything faze you, you callous bastard?*

Twenty minutes later, they entered the studio and began editing their assignments for the late night news. Concern tinged Kyle's face as he watched Karen jot some notes on a legal pad. She hadn't spoken a word since they left the restaurant parking lot. "Is anything wrong, Karen?" he asked softly.

Karen kept her eyes glued to the pad. "No," she said curtly. "*Should* there be anything wrong?"

Kyle looked on but remained silent.

She put down her pen and sighed. "It's that six-year-old boy . . . at the restaurant. I can't shake his death from my mind."

"This isn't the first fatality we've covered."

"I know." Her eyes dropped. "Maybe I should consider another line of work."

"Don't be ridiculous–you're a hell of a reporter."

"Then why can't I be *objective* about this? Nothing seems to make sense any more."

"The world's not supposed to make any sense."

She looked up sharply. "Is that why you don't . . . care?"

He ran a hand over his face and exhaled loudly. "No, it's because

I grew up in a neighborhood just like that boy and watched several of my own friends–die." His expression grew dour. "Maybe that explains why I feel the way I do. Why I no longer seem to . . . care. If something's gonna happen, it's gonna happen–and there's nothing you can do to change things."

"That fatalistic attitude may work for you, but what about the rest of the kids growing up in violent neighborhoods? What happens to them when they become adults?"

Kyle shrugged.

"What kind of *answer* is that?" she chided.

"What can we do, Karen? We can't change the way people think–or feel."

"No, of course not. But you're wrong about being powerless to act. If each of us becomes more involved–more *outraged* at what's happening–things will eventually change."

"Ahhh . . . the politicians have been promising us a better world for years. Their empty pledges never made any difference in the neighborhood where I grew up."

"That's because the violence rarely affects them personally. Our elected elite are so wrapped up in their corporate sweetened cocoons that they're totally oblivious of the carnage playing out in our communities every day."

"And just how do we make them–listen?" he asked drolly.

"We can start by changing the public's perception of violence. The rapes, the murders, the naked *butchery* we see flashed across the screen has become nothing more than background noise in Americans' daily lives. At some point, our tolerance for savagery must end. There must come a time when the people of this country stand up like Howard Beale and declare 'We're mad as hell and we're not going to take it anymore!'"

Kyle pulled on his beard and frowned. "That time may never come."

Karen gave a reluctant nod. "You're probably right." A wave of sadness washed over her face. "You know, we're partly to blame for the apathy because we continuously feed the public's craving for depravity. The so called respectable media are no more credible than the bottom-feeding tabloids anymore."

"We don't make the news, Karen—all we do is report it."

"But, we have a *choice* on what to report, don't we? Is what we feed our viewers *really* news? Tell me, how do you feel about exposing some poor bastard's misfortune to millions of viewers everyday?"

"I really don't think about it, to be honest with you."

"Well, I must be in the minority, because I think about it almost every day." Her voice softened to a whisper. "Sometimes at night, when I try to fall asleep, I'm . . . haunted by certain incidents that play back in my mind."

Kyle's eyebrow arched upward. "What are you talking about?"

"You know, the events we've seen so often that they've become etched upon our collective mind. The Kennedy assassination, the Challenger explosion, 9-11, the Seattle Slaughter . . ."

He nodded. "They're definitely . . . disturbing."

"Are *you* disturbed by them?"

"I try not to think about it too much."

She cocked her head. "Why?"

"What's past . . . is past."

"Don't you ever think about how many people's lives were changed by these events—or how they've changed our outlook on life forever?"

Kyle gave a slight headshake. "Life is confusing enough. Why complicate it even more?"

Karen smiled wanly. "Yeah, I guess you're right. Why complicate it . . . even more."

4

Andrew Landis turned from the panoramic window of his office and faced the foppish flunky who had just walked through the door. "Not one fucking cent more!" he growled. "Ron's already pissed away *enough* of my money."

Harry Bennett took a step back and frowned. "But he needs the additional funds to–"

Andrew waved him off. "I don't care *what* he needs. This project is already twenty million over budget and a month behind schedule. The only way he'll see another dime is if it comes from his own damn pocket."

"He's not going to like that option," Bennett said.

Andrew's eyes narrowed. "You *heard* me."

Bennett met Andrew's gaze and forced a smile. "I'll let Mister Burgess know how you–feel."

Andrew sneered as he watched the door close behind his director's assistant. In a past life, he would have been the messenger getting his hide roasted. *But that was a long time ago,* he mused. He lighted an imported Cuban cigar and moved his gaze across the sparkling lights of the city. *When I was a . . . nothing . . . in this town.*

Time had been kind to him since his arrival in Tinseltown nearly three decades ago. His innate ability to recognize talent and creativity made him one of the most powerful independent producers in the motion picture industry.

He took a drag from his Cohíba and blew a stream of smoke towards the ceiling. *Was it worth it?* He swiveled around and looked at the luxurious trappings of his tony Century City office. *Yes*, he thought, without any hint of doubt. His insight and business acumen had allowed him to acquire the expected accoutrements associated with an opulent lifestyle: several palatial mansions, a fleet of collectible automobiles, a sleek personal jet, and a stately yacht were the culmination of a life continuously fought from a childhood of despair.

Andrew's face tightened as he recalled a long-buried memory from his childhood. *Yes, it was a long time ago.* He moved the cigar from his face and stared at the reflection in the window. Now nearing fifty, his dark featured face and piercing eyes lent him a look of simmering intimidation. An impeccably tailored appearance reflected his attention to detail in the world of business–and in life.

But, that affinity for thoroughness was not without its price. His latest project was causing him considerable distress, despite his tendencies to micro-manage every step of the production process.

Trouble reared its ugly head since the project began. One of Hollywood's most gifted screenwriters instigated the fiasco by botching the adaptation of a novel Andrew had secured from an aspiring young writer. The subtleties and characterizations of the original story were lost in the conversion to the big screen, turning it into an unmitigated piece of trash.

He fired the hack and turned the bungled script over to a succession of screenwriters in a valiant attempt to recapture the novel's originality. Each successively failed until Andrew found an unknown writer who redrafted the novel to his satisfaction.

Finding the right actors for the lead roles also proved to be an unrelenting farce. Several A-list stars were available, but Andrew did not feel their self-serving attitude was in the best interest of the project. In the end, most of the roles were doled out to a bevy of relatively obscure actors with little previous acting experience.

Looking for a director who could bring his vision to the screen turned out to be the most demanding debacle of all. After an exhaustive search, the young, but brilliant Ron Burgess was brought on board to oversee the project. Initially, the wunderkind director adapted well to bringing his project to fruition, but the intricacies of a large-scale production soon overwhelmed him. His conciliatory style led to constant slowdowns and multiple reshoots, forcing Andrew to hire an assistant director to keep costs in line. Though progressing well from an artistic standpoint, his film was slipping further behind its projected time and budget. And now, Bennett's ill-timed news dashed any hope he had for moving the film into post-production by the end of the week.

Andrew's gaze rested on the phone atop his desk. *It's time I kicked some ass.* He placed his cigar in the ashtray and punched his director's number on the phone.

Several seconds later, Ron's nasally tinged voice chirped through the line. "Hey, Andrew. How are you–"

"Skip the *pleasantries,* Ron. What the hell's going on with my project?"

A pause. "What are you talking–"

"Why did you send Bennett over here looking for a handout?"

"Didn't he tell you? I need to shoot some additional scenes to–"

"Cut the friggin' *bullshit,* Ron. When do you expect to move this project into post?"

"Another week or two." A pause. "By then, everything should meet my . . . approval."

"Let's forget about your *personal* gratification for a moment and concentrate on the big picture. Is this extra footage that Bennett requested necessary?"

"Not *absolutely* necessary. The screenwriter, with my input, felt the new scenes would enhance the continuity of the story and provide a more credible ending. However, we had to . . . alter . . . part of the original script to make it all come together."

Andrew clutched the phone tightly in his hand. *"What?"* he growled. "You changed the script without telling me?"

"We didn't *change* things, Andrew, we only made some minor . . . modifications." He paused for several seconds. "I'm sure you'll be pleased with the results."

Andrew could barely restrain his anger. "From now on, at least have the *courtesy* to let me know before you change things." His voice hardened. "Is that *fucking* clear?"

Before Ron could reply, Andrew hurled the phone across the room and watched with smug satisfaction as it shattered against the wall. He snatched his cigar from the ashtray and turned to look at the twinkling lights of the city.

But, I'm not a nothing . . . anymore.

5

ear gripped José's face as the helicopter's searchlight seared his eyes. *There's nowhere to run! What will happen to me now?* His eyes turned wild–he had heard enough horrific tales of the Americano prisons to last him a lifetime.

Eighty feet overhead, the helicopter's pilot watched José's plight with bored amusement. "Looks like another slow night, eh Jim?" Ben Jacobs said.

Jim Hansen, the chopper's copilot, nodded as he looked at José's ghostly silhouette in the Forward Looking Infrared scope. On the scope's digitally enhanced screen, José's heat signature stood out from the cool desert background like a firefly in a pitch-black night. "Yeah, you'd think the *tonks* would have learned that we don't want them here by now."

Jacobs shot him a grin. "You know, I kinda miss the good old days when we had to go after them on foot. Now, tech-nol-o-gy roots out the beaners as soon as they step across the border." He sighed. "It just ain't the same anymore . . . the thrill of the hunt is gone."

"I know what you mean. You used to be able to shoot the SOBs and not give a rat's ass about it. Now, everything we do has to be friggin' *documented.*" He pointed through the chopper's bulletproof canopy at

José. "Does *Paco* really think the grass is gonna be any greener on this side of the fence?"

"Look at the bright side, Jim. If Paco didn't look for greener pastures, you and I would soon be out of a job."

Hansen nodded slowly. "There's nothing like a little job security–especially in this shitty economy." He switched on the radio to contact the Brown Field Station with their coordinates. "Brown Field, this is Apache SV4. We have one alien tagged near the southeast junction of sector eight. Will maintain contact until ground units have situation in hand. Over."

A gruff sounding voice crackled through Hansen's headset. "This is patrol vehicle A45. I see you trackin' to the southeast and will head over to sector eight to apprehend the suspect."

"A.J., is that you?" Jacobs inquired. "I thought you were on leave this week."

"Yeah, I thought so too until my partner done got himself hurt yesterday."

"The Chief is hurt?" Hansen asked. "How bad?"

"Oh, he'll be all right," A.J. grumbled. "He tried to take down two tonks all by himself and one was packin' a blade in his sweatsuit. When the Chief wasn't payin' attention, the beaner spun around and stuck him in the chest. The dumb spic then ran off towards the canyon but didn't manage to get very far."

"What happened?" Jacobs asked.

"The Chief was standin' there with this–*surprised look*–on his face. He's lookin' down at his chest and couldn't *believe* that this bad boy tried to take him out. Well, you know the Chief–all that shit does is piss him off. The poor spic got about a hundred yards before the Chief caught up to him and shoved his face in the dirt. By the time we caught up to 'em, half the dumb fuck's nose was scraped away."

Jacobs whistled. "Is he going be all right?"

"That depends on who you're talkin' about," A.J. said, snickering. "Yeah, the Chief was lucky this time–not much more than a scratch. A few stitches, a little rest, and he'll be his nasty ol' self in no time."

"Those Injuns are tough motherfuckers," Jacobs said. "When he gets back to work, tell him not to take the job so seriously."

"Yeah, like he'd give a shit," A.J. said. "So what's the scoop on the wetback?"

"We're tracking him in sector eight just beyond Giclee Canyon."

"All right, I'll round him up after he leaves the ravine. I hate gettin' them damn cactus thorns stuck in my ass."

"Roger on that. We'll maintain contact until the suspect is apprehended. Over and out."

A voice blared from the helicopter's outboard speakers, momentarily startling José. "Stay where you are–help will be here shortly."

José held his hand up and squinted into the searchlight, a confused expression on his face.

"No te muevas, quédate donde estás," the voice repeated in Spanish.

José nodded mutely as the chopper's blades lashed sand across his body. Seconds later, the copter doused its searchlight and climbed above the canyon walls, leaving José enveloped in darkness.

Another floodlight slashed through the darkness and focused on José. A.J. stood on the edge of the ravine and brought a megaphone to his face. "Okay, amigo–get your *asno* up here. Now!"

A.J.'s partner Tom Roberts patted José down when he reached the top of the ravine. "Just where you from–*Paco?*" he asked brusquely.

"Save your breath, Tom," A.J. said. "Paco don't understand a word you're sayin'."

Roberts nodded. "Yeah, I know." He gave a disgusted look and muscled José into the Chevrolet Tahoe's backseat. "What kind of job does this *pollo* hope to find if he can't speak *Inglés?*"

"You don't need no degree in English to pick produce or scrub down toilets," A.J. replied.

The two men clambered aboard the truck and headed towards the Brown Field Station. Through the truck's rear window, José watched with despair at the country he had tried to leave behind.

6

itting at a picnic table outside a brightly colored taqueria on Venice Boulevard, Ryan was mid-bite into his burrito when his cruiser's radio crackled to life. "All units–this is Wilshire. Code Three–shots fired–vicinity of West Pico and Cochran Avenue."

He looked at his half-eaten burrito and frowned. *It never freakin' fails.* Tossing the remainder of his meal into the trash, he scrambled inside the patrol car and yanked the microphone from its cradle. "This is unit 7L731, Wilshire. En route from LaBrea and Washington."

Switching on the siren and lightbar, Ryan swung the cruiser out of the parking lot and into northbound LaBrea Avenue–the familiar rush of adrenaline surging through his body. In less than a minute, he was hurtling west down Pico Boulevard when a maroon Monte Carlo with its headlights off shot by his cruiser in the opposite direction.

Spinning his vehicle around the roadway in a smooth 180-degree arc, Ryan smiled briefly as the stench of charred rubber filled the cruiser's cabin. "Wilshire, this is unit 7L731. Currently in pursuit of a dark red Chevrolet Monte Carlo traveling east on Pico. License number–*damn*, the plate's been removed. Suspects heading east towards Crenshaw. Requesting backup."

"Roger, 7L731," Dispatch replied. "Code one-hundred. All units near

Pico and Crenshaw respond."

Two patrol vehicles quickly joined the chase. "Wilshire, this is unit 7A694 responding from Venice and Arlington Avenue."

"Unit 7L475 southbound on Crenshaw near Olympic responding Wilshire."

Ryan's mouth turned upward in a grin as his cruiser nipped at the heels of the suspect's vehicle. *It looks like we're going to have a little party tonight.* "Wilshire, unit 7L731 proceeding south on Crenshaw. Suspects approximately a half-mile from the Rosa Parks Freeway. Any update on the 245?"

"7L731, this is Wilshire. Officers searching the vicinity right now. Current status unknown."

"Copy that, Wilshire. Keep me posted."

"Roger your location, 7L731. Maintain pursuit."

Suddenly, the Monte Carlo veered right, clipping a lamppost as it shot down the on-ramp towards the freeway.

Ryan shook his head and scowled. *What the—are those assholes out to kill someone?*

Tires squealed as Ryan swerved his vehicle towards the on ramp. The rear of his black and white spun to the left and slammed violently against the curb.

A look of disgust crossed Ryan's face. *Damn, where'd you learn to drive, Rysinski?* He mashed the pedal to the floor and the cruiser streaked down the on ramp towards its prey. "Wilshire, this is 7L731. Suspects heading west on Rosa Parks Freeway towards La Brea Avenue."

"Roger 7L731, suspects' vehicle currently headed west on Rosa Parks Freeway."

With the Monte Carlo safely in view, Ryan backed off the throttle and increased the distance between him and the suspects' vehicle. Due to a growing number of injuries and lawsuits in the Los Angeles County, the local law enforcement agencies had changed vehicle pursuit tactics in deference to civilian safety. A pursuit was to be given up if the chargeable offense was not worth injuring other drivers or the police. But in this case, the suspects were wanted for a possible homicide, so the pursuit would continue until the suspects were apprehended.

The Monte Carlo swerved abruptly across two lanes of traffic towards the Washington Boulevard exit, barely missing another vehicle as it careened down the off-ramp. When the vehicle reached the bottom of the ramp, the driver ignored the signal and shot across Washington Boulevard, clipping the rear of a Honda Accord traveling through the intersection.

As Ryan came to the end of the off ramp, he slowed and glanced at the damaged Accord. "Wilshire, send an ambulance to Rosa Parks eastbound off ramp at Washington Boulevard. Possible injury." His eyes narrowed as he watched the suspects speed down the thoroughfare. *Just one more nail in your coffin, assholes.*

The three police interceptors decreased their speed relative to the traffic as they continued their pursuit on Washington Boulevard. Several blocks ahead of the suspects' vehicle, Ryan watched smugly as six SUVs from the Sheriff's Department set up a barricade on the roadway, forcing the Monte Carlo to a crawl.

Seconds later, the Monte Carlo came to a stop and four men tumbled out of the car waving their hands in the air. The three cruisers drew cautiously behind the suspects vehicle, lightbars flashing ferociously in the still summer night.

Ryan edged his cruiser alongside the suspects' car, then climbed out of his vehicle with his pistol drawn. As he crouched behind the door and leveled his firearm, the radio suddenly sparked to life. "Unit 7L731, this is Wilshire with an update on the 245."

Ryan swiped at his shoulder microphone. "Proceed."

After Dispatch relayed the message, Ryan rose from behind the door and signaled his fellow officers for assistance. The four men were quickly handcuffed while Ryan read them their rights. "You are under arrest for attempted murder. You have the right to remain silent. Anything you say can and will be used against you in a court of law . . ."

7

Cruising up the Pacific Coast Highway to his posh beachside estate, Andrew moved his gaze across the upscale homes ringing the roadway. Lights shimmered brightly in the McMansions curtained windows; the denizens within lavishly isolated from the uncertainties of an increasingly troubled world.

Rounding a curve on Malibu Road, Andrew's eyes rested upon the familiar silhouette of home. An immense collection of ivory colored cubes and gleaming metals, it stood conspicuously against its neighbors in a town known for its hedonistic excess.

Andrew inched his Mercedes coupe into the expansive four-car garage and entered his home. The living room was a spacious affair of soaring walls, sweeping skylights and a panoramic wall of glass framing the sea. Scattered pools of light illuminated contemporary styled furniture and eclectic sculptures imported from all over the world. A collection of vibrant abstract paintings glittered brightly on the walls, lending the only splash of color to the otherwise monochromatic room.

Tossing his briefcase on a nearby chair, Andrew strolled towards the liquor cabinet and poured himself a drink. He unbuttoned his shirt and stepped onto the teak framed balcony, taking a moment to savor the cool breeze drifting off the ocean. In the distance, a sliver of a moon shimmered above the ebony tossed sea.

As he watched the waves lash against the shoreline, Andrew took a healthy swallow from his drink and reflected on life. By most measures, he would be considered a success, as wealth and power were universally admired goals the world over. And yet, there were lingering doubts about the paths he had chosen, and an ever-growing angst that he would never be content regardless of how much fortune and influence he achieved.

On the long road to the good life, Andrew governed his actions by the Consequentialistic ideology put forth in the proverb *"The ends justify the means."* Though most of his success had resulted from personal sacrifice and perseverance, there were times when individuals had been manipulated or crushed in order to achieve his long-term goals.

He took another sip from his drink and smiled. *Sure, I've made a few enemies over the years, but what successful businessman doesn't have an enemy or two?*

Turning his gaze towards the sea, Andrew mused upon his less than virtuous journey. Only yesterday it seemed, but the odyssey had begun nearly five decades ago in a dilapidated trailer park in West Virginia. His parents had divorced when he was eight, but Andrew could still vividly recall the beatings he endured from his drunken father's fists. Hard times descended after his parents' acrimonious split, and he and his mother slowly made their way west through a succession of towns best forgotten. On numerous occasions his mother begged, borrowed, and sometimes stole to keep a roof over their heads, and throughout it all, hunger was a constant companion in their lives. During this transitory time in his life he was a perpetual outcast at school and never knew the meaning of the word–friend.

They settled in Burbank when Andrew entered his teens, and he became a devout pupil of the visual arts in his junior year of high school.

To assuage his thirst for information on the movie industry, he soon found himself devouring any material he could find at the local libraries or bookstores. By the end of the year, he directed a crude movie from a script he had developed with a classmate. Critically acclaimed by his class, he was voted Best Director at the school's awards ceremony. For the first time in a life filled with solitude and rejection, Andrew knew what it meant to–belong.

Once he was able to drive, Andrew learned about the trade by garnering the friendships of crew members working on the sets of the major film studios. In time, he understood how sound, lighting, and camera effects came together in the production process.

After he graduated with honors from his high school, Andrew spent most of his time on studio lots trying to be noticed by the management elite. Before long, he secured a position as a producer's assistant and learned the value of networking in the industry. He worked his way up through the ranks using the knowledge and contacts he acquired and eventually became one of the biggest independent producers in town.

Andrew took a deep breath and exhaled. *Was it really that long ago? Sometimes, it seems like–yesterday.* He downed the last of his drink and gazed somberly at the star streaked sky. *How many times has man looked up in the heavens and questioned his place in the universe? How often has he longed to know–the answer?*

He looked into his empty glass and frowned. *And what if there is . . . no answer?*

8

osé gazed glumly at the Brown Field Station as it swept into view. A gray slab of concrete surrounded by a razor wire fence, it rose menacingly into the hazy night sky. Several shuttles loitered in the parking lot on the left of the building, their occupants faces framed against the windows in portraits of despair.

The Border Patrol truck stopped in front of a brightly lit entrance-way, and the agents escorted José into the building. Inside the sterile, beige colored interior, José saw several men sequestered inside a small holding area, but thankfully, none were from the group he befriended several hours earlier.

A sly smile crept across José's face. *I hope Paulo and the others made it through safely.*

A.J. led José towards a large wooden bench at the far side of the room. "Have a seat, Paco," he said gruffly.

Roberts looked at A.J. and hooked a thumb over his shoulder. "I'll get started on the paperwork."

"Better you than me," A.J. grumbled.

Roberts took a seat at his desk and called up the requisite forms on his computer screen. Anita Coleman, the shift supervisor, strolled over to his desk and wrapped her arm around his shoulder. "How's it going tonight, Tom?" she whispered into his ear.

Roberts grunted. "The same old shit. The beaners never learn."

"Well, they must be learning *something* because our case load has dropped significantly in the last year. Since Congress passed the National Identification Act, we finally have the resources we need to do our job."

He turned his head and nodded. "It's sure made our jobs easier. In less time then it takes to sing *La Cucaracha*, the tonks are put on a bus and sent back to where they came from."

The National Identification Act was whisked through a patriotically charged Congress after a terrorist strike at the fourth game of the World Series in Seattle revealed serious flaws in America's identification system. The creation of a national identification card–the Citizen Access Resource Document–or CARD as it was commonly known, instituted a uniform standard of authentication throughout the country. Incorporating a holographic retinal scan as the basis for secure identification, each individual's unique identification code was stored on servers throughout the country to ensure verification of an individual as needed by an authorized agency.

Passage of the act had been fought vigorously by the ACLU as an invasion of individual privacy rights guaranteed under the Ninth Amendment of the Constitution. In the landmark case *Lambert v. United States*, the U.S. Supreme Court ruled in a 5-4 vote that national security concerns overrode the rights of individual privacy. In protest of the ruling, civil rights leaders across the country declared the date of the law's enaction as 'Big Brother Day.'

Anita glanced over his shoulder at the computer screen. "What's on your log for tonight?"

"Not much," Roberts said. "Just some schmuck we snagged over in sector eight." He took a swig from his coffee mug and winced. "No CARD . . . limited English . . . what he hoped to find in this country is a mystery to me."

She patted his arm. "You don't need to be Sherlock Holmes to figure it out. They must feel it's worth the risk or they wouldn't bother coming here."

"I suppose," he muttered. "But ever since the economy tanked back in '08 there ain't *shit* out there in the job market. A friend of mine has a friggin' MBA, and the only job he could find is workin' as a cashier at a convenience store." He shook his head and frowned. "If my friend can't find a decent job, why does *Paco* think he will?"

"Desperate people take desperate chances, Tom. Sometimes you have . . . no other choice."

He looked up sharply. "Everyone has a choice, Anita. Paco just made the *wrong* choice."

Anita compressed her lips and nodded. "Perhaps." She stood upright and gave his shoulder a squeeze. "But, the Paco's of the world have a right to live their lives, too."

9

aren slept fitfully as images from the shooting earlier this evening flashed through her mind. *A young boy's life ended tonight for no reason. And yet, where is the outrage–the anger? Why aren't people out on the street demanding an end to the violence?*

She flipped over on her back and stared at the ceiling. *Was Kyle right? Has life become so complicated that people no longer care?* A frown traced her lips. *And to think I came to the big city to leave my troubles behind.*

Karen's past began nearly thirty years ago in a small eastern Nebraska town, where middle-class Americans embraced a life of peace and prosperity.

But, she had always wanted more than a life bounded by simple contentment. Armed with a degree in Journalism from the University of Nebraska, she commenced her journey as an intern at a small independent television station in Omaha, and soon began covering local news as a field reporter.

She considered a career at the station when a series of unforeseen events turned her life upside down. Her father died unexpectedly, and the boyfriend she had counted on during her time of need suddenly deserted her for another woman. Devastated, she turned towards meditation and prayer to bring purpose to her shattered life.

But faith and focus were not enough, and the opportunities presented by a major metropolitan area were a strong lure for a talented, independent woman searching for a better life. She sought employment at all the major markets in the country, and within months KNBS answered her prayers by hiring her on as a field reporter for their station.

In the three years since her arrival to LA, Karen had found some semblance of balance in her life. But some part of her still searched for a purpose. Something inside her heart still remained–unfulfilled.

As distant sirens lulled her into a fitful sleep, the answers she sought would remain unanswered until another day.

10

With the suspects from the pursuit now in custody, Ryan sat down at his desk for a well-deserved break. News about the bust spread quickly through the precinct, and several officers soon surrounded his desk to ferret out the details.

"Oh, Ryan," Tony Casperelli gushed. "What's it like to be a *hero?*" Casperelli, or Cap as he was known around the station, was a shaggy, heavy limbed brute with a broad featured face. Acerbic and opinionated, he was generally regarded as the Wilshire division's resident clown.

Ryan rolled his eyes. "When it happens, Cap, I'll let you know."

"I heard it was quite the party out there tonight," a tall, lanky officer standing next to Casperelli commented. "Washington Boulevard had to be shut down for almost an hour to catch the punks."

"If it weren't for the Sheriff's Department barricade," Ryan said, "there's no telling how long the chase might have continued. The homies might be able to outrun our cruisers, but there's no way they can outrun our radio."

Casperelli kicked his feet up on his desk and yawned. "Did you hear about the dude in Foothill who crashed his rig on the Hollywood Freeway during a pursuit last week? He's still laid up, last I heard."

"Must have happened during the graveyard shift," Ryan quipped.

"The Hollywood's so fuckin' jammed most of the time an officer could catch the offender faster on foot."

The group laughed briefly, and then stood to attention as Lieutenant Sam "The Hammer" Cullen swaggered into the room. Square-faced and broad-shouldered, Cullen wore a hardened look from twenty long years on the force.

"As you all must know by now," Cullen said sternly, "the four suspects in the Pico Boulevard shooting were apprehended earlier this evening by several members of our precinct and the assistance of the Sheriff's Department." He looked in Ryan's direction and winked.

"Fortunately, no one in the house the suspects fired on was seriously injured. Since the disturbance was on territory disputed by the Hauser Howlers and the Pico Pirus, we can assume that there's a connection between this shooting and the restaurant slaying earlier this evening on Pico Boulevard. Unfortunately, none of the suspects are willing to talk, and they've all had enough experience to request an attorney as soon as they were booked into the county jail."

"So what's the game plan, Loo?" a jowly faced officer asked.

Cullen's eyes narrowed. "Keep your eyes and ears open. Talk to the people on the street. One of the bangers is bound to open up if you lean on 'em a little."

Casperelli moved near Ryan's ear. "Like that's gonna happen," he whispered.

Ryan nodded but remained silent. Every veteran on the force knew the bangers were a closed-mouthed group when it came to ratting out their own. They were more afraid of retaliation from within their own gang than from anything California's overtaxed justice system could mete out.

Cullen's voice boomed across the room. "Was there something you wished to share with us, Cap?"

Casperelli flinched. "Ahhh–no sir. Ryan and me were just discussin' a list of possible suspects."

"And did you come up with any—candidates?" Cullen pressed.

"Yes, sir," Casperelli deadpanned. "We narrowed it down to just about everyone."

Several muffled laughs echoed through the precinct, and one of the officers stamped his feet in approval. Casperelli had crossed the line—again.

Cullen's eyes blazed. "Would you like to lead up an investigative team on the shooting, Mister Casperelli?"

Casperelli's face slackened. "Sir, I'm kinda busy with—"

"Well, now you're going to be *busier*. Select two officers from the shift and get some leads on my desk in the next forty-eight hours." Cullen looked around the room and shot a winsome smile. "All right troops, it's time for us to earn our pay." He gave a curt nod and strode briskly towards his office.

"Way to go, Cap," Ryan said, chuckling.

Casperelli shook his head and scowled. "Awww... shut the fuck up."

THURSDAY

11

Calvin Taylor gave a disgusted headshake when his BMW 5 Series sedan failed to start for the early morning commute. He looked at his reflection in the vehicle's rearview mirror and frowned. "Why me, Lord?" he groused. "Why *me?*"

He barely recognized the person staring back at him in the mirror. Now nearing forty, his lean cocoa face was finally bowing to the ravages of time. A fine spray of wrinkles radiated out from determined, black eyes and his kinked charcoal hair was starting to show flecks of gray. *Well, it could be worse,* he mused. *I could have no hair.*

Climbing out of the balky vehicle, he strode up the short stairway towards the kitchen and slammed the door. His Asian wife, Kati, looked on with concern as her husband tossed his briefcase on the counter and began pacing around the room.

"Something wrong, hon?" she asked.

"Ahhh . . . the car won't start–*again."* He glanced at the two-ton paperweight gracing his driveway and exhaled loudly. "The Ultimate Driving Machine. *Hah!"*

Kati touched his arm. "What's the problem this time?"

"I never should have bought it," he grumbled. "That's the problem." He turned towards Kati and smiled. "It looks like I'm going to have to take the Buick in to work today. Will you be able to manage without a car?"

Kati returned his smile. "I'll be fine."

"Call the dealership and have that . . . that *car* . . . towed in to be looked at. Next chance I get, I'm trading that Krautmobile in for something more practical. Like a Harley." He turned his gaze towards his two children gathered at the kitchen table. His tween daughter Toni had her face buried in a *Black Beat* magazine while his five-year old son James was in the midst of a galactic battle on his iPod. Neither had acknowledged his presence.

He shot his wife a sideways glance. "Any chance of trading them in?" he whispered.

She shook her head. "Fraid not. You're stuck with them for an unlimited amount of miles or life. Whichever comes *last.*"

Calvin gave an eyeroll. "It's too bad they don't offer them on lease."

Before Kati could reply, Calvin picked up his briefcase and bolted out of the house towards the garage. He slid into the Buick and smiled when the Detroit iron thrummed to life. *That's why you lost the Big One, Hans. Old-fashioned Yankee ingenuity trumped your vaunted Teutonic engineering every time.*

Several minutes later, Calvin's thoughts wandered as he fought his way through the Southland morning crush. His company's pending bid with Royce Industries, one of the largest defense contractors in the country, centered prominently in his mind. Winning the bid would bring financial security for the next several years. A losing bid, on the other hand, could threaten his company's long-term survival. His face tightened as he pondered his company's probability of success. *Only one thing is certain,* he thought anxiously. *We only have one shot at this, so we better not screw it up.*

Guiding the Buick into his company's parking lot, Calvin's mood brightened as the familiar blue and white SONIC ENGINEERING SYSTEMS sign came into view. Memories from the past flashed through his mind as he recalled the long, bitter struggle towards personal and financial success.

The journey began many years ago in Van Nuys, California, where his father welded sub-chassis components in a General Motors manufacturing plant. For a black man with a middle school education, his father's labors provided his family with a comfortable lifestyle in late sixties urban America. During his childhood, Calvin idolized his old man's exploits, and dreamed of working for one of the 'Big Three' when he grew up.

But, some dreams are not meant to be. His father's fortunes changed in the seventies as high oil prices and economical Japanese imports whittled away the Big Three's market share. Massive layoffs and corporate restructuring sustained solvency for the Detroit automakers, but the glory days of the past were gone forever.

In the late eighties, his father became a casualty of downsizing and soon realized his eighth grade education was inadequate for the Information Age. A succession of menial jobs followed, and his father turned to the bottle for comfort. From then on, his life was a continual slide downward, and he eventually came to blame *Whitey* for his plight.

To avoid his father's fate, Calvin earned a degree in Applied Electronics, and after several years of learning the intricacies of his trade, he eventually started his own business.

Sadness tinged Calvin's face as his gaze drifted across the sign spanning his building. *It's too bad Pop never lived long enough to see my success, but his ill-destined fate gave me the inspiration I needed to succeed.*

Ramon Sanchez, his head machinist, flashed Calvin a smile as entered the building. "Buenos días, señor Taylor."

Calvin snapped out of his gloomy mood and returned his smile. "Gracias, Ramon," he replied warmly. "Cómo estás?"

"Muy bueno, gracias."

Calvin nodded politely and strolled down the hallway towards his office, playing the just concluded conversation through his mind. *It's strange, even though I've worked with Ramon for years, I know so little about his life. And yet, I feel we're a lot alike despite the differences in our cultures.*

Both had certainly felt the sting of discrimination in their lives. Calvin's exposure had begun in the third grade, when he became an unwilling victim of the Los Angeles School District's well-intentioned student bussing program. Sent to schools where he was a distinct minority, he remembered all too well the ostracism inflicted upon him by his classmates. The hushed whispers, suspicious glances, and outright taunts were a daily occurrence in his tormented youth. *But, the one thing I never understood was . . . why?*

He soon realized there would be no answer to his query. No matter how friendly or personable he tried to be to his classmates, he would always be regarded as *different*. And being different within the already cliquish classroom environment made one a virtual pariah.

Lonely and dejected, Calvin sought his mother's solace when he was on the verge of tears from some insensitive classmate's remarks. *And though she would give me a hug and try to rationalize their actions, she could never explain why such inequity existed in the first place.*

His father, however, had a different solution for his problems. He felt his son should face his classmate's ridicule head-on. *Pop always embraced the militant ideology of the Black Panthers, maintaining that the time had come for African Americans to aggressively assert their rights in the world. He maintained those beliefs until he died, even though society had moved towards a more pacifist solution.*

Calvin planned to carry on his father's struggle towards equality, but he did not realistically expect resolution within his lifetime. Or his children's lifetime. *But someday,* he reasoned, *the world Martin Luther King envisioned will become a reality. Someday, there will be a world where people are judged not by their color, but by the content of their character. Someday, there will be a world imagined by our founders in the Declaration of Independence. A world no longer encumbered by race, religion, or economic status. A world where all are truly created . . . equal.*

12

Once his interrogation at the Brown Field Station was complete, José was herded on a bus and shuttled back to Tijuana. As the bus joined the swell of vehicles waiting to cross the border into Mexico, he caught his reflection in the grime-streaked window and was gripped by a feeling of despair. *I've failed,* he thought glumly. *Thank God Maria and the kids weren't here to witness my disgrace.*

An interminable time later, José was dropped off at Tijuana's bus depot and left to fend for himself. He watched forlornly as the Border Patrol bus shriveled to nothingness on its way back to America.

A portly man with a ragged scar bisecting his right eye strolled across the deserted depot to greet him. "Are you lost, amigo?" he asked amicably.

José looked the stranger over. His contemptuous smile revealed a set of teeth that rarely saw the business end of a toothbrush. "No, señor," he replied curtly. "I'm . . . waiting for someone."

The stranger barked out a laugh. "You do not fool me, amigo. The *immigración* shuttles stop here like clockwork every day."

José's eyes narrowed. "What do you want, señor?"

The scarfaced man smiled wryly. "Perhaps the same thing you do, amigo."

"Quit speaking in riddles–*amigo*."

"There are no riddles here." He turned his gaze towards two men standing on the other side of the depot. "Only answers."

The stranger walked towards the two men, and José, curious about the man's cryptic response, followed. Scarface began the introductions by gesturing towards a tall, sharp featured man on his left. He wore a dark green polo shirt over a pair of rumpled khakis and intricately engraved western boots. "This is Santos," he stated.

José nodded in the man's direction but remained silent.

The man on José's right extended his hand. "And I'm Ricardo." Considerably older than the other two men, Ricardo's salt and pepper hair framed a wind toughened face and austere eyes. By his bearing and brash confidence, José took him to be the group's leader.

José shook Ricardo's hand and regarded the trio with a wary eye. *What do they want from me?*

"You're probably wondering who we are," Ricardo said, "and why we've chosen to speak with you."

José's mouth turned upward in a grin. "The thought did cross my mind."

Ricardo chuckled. "As it should, señor. We are three strangers in an unfamiliar city–you have a right to be suspicious. But, we are not here to harm you, José. We only wish to offer you our . . . help."

"Help?" José's eyebrow twitched. "How?"

Ricardo glanced watchfully around the depot. "Forgive us for being cautious my friend, but the Federales eyes are everywhere. If you are interested in what we have to say, I know a place where we can speak in private."

The quartet left the depot and wandered down the Avenida Coahuila to a small diner at the end of the street. Inside the dimly lit interior, ramshackle booths lined dingy walls plastered with posters from popular tourist destinations throughout Mexico. The four men made their way to the rear of the nearly vacant restaurant and slid into a booth to talk.

"How was your trip to America, José?" Santos asked. "Not quite what you expected, was it?"

José's face soured as he recalled his experience at the Brown Field Station. "I still don't know how El Migre found me so quickly. Even in the darkest shadows of the canyon I wasn't safe."

"El Migre knows your exact location the moment you cross over the border," Ricardo said. "They have sensors embedded throughout the countryside that pick up the slightest motion or sound, making your chances of avoiding detection almost impossible. And now that they have a record of your crossing, any further attempts to enter America may land you in the *detención de immigración*, where you may never be heard from again."

José met Ricardo's eyes. "Is there some way to cross the border without getting caught?"

"There are ways," Ricardo affirmed. "Have you heard of . . . *el coyote?*"

José stiffened. El coyote's exploits were legend to all who ventured north. There were numerous tales of those who had used the coyote's services and were never heard from again. "How can el coyote possibly help me?" he asked.

Ricardo folded his hands on the table and smiled slyly. "We will discuss this matter shortly. In the meantime, allow me to buy you breakfast while we talk of your dreams for the future."

13

ndrew stood before David Levin's desk and began his pitch, hoping to gain the financial support he needed from his studio to green light his next project. "Candice Morraine has expressed interest in playing the female lead, but the male lead is still up for consideration. I'd like to see Damon or Norton in the role unless you have someone better in mind."

Levin leaned back in his sumptuous leather chair and gazed at Andrew with a bemused expression on his face. Round-faced and bald, his light blue eyes sparkled with shrewdness. Over the years, he listened to numerous souls pick Landmark Studio's pockets to bankroll their pet projects. But, Andrew's ventures always held a special place in his heart because they consistently fattened his corporation's bottom line. If he needed investment capital or the use of the studio's facilities to produce his next project, he would listen politely and cut himself in for the largest percentage possible. "It sounds promising, Andrew," he said, "but the plot seems a little farfetched–even for Hollywood."

A smile tugged at Andrew's face. "It's a little out there, but no one ever went broke underestimating the intelligence of the American public."

Levin pulled a cigar from the humidor on his desk and lighted it.

"I'm still . . . undecided. Have you worked out a preliminary budget?"

"More or less. Landmark's investment will be a hundred large, less marketing and distribution costs."

Levin pinched his lip. "A hundred mil, eh? That's a lot for a project of this size."

"Maybe the costs won't seem so *extravagant* after you gross three hundred and fifty large from the anticipated worldwide distribution rights."

"Three hundred and fifty large?" Levin whistled. "Now you're talking some *real* money here." He rolled the cigar between his finger-tips, watching the smoke curl slowly towards the ceiling. "The actor's fees are a bit troubling, however. Why use A-list actors on this project instead of your usual entourage of has-been's and wannabe's?"

"Because this project needs A-list actors to bring credibility to the *farfetched* storyline. Candice has been out of the limelight since the birth of her daughter, and she's itching to get back in the public eye again. With a little schmoozing, she might be willing to take on this role for scale."

Levin shook his head and chuckled. "Mmmm . . . it's going to take a lot more than *schmoozing* for that."

"I've talked to her agent and he feels she'd come on board for ten large and two percent of the back end profits."

Levin's eyes widened. "That's all? What's she doing–*slumming?*"

"It's not always about the money, David."

"It's not?" he asked, puzzled. "Since when?"

"This may come as a shock, but most actors are in this profession to *act*. A challenging role can mean more for an actor's self-esteem than a ten figure paycheck."

"You're right," Levin mused. "That *is* shocking."

"Think about it," Andrew said. "Established actors don't need another multi-million payday or half the back end profit to prove their worth. By this point in their careers, they're more concerned about their legacy than the studio's largesse. A challenging role allows them the opportunity to stretch their craft and ensure their place in cinematic history."

"And Candice feels the time has come to . . . stretch her craft?"

"Candice is no fool," Andrew replied. "She knows it's just a matter of time before she falls out of the public eye forever. Actors are like any other creative commodity—they need to achieve critical and financial success while they can."

"I guess I've been so busy looking out for the interests of the studio that I sometimes forget there are *real* people involved in this business." He took a drag from the cigar and blew a stream of smoke into the air. "Maybe that's the secret behind your success, Andrew. You treat the hired help with respect, and in return, they respect you for it."

Andrew smiled wryly but remained silent. *If you only knew, David.*

"Have you settled on a director yet?" Levin asked.

"There's a director I met at this year's Sundance Festival who shows promise. His touching portrayal about a woman's ordeal in a state mental institution garnered raves from–"

A loud rap on the door suddenly interrupted their conversation. Levin's secretary poked her head into the office with a harried look on her face. "Sorry to disturb you, Mister Levin, but Mister Landis has a call from his assistant. She said it was important."

A smile played across Levin's face. *"Problems,* Andrew?"

"You know how it is," he grumbled. "One damn fire after another."

"Go ahead and take the call, Andrew. It will give me some time to consider your proposal."

Andrew slipped out of Levin's office and had the call forwarded to his phone. "Erin, it's Andrew. What's so *important* that it couldn't wait until after my meeting?"

"I'm sorry to bother you, Mister Landis. The production supervisor contacted me and said there was a problem on the set."

Andrew's jaw clenched. "What *kind* of problem, Erin?"

"It's something to do with the script. Angela had a disagreement with Ron and walked off the set. Production's been shut down until further notice."

Andrew ran his hand across his face and exhaled. *Can't you do anything right, Ron?* "Tell the production supervisor I'll be right over." He disconnected and scurried back towards Levin's office.

Levin shot Andrew a crooked grin as he entered through the doorway. "Did you get the fire stamped out?" he asked dryly.

"Not this time. There's a little–glitch–on the set that requires my attention."

"This *glitch,*" Levin ventured, "wouldn't happen to be blonde with a chest out to here, would it?"

Andrew chuckled. "You know I don't kiss and tell, David. Can we reschedule my proposal for another time?"

"Sure, set it up with my secretary on your way out." He took a drag from his cigar and leaned back in his chair. "It's too bad you have to leave. That bit about Miss Morraine working for scale could have been a great story all on its own."

14

oncern tinged Kyle's face as he peered over the top of Karen's cubicle in the KNBS newsroom. "Stan wants to see you, Karen."

She looked up from her computer and frowned. "Did he tell you why?"

"I'm just the messenger. But knowing Stan–it can't be good."

"Yeah," she muttered. "That's what I'm afraid of." She rose from her desk and took the elevator to his third floor office, anxiously wondering her fate. Two minutes later, she stood before his desk with a smile smeared across her face. "Hi, Stan," she said cheerfully. "Kyle said you were looking for me."

Stan's jowly puss glared angrily in her direction. "What took you so long?" he growled. "I asked Kyle to get you *yesterday*." He gestured towards a chair in front of his desk and grinned wolfishly. "Sit down and make yourself comfortable–you're not here to get your ass reamed. As a matter of fact, I've got some news you might find . . . interesting."

She sat down and leaned forward in the chair. "Interesting?"

He nodded. "What's your take on the Pangaea Festival?"

Karen gnawed her lip and mulled his question over. "From what I've heard, it's supposed to be the largest celebration of multiculturalism in our nation's history. The festival's name is derived from the ancient supercontinent Pangaea, which roughly translates to the 'one world' theme promoted by the event."

"That's an informative summary, but you still haven't answered my question. What's your take–your personal opinion–about the festival?"

"My personal opinion?" She took a deep breath and exhaled. "It's going to take more than four days of well-intentioned *propaganda* to mend the current divisiveness in L.A. As things stand right now, this town is one slight away from exploding like the proverbial powder keg."

He chortled. "Good, you're just what I'm lookin' for."

A look of puzzlement crossed her face. "Looking for?"

"I need someone to co-anchor our coverage of the festival with Martin Strothers. Your cynicism will supplement Martin's pompous attitude nicely." He rubbed his hands together and smirked. "Are you interested in the position?"

Her eyes grew huge. *"Me?"*

"Don't you want the job?"

"It's certainly a great . . . opportunity," she stammered. "But, Julie and Leslie have more experience and–"

Stan held his hand up. "What are you afraid of?"

"Nothing," she declared. "I'm just surprised that you would select me over some of the other veterans at the studio. Despite my three years on the staff, I'm still considered the rookie around here."

"You're sellin' yourself short as far as your experience is concerned, Karen. I've watched your progress at the station and wouldn't be surprised if you're co-anchorin' one of our news slots in the near future." He smiled wryly. "And who knows, maybe one of the *national* networks will pick up your contract someday."

Karen's mind wandered at her supervisor's revelation. *A national anchor position? That's more than I ever dreamed of. To be one day mentioned with the likes of Cronkite, Brokaw, Rather, Walters . . .*

Stan snapped his fingers. "Are you all right, Karen?"

"Huh?" she said, blinking. "Oh, yeah–everything's fine."

"As I was sayin', the golden ring might be yours–*someday*. But in the meantime, I want you to promote the hell out of the event so viewers tune into our station when the festival rolls into town."

"Where do you want me to start?"

"It's up to you. Start lookin' at all the angles, and you'll have more on your plate than you could ever imagine."

"Anything else?"

"Yeah, find out if President Jennings is scheduled to attend the festival. Rumors are flyin' all over the place, but the White House hasn't said shit because of security reasons. The Secret Service might believe an impromptu schedule keeps threats to a minimum, but if you ask me, their improvised planning will bite them in the ass one day."

She nodded. "Will that be all?"

He shook his head. "Since we're short-staffed, you'll have to cover your regular assignments in addition to the Festival news." He leaned back in his chair and chuckled. "The road to stardom is bound to have a pothole or two."

Karen rose from her seat and forced a smile. "Thanks," she said curtly. "I hope I can up to live up to your–expectations." She left Stan's office and bumped into Kyle several minutes later in the break room.

"Hey, how'd it go with Stan?" he asked.

"Not as bad as I expected." She gave an impish grin. "You'll never guess what happened."

"Stan proposed to you?"

She rolled her eyes.

"You proposed to Stan."

She winced. "Get real."

He shrugged. "I give up."

"You're no fun. Take another guess."

"It's probably a long shot, but did you get a promotion?"

Her eyes narrowed. "All right, who told you?"

"I was *right?*" He let out a laugh.

"This time," she replied, giggling. "Stan asked me to co-anchor the Pangaea Festival next week with Martin."

"That's great, Karen!" His expression suddenly grew dour. "Uhh . . . don't take this the wrong way, but why did Stan give *you* the nod when there are others at the station with more experience?"

Karen's brow furrowed. "That's weird, I asked him the exact same thing."

"And what did he say?"

"That he was pleased with my progress at the station and felt this opportunity would advance my career."

"Really?" Kyle pulled on his beard and frowned. "I guess that's as good as reason as any for his decision."

"What's *that* supposed to mean?" Karen snapped.

Kyle's gaze was steady. "Just watch your back, Karen. Stan's not known around the station for his acts of generosity. There must be some other reason why he chose–"

"Why must you always suspect the worst, Kyle? Maybe what he said was . . . what he meant."

Kyle compressed his lips and nodded. "I hope that you're right, Karen," he said softly. "I really hope that you're . . . right."

15

The tires squealed in protest as Andrew barreled his Mercedes between the narrow streets on Paramount Studio's production lots. At the end of Avenue P, he let up on the throttle and swerved his vehicle to the left, barely missing a stack of props set along the sidewalk. He gunned the engine towards the redline and hurtled past several more buildings before screeching to a halt directly outside stage sixteen.

Climbing out of his car, Andrew swept past several security guards and made his way to the back of set. As he scanned the interior of the cavernous structure, his eyes rested on the cause of his impromptu visit.

Ron Burgess was tall, lean, and perpetually tanned. His long flowing locks framed steel blue eyes and a gray-flecked goatee. Surprise swept over his face as he watched Andrew storm in his direction. "Andrew!" he cried. "What are you doing–"

Andrew held out his hand. "We need to talk. *Now!*" He clutched Ron's arm and led him to a secluded area behind the set where they could speak alone.

"You could have saved yourself the trip over here, Andrew," Ron explained. "A little more time and I would–"

"That's the problem, Ron—we don't have the time. Every second this crew's idle is costing me money."

"I know," Ron muttered. "Angela's just . . ." He exhaled loudly.

"Tell me what happened," Andrew said. "From the beginning."

"This morning, the shoot was going as scheduled until we began rehearsing for the last act. Then Angela starts bitching that the script isn't consistent with the persona of the character she's playing and demands to have it changed. I tried to work out something that stayed within the framework of the script, but she stormed off the set and locked herself in her trailer, refusing to talk to anyone." He took a breath and shrugged. "That's pretty much everything. Any ideas on what to do next, Kemo Sabe?"

Looking through an open door at the rear of the set, Andrew moved his gaze across a row of trailers in the parking lot and frowned. *In one of those trailers, Angela Carson is costing me a pretty penny for every second she stays locked behind her door.* "What part of the script does she have issues with?" he asked.

"It's the scene where Corinne discovers her husband is still alive after believing he had been killed in an accident many years ago. The script calls for her to be momentarily surprised when they first meet, then she rushes to embrace him after the initial shock wears off."

Andrew nodded. "I remember the scene. How does Angela feel it should play out?"

"She feels Corinne should slap her husband across the face when they meet for the first time."

Andrew's eyes widened. *"What?"*

Ron chuckled. "Funny—that's exactly what I said. She thinks any husband who *really* loved his wife would have made every conceivable effort to contact her during their separation."

"I agree. But, the husband couldn't reveal why he disappeared because other people's lives—including his wife's—were at stake."

"I explained that to Angela, but she said it didn't make any difference. The wife didn't know the reasons behind his disappearance, so she had every right to be angry once they were reunited again."

"What does the writer think?"

"I haven't spoken with him yet. I was hoping Angela would change her mind and come back to finish the rehearsal."

"And how's that working for you?" Andrew asked dryly.

Ron sighed. "*Women.*"

A grin traced Andrew's face despite his sullen mood. "I'll go have a talk with her. Does it make any difference to you how the scene plays out?"

"I'm always willing to compromise. I want to wrap this project as soon as possible."

Andrew looked at Ron and bit his cheek. *Not half as much as me, asshole.* "Is she still in her trailer?" he asked.

"Last time I checked." He clasped Andrew's shoulder and smiled. "Good luck, *Kemo Sabe.*"

On his way towards Angela's trailer, Andrew reflected that he could have been out on his yacht today instead of wasting his time coddling an obstinate actress. Setting aside his annoyance for the time being, he strode up the steps to her trailer and rapped on the door. "Angela," he said gently. "It's Andrew. Are you there?" He rested his ear against the doorway and listened. *Nothing but the faint drone coming from the air conditioner.*

He rapped on the door again. "Angela, I know you're upset with the script. Let's talk and try to work something out." Turning, he scanned the parking lot for the recalcitrant actress. *Hmmm . . . no sign of her anywhere. Could she have skipped off the set without being seen?*

A latch was suddenly dragged back from the door, startling him. The door drifted inward, and Andrew came face to face with the cause of his concerns.

Despite her red-rimmed eyes and smeared mascara, Angela Carson retained the sultry vulnerability that made her one of the most desirable starlets in the industry today. A mop of curly blonde hair hung limply over her prepubescent face, and she stared at him with an intelligence far beyond her age of twenty-four years.

Andrew met her gaze and grinned cheekily. "Mind if I come in?"

She backed away from the door. "Watch your step, Andrew. I was a little upset and things kinda got . . . moved around."

No shit, Andrew mused as he surveyed the trailer's cramped interior. It looked like a tornado had whisked through the wood paneled room and scattered everything that hadn't been bolted down. He cleared some debris off the tan leather couch and slumped against the cushions. "I just talked with Ron about-"

Her eyes blazed. "And now you agree with *him,*" she hissed. "And to *hell* with my point of view!"

Andrew held out his hands. "Let me finish!" He paused and softened his voice to a whisper. "*Please.*"

She curled up next to him on the couch and let out a wheezy sigh. "I'm . . . listening."

"I heard you're unhappy with the way your character's scripted in the final act. There seems to be a disagreement on how Corinne is supposed to react when she discovers her husband is still alive after-"

"It just feels *wrong!*" she interjected. "No woman would *ever* act that way-regardless of the circumstances behind her husband's apparent death."

"And how *should* a woman feel in this particular situation?"

Her eyes narrowed. "Are you trying to patronize me, Andrew?"

He gave a quick headshake. *We've already seen how that works.* "No, just tell me how you really feel."

"You want to know how a woman would *feel* in that situation?" she chided. "I'll tell you how she'd feel-she'd be mad as *hell.*" She sprang off the couch and paced around the tightly confined room. "How would you *feel* if your lover hadn't made any effort to contact you–hadn't bothered to let you know he was still alive?"

"But other people's lives would be in jeopardy if he revealed his existence," Andrew pointed out. "Including his wife. Can't you see he was trying to protect them?"

"But she didn't know *why* he disappeared, she only knew that he was gone–forever. Seeing him alive after all that time was not only a shock, it was a . . . betrayal." Tears welled in her eyes. "She was in *love* with him, Andrew. Was she supposed to act like *nothing* had happened at all?"

Andrew blinked. *She has a point. The scenario she's proposing is more believable than the original script.*

Her eyes dropped. "Maybe I'm overreacting–seeing something that really isn't there."

"No," he replied. "I think you've nailed the part dead on."

"Really?" A smile lighted her face.

"Really," Andrew affirmed. "But, tell me how you feel about this story line. Corrine batters her long missing husband after the initial shock wears off from their surprise meeting. The husband doesn't push her away, but tries to console her with an embrace. She continues to strike him, but her anger soon subsides and is replaced with an embrace of her own." He rose from the couch and draped his arm around her shoulder. "Just think of the dynamics of this scene–from anger to affection–all in a matter of moments." He looked at her and smiled wryly. "Do you think you can pull it off?"

Her eyes twinkled. "What do *you* think?"

"I think you'll have the audience eating out of your hand. Let's head back to the set and show 'em how it's done."

"Are you going to stay for my performance?" she asked coyly.

He kissed her forehead and smiled. "I wouldn't miss it for the world."

16

The alarm pierced the brightly lit bedroom, urging Ryan to respond to its demands. He glanced briefly at the face of the clock, then picked it up and hurled it across the room. *Uhhh . . . eleven o'clock,* he moaned. *Half the day's already shot to hell.*

With a groan, Ryan struggled upright and found his golden retriever sitting patiently beside his bed. "Are you hungry, Bear?" He scratched the dog behind the ears and chuckled. "What a dumb question, you're *always* hungry."

Trudging into the kitchen, Ryan dumped a can of mystery meat into Bear's monogrammed bowl and stepped back as his dog voraciously attacked his meal. He then ambled into the den and sat at his desk to dispatch a growing pile of mail that had accumulated during the past week. He thumbed through the lopsided stack of envelopes and mailers and frowned. *Bill, junk mail, bill . . . it never freakin' ends,* he thought glumly. *My dog has a better life.*

Once the unpleasant task was completed, his gaze settled on a pewter framed photo resting on the edge of his desk. A late-twenties blond with striking blue eyes; a pixie haired child with a gap-toothed smile, and a fuzzy haired man with a cocky grin stared back from a touching family portrait frozen in time. *Stephanie, Ashley, and me . . .*

before the demands of The Job changed our lives forever. He picked up the intricately engraved frame and traced his fingers across the glass, a look of melancholy tinging his face when he couldn't recall the time or place when the picture was taken.

Reaching into the bottom drawer of his desk, Ryan withdrew a bottle of Scotch and a tumbler and placed them on his desk. He stared at the empty glass for several moments and pinched his lip. *Just one,* he assured himself. *Just one and you'll be . . . all right.*

He poured a generous amount of the amber liquid into the glass and breathed deeply. Looking at the picture again, he took a healthy swig from the glass and felt the familiar warmth as the Scotch washed through his body. *It's no use,* he grumbled. *I can't remember when this photo was taken, but I'll never forget the day when Stephanie and I first met.*

On a dare posed by one of his Marine buddies over ten years ago, Ryan agreed to meet his future wife at a miniature golf course for a blind date. He staked out their designated rendezvous area thirty minutes ahead of time so he could observe all incoming visitors to the links. *When your friend says your date has a great personality and reveals little else, you sure as hell want to cover your ass.*

When the time for their date arrived, he watched anxiously as a bright red Mustang pulled into the parking lot. He stood quietly behind a tree, waiting for the occupant to leave the vehicle. The Mustang's door opened and a buxom bronzed beauty spilled out of the car, her face shrouded from view by a large white fedora and oversized sunglasses.

A smile traced Ryan's face as he relived the memory in his mind. *I emerged from my vantage point and walked towards her car, hoping against hope that she would be my date.*

Several yards from his destination, he was feeling confident, care-free. But, when he drew up beside her and opened his mouth, a spasm suddenly caught his throat. "S-St-Stephanie?" he stuttered out.

She tilted her head and looked him over. "Yes?" she purred. "Ryan?"

He nodded dumbly. "It's . . . nice to meet you."

Stephanie remained silent and removed her sunglasses. Even with her countenance partially shielded by the hat, he could see she possessed the bluest eyes that ever graced a human face. A blue only observed on a clear wintry day, or in the deepest depths of a sapphire. And then, the sun caught her smile and her face was bathed in an ethereal glow that he had never seen before–or since.

She was perfect, Ryan reminisced. A shiver went up his spine. *Too perfect.*

The rest of the day went by in a blur, and he could no longer recall what was said or who even won their match. *But, I'll never forget how nice her shorts looked when she bent over to get her golf ball that day.*

He snapped out of his reverie and refocused his eyes on the photo. *I wonder what she's doing right now,* he wondered. He picked up the phone and tapped her number into the keypad. *Ashley's birthday is next week–I can always use that as an excuse to call. Not that I need an excuse to call . . .*

Six rings later, a woman's voice answered the phone. "Hello?"

"Hi, Stephanie," he said amiably, "It's Ryan. How are–"

"What do you want?" she asked coolly.

He moved the phone away from his face and frowned. *Mmmm . . . must have caught her at a bad time.* "I wanted to talk to you about Ashley's birthday next–"

"Can't this wait? I've got–"

"No, it can't wait. I've got to be at work in–"

"It's always about *The Job,* isn't it, Ryan?"

His eyebrow twitched. "The Job?"

"*Forget it.* What do you want?"

Nothing from you, he groused. "I was wondering what to get Ashley for her birthday. I don't have a clue on what eight-year old girls are–"

"You would if you spent more time with her."

Ryan bit his lip–hard. "I *do* spend time with her, Stephanie–as much as I can." He took a deep breath and exhaled slowly. "I know I wasn't always there for her . . . or you."

"Now there's an *understatement.*"

Here we fuckin' go again. "Stephanie, please don't let this escalate into the same old argument between ourselves. Contrary to what you think, I still want to be a part of our daughter's life."

"GirlTalk," she said tersely.

Puzzlement tinged his face. "Girl what?"

"Girl*Talk.* It's a two-way radio transceiver that can record high definition video and play a variety of audio and visual media."

"It sounds like your average portable media player to me."

"That's all it is. Wrapped up in girl friendly package and minus the monthly charge to a communications network."

Ryan scratched his head. "Hmmm . . . I don't know. Wouldn't she rather have a doll or a large stuffed animal instead?"

She chuckled. "Ryan–you are *sooo* far behind the times."

"You don't think those are appropriate gifts for a girl her age?"

"You *asked* for my advice."

My mistake. "I'll keep your–suggestion–in mind. Anything new going on in your life?"

"Nothing for you to be concerned with. But, I'm glad you called because there is one little thing I wanted to talk to you about."

"What's that?"

"I still haven't received my child support payment for last month."

"I . . . I already sent that out."

"That was May's payment. You're still a month behind."

"Are you sure? I thought–"

"Of course I'm sure," she said. "If you want to be a part of Ashley's life, then the *least* you can do is contribute towards her welfare. You certainly aren't here enough in *person* to make any difference."

"That's not fair, Stephanie, and you know it. I don't have your typical nine-to-five job that you can leave when your shift is over." He paused. "But, you knew that when you married me."

"I wish I knew a couple *other* things before I–"

"What's that supposed to mean?" he snarled.

"*Nothing*. Look, I'm late for my appointment. What time are you planning on picking up Ashley next weekend?"

He paused. "I'm afraid I won't be able to take her to Disneyland on Saturday like I originally planned."

The line was silent for several seconds. "You couldn't get the day off for your daughter's *birthday?*"

"All vacation days have been cancelled for next week because the department is mobilizing for the Pangaea Festival." He paused. "You know how The Job can–"

"How could I *ever* forget?"

"Maybe I can take her to Disneyland the following weekend–if it's okay with you."

She sighed. "We'll see. I guess *maybe* is better than . . . not at all."

"Tell Ashley I love her," Ryan added.

But, it was too late–the only sound he heard was the pitiless drone of the dial tone.

Ryan rubbed his temples and slumped wearily back into his seat. He reached across the desk for the bottle of Scotch and poured himself another drink.

17

Within the confines of his spacious windowed office, Calvin studied the small metallic sphere his company was developing for Royce Industries. Slightly less than four inches in diameter, its dimpled titanium surface resembled a large golf ball flecked with holes. "The crew did a great job on the prototype," he remarked as he turned the ball over in his hand. "Do the operating specs fall within the military's requirements?"

Sonic Engineering Systems chief engineer, Kevin Turner, nodded assuredly. "No problems there, boss. As a matter of fact, it surpasses their specs by more than thirty percent."

Calvin examined the sphere with a magnifying reticle. "The seams are virtually invisible. That will keep any radiant sound to a minimum—just as Uncle Sam requested."

"It's hard to believe that something so harmless looking can be so lethal."

"*Could* be lethal, Kevin—but that's not it's intended purpose. The Frequency Wave Module is just one of the military's latest weapons designed to disable rather than kill its intended victim." He juggled the silver-gray orb with one hand, watching it glint dully under the florescent lights of his office. "Instead of using a grenade against an adversary, tomorrow's soldier will lob this little sphere in their direction. Microseconds after it lands, it will emit a high frequency sound that will paralyze the nerve centers for locomotion, causing the assailant to fall to the ground in excruciating pain. Fortunately, our service personnel can deactivate the device with a special programmed code, rendering it useless if the enemy decides to use it against our troops." He tossed the sphere to Kevin. "Unless they want to bean our soldiers by using it like a baseball."

Kevin hefted the sphere in his hand and frowned. "I wouldn't want to be whacked in the head with it."

"How does our profit per unit look once we ramp up for production?" Calvin asked.

"Roughly fifteen to twenty percent, depending on the market cost of raw materials. However, it will be less if we have to outsource part of the production to other vendors."

"Do you foresee that happening?"

"Only if the military requests a large quantity within a very short time. Our facility is not large enough to supply the demands of the Army and Marines if they become involved in a rapidly escalating conflict. If that happens, we'll have to sub out some of the work and incur the costs demanded by the increased overhead."

"There's little chance of that happening in the immediate future," Calvin surmised. "The practical engineering is still under development, and the military abandons any technology if it doesn't pan out under real world scenarios. Frankly, I see this device used by law enforcement agencies in situations where crippling an aggressor is more desirable than killing them."

"Maybe we can pitch the module's benefits to the LAPD if Royce turns us down for the contract."

"There's just one small snag with that idea, Kevin. The military owns most of the patents on the technology." He shot his chief engineer a sideways glance. "Speaking of snags, is there anything I need to know before we give our presentation today?"

Kevin's face slackened. "There is one little thing . . ."

Calvin's eyebrow arched upward. "Spill it."

"There's a glitch with the power system," he said. "It's probably . . . nothing."

"Humor me."

"The Li-Ion cells don't have enough juice to vibrate the sonic transducer. When the module powers up, the high frequency sound is forced through the spherical diaphragm–"

"Let me guess–it makes a lot of noise but won't disable its intended assailant."

Kevin nodded. "I'm sure it's something we can work out before production."

Calvin slammed his hand down on the desk. "Why did you wait until the *last* minute to tell me this?"

"Roger assured me that he could get it fixed before the presentation."

"But he didn't, did he?"

"Royce isn't expecting a working prototype at this time anyway. All they want is an assurance that the technology is viable and can be brought in on budget."

"Can it?"

"Roger says . . . I think so . . . *yes.*"

A look of disgust crossed Calvin's face. "The voice of *confidence.*"

"Have I ever let you down?" Kevin retorted.

Calvin met his gaze and shook his head. "Anything else I should know about?"

"No, that should cover it." He lowered his eyes. "Sorry I didn't bring this to your attention earlier."

"What's done is done," Calvin groused. "We'll have to make the best of it." He tossed several files into his briefcase and snapped it closed. "Are you ready for the meeting?"

"I need to get a few things from Roger and I'll be set."

Calvin hooked a thumb over his shoulder. "Meet me at my car when you're ready."

After their gear was tossed in the trunk, Calvin and his chief engineer barreled down the freeway towards Royce Industries. An uneasy silence filled their commute, as they were keenly aware of this contract's significance on Sonic Engineering Systems future.

Two hours later, Calvin summed up months of engineering and innovation to a small group of people gathered around a mahogany table in the Royce Industries conference room. "As you can see," he concluded, "Sonic Engineering Systems has exceeded the original military specifications and brought in a working prototype below initial projected costs. The harmonic disruption issues have been solved by the engineers at my company, and the example you hold within your hands could be production ready within a matter of months once our bid is confirmed for the contract." He glanced around the room, looking to field any concerns from Royce's staff. "Does anyone have a question?"

A production manager raised his hand. "Will your company be able to satisfy the military's needs if it becomes involved in a large scale conflict?"

Calvin pinched his lip. *Mmmm . . . straight for our Achille's heel.* "If we use the military's current inventory projections as a guideline," he deflected, "SES will have no problem meeting their demand." One last glance around the room yielded no further questions, so he wrapped up the presentation. "If that is all, I'd like to thank each of you for coming today and I hope we can work on this project together in the future."

After the conference room cleared, Morgan Styles, the senior vice-president of Royce Industries, clapped Calvin on the back. "Great presentation, Cal. It's the first I've heard in a while that didn't put me to sleep."

Calvin smiled but remained silent. After several joint ventures with his company, Morgan Styles was more than a business acquaintance, he was one of Calvin's most trusted friends. Wide shouldered and trim waisted, Styles moved with the fluid athleticism of a man half his age. A white mane of hair billowed from a face weathered by years of sun and hard drinking. Today he wore his usual conservative navy suit, crisp ivory shirt, and the obligatory power tie requisite for his position in the company. "Thanks Morgan," Calvin replied. "I hope our presentation cleared up any doubts about the viability of this project."

"More than cleared it up," Styles affirmed. "Do you have time for a little private chat in my office before you leave?"

"Sure. I'll make arrangements for Kevin to take the presentation materials back to SES and I'll join you."

A few minutes later, Calvin accompanied Styles down a long corridor to his well-appointed office. Looking around the glass-paneled office, he noticed little had changed since his last visit. Three cherry bookcases filled with personal mementoes lined one wall, while a large hand-painted mural illustrating the history of flight plastered the wall behind Styles' massive Mission styled desk.

Styles closed the door to his office and sat on the edge of his desk. "It's been a while since we last talked, Cal. How's your family doing?"

"James has just started school, and Toni's acting like a teen I'm sorry to say."

Styles chuckled. "Yes, they grow up before you know it. One minute you're watching them take their first steps and the next, they're out in the world starting their own families. I've already got two grandkids, but I don't feel anything like a granddad yet."

"How does Natalie like being a grandmother?"

"Oh, she *loves* it—whenever she gets a chance she spoils our grandkids rotten. My daughter doesn't like it, but let's face it, Sharon is no match when it comes to her mother."

"She's definitely a strong willed woman."

Styles rolled his eyes. "Don't I know it. I can't get away with *anything* now that the kids have left. Speaking of strong willed women–how's Kati?"

Calvin shot him a crooked grin. "The glue that holds the family together. I don't know what I would do without her sometimes."

"She's a keeper." Styles strolled to a small credenza to the left of his desk and plucked two tumblers from a glass shelf. "It's a little early in the day, but as the old adage goes, it must be five o'clock–somewhere. Care to join me in a midday toast?"

"Why not? I'll have a bourbon–neat."

"A man after my own heart. A fine bourbon should *never* be diluted with water." He poured a healthy shot into the tumblers and handed one to Calvin. "It kind of defeats the whole purpose behind drinking in the first place, wouldn't you say?"

Calvin took the glass and smiled. "What should we toast to?"

"I don't know," Styles said, shrugging. "Do we particularly *need* a reason?" He held his glass out. "To old friends . . . and new partners."

Calvin toasted Styles then took a healthy swig of his drink. "It's very smooth, with just a hint of pepper." He studied the label on the bottle. "I'm not familiar with this brand–is it available locally?"

"No, it's made exclusively by a small distiller just outside New Orleans. My brother lives in the area and ships a case to me every Christmas."

"If it's not too much trouble, do you think you can put me on his list this year?"

Styles chuckled. "I'll see what I can do." He refilled their glasses and stoppered the bottle. "Calvin, I wanted to meet with you privately so we could discuss your company's role on this project. As I said earlier, I was impressed with your presentation, and judging from the general reaction of the managers and engineers at the meeting, the feeling was mutual."

Calvin nodded politely but remained silent. *That's a relief. Up to now, I was beginning to feel like the blindfolded prisoner smoking his last cigarette.*

"There are two other companies actively bidding on this contract, but in my opinion only one will offer your company any real competition. Sonic Engineering Systems has contracted with us in the past, and the quality of your work has always been top notch. On time, and more important—on budget."

But—Calvin mused. *There's always a but.*

"But, in the last several years, there have been significant changes in military procurement procedures as the federal budget has turned its attention to the increased cost of our nation's entitlement programs. There's no longer a tolerance for budget overruns, unspecified cost-cutting procedures and negligence in general. After the *Annihilator* fiasco at Phoenix Aerospace two years ago, Congress and the military have put the bite on defense contractors, holding executives criminally liable for any malfeasance arising during their tenure."

Calvin had heard about the Annihilator debacle while socializing with some Phoenix engineers at a local watering hole several months ago. Most of what he had heard before that meeting was unverified or hearsay, but the engineers confirmed most of his suspicions once the alcohol had loosened their lips.

The FX-40 Annihilator was to be the nation's next generation tactical stealth fighter—a state-of-the-art aircraft designed to carry the diverse needs of the military through to the second half of the century. Utilizing a propulsion system based upon experimental electro-magnetic theories, the aircraft was a classic example of untested concepts combined with leading edge technologies before either was proven viable in the field. In simple layman's terms—the proverbial recipe for disaster. After the contracts were awarded and pilot testing had begun, it soon became apparent that the program was flawed from the start.

After a period of unexplained failures cost the lives of over a dozen test pilots, the media 'uncovered' a slew of documents from Phoenix engineers questioning the mechanics of the propulsion system and the composites used in the structural composition of the aircraft. When it was subsequently 'discovered' that the engineers' concerns were suppressed by Phoenix management, the wrath of Congress turned directly upon the operating officers of the company.

In secret closed-door sessions with Congress, the executive officers denied any knowledge of wrongdoing or avoided controversy altogether by invoking their fifth amendment rights. Soon thereafter, a major shake-up ensued in the ivory towers at Phoenix Aerospace and Congress enacted legislation making the executives of a company criminally liable for negligence directly under their oversight.

Within days, defense contractors throughout the country cleaned house, executing major organizational changes to avoid the possibility of any similar incidents in the future. The total costs to the taxpayer from the Annihilator debacle were never officially calculated, but for fourteen pilots and their families, the final bill would always be much too high.

"How does the Congressional ruling on Phoenix Aerospace impact this particular program?" Calvin asked.

"The Annihilator fiasco was a major clusterfuck to the nth degree. Unfortunately, the safeguards Phoenix had in place were virtually identical to those at all the major defense contractors. Including–*us*."

"Royce has never been involved in any scandals that I'm aware of."

Styles gave a wan smile. "That's the operative word–that you're *aware* of."

Calvin's eyes widened. "Care to elaborate?"

"Sorry–not a snowball's chance in hell. I've got a huge mortgage hanging over my head and enough debt to last me a lifetime." His eyes shifted to the right. "And what you've just heard remains confidential, comprendé?"

"Don't worry, Morgan," Calvin confided. "Your company's interests are safe with me."

"I know," Styles said. "As long as we're talking about the truth, I want your honest analysis on the Frequency Wave Module. Is there anything your company has discovered that wasn't revealed to us today in the presentation?"

Calvin met his gaze. *Should I reveal everything I know? I'm sure we can work out any existing problems before we ramp up for production.* "There's nothing I'm aware of," he lied. "Everything we've disclosed so far is strictly by the book." *There's no need to tell him I'm writing it as I go along.*

"Good, that's what I wanted to hear. I don't want any unexpected problems cropping up before production. Unlike their namesake, Phoenix Aerospace never recovered from the Annihilator debacle, and I'll be damned if I'm going to let that happen to Royce under my watch." He clapped his arm around Calvin's shoulder and smiled broadly. "We'll take a hard look at your presentation later today, and if all appears satisfactory, I suspect the two of us will be spending a little more time together."

Calvin forced a smile. *I guess that's my cue to leave.* He shook Styles hand and trudged out of the office, feeling less sure about his company's future than before he entered.

18

After their meeting concluded at the diner, Ricardo and his cohorts led José to a nearby industrial district several blocks away. They strolled to the end of a dead end street, and Ricardo ushered the group towards the back of a sooty windowed warehouse scrawled with colorful swirls of graffiti.

An eight-foot high razor wire fence surrounded the rear of the warehouse. On the other side of the rust-tinged fence, several burned out vehicles competed for space with moldering mounds of trash on a crumbling asphalt parking lot.

Ricardo fumbled with the balky lock to the gate for several moments, and then steered the group towards a dented steel door at the back of the warehouse. He rapped several times on the doorway in a rhythmic manner and stepped back to wait.

Moments later, the door drew inward to reveal a well-dressed man with a saturnine face and dark, searching eyes. He regarded the quartet cautiously for several moments and motioned for José to come inside.

Ricardo placed his hand on José's shoulder. "We have reached the end of our journey, José," he said. "And you are about to start the beginning of yours." He shot him a lopsided grin. "Be safe, my friend."

The saturnine faced man stepped away from the door and José

entered the dimly lit interior of the warehouse. Overhead, several rows of lamps hung from the ceiling, casting faint circles of light on the gray concrete floor. As his vision acclimated to the gloomy surroundings, he noticed several large cargo trucks parked in the back of the otherwise vacant building.

"Welcome to my humble *establecimento*, señor," the coyote said warmly. "Shall we skip the usual pleasantries and get down to business?"

José looked the coyote over. "A question first, if I may, señor."

The coyote nodded and flashed a smile. "Go ahead and ask your question, amigo."

"Where will you be taking me and how much will it cost?"

The coyote chuckled. "That is *two* questions, señor. No matter, I am feeling *generoso* today." He twirled his moustache and studied José with a watchful eye. "In answer to your first question, you will be taken in one of my trucks to a location across the border. A location I cannot reveal at this time because the eyes of El Migre are everywhere. As for your second question, the price to take you across the border will be five-hundred U.S. dollars." He gave a sly smile. "Payable in advance."

José's face slackened. "I don't have five hundred U.S. dollars, señor."

"How much *can* you pay, amigo?"

"I'm a poor dirt farmer from Jiquilpan. Five hundred dollars is more than I make in a year. I could give you half–"

"Four hundred," the coyote countered.

"Three hundred," José offered.

"Three fifty," the coyote said firmly. "My *final* offer."

José stuck out his hand. "Agreed." He pulled a battered billfold from his pocket and handed the coyote seven well-worn fifty-dollar bills. Unbeknownst to the smuggler, José had several thousand dollars hidden in the soles of his boots and was prepared to pay the original asking price if necessary.

The coyote took the money and gestured towards a group of people gathered at the far side of the warehouse. "Join the others and I will let you know when we are ready to leave."

José nodded gratefully and strolled towards the waiting group of migrants, wondering when his strange journey to the land of opportunity would reach its end.

19

S itting at a curbside table outside a trendy Westside bistro, Karen popped a salsa slathered tortilla chip into her mouth and smacked her lips. "Mmmm, aren't these nachos delish, Kyle? You can't find anything like this back in my hometown in Nebraska."

Kyle swirled some salsa on a chip and took a hesitant bite. "They're okay, I guess."

"I know," Karen ribbed. "You've had *better* at some hole-in-the-wall joint in Santa Ana. Or was it Huntington Park?"

"Or a million other hole-in-the-wall restaurants scattered throughout the Southland." He sampled the guacamole and winced. "Let's face it, if you want *real* Mexican food, you need to go to a place where the menu's written in Spanish."

"That might work for you–or anyone else who's bilingual. But, what are the rest of us gringos supposed to do?"

"I'm just as much a gringo as you are, Karen. I've picked up some of the language here and there, but I'm not fluent by any means. If you really want to learn a language, you need to live where it's spoken every day."

"You don't need to look very far for a place like that in L.A.," Karen quipped. "There's so many communities where English isn't the native language that I'm beginning to feel like a foreigner here."

"It certainly seems that way sometimes. But, after the Pangaea Festival blows through town, we'll all learn to live like one big, happy family."

Karen chuckled. "And if you believe that, there's a nice bridge in Brooklyn I can sell you." Her expression grew dour. "Do you think we've passed the point where we can no longer love our neighbor?"

"Are you kidding? We passed that point a long time ago." He shook his head and laughed softly. "Love thy neighbor? Most folks don't even *know* their neighbor."

"My, aren't you the voice of *optimism* today. What ever happened to the happy-go-lucky Kyle I used to know?"

"I haven't changed, Karen–it's the whole friggin' world that's changed. We're so busy looking for the next big thing that we never stop to see why we want–or need–it. We've been bombarded by so much institutional and corporate propaganda that we don't know who we are anymore. As a matter of fact, if most of the people in this country took a good hard look at themselves, they'd find a complete stranger staring back at them in the mirror."

"And what would you change–if you could?"

"You mean if I could be–God–for a day?"

She gave an impish grin and nodded.

Kyle ran a hand through his scraggly beard. "Since the forty days and forty nights of rain strategy has already been used, I guess I'll have to think of a more . . . compassionate solution."

Karen smiled wryly. "It's easy to sit on your ass and find fault with the world when you don't have a plan of your own."

"Who says I don't have a plan?" he groused. "Even *God* had six days to bring his little project to fruition."

"All right, I'll give you five more days to solve all the world's problems," she teased. "And not *one* day more." Her eyes widened as she glanced at her watch. "We'd better get moving or they'll be hiring two new faces at the station."

Kyle tossed some money on the table and the pair dashed back to the studio. Twenty minutes later, they were editing the day's assignments in the production room when the phone rang.

Karen reached across the console and picked up the phone. "Karen Mitchell here."

"Where the *hell* have you been?" Stan snarled. "Are you gonna have the Neidermeyer interview ready for the six o'clock lead-in?"

Karen shot a worried look at Kyle. "Will the Neidermeyer interview be ready for the six o'clock lead in?"

Kyle looked up from the computer screen and shrugged.

"Don't worry, Stan," she said calmly. "Everything's under control."

"Get up to my office. You and me need to have a little *talk*."

Karen stared anxiously at the phone. *Shit–what's wrong now?* "I'm on my way," she muttered.

As the elevator made its ascent to her supervisor's office, Karen reflected that the trip seemed to take a lot longer than usual. *Or does it always seem that way when you're about to get your butt chewed out?*

Sixty too long seconds later, she paused briefly in front of his door to regain her composure. *Just remember to keep your cool, Karen. Stan's bark is always worse than his bite.* Temporarily emboldened, she pushed open the door and flashed her thousand-watt smile. "You wanted to see me?" she asked sweetly.

Stan waved her towards the chair in front of his desk. "Make yourself *comfortable*." He lighted a cigar and blew a stream of blue gray smoke towards the ceiling. "You know Karen, I'm beginnin' to have doubts about you co-anchorin' the Pangaea Festival with Martin next week."

She sat upright in the chair but remained silent.

A sly smile curled her supervisor's mouth. "Do you think you're the right person for the job?"

She bit the side of her cheek and nodded.

Stan tapped the end of his cigar into his coffee mug and leaned back in his chair. "I hope so," he said. "Some of the suits didn't think you were ready, but I stepped up to the plate and convinced them otherwise." He took another draw on his cigar and exhaled. "Don't you think I deserve some . . . gratitude . . . for puttin' my job on the line for you?"

"Ummm . . . sure. Thanks for your support, Stan."

He leveled his gaze in her direction and shot her a wicked grin. "Surely you can do *better* than that."

The hairs stood up on the back of Karen's neck. "Maybe you could be more . . . specific."

He let out a short, harsh laugh. "You're an investigative reporter, Karen. You should be able to figure it out."

A spasm convulsed her stomach. *Damn! Why didn't I see this coming?* "I . . . I need to help Kyle with the Neidermeyer story," she said weakly, "if you want it ready for the six o'clock lead-in."

Stan bared his mouth in an oafish leer but remained eerily silent. Karen rose slowly from her seat and edged unsteadily out of the office. Any moment now, she expected her boss to morph into a wolf and leap across the desk flashing a set of long, sharp fangs. *My Stan, what big teeth you have . . .*

Once in the relative safety of the hallway, Karen leaned against the wall and tried to relax. She took a deep breath and exhaled as a cold sweat broke out across her face. At the moment, she was torn between smashing every tooth out of her supervisor's leering mouth or curling up in a cozy, secure spot where she could drift away forever.

She set off towards the elevator, rehashing the meeting in her mind. *Could I have misunderstood what he said? Maybe all he wanted was some token of thanks for selecting me for the position.* Her face quickly contorted in rage. *No, don't make excuses for him, Karen. Though he never said anything specific, you don't need to be an investigative reporter to figure it out.*

When the elevator tolled for her floor, Karen darted inside and pressed the button for the ground floor. Her head swam with a million questions, and she didn't have an answer for any of them.

20

Still feeling the aftermath from his drinking binge earlier in the day, Ryan was tailgating an early sixties Chevy lowrider when his cruiser's radio squawked to life. "Wilshire, all available units respond. Code Three."

Ryan snatched the microphone from its cradle. "Unit 7L731 responding, Wilshire."

"Tanker fire reported near the intersection of Santa Monica Freeway and La Cienega Boulevard. Emergency and hazmat vehicles en route to scene."

"Affirmative, Wilshire. 7L731 out."

Ryan switched on the cruiser's alarm and barreled west down Pico Boulevard. Minutes from his destination, his face tightened as he watched viscous black smoke curl upward from the vicinity of the freeway.

Turning onto La Cienega Boulevard, he threaded his vehicle through the ever-tightening gridlock until a semi truck blocking the intersection halted his progress. He quickly surveyed the area but couldn't find a way past the vehicle. *Damn,* he groused to himself. *I guess I'll have to go the rest of the way on foot.*

Killing the lights and siren, Ryan moved the black and white to the curb. He fetched a first aid kit and bullhorn from the trunk and began to sprint towards the freeway. Stalled motorists honked their horns and hurled obscenities in his direction, but he ignored their taunts and pushed onward, fully aware that every second lost could cost someone their life.

As he rushed up the on ramp to the freeway, the stench of burning fuel, melting tires and other grisly scents nearly made Ryan lose his lunch. He fought off a wave of nausea and scurried up the steep embankment towards the freeway. Within seconds, he reached the top of the slope and hurtled over the guardrail, but even he was unprepared for the devastation that played out before his eyes.

A curtain of flames raged across the westbound lanes of the freeway, turning the vehicles near the ruptured tanker into a molten pile of slag.

Ryan's mind raced, calculating the odds on pulling any motorists from their vehicles before the superheated air from the blaze ignited their gas tanks. Without protective gear or a rapid change in the inferno's intensity, his chances of mounting an effective rescue rapidly slipped to zero.

But, he wasn't ready to quit yet. Moving back an ever-growing mob of stranded drivers and lookie-loos, Ryan broke away from the crowd and charged up an aisle of stranded vehicles to look for survivors. As he drew closer to the flames roaring from the tanker's ruptured shell, waves of heat rippled the atmosphere and sent rivulets of sweat trickling down his face.

Overhead, several choppers dumped powdered retardant on the blaze while a group of firefighters in the eastbound lane braved the roiling flames to rescue any motorists trapped near the overturned truck. Ryan watched sadly as the charred remains of a family were pulled from the interior of a blackened van.

Suddenly, a pickup exploded in a blinding flash of light and slammed

Ryan against the hood of a car. A red hued fireball soared into the sky, and Ryan rolled off the hood as the truck's steering column hurtled through the air and pierced the car's windshield like an eggshell.

He took a deep breath and exhaled. "Shit!" he hissed. "That was too damn close!"

Anticipating another explosion, Ryan scrambled to his feet and backed out the way he came. As he moved past the front of a silver sedan, he heard someone pounding on the windshield behind him.

Turning, Ryan found Calvin staring wide-eyed from the driver's seat. "The door's jammed!" he hollered. "I can't get out."

Ryan ran around the front of the car and found the problem–a crumpled fender. "Can you lower the windows at all?" he shouted.

"No. The electrical system's dead."

A black Mercedes sedan ignited thirty yards away and sent an orange colored ball of flame into the air.

Ryan ducked behind the Buick as shrapnel showered the area. *Where's the fuckin' backup?* he groused. *Am I the only one dumb enough to be out here today?*

In answer to his rhetorical query, a Chevrolet Tahoe burst apart with a thunderous roar and fell to the ground with a thud.

Ryan's face slackened as he watched the remnants of the Tahoe blaze out of control. *The explosions are getting closer. There's not much time to get him out of here.* He dashed around the car to the passenger side of the Buick. "Cover your face–I'm gonna break the glass."

Calvin turned away as Ryan slammed his baton into the window. The glass crazed on impact, but didn't shatter.

Ryan brought his arm back to try again when a Honda Accord gave up the ghost to the blaze. The blast whisked him off his feet and tossed him in a heap on the roadway. He rose groggily to his knees, trying to clear the cobwebs from his head. "Uhhh," he groaned. "I guess I am the only one dumb enough to be out here today." Struggling to his feet, he leaned against Calvin's car for a moment as nausea swept over him.

Calvin watched anxiously as Ryan teetered on his feet. "Are you all right, officer?"

Ryan nodded weakly and slammed his baton against the window a second time, spraying the interior with glass. He hammered the remaining fragments from the window frame and leaned into the cabin. "Feel like blowin' this popsicle stand?" he asked drolly.

Calvin shot him a crooked grin. "You don't have to ask me twice." He propped himself upright and tried squirming out of his seat.

"Let me give you a hand," Ryan offered, mindful of their dwindling escape window. He grasped Calvin under the arms and pulled him free from the car. "Let's get out of here!" he shouted. "We don't have much time before–"

"Wait!" Calvin cried, reaching into the car. "I need to get my–"

Ryan clutched his arm. *"Leave it!"* he growled. "One of these vehicles could explode any second now!"

Calvin shook free from his grasp and reached through the shattered window to retrieve his briefcase. Though it would likely be destroyed in the fire, the working blueprints for the Frequency Wave Module could not be allowed to fall into unauthorized hands.

Ryan glared at him. "Whatever's in that briefcase better be worth *both* our lives." He tugged Calvin's arm, and they fled down a row of vehicles towards safety.

Twenty steps later, a deafening blast erupted behind them. Ryan reached out and hurled Calvin to the ground. "Get down! *Now!*"

As they fell to the pavement, the remains of the Buick's exhaust system whizzed overhead and slammed into the ground several feet in front of them.

"It's a freakin' battleground out here!" Ryan snarled. He bolted upright and yanked Calvin to his feet. "Come on, we gotta keep movin' or we'll be next."

Calvin cringed as another explosion went off behind them. He glanced over his shoulder, whistling aloud as a Dodge Caravan shredded to pieces in a cloud of destructive fury.

A few moments later, they reached the shoulder of the freeway and paused to catch their breath. To Ryan's relief, the back up he yearned for had finally arrived on the scene. Police and medical personnel were moving the stranded motorists into a waiting fleet of emergency vehicles parked alongside the roadway. Near the burned out shell of the tanker, a towering mound of foam flowed across the freeway as firefighters gained the upper hand in extinguishing the blaze.

A smile touched Ryan's face as he watched the operation unfold, noting with a bit of satisfaction that their exhaustive training had come together to save lives in the end. But, the smile quickly turned to a frown when he saw several blackened limbs protruding from the carcass of a melted car. Despite their best efforts, there was still much to learn.

"Officer?" A voice. Near–yet very far away.

Ryan turned his head towards the sound. *It's the man I pulled from the car. A little worse for wear, but he'll go home to his family tonight. Unlike some of the . . . others.* "Yes?" he asked.

Calvin smiled weakly. "I just wanted to thank you. For saving my life."

"Don't mention it," he muttered. "It's all just part of The Job."

"It never gets any easier, does it?" Calvin asked gently.

"Easier?"

"Watching people . . . die."

Ryan eyes dropped. "No . . . it doesn't."

"You did your best. There's only so much one can do."

Ryan looked up sharply. "Then next time, we do more. Until we get it–*right.*

21

Kyle flinched as the door slammed shut in the production room. "Rough meeting?" he asked dryly.

Karen hurled her purse into a chair and paced around the room. "No," she snarled. "The meeting went *fine*."

"Is something wrong, Karen?"

"*Should* something be wrong?" she snapped.

He shrugged. "Just thought I'd ask."

She ran a hand across her face and exhaled loudly. "Sorry, Kyle. I shouldn't take my problems out on you."

"Anytime you need to talk . . ."

Karen squeezed his shoulder. "I may take you up on that–sometime." She leaned over his frizzy topped head and glanced at the monitor. "How's the Neidermeyer segment coming along?"

"It's almost done. Are you ready to do the voice over?"

"Let me get my notes, and I'll–"

The phone suddenly pealed, and Karen reached across the console to pick it up. "Karen Mitchell."

"It's Stan. We just got word there's a major Sig-Alert on the Santa Monica Freeway near La Cienega Boulevard. Grab Kyle and head over there in Mobile Three to get the story."

"But, we're not done with the Neidermeyer–"

"Screw that," he barked. "No one gives a rat's ass on what politicians have to say these days anyway."

She rubbed her temples and sighed. *A Sig-Alert. Now my day is complete.*

"Are you still here?" he roared. "Get your ass out there. *Now!*"

Karen glared at the phone. "We're on it." *Asshole!*

Kyle looked up from the monitor. "What's up?"

"Sig-Alert on the Santa Monica Freeway. Grab your gear and meet me in Mobile Three."

"But what about the Neider–"

"*Forgetaboutit!* Stan said this is lot more important."

Twenty minutes later, the intrepid newshounds were hopelessly mired in gridlock ten blocks from their destination. Karen rapped her fingers on the dashboard, wondering anxiously if their report would be ready before the nightly news deadline. She pointed to an empty space on the side of the street and urged Kyle to pull over. "We're going to have to hoof it, Kyle. We can't wait here any longer if we want to meet our deadline."

His face slackened. "Are you kidding? We're half a mile from the freeway. We'll miss our deadline for sure."

"Do we have any choice?" she hissed. "At the rate we're moving, we can get there faster on foot."

Kyle shook his head and inched the van over to the curb. They snatched their equipment from the cargo area and headed towards the freeway on foot. From their location, the Sig-Alert looked like a broad charcoal smudge smearing the azure sky.

Hiking six jam-packed blocks towards the La Cienega on-ramp, they passed a multitude of frustrated motorists and curious onlookers caught up in the spectacle. The law enforcement agencies were out in force, cordoning off areas from rubberneckers and trying to restore order to the traffic clogging the streets.

Pushing through the mob, Karen waved her media pass overhead to get the attention of one of the officers guarding the on ramp. Several minutes later, she caught the eye of a young Latino officer holding back some unruly people from the crowd. "We're with KNBS," she shouted. "Who do we need to talk with to pass us through?"

The officer glanced at her credentials and smiled. "I'll have one of our men escort you to an area they have set up for the media, Miss Mitchell."

"Thanks." She looked at his badge and flashed a smile. "Officer Hernandez."

He shot her a roguish grin. "My Mom's a big fan of yours–she won't believe I actually met you today." He tore a ticket from his citation book and handed her a pen. "Would you mind giving her your autograph?"

Karen's cheeks reddened. "Sure, who do I make it out to?"

"Paulo."

"Paulo?" she asked, puzzled.

"My Mom's . . . nickname. Short for . . . uhhh . . . *Paulina.*"

Karen smiled wryly. "Of course–Paulina." She scrawled a few lines on the back of the citation and handed it back to the officer. "This must be a first–a civilian giving a ticket to a police officer."

Hernandez chuckled. "Please don't say anything about this–the crew at Rampart will never let me live it down."

"I think we can keep it off the late night news," she said dryly.

Hernandez instructed an officer to escort Karen and Kyle to the site reserved for the media. The trio scampered up the xeriscaped embankment, leaving the frenetic crowds and motorists behind. When they climbed over the guardrail at the top of the slope, they had their first clear view of the evening's carnage.

Surrealistic was the only word that came to Karen's mind. It was as if a scene had been lifted directly from a Hollywood disaster flick. Except this was all too real–Hollywood had not figured out how to recreate the malodorous stench of death in its movies.

The escort swept his arm across the pavement. "Be careful when you set up your equipment," he warned. "There are still some pools of unburned fuel scattered along the freeway. All it takes is a single spark and we may have another blaze on our hands."

Karen nodded politely while she surveyed the freeway. At the center of the scene, firefighters sprayed mounds of foam over the still smoldering tanker while hazmat personnel neutralized the fuel and toxic elements left over from the blaze. Paramedics and EMTs scavenged through the badly charred vehicles, recovering bodies for later identification. Law enforcement officials scurried throughout the grim tableau like a horde of ants, gathering information and considering how to bring the freeway back on line as quickly as possible.

After Kyle shot a few establishing shots of the tragedy, their escort led them towards a familiar flock of reporters that Karen frequently encountered at newsworthy events throughout the Southland.

Ken Orstein, a national reporter for CBS News, sneered at Karen as she approached the group. "Well, look who's here–the *inscrutable* Miss Mitchell. What's a nice girl like you doing in a place like this?"

"Now I know why you're such a ladies man, Orstein," Karen chided. "Your charisma is almost surpassed by your intelligence. *Almost.*"

Several reporters chuckled, but Orstein remained unfazed. "Retract your claws and relax, Miss M," he replied. "Or haven't you learned how to take a joke?"

Karen blinked. *He's right. My meeting with Stan has put me on edge all day.* "Sorry. Any word from the brass on what happened tonight?"

"Miss M, you know that a reporter never reveals his sources to the competition."

"Would it be asking too much to reveal who's acting liaison for the media?"

"Some joker named Rysinski is running interference for the department. But, he hasn't said shit to us up to now."

Karen glanced at her watch. *There's not much time left if we want to make our deadline.* "Did he give you any clue when we'd be briefed?"

"Nada. But, maybe you can turn on some of that legendary *charm* and he'll fall over backward to hand you the story."

Karen smiled wanly. *Like that's ever going to happen*, she mused. *If someone were to write a book about my love life lately, it would be a single blank page.* "Any idea where I can find this officer Rysinski?" she asked.

Orstein hooked a thumb over his shoulder towards a cadre of black and whites. "The last time I checked, he was over there conferring with some of the brass. You can't miss him—he looks like he stepped out of a war zone."

Karen wandered away from the group and snagged her cameraman's arm. "Follow me, Kyle" she urged. "I may be able to get the scoop on the Sig-Alert."

Standing near the blackened remains of the tanker, Ryan watched warily as a pair of reporters scurried across the freeway in his direction. He excused himself from a group of investigators and made a beeline in their direction to head them off. "You're going to have to leave, Miss," he said tersely. "This area is off-limits to unauthorized personnel."

Karen held out her credentials and smiled. "Are you officer Rysinski? I heard he's–"

"Please return to the area set aside for the media, Miss . . . "

"Karen Mitchell, from KNBS News." She flashed her thousand-watt smile. "Perhaps you've seen me on the air?"

"I don't have time to watch the local news on television, Miss Mitchell. I see enough bad news on my job every single day."

Karen inched the microphone towards his face. "And that's why I wanted to talk to you, officer Rysinski. Can you give me a statement on what happened here–"

He nudged the mike away. "I'm sorry, Miss Mitchell. The department is not ready to issue an official statement at this time."

"Well, what about unofficially?"

"There's no unofficial statement, either. When the data from the accident is analyzed and verified, the department will reveal their findings to the community."

Karen looked at Ryan and frowned. *This is going nowhere fast. A few minutes ago, I could've gotten officer Hernandez's life story without batting an eyelid. This Rysinski character, on the other hand, has all the warmth of a French waiter.* She cast a furtive glance in his direction. *On the other hand, he is pretty easy on the eye. A little soap and water . . . some nice, stylish clothes . . . and I could teach him a thing or two on how to protect and serve.*

Pushing aside her salacious thoughts, she pressed on with the interview. "Would you care to relate any personal experiences from tonight's tragedy to our viewers?"

"I can't give a personal account at this time either, Miss–"

Karen shoved the microphone in his face. "Can't? Or *won't?*"

Ryan's face tightened. After all the abuse he dealt with earlier in the day, the last thing he needed was a third rate reporter with an agenda for furthering her career. *But, if we had met under more–suitable–circumstances, things might have turned out different. I've never seen Miss Mitchell before, but I may have to start watching the local news channels a lot more often.* "I can't issue a statement of *any* kind, Miss Mitchell. Until all the facts are confirmed, any opinions I have could prove detrimental to the investigation. Surely, even you must understand that."

She lowered her mike and sighed. "Yeah, I understand. It's the same old bureaucratic *horseshit.*" She looked up sharply. "When do you think the department will be ready to issue a statement?"

"It's hard to say. The evidence needs to be analyzed to find the cause of the accident. Then, eyewitnesses must be interviewed and the facts corroborated by our department for accuracy. After that, the legal–"

"How *long?*" she groused.

"As one from your profession might say–stay tuned for further details." He broke into a broadfaced grin.

Karen's face went hot. *What a prick. If you weren't a cop I'd slap that silly smirk right off your face.* She turned suddenly and stalked away, leaving Ryan with a bewildered expression on his face.

Kyle hastily thanked Ryan for his assistance and ran down the freeway after Karen. "Hey! What's going on?" he hollered. "Why'd you take off like that?"

She ignored his query and climbed over the guardrail, carefully watching her step as she plunged down the embankment towards the La Cienega off ramp. Thirty feet behind her, she could hear Kyle pleading for her to stop.

She continued scrambling down the slope, pausing at the La Cienega on ramp just long enough for Kyle to catch up.

"What the hell's wrong, Karen?" he asked. "You got a bug up your ass or something?"

She crossed her arms and stared calmly in his direction. "Nothing's wrong, Kyle," she said softly. "Nothing at all."

"Then what do want to do with the video I shot between you and officer Rysinski a few minutes ago?"

Karen's eyes blazed in the waning evening light. "Frankly Kyle, if I never see or hear from Mister Rysinski again, it will be too damn soon!"

22

osé watched with bored amusement as a moth fluttered near one of the lamps hanging from the warehouse ceiling. The winged insect had darted in and out of the lamp's glow for over five hours now and had yet to grow exhausted from its efforts. The same, however, could not be said for José. Five hours waiting in the sweltering heat of the warehouse had become a true test of his patience.

Since his arrival, a dozen more migrants had drifted into the warehouse, bringing the total number in the group to twenty. The gathering was an eclectic mix of men, women, and several families from scattered regions of Latin America.

A young woman tending her infant daughter had befriended José while he had whiled away the time. Elena Sanchez was a bubbly brunette with doe-like eyes and a disarming smile. She planned on reuniting with her husband in Los Angeles once they were ferried across the border.

During their brief time together, they discussed their families, their hometowns, and the dreams they held for the future. Both shared similar lives and aspirations, and within hours a budding friendship had begun to grow between them.

José continued to watch the moth's monotonous journey when a door on the far side of the warehouse opened. Two large men scanned the dimly lit interior and then stepped quickly towards the waiting migrants. A short time later, the coyote strolled through the doorway and came over to greet them.

"Thank you for waiting," the coyote said amiably. "Gather up your belongings and follow my men to the white cargo truck at the back of the warehouse."

Several minutes later, the migrants joined the two hulking smugglers at the rear of the truck. The smuggler to the left of the truck sported languid eyes, close-cropped hair and a stubbly beard. A line off prison tattoos extended down one side of his neck and disappeared into a black sleeveless t-shirt. The other man was several inches shorter, with the stocky build of a rhino on steroids. A patch covered one eye on his craggy face, and his paper cut of a mouth was turned upward in a perpetual sneer.

The tattooed man cranked the back door of the truck upward, unveiling a pair of metal benches extending the length of the cargo area. Under each bench were several water filled jugs and a small lantern. At the back of the truck's cargo area, a five-gallon bucket served as a makeshift latrine.

A ramp was lowered to the ground, and the migrants trudged into the cargo compartment single file. After they had been seated, the tattooed man lowered the door and sealed them inside. The migrants shifted anxiously on the bench while their eyes adjusted to the compartment's dim interior.

A short time later, the engine started with a muffled roar and the truck rumbled out of the warehouse and on to one of the many roads leading from the city. The migrants stared numbly into each other's eyes, with only an occasional word of conversation breaking the gloomy mood in the cargo area.

An hour into their journey, the ride became noticeably rougher and José realized the truck was no longer traveling on a paved surface. The cargo area had become increasingly uncomfortable when the ventilation system failed to keep up with cigarette smoke and body heat generated in the heavily insulated compartment. As his gaze wandered over the somber faces of the migrants, he could see that fear and exhaustion had slowly taken their toll.

The truck rolled to a stop thirty minutes later. Two doors slammed shut, and the sound of crunching footsteps filtered into the cargo area. The rear door creaked slowly upward, and the migrants looked out on a dark desert landscape stretching desolately towards a mountain range on the horizon. A silver slash of a moon hung just above the jagged peaks, its feeble light providing little comfort in the bleak-looking environment.

The tattooed smuggler leaned into the cargo area and pointed the business end of an assault rifle at the immigrants. "End of the line, amigos," he growled. "Everybody out."

The migrants disembarked quickly from the cargo area and were herded a short distance away from the truck. The one-eyed smuggler shot a contemptuous look in their direction and chuckled. "Welcome to America."

A tall, fox-faced man stepped from the crowd and leveled an angry finger at the smugglers. "Where are we?" he groused. "I didn't pay *mucho dinero* to the coyote to be brought here!"

Several other migrants quickly voiced their dissent, their fear and confusion temporarily displaced by rage. The tattooed man aimed his rifle at the crowd and the outburst quelled as soon as it had begun.

"This is as far as we can go without being detected by El Migre," the one-eyed smuggler explained. "From this point on, you're on your own."

An obese, middle-aged woman shot the smugglers a disapproving look. "How far away is the nearest Americano town?"

The one-eye man gestured casually towards the horizon. "A single day's journey to the north."

"Why should we believe you?" José asked. "We could wander for days in the wrong direction if you're not telling us the truth."

The tattooed man marched forward and pressed the barrel of his rifle into José's neck. "The truth–*amigo*–is you have no other choice." He stepped back towards the truck and looked the migrants over. "Take whatever path you wish–it makes no difference to me."

"*Wait!*" Elena shouted. "You can't leave us here without any food or water."

The tattooed man smiled slyly. "Is it water you want?" He reached into the cargo area and hurled a plastic jug towards the crowd. "Then water you shall have!" As the container skittered across the graveled surface, the smuggler blasted a hole through its side and showered the startled migrants with water.

The one-eyed man let out a short, hard laugh. "Good luck, amigos. You'll need it."

The smugglers climbed into the truck and drove off into the darkness, leaving the migrants to face a grim and uncertain future.

23

Kati whipped open the kitchen door and wrapped her arms around Calvin. "Are you sure you're all right?" she cried. "I saw the accident on the news and–"

Calvin hushed her with a finger on her lips. "I'm *fine*, honey," he said gently. "But your car is another story."

She pushed him away. "That's not funny, Cal. You could have been killed out there tonight."

"You're right, Kati," he muttered. "There's a lot of people tonight who won't be going home to their families." His eyes dropped. "Ever again."

Tears welled in Kati's eyes. "I don't know what I would have done if you never . . ."

He pulled her close. "With the Lord's blessing, you won't have to worry about it for a long, long time." He looked around the kitchen and frowned. "Where are the kids?"

"They're around," she said coyly. "Right now, I want you all to myself."

Calvin kissed her on the lips. "Mmmm . . . remind me to get stuck on the freeway a lot more often." He looked at his wife, as if seeing her for the first time. She had aged well since their exchange of vows over a decade ago, her ivory complexion and glossy black hair showing nary a trace of the intervening years. Her assertive face framed almond shaped eyes that perpetually projected her quick wit and curiosity. He held her tightly in his arms and smiled wryly. *No doubt about it,* he mused. *They broke the mold right after they made Kati.*

A puzzled look crossed her face. "What's on your mind, dear?"

"Not much. I'm just thinking how good it is to be alive."

"That makes two of us." She stroked him gently on the cheek. "You must be starving by now. Sit down and I'll fix you something to eat."

He pulled a chair away from the kitchen table and sat down. "I'm not really that hungry, but I'd practically kill for a beer right now."

Kati got Calvin his beer and snuggled into his lap. "So how did your presentation go at Royce today?"

"It's hard to say. They seemed receptive to our presentation–"

She touched his lip. "But–"

Calvin chuckled. "There's always a but, isn't there? After our presentation was over, Morgan confided that my company has a better than even chance of getting the contract."

"Good news, then."

"Mmmm . . . it only means we're still in the ballgame." He took a swig from the bottle and frowned. "I hope Royce awards us this contract because my company won't be able to weather this downturn for much longer."

"*Our* company," she amended. "And don't worry about the contract–things will work out for the best regardless of Royce's decision."

"I'm glad *you're* the optimist in this family," he said. "But enough about me. What went on in your world today, Missus Taylor?"

"After you left this morning, I had the dealer tow the car to their service department. The service advisor suspects it's a malfunctioning sensor and quoted me a price of seven hundred and forty dollars to get it fixed."

Calvin groaned. "Anything else?"

"Not really. Compared to your day, mine was pretty . . . dull."

"I'll take your dull, routine day over mine, anytime. I've had enough excitement today to last me a lifetime."

"Oh, that's too bad," she teased.

His eyebrow rose. "Too bad?"

"It's too bad you had too much excitement today. I guess you won't be interested in any excitement later *tonight*."

"You know, I could take a *little* more excitement in my life."

Her eyes twinkled. "Are you sure? I wouldn't want you to get too excited or anything."

"You can excite me as much as you'd like," he whispered. "*Please.*"

She nuzzled his cheek and smiled. "I think it can be arranged."

He chuckled. "Well, now that we have *that* settled, what have the kids been up to today?"

"All Toni's been talking about lately is the new song that's out from Tangent."

"Tangent?" he asked. "Who's that?"

"You've got to be more in touch with your kid's lives, Calvin. Tangent is the latest boy band–"

"The latest? Who was the *last* one?"

"Does it matter?" she asked dryly. "You know really what scares me? In a few more years, she'll be a full-fledged teen. What will we do then?"

He shot her a crooked grin. "Be afraid, Missus Taylor. Be very afraid."

"Maybe we'll get lucky and she'll lead a relatively normal life."

"Ever known a teen to be anything *close* to normal?" Calvin asked.

"From what I've heard, the word teen is usually preceded by the word *problem*." Her face clouded. "Speaking of . . . problems, I think you need to have a talk with your son."

Calvin's forehead furrowed. "Oh? What's wrong now?"

"I don't know, but he hardly touched his dinner tonight. And it was his favorite–spaghetti and meatballs."

"Is he sick?"

"He's definitely not sick," she replied. "But when I asked him if something was wrong, he looked me straight in the eye and said everything was fine." She pinched her lower lip. "I know James, honey, and he's not a very good liar–yet."

"So what do you think is wrong?"

"I'm not sure, but it might be something that happened at school today. You remember how scary the world was at that age."

Calvin's mouth tightened. *It's still scary.* "Did his teacher call you today?"

She shook her head. "Talk to him. He may open up for you."

"It's worth a shot. Where is he now?"

"In his bedroom. He went there right after dinner and I haven't heard a peep from him since."

"No television, or video games?" His eyes widened. "That is strange."

Rising from the table, Calvin strolled down the hallway to James' bedroom and rapped on the door. When there was no reply, he pushed open the door and found James sitting on the edge of his bed in a dark, shadow streaked room.

He switched on the light and smiled cheerfully. "Hey, champ! How's it going today?"

James blinked briefly but remained silent.

Calvin's smile slackened. *Kati's right. There's something definitely going on here.* "So . . . who do you think's going to win the World Series this year?"

"I dunno," James muttered, lowering his eyes.

"You know, I think the Dodgers have a good chance of taking it–"

James looked up sharply. "Dad, the Dodgers *suck* this year!"

"Then who do you think—"

"Maybe the Indians."

"The *Cleveland* Indians?" Calvin quipped. "They blow chunks!"

James began to giggle, and Calvin sat on the bed and began tickling him. Within moments, they were engaged in a playful wrestling match. Toys and comic books tumbled off the bed and joined the rest of the playthings scattered though out the room. At the match's conclusion, they both gasped for breath—Calvin's distress more an act than the result of exertion.

"Whew!" Calvin wheezed. "A few more years and you'll be able to whup the old man for sure."

"You're not old, Dad."

"I wouldn't be so sure. I'm almost forty-years old."

"Forty!" James eyes grew huge. "That's old."

Calvin flinched. "At least I'm old enough to not suck my thumb."

James jumped up on the bed. "I don't suck my thumb!"

"You sure?"

James nodded emphatically.

Calvin grasped his son under the arms and lowered him to the bed. *He seems like his old self again. Or is he?* He searched his son's face and nibbled on his lip. *Kati feels something might have happened to him at school today. I guess there's only one way to find out.* "So, how did things go at school today?" he asked.

He shrugged. "We got to do some finger painting, and Miss Grant is teaching us how to read."

Sounds pretty normal so far. "Anything else?"

"I ate lunch in the cateferia and—"

"Cafeteria," Calvin corrected.

"Ca-fe-ter-i-a," James repeated slowly. "You should have been there, Dad!" he exclaimed. "Tommy sucked milk through a straw and blew it out of his nose! It was *cool!*"

A smile traced Calvin's face. *The frivolities of childhood.* "Did you get a chance to work on your fastball during recess today?"

James' face spasmed so quickly that Calvin thought he imagined it. "James?"

He looked up slowly. Tears welled in his eyes.

"What's wrong, son?"

"One of the kids . . . in third grade . . ."

"What happened, James?" Calvin pressed. "Did he beat you up?"

He shook his head and sniffed. "When I asked . . . if I could play on his team . . ."

Calvin leaned closer but remained silent.

"He said . . . he said he didn't want no *niggers* on his team." He buried his face in his hands and burst into a loud, wracking sob.

Calvin's head snapped back, as if struck. He reached out and wrapped his arms around his son. "It's all right, James," he said softly. "It's . . . all right."

The sobs grew more quiet, the breathing less labored, and James looked up at his father with red-rimmed eyes. "*Why* did he say that to me, Dad?"

Calvin took a breath and exhaled slowly. It was though he was reliving his own childhood again. He remained silent as he gathered his thoughts. *Just how do I explain racism in words that a five-year old child can understand? Will any explanation be possible without sounding like a racist myself?* After several considered responses, he chose to explain the principles behind racism in terms a young boy could understand. "James, sometimes people become . . . confused . . . about things they don't understand. And what they don't understand can sometimes make them . . . afraid. Does that make any sense to you?"

James' eyes squinted in puzzlement. "I . . . I think so."

"It's kind of like the monsters that hide under your bed at night–"

James eyes widened. "There are monsters, Dad! I've *seen* them!"

Calvin suppressed a smile. "I know they seem real to you now, but one day you'll understand a lot more about the world. And when that time comes, the monsters under your bed will be gone forever."

James scratched his head. "So the boy in the third grade thought I was . . . a monster?"

"No, not a monster," he assured. "Just . . . different. And because he really doesn't know you, it makes him–afraid."

"Why should he be afraid? He's a whole lot bigger than me!"

"It doesn't matter. His fear makes him lash out at you in a hurtful way because it makes him feel better about himself and a little less afraid of you."

"But I never did anything to hurt him," James countered.

"I know, son. But he is afraid nonetheless." Calvin placed his hand on his shoulder. "Are there any kids in your class that you don't know very well?"

James gnawed on his fingertip. "Just the *retards* that don't speak any English. Everyone at school makes fun of them because they talk funny."

"*James,*" he scolded. "How often have we taught you not to make fun of other people?"

"But *all* the kids make fun of them."

"Does that mean you have to act like every kid in your class?" he growled. "Making fun of someone because they're *different* is wrong."

James bit back tears. "I won't do it no more, Dad. Promise."

Calvin's jaw clenched. *Damn it, Cal! You're here to help, remember?* "I'm the one who should be sorry, son. I didn't mean to yell at you." He wrapped his arm around James and smiled. "From now on, try to treat everyone you meet in the same way you would like to be treated. And if you come across someone who doesn't want to take the time to know you better–then to *hell* with 'em. You're better off not having someone like that as your friend."

James nodded wearily and yawned.

Calvin's mouth tightened. *Looks like tonight's little sociology lesson is over.* "I think someone's up past their bedtime. Get into your jammies and I'll tuck you in for the night."

Several minutes later, Calvin flipped off the light and watched as James slept peacefully in the dimly lit bedroom. He turned his gaze out the window at the homes in his neighborhood and wondered what kind of lives the families led behind the protective glow of their windows. Were they the close-knit, loving families found on *The Waltons* or *The Cosby Show?* Or were they more like the dysfunctional families portrayed on *The Simpsons* or *Married with Children?*

He wondered how many families had to teach their children how to survive within a society where they were different. How many had to teach their children to adopt the language and traditions subscribed by the majority of society? *This was the premise on which our country was founded. A union born of diversity—where one's race, religion, or creed would meld with others in a utopian 'melting pot' and become greater than the sum of its individuals. A noble idea in concept, but more often than not our differences simmered angrily until some injustice brought the pot to an explosive boil.*

A tear drifted down his cheek as he watched his son slumber blissfully in the relative safety of his bedroom. *Today will mark an important turning point in James' young life. Today, he'll become another casualty in the collective conceived as America.* His expression grew dour. *How he'll fare will be anyone's guess.*

Kati stepped quietly into the room and embraced him from behind. "We can't always be there to protect him, Calvin," she whispered. "Sometimes the monsters *are* real."

He cocked his head. "How much did you overhear?"

"Enough. Do you think he understood?"

"I don't know," he muttered. "I'm a helluva lot older than he is, and I still don't understand it myself."

They stared at each other in the darkened room; the only sound was James gentle snoring.

Kati reached out and squeezed his hand. "You've had a long day, honey," she said softly. "Let's go to bed."

24

Andrew inched his gullwinged Mercedes coupe into the garage, breathing a sigh of relief that he had made it home without incident. He turned off the motor and stared groggily at his reflection in the rearview mirror. *You look like hell, Andrew. You better lay off the carousing or your mug shot will be plastered across every tabloid in town.*

Clambering out of his car, he fumbled his way into the house and poured himself a Scotch to wash his troubles away. As the golden elixir worked its magic, he mulled his current project's nearly endless litany of problems in his addled mind. Unlike most of his ventures, his production company had bankrolled the entire cost of his current project. The eighty million he budgeted had been exhausted several weeks ago, and additional funding would be almost impossible to find in today's financially constrained world.

He splashed another shot of liquor into the tumbler and downed it in one gulp. *This is all Ron's fault,* he fumed. *His constant fuck ups and capitulations have nearly brought my company to its knees.* A scowl crossed his face as he moved his gaze across the plushly decorated interior of his house. *I could lose everything if things don't work out, but I'm in too deep to back out now.*

As the alcohol dulled his rage, Andrew filled the glass to the brim and headed towards his media room. Modest by some standards in town, his entertainment chamber was a semicircular affair of birds-eye maple panels adorned with brushed aluminum trim. A state-of-the-art sound system and eight-foot wide plasma screen were concealed behind the sliding panels, giving the room a look of restrained minimalism.

Andrew sprawled across an ivory sofa in the center of the room and powered up the system with the remote control. Within moments, the lights in the room dimmed to darkness and the panels accordioned back to reveal the screen.

Surfing through a slew of pretentious pap, he was eventually drawn to a movie he hadn't seen in years. Starring Robert DeNiro and a young Leonardo DeCaprio, it was the true tale of an abusive stepfather's influence on *This Boy's Life.*

Sadness touched Andrew's face as the drama unfolded across the screen. Memories he had suppressed for years suddenly found their way into his troubled mind.

Roger Kinsey was no different from most of the losers his mother had met over the years, and like DeNiro's domineering character, had done everything he could to control their lives. At seventeen, Andrew neither wanted nor needed the advice of an abusive boyfriend who felt he would never amount to anything.

As the relationship between his mother and Kinsey plunged from bad to worse, Andrew could no longer turn a blind eye to the constant abuse his mother endured in the name of love. After years of watching the same rancorous relationships, he confronted his mother one fateful day on the choice of men in her life–and on Kinsey in particular. Their argument eventually became so heated that they failed to notice when Kinsey stepped into the house after a night of barhopping. Another argument quickly ensued, and Andrew pressed his mother to make a choice between him and her freeloading lover.

Andrew's hands clenched as he recalled the tortured expression on his Mother's face. *Her silence told me all I needed to know, so I made the choice and left her and her low-life boyfriend behind forever.*

As he watched DeNiro and DeCaprio duke it out on the screen, Andrew reconsidered the decision that changed his life forever. *Though much has transpired in the last thirty years, I have never regretted my choice. But I bear her no malice, and I only hope she found the peace she sought for most of her miserable life.*

Downing the last of his drink, Andrew settled back in the couch and watched as mother and son reconciled their differences in the film's final scene. Once the movie concluded, he turned off the television and stared mutely at the darkened screen.

If only real life could always end happily ever after.

25

Ryan exhaled loudly as he collapsed behind his desk at the station. "Man, what a fucked up day." He gave an anxious glance at his computer, dreading the task that lay before him. The paperwork. *Might as well get it over with,* he groused to himself.

His mood soured further as he typed the first snippets of information into his report. *Twenty-two dead–another thirty injured. Real people's lives distilled to nothing more than a line or two on some impersonal government chart.*

After completing half of the document, he suddenly realized he was spared the most difficult task of all–notifying the next of kin of their loved one's demise. *The only time I did this thankless chore, the vic's wife collapsed into my arms and left me with two terrified kids on my hands.* His face tightened as he recalled the incident in his mind. *I'd rather face a thousand infernos than deal with that shit again.*

He wondered how his own family would react if he were to die unexpectedly. *Ashley would be devastated by the news, but my ex would probably dance a jig upon my grave.* He gave a brief shudder and sighed. *I hope–if only for self-preservation's sake–that the situation never presents itself.*

Casperelli stumbled towards his desk with a box of doughnuts in his hand. "Hey dude, you look like shit. Has The Job finally caught up with you?"

Ryan smiled weakly. "Not yet. But some days it can be a little . . . overwhelming."

"Ain't that the truth." He pawed through the box of doughnuts and shoved one into his mouth. "I heard it was a real clusterfuck on the Santa Monica tonight," he sputtered between bites. "The crispy critters were stacked into the meat wagons like firewood."

After all his years on the force, Ryan could not understand why some of his associates regarded human life with such dispassion. "Yeah, it wasn't *pretty*," he grumbled. "Come to think of it, where the hell were you tonight?"

Casperelli slammed his hand on the desk, scattering a stack of papers across the floor. "Ahhh . . . the Loo's got me out on the street investigatin' all this gangbanger horseshit."

"Any clues so far?" Ryan asked dryly.

"Are you fuckin' kiddin' me? The homies ain't sayin' *dick*." He popped another sugared wad of dough down his maw. "We all know the bangers are more afraid of their own than anything we might toss at 'em. So they lay low, keep their yaps shut, and wait 'til we move on before they start terrorizin' the hood again." He shook his head and frowned. "Talk about your fuckin' circle jerk of life."

"Mmmm . . . sounds like The Job has caught up with *you*."

"Maybe so," Casperelli quipped. "But you can't beat the benefits."

Ryan's eyebrow twitched. "There's *benefits*?"

Casperelli chuckled. "Hey—if you ain't doin' nothin' later tonight, I'm lookin' for a few warm bodies to join me at the Cheshire Lounge. Interested?"

"I don't know. It's been a pretty fucked up day and I still have all this paperwork to do before I leave."

Casperelli clicked his tongue. "Dude, you need to get out more.

That triplicate shit can wait until mañana."

Ryan's gaze drifted wearily across the computer screen. *He's right, I do need to get out more. Maybe a couple—or a dozen—brewski's would be just what the doctor ordered.* "All right Cap, I'm in. Let me make a dent in these forms and I'll meet you at the club when the relief rolls in."

"That's the spirit, lad," he said. "Just remember to thank me in the morning." He stuffed another doughnut in his mouth and jogged off to the break room, leaving Ryan to finish his paperwork.

A smile tugged at Ryan's face as he watched Casperelli head down the hallway. *If I know Cap, he'll be lucky if he can remember his name tomorrow.*

26

J osé moved between two squabbling migrants and grasped Elena's hand. "Come on, Elena," he urged. "Let's get away from here for a while."

A puzzled look touched her face. "Where will we go, José?"

He remained silent and led her towards a group of boulders several hundred feet away. "Forgive me, Elena," he said softly. "I needed a few minutes away from those *idiotas* so I could think about our–situación."

"Did you find a way to the nearest town?" she asked excitedly.

He turned his gaze up towards the sky and smiled. "Perhaps."

She followed his gaze and frowned. "I don't understand, José. What's in the sky that could possibly help us?"

"It will all be made clear shortly." They retraced their steps back to the migrants and José stepped in front of the group to make an announcement. "May I have your attention, please? I may have found a way for us to get out of here."

The group temporarily stopped bickering and looked in José's direction. A tall, well-dressed man stepped out from the crowd and shot him a contemptuous sneer. "Forgive me for being *blunt*, señor, but what makes you so fucking sure?"

José ignored his derisive remark and leveled his gaze at the crowd. "When I was a boy, my grandfather showed me how to look for patterns of stars in the sky. These star patterns–or constellations as they are more commonly known–can be used as a guide to find your location on Earth."

The well-dressed man shook his head and chuckled. "So what do your stars tell you, amigo? That we're stranded in the middle of nowhere?"

Several migrants laughed and hurled taunts in José's direction. He ignored their ridicule and swept his arm towards the sky. "See those two bright stars just above the horizon? If you draw a line upward through them, you'll come across the North Star."

Elena pushed through the migrants and stood next to José. "And why is this North Star important?" she asked.

José flashed Elena a smile, thankful for her support. "If we head in the direction of the North Star, we'll continue to travel northward as though we had a compass to guide us. Sooner or later, we're sure to find someone who can help us out."

"Let's hope it's not El Migre," a teen joked from the back of the crowd. Several migrants in the group laughed nervously at the quip, keenly aware of their vulnerability in the wide open space of the desert.

After several minutes of wrangling between the migrants, they acceded to José's advice and trudged out into the desert in the direction he indicated. They made slow but steady progress across the desolate landscape, passing clumps of scraggly creosote bushes punctuated by the occasional mesquite or yucca tree. In the distance, giant saguaros stood guard like many limbed soldiers overlooking the hostile environment.

After several hours of hiking, the group's progress was halted by a steep sided gully carving a trough across their path. The gully's parched bed was only twenty feet below the surface, but the sharp drop-off made access impossible without the use of a rope. Undaunted, the group paralleled the edge of the ravine for several hundred yards until they found a break in the slope that would allow them to descend safely. A human chain was formed, and the migrants carefully descended to the bottom of the dried out riverbed. A navigable course was soon found up the opposite embankment and José suggested the group rest in the basin for the night.

The overweight woman pitched her knapsack to the ground and looked disapprovingly in José's direction. "Why are we making our camp down here and not along the banks of the ravine?" she groused.

"The gully's walls will shelter us from the weather," he replied. "And the animals that look for food at night will be less likely to look for it down here."

Elena shuddered. "That's a good enough reason for me."

The migrants scoured the gully for firewood and were soon soothing their weary bodies around a blazing fire.

Elena settled next to José and began to rock Angelina in her arms. "I don't know about you, but I'd give almost anything for a nice, hot shower right now."

José nodded but remained silent. He watched the cinders from the fire whirl upward in the sky and wink out in the cool, dark night.

Elena nudged his shoulder. "What's on your mind, José?" she asked gently.

"Just thinking about . . . my future. But considering our current situation, I may not have much to worry about."

"Don't you think we'll make it out of here?" she asked, anxiety tinging her voice.

He smiled wanly. "I think so, but–"

"No *buts*, José. There are too many people counting on us."

"Marriage has taught me not to argue with a woman once she has made up her mind."

"And you have learned well," she said, grinning. "As long as we don't give up hope, there's always a chance we'll succeed."

Forcing a smile, José turned his gaze back towards the fire, hoping Elena hadn't sensed the despair he felt in every fiber of his body.

FRIDAY

27

Kicking off the bedspread, Karen stared angrily at the ceiling in the dimly lit bedroom. On the nightstand to her left, she watched with frustration as the clock ticked away another second until daylight.

Several minutes later, she gave in to her anger and switched on the lamp. *Ahhh . . . it's no use,* she griped to herself. *Between my jerk of a boss and some wiseass cop, I'm too wound up to sleep tonight.* She rubbed her temples and sighed. *What did I do to deserve this abuse?*

Karen continued to stare at the ceiling, wondering how she was going to solve her problem with Stan. *If only I had someone to talk to . . . someone who understood how–Wait! Jen will know what to do.* She glanced at the clock face and frowned. *Mmmm, I hope she's still awake.*

She snatched her cellphone off the nightstand and punched in her friend's number. *Come on, Jen–pick up. Please pick–*

A voice blared angrily in Karen's ear. "Who the *hell* is this?"

Karen flinched. "Hi Jen, it's me . . . Karen."

A pause. "Karen?"

"I hope I didn't wake you up."

"Not at all," she said. "I always expect people to call me at . . . at . . . *three-thirty in the friggin' morning.*"

Karen's face slackened. *Damn, I forgot she's in a different time zone.* "Sorry, Jen. If you want to go back to sleep–"

"*Sleep?* When you're the mother of two-year old twins, you can't even *think* about sleep."

"So how are the boys doing?" Karen asked.

"They're fine," she muttered. "*I'm* the one who's a raving lunatic."

"And Robert?"

"Ahhh . . . he's sleeping–*the rat.* He'll sleep through anything short of a tornado ripping the roof off the house. And probably that too, now that I think of it." She paused. "So what's up? You didn't call me in the middle of the night just to find out how my family is doing."

Karen stared at the phone. "I'm not sure . . . where to start . . ."

"How about the beginning?" she said drolly. "Usually works for me."

Karen paused. "Have you ever had one of those days where everything turns to shit?"

"Are you *kidding?* That pretty much describes my average day. Not only does it turn to shit–I've got to look at it and smell it, too."

Karen tittered. "I thought we were going to talk about *my* problem."

"I've got issues too, you know."

"We can talk about those later."

"Why do I always play second fiddle to the glamorous reporter–"

"My life's not as *glamorous* as you think," Karen interjected.

"Mmmm . . . sounds like you might have a real problem here."

"It's not a matter of life or death," Karen said. "But I wouldn't mind–"

"–getting another opinion?"

Karen smiled. "Right. Anyway, back to my–problem. This morning, my boss asked me if I would be interested in co-anchoring the telecast of a nationally televised event. At first, he said he was giving me an opportunity to advance my career, but later in the day I found out the *real* reason why he picked me for the position."

"And what would that be?" Jennifer asked.

"Let's just say he wanted something in return for getting me the job."

A pause. "Are you saying what I *think* you're saying?"

"He never said anything specific, but the *message* was definitely there."

"Karen, are you sure? He may have had something else in mind entirely–like dinner at a fancy restaurant or tickets to the ball game. I can't believe someone in his position could be so clueless about the laws concerning sexual harassment."

"So what do you think I should I do?"

"Did you consider giving him a quick kick to the *cojones?*"

Karen laughed. "Don't you think that's a little harsh?"

"Not at all. It would be a symbolic blow for every woman who's been screwed over in the workplace."

"There's just one tiny flaw with your plan. I was hoping to keep my job after the issue was resolved."

"Oh, that changes things." She paused. "What about talking to his supervisor? Maybe they can help you out."

"I'm not sure that's such a wise idea, Jen. I don't have any proof to back up my claims, and it would quickly become your typical 'he said, she said' dispute." She took a deep breath and exhaled. "No, I need to nip this in the bud right now. Do you think I should confront him directly or just ignore his comments entirely?"

"That depends. Does your boss remind you more of James Bond or . . . Genghis Khan?"

Karen snorted. "Isn't there some other choice?"

"Not in my experience."

"If those are my *only* choices, I'd say he's more like good old Mister Khan."

"That's not so good for you, my dear. Good old Genghis tends to view the world in black and white–he's your 'if you're not with me, you're against me' kind of guy. Confrontation is out of the question because he'll find some way to retaliate against you the first chance he gets. I'd suggest a more . . . subtle approach . . . that allows him to walk away with his machismo intact."

"And what *devious* plan did you have in mind, Jen?"

"Ahhh, Grasshopper," she replied, "it's time you learn from the Master. In my younger days, I had many ways of discouraging over-eager men from staying out of my pants."

"Oh, really? That's not what I heard."

"And how would you know, *Miss Bookworm?* As I recall, you wouldn't date anyone with an IQ of less than a hundred and thirty."

"And as I recall, you used another part of the anatomy to measure your men."

Jennifer laughed. "A woman's got to have some standards, you know."

"So what is your plan of enlightenment, Master?"

"What I am about to say is strictly confidential, Grasshopper. In the wrong hands, such knowledge could have unfortunate consequences." She paused. "The Master advises Grasshopper to . . . to . . . become undesirable to his heart."

"Huh? What kind of *advice* is that?"

"The answer is obvious, Grasshopper. Getting involved with you is not an option."

"And how–"

"Haven't you figured it out?" she chided. "Just tell the jerk you have a sexually transmitted disease and he'll drop you like yesterday's news. No pun intended."

Karen sighed. "Why don't I just tell him I'm really a man and see how that–"

"That was my going to be my *second* choice, Grasshopper, but one look at you and it will never fly. Look, when it comes to emotional issues, men always take the path of least resistance. Once your boss knows what the score is, he can bow out with dignity and your problem will be solved."

"I guess I shouldn't question the Master's wisdom . . ."

"Damn right, Grasshopper. I might be married now, but that doesn't mean I've forgotten what it's like to be a swingin' bachelorette." She yawned. "Does Grasshopper need any more advice tonight because the Master is up way past her bedtime."

Karen paused. "I could use your help on something else–now that you mention it."

Jennifer groaned. "Who needs sleep anyway? Continue Grasshopper, you have my undivided attention."

"This isn't really a . . . problem, but I'd like to get your opinion just the same." She paused to gather her thoughts. "Earlier tonight, I had to cover a grisly Sig-Alert for the late night news. When I tried to interview the LAPD's liaison about the accident, he jumped all over my case like–"

"Excuse me for interrupting, but did he have a reason to do so?"

"Of course not. My behavior was strictly professional."

"Does strictly professional mean badgering your interviewee in a confrontational manner?"

Karen bit her cheek. "I may have been a . . . little demanding."

"A little?"

Karen frowned. "Okay, *a lot*."

"Hmmm . . . there's something more going on here, isn't there Grasshopper? You wouldn't bring this up just because someone blew you off for an interview. In your profession, that must be something you have to deal with everyday."

Karen took a breath and exhaled. *She knows me better than I know myself.* "You're right, Jen–there is more. Rysinski was a total pain in the ass, but *something* passed between us. I think he sensed it, too."

"Maybe it was gas," Jennifer quipped.

"You know what I think? I think the Master has lost her touch."

"Bite your tongue, Grasshopper." She paused. "Is this officer Rysinski . . . good looking?"

"You might say that."

"Oh, a real stud-muffin, eh?" Jennifer said, chuckling. "Any chance of seeing him again?"

"I doubt it," Karen muttered. "We're just two ships passing in the night." A look of sadness touched her eyes. "I wonder sometimes if I made the right choice when I moved to L.A. If I had never left Norfolk, would I have settled down and raised a family like you?"

"We'll never truly know, Grasshopper. But, you never would have been satisfied with my way of life. You've always been on a quest–searching for answers–ever since I've known you. I wasn't the least bit surprised when you left this Podunk town to find something better in your life. My only fear is when you do find what you're looking for, you'll fail to appreciate it and your life will remain unfulfilled."

"But, isn't that the irony our existence? To never know fulfillment?"

"It's the sad truth, Grasshopper. Most societies in today's world have equated contentment with materialism, but happiness is not defined by what you own. It's a feeling of peace; a spiritual acceptance of one's self in the world. The promise that hard work and determination will bring you contentment and prosperity–the so-called *American Dream*–is nothing more than glorified Madison Avenue propaganda." She paused. "In your quest for fulfillment, the only advice I can give is to keep your search focused, and hopefully you'll find what you're looking for one day."

"You are most wise, Master," Karen said dryly. "Or full of bullshit."

"Perhaps a little of both, Grasshopper. For isn't wisdom nothing more than bullshit that has passed the test of time?"

28

While he waited outside the door to enter the Cheshire Lounge, Ryan could feel the music inside the club resonate through every bone in his body. After a quick shower and change of clothing at the station, he was eager to leave the day's troubles behind him.

After the hired muscle passed him through the doorway, Ryan beat a circuitous path through the dimly lit interior to reach his comrades. Moving his gaze through the smoky room, he noticed that little had changed since his last visit. A large sit-down bar and bevy of topless dancers gave the testosterone crazed crowd the solace they needed after a lonely day.

Casperelli waved his hand to catch Ryan's attention. "*Hey!* Over here, dude!"

Ryan strode up to Casperelli's table and clapped him on the back. "You're still conscious?" he asked dryly.

Casperelli held up a half filled glass and looked at Ryan with glazed eyes. "Just gettin' warmed up, dude," he slurred. He swept his arm around the table in a drunken whirl. "Let me introduce you to the rest of the gang."

Glancing around the table, Ryan noted that half the group needed no introduction as he had worked with them for years.

Jerome Biggers had been aptly named at birth. Standing nearly seven feet high and weighing three hundred pounds, Biggers was a former Chargers lineman who entered law enforcement after a bad block ended his career. His intimidating appearance belied a gentle manner that endeared him to everyone at the division and to the communities he patrolled.

Kyle Reed, on the other hand, barely squeaked by the LAPD's minimum height requirements and carried a chip on his shoulder twice as wide. With his cowboy attitude and trigger point temper, Reed's reputation as an enforcer was well known throughout the precinct.

The two other men at the table were Casperelli's former associates at the Rampart Division. William Deland had served on the force for over two decades, and every year of tenure was clearly etched into his face. A rat's nest of white hair framed a florid face and bloodshot eyes that darted nervously around the room.

Kelly Marsh's block shaped head was topped by a blonde curly mane clipped fuzzy at the sides. A nervous tic caused his face to spasm every time he smiled.

"Cap's been cluing us in on the freeway fiasco tonight," Deland said. "Just how bad was it?"

Ryan looked at Deland and pinched his lip. *The last thing I need right now is another reminder of what went down on the freeway tonight. Even after a long hot shower at the precinct, I still haven't gotten the stink of diesel fuel and burnt flesh off my body.* "Bad enough," he muttered. "But thankfully, most of the vic's had stopped screaming by the time I arrived on the scene."

A busty brunette with a vacant stare bounced over to the table to take Ryan's order. "What would you like to drink, sir?"

"Bring me a double Chivas–straight," he replied. "I've got a lot of catching up to do." After the waitress left the table, Ryan reached across the table and snagged Casperelli's arm. "Who's topping tonight's bill?

"You're in for a real treat, dude. Blossom is one of the hottest dancers on the circuit."

"Blossom?" Ryan's eyebrow lifted upward. "Is she new here?"

Casperelli shook his head and smiled wryly. "She's . . . unique."

"What's she do that's so unique?"

Biggers shot him a crooked grin. "We could tell you, but then we'd have to kill you."

The waitress returned with Ryan's drink. "Here you are, sir. Twelve dollars, please."

Casperelli snatched her arm. "It's on me, babe. And while you're at it, bring everyone here another round." He tucked a fifty between her breasts and chuckled. "Keep the change."

She flashed him a smile. "Anytime, big guy."

Casperelli wore a hangdog look after she fluttered away. "I'm in love."

Ryan rolled his eyes. "*Again?* That's the third time this month." He reached over and patted Casperelli on the back. "Don't worry, Cap. Another one will come along to take her place."

Casperelli sniffed. "There'll never be another one like *her.*"

Before Ryan could finish soothing his hammered friend's ego, the room darkened in anticipation of Blossom's arrival. The gentle strains of the Eurythmics *Sweet Dreams* swept through the room, barely audible over the howls of the nearly maniacal crowd. A red spotlight speared the rhinestone-flecked curtain, showering the room with tiny sparkles of light. A hand undulated outward between the curtains like a rhythmic human snake, followed by a body rippling in beat to the music.

Though Blossom wasn't particularly attractive in Ryan's eyes, there was an exotic element about her that was—for lack of a better word—unique. *Maybe it's her gold lamé costume,* he wondered. *Or the way she moves across the—*

Casperelli shot an arm into his side. "You ever seen anything like that, dude?" he screeched. "That bitch don't have a friggin' bone in her body!"

Ryan nursed his ribs and watched raptly as Blossom slinked languidly down the runway. Scores of men rose from their tables and swarmed towards the stage, vying for the best vantage point possible. Blossom leaned towards the frenzied crowd and caressed their faces with long curved fingers while they slipped money inside her continually gyrating thong.

After several minutes of playful banter with the audience, she wrapped her legs around the pole at the center of the stage and arched her back towards the floor. She inched one leg provocatively upwards until she was vertically spread-eagled against the pole. Encouraged by the rowdy crowd, she peeled off her top and flung the strip of flimsy fabric into the audience. A skirmish quickly ensued until one hardy soul raised the golden strip of cloth above his head, victorious.

The audience roared their approval and Blossom flipped onto her back, arching her legs until they were behind her head.

Casperelli's jaw dropped. "Can you fuckin' believe that? She must be double jointed or somethin'!" He jumped on top his chair and whistled. "This time I know it's real, Ryan," he howled. "I'm in love. *I'm in love!*"

Ryan watched Casperelli's antics and smiled wanly. To his buddies, he appeared to be having a good time, but inside he felt strangely unfulfilled by tonight's performance. His thoughts drifted to an encounter he had several hours earlier–but what now seemed a lifetime ago. *How hard would it have been to grant her an interview? But no, you had to do everything by the book and force her off the freeway–and out of your life–forever.* He downed the rest of his drink and frowned. *Let's face it, you never get a second chance to make a good first impression.*

His face clouded. *Or do you?*

29

Exasperation tinged Calvin's face as he tried to fit a baseball cap on his son's fidgeting head. "Hold still for a minute, James, so I can put your cap on." He tugged the bill downward and looked him over. "Now you look just like your favorite slugger, Tyler Lewis."

James twisted the cap's bill backward and grinned at his father.

Calvin sighed. "I give up. Is that the way you guys wear your caps these days?"

James wiped his nose with the back of his hand and nodded.

"Do you remember what we talked about last night?" Calvin asked.

"Don't make fun of people who are different from me?"

Calvin nodded. "And?"

"Treat everyone like I'd like to be treated?"

Calvin's mouth curled upward in a smile. "That's right. And if someone ever picks on you, walk away unless you have no other choice. When I was your age, we had a rhyme we'd use on kids that called us names. Sticks and stones may break my bones—"

"But words will never hurt me!" James screeched. "I know it, Dad."

Kati handed James his lunch and kissed him on the cheek. "Some things never change, dear."

"Maybe not," Calvin muttered, "but I wouldn't mind if that phrase faded from use forever." He glanced around the kitchen and frowned. "Where's your sister, James?"

He shrugged.

Calvin cupped a hand over his mouth. "Hurry up Toni, or you'll be late for school!"

A door slammed loudly at the rear of the house, and his daughter trudged into the kitchen with a sullen look on her face.

"Glad you could grace us with your presence, Toni," Calvin said dryly. "Make sure you drop your brother off at the bus stop on your way to school today."

Toni gave a disgusted look. "Do I *have* to, Dad? I don't want my friends seeing him tag along with–"

"Yes–you *have* to," he chided. "And don't worry about what your friends think–all that matters is what you think of yourself."

She scowled. "Oh, *alright!*" She reached out and snatched James' hand. "Come on, butthead–I haven't got all day!" She kissed her mother on the cheek and paused by the door to look at Calvin.

"Don't I get a kiss, too?" he asked sweetly.

Toni stared at her father for a moment, then bolted out the door.

Calvin winced. "All right–what the hell did I do now?"

Kati sat next to him at the kitchen table and smiled. "Not a thing, dear. Your little girl is growing up. In a few more years, she'll be bringing home boys for you to give the third degree to."

"Don't *remind* me," he grumbled. "They're growing up so fast that I can't keep up with them anymore."

"You didn't have any problem–keeping up–last night."

He smiled wryly. "Well . . . you're never too old for *some* things."

"Still, after your third time, you should have called it a night." She rubbed her back and grimaced. "Some parts of me are still sore."

Calvin chuckled. "Oh really, Missus Taylor? Care to elaborate?"

"That's strange, weren't you there at the time?"

"I'll always be there for–" His face suddenly slackened.

"What's wrong, hon?"

"Your remark. I wasn't there for James . . . when he needed me."

She shot him a puzzled look. "Maybe it's your turn to elaborate."

"Last night, you said we couldn't always be there to protect him. That sometimes . . . the monsters are real."

"Our kids can't live their lives inside a bubble, Cal. They need to experience the good, the bad, and the ugly in life firsthand. James childhood may be a little more difficult than most, but with our love and support he should do all right in the end."

"And if he doesn't?"

"We'll cross that bridge when we come to it. *If* we come to it. He'll soon realize that racial taunts reflect more shamefully on the person directing the comment than the one they are directed at."

"You're probably right," he replied. "But words can definitely hurt you, despite what the rhyme from our childhood implies. The *wrong* words can change how a child looks at the world for the rest of their life."

"Let's face it," Katie said. "Kids can be downright cruel sometimes. We'd like to believe they're sugar and spice and everything nice–but we were kids once–and we *know* better. I'm sure every adult can remember a time from their childhood when they were at the wrong end of some classmate's vicious put-down."

"I certainly can," Calvin reflected. "And unfortunately . . . so will my son."

Kati gave a sour smile. "Let's hope his childhood takes a less troubled path than yours."

"I doubt that it will. Even though we've made great strides in the last hundred years, I don't think bigotry will ever be eliminated from our lives. One look at the news or the history books and you'll see countless examples of man's inhumanity to man."

"And what does that say about us?" Kati asked. "Are we headed on a path towards extinction?"

"I don't know," he said softly. "Lord knows we've made plenty of mistakes so far." His gaze grew distant, unfocused. "Sometimes I wonder if the melting pot envisioned by our founders is nothing but an idealistic dream. If your average couple can't always see eye to eye, how can we expect three hundred million individuals to live in complete harmony?"

"We've managed so far."

"Not everyone is like us, Kati. Neither of our family's have yet to truly accept our marriage."

"They'll come around someday."

Calvin shook his head. "It's too late for them–and probably for most of our generation as well. Our kids will have to continue the struggle towards equality, and perhaps their children or grandchildren as well."

"You make it sound so . . . so hopeless."

"It's not hopeless," he replied. "In each generation, there are always a few who are willing to carry on the dream towards peace and equality. And as long as *one* of us believes–that dream will never die."

Kati squeezed his hand. "Never is a really long time."

"And belief in one's faith," Calvin affirmed, "is forever."

30

The morning sun sliced over the gully's edge with the fury of a blast furnace, awakening the immigrants to a brutally hot day.

José rose from the dried out riverbed and ruffled the sand from his clothing. His eyes crawled with grit, and his tongue squirmed inside his mouth like a warm lump of clay.

Elena opened a bleary eye to the world. "Mmmm . . . what time is it, José?"

He glanced at his watch. "It's almost eight. If I were back in Jiquilpan, I would have already been out in the fields long before the sun squeezed the life out of you for the day."

She propped herself upright and tousled her hair. "What's on your schedule today?"

"The first thing we need to do is find some kind of shelter away from the sun. Without it, we won't last more than a day out here in this heat."

"I saw nothing last night that we could use for shelter except the mountains on the horizon." Her face slackened. "You're not thinking . . ."

"It's our only chance, Elena. The gully will provide us with shade for another hour or so, but after that we'll be at the mercy of the sun."

He wiped his forehead with the back of his hand. "If we head towards the mountains, we may be able to find a ledge or cave to protect us from the heat. And with any luck, we might find water underneath a dried out stream bed at the base of the mountain range."

Her eyebrow rose. "How do you know of such things, José?"

"My grandfather taught me many things about the world when I was a little boy. But until now, I haven't had the opportunity to test his teachings."

"Let's hope he was right," she said. "Our lives may depend on it."

A man's voice suddenly interrupted their conversation. "Where do we go next, señor?" he jeered. "Or do we need to wait until the stars come out tonight to find our way out of here?"

José and Elena turned towards the source of the derisive remark. The well-dressed man who taunted José earlier glared in their direction with baleful eyes.

José inspected the stranger's wardrobe and suppressed a smile. His tailored gabardine suit and oxford shoes were ill-suited for a trek across the desert. "I don't need the stars to find my way around, señor. We'll continue on our present course until we find something that–"

A gangly teen with buzz cut hair laughed harshly. "How can you find your way without the stars to guide us?"

"It's simple," José explained. "We'll use the sun as our guide. We'll keep it to our backs as we travel across the desert and that will keep us moving in a northward direction."

"And how long before we reach the nearest town, amigo?" the well-dressed man demanded.

José's eyes narrowed. *He's testing me,* he thought to himself. *He's probably used to ordering people around where he came from. Well, he's about to learn that things have radically changed.* "I don't think we've been introduced, señor." He held out his hand. "I am José Torres."

The stranger looked at José's hand and sniffed. "Miguel," he growled.

"Miguel Rios."

José dropped his arm and met Miguel's eyes. "The question is not how long it will take to reach the nearest town, Miguel, but whether we can reach the nearest town at all. Since none of us brought any provisions for our trip, we'll need to find water if we–"

"And where we will find water in the middle of the desert, señor?" the buzz cut teen cut in. "I haven't seen a single McDonald's since we've been dumped here."

José stiffened as several migrants listening to their conversation burst into laughter. *Am I the only one who realizes the danger we're in?* Moving his gaze across the group, he saw several migrants who were not amused by the teen's wisecrack. In their expressions, José clearly saw anxiety, overlaid with a trace of fear. *They know,* he fretted. *They know we're only a day or two away from dying out here.* He waited for the laughter to subside before he continued. "Now that everyone's had their little laugh," he said curtly. "Let's talk about getting the hell out of here."

"What did you have in mind, señor?" a portly man with a Dutch-boy haircut and bushy eyebrows asked.

"The gully will keep the sun away from us for another hour or two, so we need to find shelter as soon as possible. If we head east towards the mountains, we might come across a cave or a ledge to protect us from the heat. Then at night, when it's cooler, we'll continue to head north until we come across a town or a roadway leading to civilization."

An overweight woman wearing a red and green scarf cast a stern look in José's direction. "Must we go all the way to the mountains, señor?" she griped. "Can't we just head north from the gully?"

"There's nothing north of here we can use for shelter," José replied. "We must conserve our strength for the next few days if–"

"You expect to be here *more* than a day?" the woman chided. Her face suddenly grew pale.

"I don't know," José replied. "But, we should prepare ourselves for the worst." He glanced up in the sky and pursed his lips. "We're wasting time. If any of you wish to join me, grab your gear and be ready to head out in the next few minutes."

Though some doubted the soundness of his plan, the group put aside their misgivings and decided to follow José. Several minutes later, with José and Elena at the lead, the migrants trudged out of the gully and headed towards the mountains.

"You sure showed them who's boss today," Elena said proudly.

José gave a sour smile. "It doesn't matter who has the biggest cojones in our group, Elena. We're all going to have to work together if we want to survive."

She clutched his arm and smiled broadly. "And with you as our guide, we just might make it."

31

A ndrew scanned the menu from his plushly upholstered seat and smacked his lips. "Have you ever tried Antoinne's seafood omelet, David?" he asked. "It's quite good."

David Levin glanced at Andrew's endorsement and frowned. "Mmmm . . . any other recommendations?"

"You can't go wrong with the crepes," Andrew professed. "They're pleasantly light–with a sweet, buttery taste that melts in your mouth. And the fillings–if you'll forgive the cliché–are to die for." He waved his arm above his head to get the server's attention. "Let's order a round of cocktails while we mull it over."

The server soon returned with their drinks, and Andrew stretched out in his chair and got down to business. "Thanks for fitting me in on such short notice, David. I know you're juggling a million things at the studio right now."

"Always glad to be of service," Levin quipped. "Especially when I've got the chance to sign Miss Morraine on for scale."

Andrew chortled. "I think it's going to be a little more than scale, but her agent has confirmed that she'll come on board for ten large and two percent of the back end profits."

"If you think it's a done deal, I'll have my lawyers work up a contract." He took a swig from his drink and smiled wryly. "Speaking of actresses, we're you able to douse the fire on your set yesterday?"

"Oh, that?" Andrew replied nonchalantly. "Just your usual . . . creative differences."

"I heard Angela shut down production for close to six hours yesterday. That must have cost you a pretty penny–or two."

Andrew downed half of his Bloody Mary and smiled sourly. "Things were down for a while. But in the end, Angela delivered one of the greatest performances of her career."

"Was it worth it?"

Andrew shrugged. "Business is business."

"Except when it affects your bottom line," Levin said drolly.

"That's one of the reasons I like working with you, David. You run your studio like a business and not some Tinseltown whorehouse where everyone gets fucked in the ass. I've learned more from you through the years than from everyone else in this industry *combined*."

"Though flattery will get you everywhere in this town," Levin smirked, "you've advanced far beyond my–enlightenment. You have an uncanny eye for talent, and a sixth sense for what sells on the silver screen. There's a long list of people in town who owe their success to your insight and inspiration."

"And an even *longer* list that thinks I'm the biggest a-hole around."

"That's the problem with the talent today, Andrew. They're all a bunch of whiny prima donnas with a sense of entitlement." He shook his head and chuckled. "But as you and me both know, an actor's bankability is only as good as their *last* performance."

"That's why I usually work with the lesser-known people in town. I get twice the performance–and half the headaches–and still manage to add millions to my company's bottom line every year.

"And don't think I haven't noticed," Levin said. "Your track record speaks for itself. But clever marketing and speculation can't always be a predictor of success."

"If there was a formula for making a hit," Andrew mused, "don't you think we would have found it by now?"

"The public's too fickle for formulas. What worked for today's blockbuster will be tomorrow's bargain basement download." He gave a bitter laugh. "As goes life, so go the fortunes of Hollywood."

Andrew shot him a puzzled look. "So everything we strive for and hope to accomplish in life is left to the whims of Fate?"

"All we have is *now*, Andrew. Nothing more, nothing less."

Andrew searched his mentor's eyes, hoping to discover the meaning behind his cryptic response. Seeing nothing, he returned his gaze to the menu. "If that's the case," he said dryly. "I think I'll have another drink."

32

Karen squirmed in her seat as she wrapped up the last few items to her Pangaea Festival outline. Several minutes from now, she'd take her proposal to Stan's office for feedback. It was a meeting she was trying to avoid until the last possible moment.

Though last night's conversation with Jennifer had allayed some of her fears, Karen was still unsure on how she should resolve her problem with Stan. Jennifer's scheme sounded promising at first, but she would still be subject to her supervisor's retaliation in the future. What she needed was a way to walk away unscathed and yet allow her boss to retain his dignity.

Karen glanced at her watch and sighed. *Time to face the music.*

She left her cubicle and headed towards Stan's office. As she stepped inside the elevator and pressed the button for the third floor, the station manager squeezed between the closing doors to join her.

Karen flashed him a smile. "How are you today, Mister Beckman?" she asked affably.

Howard Beckman adjusted his gold-framed glasses and returned her smile. Today he was wearing a blue polo shirt and beige slacks in a nod to casual Fridays, but he always looked more comfortable in the starched and creased attire favored by corporate America. "Couldn't be better," he crowed. "And you?"

"Things are looking up."

"That's great," he said. "By the way, Stan's been keeping me apprised of your progress and has nothing but praise for you."

Karen nodded politely. *Mmmm . . . I bet.* "He's the *best*," she gushed. "I've learned so much from him since I've been here."

Beckman leaned in closely. "Has he ever told you how he kicked Saddam's ass in the first Gulf War?"

That explains why everything's still screwed up over there. "I'm afraid not," she said, chuckling. "But I'll be sure to ask him about it some time."

"We're really looking forward to you and Martin covering the Pangaea Festival next week." He gave a wry smile. "And so are our sponsors."

The bell chimed for her floor and Karen stepped out of the elevator. "Thanks, Mister Beckman. I'll try not to let you down."

A few moments later, a feeling of dread surged through Karen as she stood in front of Stan's office. *You're almost out of time here*, she fretted. *Think!*

Pushing the door inward, she saw Stan staring lecherously in her direction from behind his desk. "Hi, Stan," she said cheerfully. "I've been working on–"

"Have you thought about what we discussed yesterday?" he asked brusquely.

Karen met his leer and stiffened. "You mean on the Pangaea Festival? I've got my outline right–"

"Not that," he groused. "The *other* discussion we had."

"Oh, that." Her face slackened. *Shit–I'm going to have to wing it.* "You know, I did give it some thought, but my . . . my . . . boyfriend–"

"Boyfriend?" Stan's eyebrow rose. "The poop around the office says you're single."

Karen frowned. *I wonder what else the gossip queens at the station are saying about me? Probably that I'm having Elvis' alien baby.* "I didn't know it was company policy to reveal my personal life to everyone at the station," she said curtly.

"Don't get your bowels in an uproar," Stan replied. "I guess my sources were wrong." He leaned back in his seat and smiled roguishly. "So how long have you two–been together?"

She regarded him anxiously. *Uh-oh, he ain't buying it.* "Just a couple of months. A friend of mine introduced us at his . . . workplace."

"That's interesting," Stan said. "What's he do?"

What's he do? Karen pinched her cheek. *How the hell should I know?* "He's in . . . uhhh . . . law enforcement." *Huh? What hat did you pull that from, Karen?*

Stan blinked. "A *cop?* I didn't know you were into cops."

No–I'm into clueless Neanderthals like you. "Well, I guess you don't know me as well as you thought."

"Does this *boyfriend* of yours have a name?" he pressed.

What is this–Twenty Questions? "Of course he's got a name," she quipped. "Do you think I would date someone for two months without learning their name?"

Stan chuckled. "Beats me. I don't know you that well–yet."

And you never will, asshole. "I'll bring him around sometime. I'm sure he'd like to meet you, too." She held out her outline. "Here's my proposed summary for the Pangaea Festival. Would you like to go over it now?"

He took the paper and tossed it on his desk. "You can add a briefing at City Hall to your *proposed* schedule. The Mayor's office is layin' the groundwork for the Festival at two this afternoon."

Karen moved towards the door. "Anything else?"

"Yeah, ask your *boyfriend* if he'd like to lunch with us at Marinello's next week." He laughed softly. "I'm buyin'."

Karen rocked uneasily on her heels. *He still thinks I'm feeding him a crock of shit.* "I'll let you know." She stepped out of his office and exhaled loudly. *Damn it, Karen—what have you gotten yourself into now?*

She walked quickly down the hallway towards the elevator, a frown tracing her face. *Oh, what a tangled web we weave, when first we practice to deceive . . .*

33

Opening a cloudy eye to the world, Ryan spotted his golden retriever staring at him by the side of his bed. He rubbed a hand over his face and yawned. "Are you here to keep me company, Bear, or are you looking for something to eat?"

His dog's ears perked to attention at the word *eat*.

Mmmm, I thought so. He chuckled. *At least I know where I stand.*

Straggling into the kitchen, Ryan put out a bowl of kibble for his canine friend and flipped on the television. A clip of last night's tanker fire greeted him on the screen.

As he watched the bird's eye view play out on the late morning newscast, he could almost feel the acrid smoke stinging his eyes; smell the burning fuel assaulting his nostrils; and hear the eerie howl of the fire as it ripped through every fiber of his body.

Ryan's hands balled into fists as the Caltrans spokesman deflected the anchor's questions on the safety of the transportation system. Par for the course, the bureaucrat distanced himself from anything remotely resembling responsibility.

As usual, Ryan groused, *no one will be held accountable until a scapegoat is found. Committees will investigate, bureaucrats will obfuscate, and the whole process will drag on until something more outrageous takes its place.*

The screen cut back to the anchor, still in the midst of interrogating the bureaucrat. A close-up of the official as he issued a denial. The anchor again briefly, then another clip from the disaster.

Sadness tinged Ryan's face as he watched the process unfold in a series of well-spun sound bites. *Why doesn't the station show the whole story to their viewers? Why don't they show the survivors sad spiral into depression as they try to get on with their lives? Why don't they show the families that splinter apart because of death and despair? Why don't they show how our flawed bureaucracy fails to safeguard the very citizens they are sworn to protect?* He took a breath and exhaled. *Aren't these stories just as important, too?*

His eyes widened as a familiar face flashed onscreen. *Hey! It's the reporter I met last night. The one with the . . . attitude.* Suddenly, the half-drunken musings he made at the Cheshire Lounge the previous evening weighed heavily on his mind. *Can you really get a second chance to make a good first impression?*

Ryan sat down at his computer and logged onto the Internet. A few beats later, he was sifting through the KNBS website until he came to her profile:

> Karen Mitchell joined the KNBS news staff three years ago as a general assignment reporter. A native of Norfolk, Nebraska, she graduated cum laude from the University of Nebraska with a Masters degree in Communications and Journalism. Currently, she is a member in good standing of the National Academy of Television Arts and Sciences and the Society of Professional Journalists.
>
> She began her journalism career as an investigative reporter with the OUS Newsletter, the University of Nebraska's official student publication. During her tenure as the newsletter's editor, she received citations

for her coverage of flawed agricultural practices in the North Platte River valley and improper processing procedures at the Culpepper Beef slaughterhouse that led to the deaths of 14 people in the Midwest.

Following her graduation, she worked for two years at Lincoln's KLNS affiliate to gain experience in the broadcasting industry.

She enjoys cycling in her spare time and is currently writing a book about the history of women in politics.

Ryan studied her thumbnail sized photo on the laptop's screen. Late twenties, with assertive green eyes and tawny hair. An impish smile stared out from her portrait—mocking him.

His jaw clenched. *What are you waiting for, Ryan? You're never going to know unless you try.* Snatching the phone off his desk, he punched in the number for the studio and waited.

Several seconds later, a cheerful voice came over the line. "KNBS. How can we help you today?"

Ryan pinched his lip. "Hi, I'd like to speak with Karen Mitchell, please."

"May I ask who's calling?"

"This is officer Rysinski from the LAPD. I have some information on a story that Miss Mitchell is investigating." *That's right, Ryan—keep it official.*

"One moment please, while I page her."

The phone in Karen's cubicle trilled, and she reached across her desk to pick it up. "Karen Mitchell."

"Hi, Karen," the receptionist said. "There's a Mister Rysinski on the line for you."

"Who?" she asked, puzzled.

"Officer Rysinski. From the LAPD."

The name struck her with the fury of an exploding mortar round.

HIM! What the hell does he want?

"Should I transfer him?" the receptionist asked.

"Uhhh . . . sure." *This should be—interesting.*

A warm, friendly voice came through her handset. Not quite the way she remembered it last night. "Hello, is this Karen Mitchell?" Ryan asked.

"This is Karen," she replied curtly. "What can I do for you, officer Rysinski?"

A pause. "I wasn't sure if you remembered me, Miss Mitchell. We didn't have much of an opportunity to talk last night."

And whose fault was that, you smug prick? "You seemed a bit *preoccupied*, officer."

"Yes, it was rather hectic out there last night. But, I should have been a little more . . . considerate . . . in granting you an interview."

A frown tugged at Karen's face. *Oh—my—God! Is he actually trying to apologize to me?* "And I should have been a little more . . . understanding . . . about the situation. The last thing you needed was a reporter butting in while you were in the midst of an investigation."
Why are you apologizing, Karen? Tell him the truth. Tell him what a jerk he was last night . . .

"I was wondering if I could make up for my conduct last night? If you're . . . free this evening, I might be able to update you on the investigation."

"Will this be for the *record*, officer Rysinski?"

A chuckle. "I don't see why not. Just put me down as an official source."

Why is he being so nice to me? Karen wondered. *He must be up to something.* "I'll be away from my desk for the next several hours, but I could make some time for you around six-thirty this evening."

"That works for me. Just name the place and I'll meet you there."

Mmmm . . . what's the most expensive restaurant in town? "How about *Ráisons* on the Westside? We can have a drink or two and talk over old times." *That should be the shortest conversation in history.*

"Great. I look forward to seeing you again."

Yeah, I bet. "Ciao, Mister Rysinski."

34

organ Styles' secretary glanced up from her computer as Calvin entered the office. "Mister Styles will be with you shortly, Mister Taylor," she said amiably. "Would you care for some coffee while you're waiting?"

"No, thank you. I'll just have a seat and make myself comfortable until Mister Styles is ready to see me."

In truth, Calvin was anything but comfortable at the moment. Sonic Engineering Systems future rested on the outcome of today's meeting. Though his company's reputation had always been unassailable, there was no assurance he would win the contract in a world rife with corruption and greed.

Studying the pedestrian paintings that decorated the walls of Styles' outer office only exacerbated his feelings of anxiety. Unobtrusive and unimaginative, the illustrations were cranked out by aspiring Picassos in some third-world sweatshop.

At least they're working, he thought glumly.

Employment had dropped sharply throughout the world when the financial markets tumbled into the abyss in the fall of 2008. Adding to the American workers misery, the few jobs that were being created rarely paid a living wage.

His expression grew dour. *If the outcome from today's meeting doesn't go as planned, I may have to pick up a brush and do my best Van Gogh impression.*

The secretary's voice snapped Calvin from his somber mood. "Mister Styles will see you now."

Rising from his seat, Calvin strolled uneasily into Styles' office, hoping against hope that his fears were unfounded.

Styles came from behind his desk and extended his hand. "Hi, Cal. How are you today?"

"Not bad," Calvin replied as he grasped his hand. "And you?"

Styles shot him a crooked grin. "Just another day at the salt mine." He sat on the edge of his desk and folded his hands into his lap. "Your presentation was well received by everyone at the company, Calvin. Your grasp of the procedures needed to bring the Frequency Wave Module online were insightful and thorough."

Calvin stiffened. *Uh-oh . . . this doesn't look good. It sounds like he's buttering me up right before he makes the sacrifice.*

His suspicions soon proved to be correct as Style's admiration veered towards the outcome he was dreading. "However, after the final costs and production capabilities were taken into account, Royce has decided to award the contract to Synewave Technologies."

Calvin's heart sank. Any plans he had for his company's future would have to be shelved indefinitely. Despite the grim news, he maintained his professional demeanor. "I understand," he said steadily. "Can you reveal why my company didn't win the bid?"

The lines in Style's forehead deepened. "I . . . I don't know. The final decision was made by the Board of Directors based on the recommendations of our engineering and management staff. Frankly, I'm just as surprised by the result as you must be."

Calvin nodded but remained silent. *Move over, Mister Gogh. It looks like I'm going to need that paintbrush after all.*

"There's still a chance for your company to be involved with this project," Styles confided, "but it's a . . . long shot . . . at best."

Calvin forced a smile. "Shoot."

"Neither of your firms can meet the production demands of a full scale conflict. In that event, there's a good chance Synewave will subcontract out a portion of the production to your facility."

"I guess a *piece* of the pie is better than nothing," Calvin said gracefully.

"That's one way to look at it. And if Synewave fails to maintain the standards we expect during production, your piece of the pie could grow even larger."

Calvin gave a sour smile. *Not much chance of that–Synewave's standards are just as high as my own.*

"I'm sorry things didn't work out, Cal," Styles said. "But there will be opportunities for us to work together in the future."

Calvin put out his hand. "Thanks, Morgan. I know you tried your best."

Styles shook his hand and smiled wanly. "Sometimes your best . . . is not enough."

A short time later, Calvin got into his vehicle and left the Royce Industries facility. As the complex faded from view in his car's rearview mirror, Styles parting words brought the closing stanza of a favorite childhood poem to mind:

Oh, somewhere in this favored land the sun is shining bright,
The band is playing somewhere, and somewhere hearts are light,
And somewhere men are laughing, and little children shout;
But, there is no joy in Mudville - mighty Casey has struck out.

35

Elena offered half her candy bar to José as the migrants trudged towards the mountains in the fierce afternoon heat. "You must be starving by now, José," she said. "Would you like something to eat?"

He looked at the candy bar and smiled. "No thanks, Elena," he replied. "Besides, don't you have another mouth to feed?"

She chuckled. "I've got *more* than enough for her," she declared. "But you haven't eaten a thing since we've been dumped here."

"I'm fine, Elena. Really." He paused from his trek to stare at the mountain range on the horizon. *We've been hiking all morning, but the mountains don't look any closer than they did five hours ago.*

"Why are we stopping, amigo?" Miguel grumbled. "It's still a long way to the mountains."

José turned and glared at Miguel. "We'll be there soon enough, padré. We need to take a break every now and then to conserve our strength."

Miguel gave a disgusted look. "Speak for *yourself*, José. I have no problem hiking to our destination."

"In case you didn't notice, Miguel–there are other people here besides *you*."

The heavyset woman stopped and wiped the sweat from her face with a handkerchief. "He's right, Miguel. I need a few minutes . . . to catch my breath. I'm not used to this much . . . activity."

José looked the portly woman over and suppressed a smile. *Judging from your size, you're not used to any physical activity.*

Miguel sat on a boulder and flung his knapsack to the ground. "All right, I'll rest," he griped. "Even though I don't need to."

A grin traced José's face as he watched Miguel remove his ill-fitting shoes and massage the soles of his feet. *You don't fool me, Miguel. You want to rest as much as the rest of us.*

The buzz-cut teen sat on the ground and stretched his legs. "How much farther to the *montañas*, señor?"

"Five or six kilometers, give or take," José replied. "We should be there before nightfall if we continue at our present pace."

"Do you think we'll find water there?"

José wasn't hopeful, but didn't want to convey his doubts to the teen. "There's a good chance, but we won't know until–"

Miguel laughed harshly. "Why don't you just tell him the truth, amigo? We're not going to find *mierda* there."

José bit his cheek. *Maybe I'm not telling him the truth, Miguel, because I don't want to dash his hopes.* "You're wrong, Miguel. We might find water trapped under the sand of a dried out streambed."

"That's a pretty big *if*, José," Miguel chided. "Are you willing to gamble that possibility with our lives?"

"I'm willing to gamble *my* life. If you want to tag along, then that's up to you."

Elena clutched his arm. "I'm still willing to follow him."

The group murmured their agreement, and José knew he had their faith to guide them. Miguel was eerily silent, but his eyes blazed like coals in José's direction.

José studied the contempt in Miguel's face and frowned. *You had better watch your back, because Miguel will put a knife in it every chance he gets.* He shifted his knapsack to the other shoulder and faced the group. "All right, gang," he commanded. "Time for us to head out."

36

Karen and Kyle barged into the City Hall pressroom and scrambled for a spot among the throng of reporters gathered for the Mayor's conference.

"Damn! Get a load of this crowd, Kyle," Karen groused. "See if there's a spot near the podium or Stan will chew us a new one for sure."

Kyle craned his neck above the crowd and pointed to his right. "Over there–just to the right of the podium."

They jostled through a swarm of media junkies until Peter Haskell, the local beat reporter for the L.A. Times, stepped into their path. "Why the rush, Miss Mitchell?" he said tartly. "Don't you have time for a little chat?"

Karen forced a smile. "Mind letting us through, Peter?"

He stood his ground and chuckled. "You're not missing anything, Karen. It's just the same old shit, churned out for a different day."

Kyle smiled wryly. "See? He knows."

Karen shot him a puzzled look. "What are you talking about?"

"The reality we perceive," Haskell explained, "is nothing more than a well choreographed scheme designed to keep the *Illuminati* in power. All that we see, think, and hear has been manipulated by a covert society to keep us from knowing the truth."

Karen glanced at Kyle. "Do you really believe this nonsense?"

Haskell clutched her arm. "It's *not* nonsense. Disinformation is alive and well in America. And if we don't find a way to uncover the truth, the principles that our nation was founded on will disappear forever."

She broke free from Haskell's grasp. "Let's go, Kyle. We've got *work* to do."

Karen and Kyle settled near the podium as Mayor Camellia Santos burst into the pressroom with a small posse of bureaucrats in tow. Within moments, the room quieted down and the crowd collectively turned to face the podium.

At five feet two inches high, Camellia Santos was short in stature, but what she lacked in height was compensated for by shrewd political insight and a tireless dedication to service. Winning office in a landslide vote, she was universally admired in a city historically divided by racial, political, and cultural strife.

"Thank you for coming today," she began politely. "My office, in conjunction with the Chief of Police and the regional Caltrans director, will update you today on the logistics, transportation directives and security precautions planned for the Pangaea Festival. At the presentation's conclusion, there will be a ten-minute period to field questions from the media."

"As you know, the Pangaea Festival is a four day corporate and city sponsored event celebrating the multicultural diversity of the Southland. One cannot underestimate the opportunities this nationally publicized event will mean to the long term fortune of our city and its economy."

"To insure the festival's success, the officials of this city have examined potential problems and enacted the necessary procedures to make this event something to be remembered for years to come."

"Donald Baxter, our City Manager, will now brief you on the general layout of the festival."

A smattering of applause greeted Baxter as he stepped toward the podium. Preppy chic, his prematurely gray hair and sun wizened face made him look older than his forty years of age.

"The Pangaea Festival will mark the debut of Liberty Plaza to the general public," he stated. "Begun several years ago, the Plaza is the last phase of the Genesis redevelopment project geared to revitalizing the area east of downtown L.A."

He gave an easy smile as he looked out on the audience. "There will be seven internationally themed pavilions for the festival, each representing a major continent of the world. They will be interspersed throughout the Plaza while the entertainment venues will be primarily located near the north end."

"The center stage for the entertainment venues is 125 feet wide with an eighty-foot high tower at each end of the stage. Each tower will support several large video screens and a coliseum capacity sound system so even those far from the stage will be able to enjoy the performance."

Mayor Santos joined Baxter at the podium. "Thank you, Donald," she said. "Robert Iwasaki, the regional director for Caltrans, will now provide an overview of the transportation directives set up for the event."

Iwasaki moved behind the podium to begin his presentation. He was just two years younger than Baxter, but looked much younger. An athletic gait and burly build suggested he worked out regularly.

"As with any event of this size," he commenced, "traffic estimates can be difficult to gauge accurately. The average Angeleno's reluctance to use public transportation can make that estimate even more difficult to determine." Several people in the audience chuckled.

"Since the festival has been heavily publicized, Caltrans projects that people will seek alternative routes around the area, thereby easing our fears of gridlock on the streets during the event."

"Approximately twelve hours before the festival opens its gates, all surface streets surrounding Liberty Plaza will be closed to unauthorized traffic. Two hours before showtime, the ten parking structures surrounding the Plaza will be opened to guests on a first come, first serve basis with the outflow directed to five designated areas set specifically aside for this event. A series of shuttles will ferry visitors from these areas at ten minute intervals to the Plaza. Additional parking will be allocated for late arrivals along Liberty Expressway and National Boulevard in specially selected facilities. With luck, our planning and coordinating efforts will keep any transportation and parking issues to a minimum."

Iwasaki stepped back from the podium, and the Mayor moved forward to introduce the next speaker. "Our last spokesman needs no introduction, as he's a familiar face to most of you in this room. Our city's Chief of Police will now brief you on the security measures put in place for the festival."

Derrick Thomas strode confidently to the podium and cast his steely gaze upon the audience. His ebony shaven skull, fiery eyes and snarling mouth made him look more intimidating than most of the thugs his department incarcerated.

"One cannot underestimate the ramifications of security at an event of this magnitude. The exposure generated by the festival is certain to draw the attention of terrorists from all across the world. Any failure on our part to stop their efforts could lead to disastrous long term consequences for our city."

"Fortunately, the current security procedures put in place have enabled us to thwart all but one large scale terrorist attack during the last decade. That unfortunate exception in Seattle demonstrated the shortcomings of biometric analysis over the more effective measures of human detection in ferreting out a potential terrorist."

"To avoid a similar fate at this event, several hundred plainclothes and undercover officers will be interspersed throughout the Plaza to watch for miscreants bent on disrupting the festival. Every patron entering the gates will be screened and subject to a secondary search once they are within the confines of Plaza."

"We will also employ the latest technologies to monitor every activity as it transpires within the Plaza. Digicams, motion sensors, infrared and x-ray devices will all be deployed to track the movements of every visitor as they enter and leave the plaza. In addition, a squadron of Apache helicopters will patrol above the Plaza on a continual basis to avert any chance of aggression from the sky."

"For obvious reasons, I cannot reveal all our security tactics to the public, as our department must have discretion in dealing with those who wish to do us harm. Needless to say, I'm confident that every possible effort has been employed so we don't repeat the mistakes of the past."

Mayor Santos walked to the podium and clutched Thomas' arm. "And that concludes our briefing for today. Handouts detailing the entertainment and activities are available from my staff on your way out." She swept her gaze across the crowd. "Are there any questions?"

A balding, middle-aged man shot his hand in the air. "Why aren't security officials using the CARD to positively ID visitors as they enter the festival?"

Thomas leaned close to the microphone to field the question. "There are still some bugs to be worked out in using the CARD for large scale events. Preliminary tests at the theme parks and sports arenas have indicated the government servers are too slow in clearing individuals through security in a timely manner."

The Mayor pointed towards a silver haired woman dressed in an ill-fitting pantsuit. "Yes?"

"Has your office confirmed if President Jennings will be attending the festival?" she asked.

The Mayor gave a wry smile. "I spoke with Mister Jennings less than an hour ago and I am pleased to announce that he will deliver a speech to commemorate the opening of the festival."

A towheaded reporter shouted a question from the back of the room. "How do you plan on keeping out the crackpots and weirdos that inevitably show up for these events?"

The Mayor shook her head and chuckled. "And where exactly do we draw the line on that, Mister Robinson?" she asked dryly. "After all, this is L.A. we're talking about."

37

Sitting at a small table in Ráisons candle-lit lounge, Karen glanced at her watch and frowned. *Six-forty, and still no sign of Mister Rysinski.*

Irritation tinged her face as she scanned the walnut paneled interior for her date. *There's probably a perfectly good reason why he's late,* she reflected. *He could be stuck in traffic, or called unexpectedly in to work, or . . .*

Then she caught sight of him—you'd almost have to be blind not to. Smartly dressed in a dark blue suit and beige toned shirt, he stood half a head taller than most of the people in the jam-packed lounge. Dark brown eyes probed the room from a squared jawed face, and his mahogany hued hair was cropped short in deference to his career. He moved effortlessly through the room, hustling people from his path as though they were chaff before the wind.

Karen gave a wry smile. *He cleaned up nicely after all.* She raised her arm to attract his attention.

Ryan cast a furtive glance at Karen as he made his way to her table. Dressed in a lavender dress that contrasted with her amber colored hair, a single strand of pearls dangled provocatively above the swell of the dress's low cut neckline. "Sorry I'm late, Miss Mitchell," he said, extending his hand. "I hope you haven't been waiting long."

She took his hand and smiled. "Not too long. And please, call me Karen."

Ryan took a seat next to her and grinned. "And I'm Ryan," he replied. "Though I've been called worse from time to time." He swept his gaze around the darkened room and frowned. "I hope they seat us soon because I'm hungry enough to eat a horse."

"I believe this restaurant is too upscale for equine fare," Karen said dryly. "But we can probably find a side of beef on the menu that will satisfy your appetite."

A short time later, a hollow-cheeked hostess led Ryan and Karen to a linen-topped table near the large Roman fountain at the center of restaurant. She handed them menus and flashed a toothy smile before whirling back to the waiting throngs in the lobby.

Ryan settled back in his seat and opened his menu. "You know, this is the first time I've been on a date with a *celebrity*."

Karen's eyebrow rose. "Mmmm . . . apparently I'm not that well-known, or you would have recognized me when we met last night."

Ryan's expression grew dour. "I guess my mind was . . . elsewhere at the time."

She reached out and touched his hand "It's all right, I understand," she said softly. "Has the department determined the cause of the accident?"

Before Ryan could respond, a thin, pimply-faced man with a nervous twitch drew up next to their table. "*Bonsoir*, welcome to Ráisons," he said cordially. "My name is Will and I'll be taking care of you this evening. Would you like something from our bar before dinner?"

Ryan looked up from his menu. "I'll have a draft from your microbrewery, and the lady will have–" He looked in Karen's direction.

"Lime daiquiri, straight up."

"What kind of beer would you like, sir?" the server asked. "We have over a dozen selections to choose from."

Ryan frowned. "I don't know. Surprise me."

The server nodded and scribbled a few words on his pad. "Would you like to try one of our appetizers before dinner?"

"What would you suggest?" Ryan asked.

"Our seafood platter is quite good."

Ryan nodded his approval. "We'll order our meals when you bring out the appetizer."

"Very good, sir," the server said. "I'll be out with your cocktails shortly." He folded his pad and shuffled off towards the bar.

"Where were we?" Ryan asked.

"The accident . . ." Karen prompted.

"Oh, right." He shot her an impish grin. "Aren't you going to pull out your recorder to take my statement?"

She glared at him but remained silent.

"All right," he said, "I don't want a repeat of last night's–misunderstanding–so it will be just the facts, ma'am." He sat up in the chair and folded his hands on the table. "The CHP and Caltrans are still processing information from the accident site and syncing it with the downloads from the freeway digicams. So far the evidence points towards a white Ford Taurus as the probable cause of the accident. The sedan veered in front of the tanker, causing it to jackknife and clip a Nissan Pathfinder in the adjoining lane. The Pathfinder flipped over and detonated the fuel tank, killing the people in the SUV and the tanker driver instantly. A swarm of tailgating drivers collided with the wreckage and within seconds there were twenty-six vehicles consumed by the blaze."

Karen's eyes widened. "*Jesus!* What did you do once you arrived on the scene?"

Ryan's face tightened as last night's carnage flashed through his mind. "There really wasn't much I *could* do. Dozens of vehicles were burning out of control and scores of people were . . . toast. So I moved the lookie-loos and stranded motorists away from the blaze and looked for any drivers still trapped in their vehicles."

"What happened to the car that caused the accident?"

Ryan gave a disgusted look. "That's the real pisser. There was no tag on the front of the Taurus, and a rearview image of the sedan was unavailable because the explosion took down the entire digicam network along that stretch. The bastard probably got off at next exit, as there's no sign of the sedan anytime after the accident. The CHP will release some photos to the public tomorrow in the hope that someone might be able to ID the vehicle."

"My station can help if you need to get the word out."

"The investigation is outside my division's jurisdiction, but I might be able to put in a word with the brass so your station airs the tape first." His mouth turned upward in a smile. "I figure it's the least I could do after last night."

Her eyes twinkled. "It's a . . . start."

The server arrived at the table with their drinks. "I think you will enjoy this selection, sir. It's a smoky flavored ale with a crisp, clean finish."

Ryan took a sip from the glass and settled back in his seat to savor the taste. The server leaned expectantly over the table, a worried look on his face. Karen watched the server's unease and raised a hand to her mouth to refrain from laughing.

After what must have seemed an excruciating time to the waiter, Ryan set the glass on the table and met the server's eyes. "*Excellent,*" he proclaimed. "Succinctly dry with a distinct hop bouquet."

The server visibly relaxed. "I'm glad you like it, sir. Your appetizer will be ready shortly." He spun around and headed towards the kitchen.

"So is it *really* succinctly dry with a distinct hop bouquet?" Karen asked, sarcasm tinging her voice.

Ryan shrugged. "Hell if I know. It tastes like beer to me."

"So why'd you give the waiter such a hard time?" she chided. "The poor guy looked like he was about to piss his pants."

"Just having a little fun." He shot her a crooked grin. "Besides, it looked like you were about ready to bust a gut over there."

Her eyebrow arched upward. "I don't know about you, Ryan . . ."

"Hey—what's to know? My good looks are exceeded only by my charm and intellect."

"Not to mention the huge burden of *humility* that must go along with having such a large ego," she said drolly.

"But of course—that goes without saying." He took a swig from his glass and chuckled. "All kidding aside, what do you want to know?"

"I guess the obvious question. Why did you become a cop?"

Ryan twirled his glass between his fingers as he gathered his thoughts. "When I was young, and more . . . naive, I thought a career in law enforcement might help change the world in a more positive way."

"That sounds like a pretty noble reason to me."

Ryan nodded slowly. "It started out that way. But, as time went on, and I grew less naive, I began to see that my reasoning was . . . flawed." His eyes grew distant, unfocused. "I soon realized our world was on a downward path to self-destruction, despite our best efforts to maintain order in what we laughingly call civilization. And the longer I stay in what we call The Job, the less certain I am about humanity's chances of survival."

Karen whistled. "Talk about *burnout*. Do you ever think about getting out?"

"It's crossed my mind," he said. "At least a thousand times a day. The only problem is . . . I don't know what I'd move on *to*."

"There must be something you can do with–"

He waved her off. "I'll make a decision at some point. Or fate will make it for me. But until that day arrives, I'll continue to keep up the fight. I may not be making the difference I hoped for, but there's a virtuous streak in me a mile wide that won't allow the dark side of humanity to triumph."

Karen took a sip from her drink and smiled wryly. *Well, well, well— you can't always trust your first impressions. Under that brash veneer of yours lies an actual heart of gold.*

"So, what about you?" Ryan asked. "Tell me something about yourself."

Before she could reply, the server arrived with their appetizer and placed it on the table. "Are you ready to order your meal now, sir?" he asked.

Ryan nodded. "The lady will have–"

"The lady," Karen added, "will have the poached salmon with spicy cucumber sauce, the Parmesan potato cake, and the grilled asparagus."

"Excellent choice, madam," the server replied. "Our salmon is flown in fresh daily from Alaska. And you, sir?"

"Bring me your biggest steak–medium rare. Throw a loaded baker on the side with some green beans and I'll be a happy camper."

"And what dressing would you like for your salad, madam?" the server asked.

"Let's give your House dressing a try."

"Sir?"

"Blue cheese."

The server nodded politely. "Thank you. Enjoy your appetizer."

After the server vanished, Karen plucked a large, succulent shrimp from the platter and popped it into her mouth. She chewed slowly, mindful of the fact that she couldn't answer any questions as long as her mouth remained full.

Ryan waited patiently until Karen washed down the last of

her shrimp before repeating the question. "So–tell me a little about yourself."

Karen pinched her lower lip. *I heard you the first time, Ryan.* "It's your typical story," she said casually. "Small town girl comes to the Big City and lives happily ever after. The end."

"Happily ever after?" His brow furrowed. "What's the secret to your success?"

"I was being facetious. My life really isn't all that interesting."

"How can that be?" he quipped. "A celebrity like–"

Her eyes grew fierce. "I'm *not* a celebrity, Ryan. I'm just working stiff like you."

"But, your line of work seems like it could be glamorous. You get to report on breaking news, travel to exotic locales, interview VIP's . . ."

She gave a sour smile. "I don't know what you've been smoking, but it's nothing like that at all. I rush around most of my day just to get a few precious sound bites on the air."

"Maybe it's not that glamorous after all," Ryan agreed.

"Let's face it," Karen said. "Most news is not news at all, but hyped up drivel made to sound important. Ten minutes of news becomes an hour long broadcast so we can sell the advertising–the true king of all media."

"Hmmm . . . who sounds disillusioned now?"

"I'm not disillusioned, Ryan–I knew things were like this long before I entered the field. Without advertisers there would be no newspapers, no newscasts, no news websites–probably no news at all." She sighed. "Advertising rules–it's as simple as that."

"And despite knowing all that you still wanted to become a reporter?" he asked.

Karen nodded. "And ironically, for the same reason you became a cop. If my actions can make our world a better place, than everything I've sacrificed and worked for will be worth it."

"So when you get down to it, we both share a mutual goal in life?"

Her face clouded. "I . . . I guess so."

Ryan raised his glass. "Let me propose a toast. To those who want to make the world a better place–I salute you."

Karen lifted her glass and smiled. "I'll drink to that."

38

Thirty feet from Ryan and Karen's table, Andrew sat impatiently in Ráisons lounge waiting to be seated for dinner. He looked at his Rolex for the tenth time in the last five minutes and frowned. "Martin," he grumbled, "why haven't they called on us to be seated?"

Martin Sandersen, a tall, stoop shouldered man with a graying comb-over and well trimmed goatee, scanned the lobby from his bar seat and shrugged. "Have another drink and relax, Andrew. We just walked through the door a little over twenty minutes ago."

Andrew gestured towards a vacant dining room on the other side of the lounge. "That whole section of the restaurant is empty," he griped. "Why can't they seat us there?"

Martin looked at Andrew and nodded sympathetically. *He's changed little since the last time we met several years ago. If anything, he's grown even more arrogant during that time.* He studied the anger creeping across Andrew's face and compressed his lips. *Success does that to people sometimes.*

Andrew gulped down the last of his drink and exhaled in exasperation. "I'm going to see what's holding things up. I'll be back in a minute."

Rising from his seat, Andrew shoved several tipsy patrons from his path as he charged towards the lobby. Upon entering the ornately decorated alcove, he saw a small group of men bantering with the hostesses at the podium.

Andrew's eyes narrowed. *No wonder it's taking so long. The hostesses are all standing around with their heads up their ass.*

Barging past the group of men, Andrew glared at a rail-thin hostess at the podium. "Excuse me, miss," he said brusquely. "How much *longer* 'til we're seated?"

The hollow cheeked hostess flashed a smile. "Your party's name, please?"

"Landis. *Andrew* Landis."

The hostess ran her finger down the reservation list until she found his name. "It should be any minute now, Mister Landis."

"You told me that *twenty* minutes ago."

The hostess's smile slackened. "I'm sorry for the delay, sir. I'll see what I can do to get you seated."

"That's not good enough, miss," Andrew replied. "I'd like a word with your manager."

The hostess continued to smile, but the first cracks were showing through her cordial veneer. She excused herself and returned shortly with a squat, middle-aged man at her side. The man's dark, genial eyes quickly met Andrew's angry gaze in an effort to diffuse the situation.

"Bonsoir, monsieur," he said warmly. "I am Philipe, the maitre d' for Ráisons. What can I do for you this evening?"

"You can lose the phony French accent for starters–*monsieur*. I've been waiting for over twenty minutes to be seated and your hostess is doing her best to jerk me around."

Philipe nodded. "And you had reservations, mon–er, sir?"

Andrew's face grew hot. "Of course I had *reservations*, you Parisian putz. For seven friggin' o'clock." He tapped his fingertip on his watch.

"I don't know how they tell time in *France*, but in *this* country I should have been seated over twenty minutes ago."

Philipe bit the side of his cheek. "I apologize for the delay, sir. Would you come with me, please?"

Andrew followed the portly man into the empty dining room off the lounge, expecting to be seated at once. Philipe, however, had other plans. As the maitre d' of one of L.A.'s premiere restaurants, it was his responsibility to maintain the discretion and high standard of service his patrons demanded.

Andrew looked around the empty dining room with a puzzled look on his face. "Aren't you going to seat us?"

"Oui, monsieur. As soon as your table is ready."

Andrew frowned. "Why can't you seat us here? All these tables are empty."

"You're right. But, no one from our staff is available to work this section right now."

"Fuck that," Andrew hissed. "Just find me a friggin' table." He stepped towards Philipe and jabbed a finger in his chest. *"Now!"*

From the lounge, Martin sighed as he watched the drama between Andrew and the maitre d' unfold. Though he was too far away to hear the specifics of their discussion, he sensed that things were rapidly deteriorating as Andrew's mannerisms became more animated.

Deciding to intervene before things spiraled out of control, Martin dashed into the dining room and hooked his arm around Philipe's shoulder. He quickly spun the steward around so his back was towards Andrew. "Excuse me, sir," he said softly. "Is there anything I can do to help?"

"Stay out of this, Martin," Andrew chided. "Everything's under control here."

Philipe shot Martin a sideways glance. "There's no need for you to get involved, monsieur. Like the gentleman said–everything's under control here."

"I know," Martin whispered. "I just thought I could help move things along a little *faster*." With their bodies blocking Andrew's view, Martin palmed a hundred dollar bill into Philipe's open hand.

Philipe smiled wryly at Martin and turned to face Andrew. "I apologize for the inconvenience, sir," he said politely. "I will take you to your table at once."

The maitre d' led the two men to a booth at the far side of the vacant dining room. A short time after they were seated, Andrew looked at his friend with a puzzled expression on his face. "I don't get it, Martin. Just when Frenchie and me were about to duke it out, you butt in and a table mysteriously materializes out of nowhere." He shook his head and frowned. "What'd you say to him, anyway?"

A smile played across Martin's face. "Sometimes Andrew, it's not *what* you say, but *how* you say it that makes all the difference in the world.

39

Under the pale glow of the crescent moon, Elena watched with concern as José clawed at the ground with a flattened stone. "It's time to stop, José, you're just tiring yourself out." She placed a palm on his shoulder and squeezed. "Please . . . stop."

José let out a breath of air and flung the stone aside. *She's right,* he groused. *All I'm doing is wasting my time.*

This was the third hole he dug at the base of the mountainside, and the third hole that came up dry. The ground was damp two feet beneath the dried out streambed, but nothing that would remotely slake the migrants' thirst.

He snatched up a handful of the moistened sand and let it trickle through his fingers. "You're right, Elena," he muttered. "Why I ever thought water would be found in this hellhole I'll never know."

"Don't give up, José," she said softly. "You've already done more to help our group than anyone else here."

He gave a sour smile. "If you could call what I've done–help."

"We're still alive," she pointed out. "There's something to be said for that."

"I suppose . . . but for how long?"

"Let's not worry about that now." She reached down to help him up. "Come on, let's get back to camp so you can rest."

José grabbed his makeshift shovel from the pit and struggled to his feet. They trudged the short distance back to camp and found the migrants gathered around a glowing fire.

Miguel shot José a contemptuous smile as he entered the firelight. "Well, if it isn't our *savior*," he sneered. "Any luck finding the Fountain of Youth, amigo?"

José spun the stone slowly between his hands and glared at Miguel. *Keep giving me shit, Miguel, and I'll smash your head until it's as flat as this stone.*

Miguel met José's stare, and sensing his thoughts, moved towards the edge of the campsite.

The buzz cut teen looked up at José. "Any luck, señor?"

José shook his head. "Nada. Just damp sand."

A monkey-faced man prodded the fire with a branch. "Maybe you're not digging in the right place, amigo."

José hurled the stone at the migrant, causing him to leap out of the way. "Then show me *where* to dig–amigo."

Elena stepped in front of José. *"That's enough!"* she cried. "All this bickering won't get us anywhere."

José lowered his eyes. "I'm sorry, Elena. I shouldn't have let my emotions get–"

She held out her hand. "You're not to blame, José. We're tired, thirsty and haven't eaten in days. But that doesn't mean we have to act like *animals*."

From the rear of the camp, one of the teens grunted like a pig. A swell of laughter quickly echoed among the migrants.

"Go ahead and laugh," Elena scolded. "We might not have found any water yet, but at least José's out there trying." She stared coldly at each of the migrants. "Which is *more* than I can say for the rest of you."

An uneasy silence fell across the group. José picked up his knapsack and settled underneath the spreading limbs of a giant saguaro far beyond the campfire's glow. Elena followed him to the secluded spot and sat down beside him.

"Maybe we'll find some water tomorrow, José," she said, encouragement tinging her voice.

José stretched out his legs and stared at the star-streaked sky. "I hope so," he said wearily. "Because if we don't, you'll soon see how *ugly* this group can get."

40

Calvin let out a groan as he straggled into the kitchen. "Arghh . . . it's finally good to be home."

Kati leaned up and pecked him on the lips. "So how'd it go at the office tonight?"

"Not so good. The accountant crunched the numbers and we're going to have to lay off some of the staff."

"No!" she exclaimed. "Isn't there anything you can do?"

"I'm afraid not. Since I lost the bid with Royce, I can't keep my entire crew on indefinitely without any new revenue coming in."

"It's going to be rough on their families, especially the way the economy is these days."

"I know honey, but what can I do? Our company makes specialized products in an industry decimated by cutbacks and overseas competition. There's no other choice but to let people go."

"Who's going to be . . . cut?"

"Roger and Carlos have been singled out from engineering, and Laqueesha and Eric will be laid off our administrative staff."

"Not Laqueesha, Calvin. Our families have known each other for years." Her face slackened. "How can I ever face her again after this?"

"How do you think *I* feel?" Calvin groused. "Carlos has worked for me since I started the company, and now he'll be out of a job through no fault of his own." He gave a look of disgust. "I don't know what pisses me off more–the fact that I'll have to lay people off or that I couldn't do anything to prevent it."

Kati stroked his arm. "I know how hard this must be for you. Is there anything I can do to help?"

He gave a wan smile. "Just be there–like you always have. We'll get through this bump in the road . . . somehow."

Kati nodded and changed the subject. "Did you know James got an 'A' on his fingerpainting today?" She pulled a sheet of paper off the refrigerator door and handed it to Calvin.

Calvin looked the drawing over and scratched his head. "It's certainly . . . different. The teacher gave him an 'A' for *this?*"

"You've got it upside down, silly." She plucked the paper from his hand and turned it around. "Now can you see what it is?"

His face clouded. "Not really."

"It's a picture of our family. That big, squiggly figure in the center of the drawing is supposed to be you."

"You mean that . . . that *thing* that looks like a giant black crab?"

She giggled. "Yeah, the giant black crab. That's because you're a big, old *crab* most of the time."

Calvin pointed at another figure on the drawing. "And is that supposed to be you?" he asked dryly. "The funny looking blob that looks like a big fat ass?"

"Big fat ass?" She frowned. "Are you *implying* I have a big fat ass, Mister Taylor?"

"Yessum." He leaned down and gave her a playful slap on the rear. "And I done like dem big fat asses, Miz Taylor."

She gave a wry smile. "Good save, Mister Taylor. But don't think you're going to get off that–"

Toni strolled into the kitchen, temporarily saving her father's bacon. "Hey, Mom. Dad," she said casually.

"How's my favorite daughter today?" Calvin asked.

She rolled her eyes. "Dad, I'm your *only* daughter."

"Then that must be why you're my favorite," he said, grinning. "Learn anything new at school today?"

"Not really. Just the same dumb stuff we learn everyday."

"I thought you went to school to get smarter–not dumber."

"We do. But, its dumb stuff like history and math." A scowl swept across her face. "Why do we need to learn that crap anyway?"

"So you'll learn about the world we live in," Calvin lectured. "Some subjects won't make sense, and others you'll love to hate, but in the end your education will help you deal with the problems you'll face in life."

She pinched her lip. "Even the math?"

"*Especially* the math."

"I wish you were my teacher Dad, cuz I'd never get a bad grade from you."

Calvin smiled but remained silent. *I wouldn't be so sure about that, young lady.*

"It's time for you to get ready for bed," Kati said. "Kiss your father goodnight and I'll spend some time with you before you go to sleep." She leaned over and whispered into Calvin's ear. "After I get the kids off to bed, why don't you show me just how much you like those big fat asses, Mister Taylor?"

41

"Guess who?" Karen squealed over the phone.

"George Clooney?" Jennifer asked.

"*George Clooney?* Do I sound like George Clooney to you?"

"A girl can dream, can't she?"

"Isn't he too old for you?" Karen asked. "Besides, what would your husband think?"

"If I were with Mister Clooney, I could care less what he's thinking."

"Mmmm . . . it's always nice of you to reaffirm my faith in the institution of marriage."

"If you ask me," Jennifer quipped, "there isn't much difference between being married and being institutionalized."

Karen snickered. "I didn't wake you up again, did I?"

"Nah, I probably won't go to bed for another hour or so. Tommy's been running a fever all day, and I just want to make sure it doesn't get any worse."

"Isn't Robert giving you a hand?"

"A hand?" She snorted. "Most of the time I'm lucky if I get a *finger.*"

"It's good to know things haven't changed. Anyway, I wanted to let you know how things worked out with my boss today."

"So how are things with Mister Khan? Did you give him a quick kick in the cojones like I suggested?"

"Ahhh . . . no. Sorry to disappoint you."

"Not as *sorry* as I am. Were any of my other suggestions useful?"

Karen paused. "You know, just before I walked into Stan's office for a meeting today, I was looking for a way to resolve the issue so it wouldn't affect my job. Then I decided to hell with it–and let the chips fall where they may."

"That must have been a pretty short meeting," Jennifer said dryly.

"No, I didn't get fired, if that's what you mean. But, when the conversation drifted towards his . . . expectations, I just came out and said I was involved with someone."

"And he believed you?"

"I think he still has doubts. But as I rambled on, my story began to take on a life of its own. And before I knew it, my fictitious boyfriend was employed in a law enforcement career."

"*A cop?* What the hell were you thinking?"

"I know, I know, it sounds . . . *crazy.* But, as the words kept spilling out of my mouth, the bigger the deception grew."

"Maybe you should have taken my advice after all, Pinocchio." She paused. "What are you going to do if your boss decides to check up on your story?"

"I may already have an answer for that."

"Huh? What are you talking about?"

Karen paused. "Do you believe in . . . coincidences?"

"I believe in the Father, the Son, and the Holy Ghost because of my Catholic upbringing. But coincidences? Not a chance."

"Then you can add this to your list of things to believe in," Karen said. "Guess who called me not too soon after my meeting with Stan?"

"I don't know. George Clooney?"

Karen simulated a game show buzzer. "Try again."

"Come on, Karen. It's too late for games."

"Remember that cop that I told you about last night?"

"You mean the one that pissed you off?"

"The one and the same."

"He called?" Jennifer asked. "What for?"

"To apologize."

"He called you to apologize. Yeah . . . *right.*"

"I'm not kidding," Karen said. "And, get this–not only did he apologize, he asked me out to dinner last night."

"And you politely told him what he could do with his baton?"

Karen giggled. "No, silly. I accepted his invitation."

Jennifer paused. "Wait a sec. I need to check the thermometer."

"What for?"

"To see if Hell froze over."

"Why am I beginning to think you don't believe me, Jen?" Karen asked drolly.

"What makes you think that? Is it because you went out with a guy you couldn't stand less than twenty-four hours ago? Or is it because I'm the most cynical person you know, after you?"

"Well, it's true–whether you want to believe it or not." She paused. "Oh, and here's one more thing you won't believe–I actually had a good time last night."

"I think *Ripley* would have a hard time believing that," Jennifer said. "So what did he do that changed your mind?"

"Nothing in particular. He kind of grows on you after awhile."

"So what's he like? Just another washed up jock with anger management issues?"

"Well, he's got this really nice body . . ."

"So now we're checking out the body, are we?"

"It's kind of hard *not* to. He's must be close to six and half feet tall with a perfect male physique. Oh, and did I mention what he was wearing?"

"Uhhh . . . no–I kinda got lost after that physique thing. So what's he like–as a person?"

"He's a little rough around the edges, but he has this . . . righteous quality about him that's hard to describe." She paused. "This probably sounds silly to you . . ."

"It sounds to me like you're smitten."

"Smitten." Karen gave a fleeting smile. "I haven't heard that word in a long, long time."

"Frankly, this whole affair sounds much too good to be true. And speaking of affairs–is he married or involved with someone?"

Karen paused. "I don't think so. He certainly didn't act like he was married."

"You mean married men act differently from single men? I thought all men acted like animals."

"They're not all that way, Jen."

"Boy, some of us have short memories. Have you already forgotten how John–"

"I haven't *forgotten*," Karen snapped. "There was no reason for me to think John was married when we first started dating."

"Was he supposed to have a sign taped to his back declaring his marital status?"

"No–*damn it!*" She took a deep breath and exhaled. "I just didn't get the impression that Ryan was married."

A pause. "And what kind of impression did you get?" she asked softly.

"How much can you *really* know about someone after one date? We talked about our childhoods, our careers, our goals in life–the usual chitchat two people exchange when they are getting to know one another."

"And during this–chitchat, did you bring up your little problem at work?"

"No, it never came up. But here's where the coincidence I brought up earlier comes into play."

"Oh, I see now. Your boss thinks you're dating a cop. And by a strange . . . *coincidence*–you are dating a cop."

"No shit, Sherlock." She paused. "And if there's one thing I learned today, you can't always trust your first impressions."

"Any possibility he might turn out to be The One, Karen?"

"I don't know, Jen," she said. "That might be one coincidence too many."

SATURDAY

42

Leaning over the railing of his yacht, Andrew waved at a tall, striking brunette strolling up the marina walkway. A pair of tan designer jeans clung tightly to her hips and a green low-scooped tee emphasized every curve of her cleavage.

"Candice!" he shouted. "I'm up here." He pointed towards the stern of the ship. "There's a stairway at the rear of the ship where you can climb aboard."

A smile traced Candice Morraine's face as she strolled past the 135 feet of sleek, white fiberglass and polished metal that comprised Andrew's yacht. *Men and their friggin' toys.*

Andrew pecked her cheek as she joined him on the deck. "It's been a long time, Candice." He shot her a roguish grin. "*Too* long."

She flashed a smile, revealing a set of white, sparkling teeth. "For me, too."

Andrew looked her over. *She hasn't changed a bit since she left the limelight to have her daughter. The same sultry eyes . . . the same provocative smile that made her the darling of the motion picture industry over a decade ago.* He stepped back and swept his arm across the deck. "So, what do you think?"

Candice moved her gaze across the varnished teak deck and

burnished brass fixtures and nodded approvingly. "Not too shabby, Andrew," she replied. "This must have set you back a fortune or two."

Andrew chuckled. "Not really–just the expected profit from my next two projects."

"Oh, is that all?" she quipped. "How long before you have to apply for welfare?"

"It's hard living on the edge," he said humbly. "But I wouldn't have it any other way. Speaking of welfare, since I primarily use the yacht for business, Uncle Sam lets me take a big, fat deduction off my taxes at the end of the year."

She gave a wry smile. "Is that all I am to you, Andrew–*business?*"

Andrew draped his arm around her shoulder. "You've always meant more than that to me, my dear." He gestured towards a lavish wet bar at the edge of the deck. "Care for a little pick-me-up this morning?"

"A Tom Collins would be nice."

A short time later, he returned with the drink and took her hand. "Before we get down to business, let me give you the grand tour."

Andrew led her down a polished brass stairway into the living quarters. An eclectic mix of pastel hued furniture and potted tropical plants contrasted nicely with the dark cherry paneling and nautical fixtures adorning the walls. A large expanse of panoramic windows on each side of the room gave stunning views of the marina.

Candice swept her gaze though the room and whistled softly. "It's lovely, Andrew. Who did the interior design?"

"Raoul Estaveras, of Zeitgeist Designs. I've used his firm for years."

As they wandered through the plushly decorated room, an ornately framed photo atop a credenza caught Candice's eye. She moved in for a closer look. "Is that Corrine Rogers under the pancake make-up?"

Andrew nodded. "I wanted her for *Taming the Beast,* but she had a prior commitment at the time."

"She should have broken her contract. *The Beast* was a huge critical and financial success, and gave Emma Morrison the Best Actress Oscar for the year."

Andrew lifted another photo off the credenza. "Here's a picture we took at Ráisons following the Oscar ceremony." He ran his fingers across the black and white photo and smiled. "Miss Morrison was virtually unknown when I asked her to star in *The Beast*," he reflected. "But since her Oscar win, even I can't afford her anymore."

"How *lucky* for her," Candice said dryly.

"It's not entirely luck," Andrew pointed out. "Talent plays a large part–and there's more politics involved than most of us would like to admit. But ultimately, an actor's interpretation of the script will decide whether a performance is worthy of the Academy's recognition. A modest actor can perform miracles with a well-written script, but Tinseltown's finest couldn't salvage most of the shit churned out by the studio hacks today."

"Everything you've touched has turned to gold, Andrew. Is there some secret behind your success?"

Andrew rubbed a hand across his chin. "I believe it's my ability to recognize marketable properties and hire on the right people to bring my dreams to fruition. The role the actor plays must be an extension of their persona, rather than the actor performing the role as it is written. I believe this results in a more natural and believable performance."

"Is the real Emma anything like the character she played in *Taming the Beast*?"

Andrew's eyebrow arched upward. "Have you ever met Emma in person?"

"No, but I'm a big admirer of her work. She seems to instinctively pick roles that enhance her career."

"I met Emma about four years ago at some studio bash in Holmby Hills. She had appeared in an indie or two, and we discussed what kind of roles she would be interested in doing in the future. I had just bought the rights to *The Beast,* and was looking for a cast and crew to bring it to the silver screen."

"And you originally wanted Corrine Rogers to play the role of Celeste in the film?" Candice asked.

"That was my intent. But, she was under contract to another studio and would not be available unless I moved production to the following year."

"Mmmm . . . four years ago–that's about the time *Recognizing Millie* came out. Right?"

"That's right," Andrew replied, chuckling. "Millie was panned by almost every critic in town–although in Corrine's defense she turned in an admirable performance. But, the script was atrocious, and the directing . . ." He turned his thumb downwards.

"I actually *paid* to see it," Candice stated. "I'll never get those two hours of my life back."

"In hindsight, Miss Rogers probably regrets not coming aboard my project, considering the roles Emma has been offered since her Best Actress win."

"I don't know, Andrew. Corrine's not exactly *starving* for work. And with an Oscar win already under her belt, another one probably won't make all that much difference to her."

Andrew laughed softly. "I don't think she would agree with that." He put the photo back on the credenza and met Candice's gaze. "After Miss Rogers turned down the role, I was forced to look elsewhere for an actress. As fate would have it, I asked Emma if she would be interested in the role not too long after meeting her at the party."

"What influenced your decision?"

"As I said earlier, the role of a character works best when it is a natural extension of the actor's personality. Miss Morrison was blessed with the energy and quirkiness that I had envisioned for role of Celeste. And with Mayhew's excellent script and a superlative supporting cast,

Taming the Beast became one of those rare productions where the synergy exceeded the sum of its parts."

"I enjoyed it," Candice said. "A role like Celeste's doesn't come around everyday."

"No, they don't," Andrew agreed. "But today may be one of those days. Have you ever read *Finding Divinity*?"

Candice nibbled on her lip. "No. Should I have?"

Andrew shrugged. "I doubt most people have heard of it, much less read it. The author, Peter Denolt, is relatively unknown outside a few fiction writers groups. I bought the movie rights to his novel not too long ago and had George MacNeil adapt the story for the screen."

"MacNeil has done some work for you in the past, hasn't he?"

"Two other screenplays, one of which was nominated for an Academy award. This current script is without doubt the best work I've seen roll off his pen. The part I'd like you to play is that of a well-heeled matriarch who finds faith when the world she has known suddenly collapses around her. As she struggles to cope with homelessness and despair, her beliefs carry her through some of the most depressing experiences a person can suffer."

"Mmmm . . . a riches to rags story?"

"In a most rudimentary way. But my synopsis barely touches on the nuances of the book and its successful adaptation by MacNeil." He met her gaze. "Does it sound like something you might be interested in doing?"

Her eyes twinkled. "*Maybe.*"

"I brought you a copy of the screenplay to look over while we take a leisurely cruise up the coast. Meanwhile, let me finish with my tour of the ship before we embark." He began to descend the stairway to the next level and beckoned for her to follow.

Candice brushed her fingertips across a parquet-paneled wall, admiring the warm glow of the wood in the early morning light. "It's a beautiful ship, Andrew," she said. "What did you wind up naming her?"

"Ahhh, that was easy. Her name reflects my own personal philosophy on life."

She shot him a puzzled look. "And what might that be?"

He chortled. "What else, but–*No Regrets*."

43

osé's jaw clenched as he watched several migrants venture out from the safety of their cave into the torrid morning sunlight.

When will you fools learn? You need to adapt to your environment like the animals that make this place their home. You won't see them out in the middle of the day, losing precious moisture to the sun. He shook his head and scowled. *Ahhh . . . what difference does it make? We're all probably going to die anyway.*

Elena touched his shoulder, jerking him from his gloomy mood. "Is everything all right, José? You look kind of . . . down."

He shot her a weak smile. "I'm fine, Elena. I'm just wondering if I'll ever see my family again."

"What are you talking about? Of course you'll see them again."

"I hope so," he muttered. "I won't let the desert take me without a fight."

Her mouth curled upward in a smile. "That's the spirit. Have you made any changes in your plan since last night's . . . discussion?"

He gave a quick headshake. "We'll keep heading north, and we should eventually come across a town, or a road *to* a town."

"How do you know–"

"He *doesn't* know, Elena," a voice growled from behind them. "He's making it up as he goes along."

José and Elena turned towards the voice. In the shadows of the cave, Miguel stared balefully in their direction and chuckled.

José struggled to his feet, but Elena seized his shoulder and kept him from rising. He caught the look on her face and stiffened. *Think about it.* "What do you want, Miguel?" he groused.

Miguel looked him over and smiled. "What makes you think I want something, José?"

"I'm not sure, but if you're here it usually means trouble."

"I'm not here to cause you trouble, amigo. As a matter of fact– *trouble* is the last thing on my mind."

"Spit it out, Miguel," Elena demanded. "Just what are you trying to say?"

"I will cause you no further trouble after today, José. I've been discussing our situation with several members of our group, and we've decided to head out on our own."

José's eyebrow rose. "Don't be an *idiota*, Miguel. Our chances of making it out alive are better if we stick together as a team."

"You don't have all the answers, José. We've let you lead us up to now, but your–"

"I never asked to be the leader of our group," José snapped.

Miguel met José's eyes and nodded. "No, I suppose not," he replied. "Just the same, there are some of us that have questioned your ability to find a way out of here."

José shook off Elena's hand and rose to his feet. "And what makes you think you have all the answers, Miguel?"

"Look at you," Miguel sniffed. "What kind of job did you have back in Mexico? Were you a laborer? A farmer?" He shook his head and sneered. "Did you even graduate from high school?"

José glared harshly at Miguel. "And what did your *education* teach you, Miguel? Did it teach you anything about *survival?*"

"I learned far more at the schools I attended than what you learned at your *grandfather's* knee," he replied. "I graduated with a business degree from Universidad de Las Americas in Mexico City and then went on to earn my Masters Degree at the Universitat de Barcelona in Spain. At my previous job, I managed a division at a large manufacturing conglomerate with sales of ten billion pesos a year."

"And for all your–*braggio*," José mocked. "Here you are–the same as I. A lowly farmer from Jiquilpan who barely passed high school."

"It wasn't my fault the economy collapsed and sent my company into bankruptcy."

"Yes, Miguel–it's always *convenient* to blame someone else when things don't work out the way you planned. You could at least come up with a better excuse for your mismanagement and incompetence."

"But, I am telling you the truth," he asserted.

"The *truth* is your company failed to adapt to the changing world economy. It was easier to declare bankruptcy than to search for a solution towards solvency."

"I am not to blame for my company's–"

José laughed softly. "Of course not. I may not be as rich and educated as you, Miguel, but even I understand the principles of basic economics. When I could no longer compete with the cheap produce imported from overseas, I chose to leave my life behind and go to America." He gave a sour smile. "Yes, life will be difficult at first. But, one must do what is necessary in order to survive."

"A life of poverty may be acceptable for *you*, but I could never–"

"Why?" José chided. "Because you think you *deserve* your luxurious lifestyle? You may have been a big man in a big company at one time, but in case you haven't noticed, we are no longer there. And for all your talk–all your conceit–you haven't the slightest clue on how to get out of here."

Miguel's eyes narrowed. "How do you know what I can or cannot do, José?"

José reached out and grabbed Miguel's hand. "This is how I know, Miguel. Just look at your hand. Go ahead–*look at it!* This is a hand that's *never* seen an honest day's work in its life. It's just like you–soft, flabby, and . . . weak." He shook his head and chuckled. "You think you can find your way out of here? You won't last a *day* without my help."

Miguel wrenched his hand from José's grasp. "I don't need to listen to your–"

"Do you think hiking across the desert will be like driving to your glass walled office in the city?" He swept his hand across the desolate landscape. "Look out there, Miguel. Take a good, hard *look.* Everything you see has had centuries to adapt to its surroundings. Do you expect to survive with a few *years* of higher education behind you?" He barked out a laugh. "Good luck, amigo. You're gonna need it."

Miguel raised his fist, but thought better of it and turned to leave.

"Go ahead and leave, Miguel. I've spent most of my life being looked down on by people like you. Your kind will never admit to being wrong because you believe you're better than everyone else. So take your high-priced education and your patronizing attitude and see if you find your asno from a hole in the ground."

Miguel turned and shot him the finger. "Go to Hell, *pendéjo!*"

José chuckled as Miguel strode away. "I'll make sure they put those words on your tombstone, Miguel. That's if they ever find your dry, bleached bones in the desert."

Elena embraced José from behind. "*Mierda!* I've never seen you like this, José. I thought you two were going to go at it for sure."

"Another time, another place–I very well may have. But, I can't afford to waste what little energy I have on the likes of him. If he wants to leave, it makes no difference to me. He's been nothing but a thorn in my side since we've been dumped here."

"Do you think his leaving will affect our chances of making it out of here?"

"Not at all," he replied. "If anything, it will improve our chances because he won't be around to lower morale with his insults and pessimism." His expression suddenly grew dour. "But, I suspect this won't be the last of our group to split off on their own."

She squeezed his shoulder. "You'll always have my support, José."

His lips turned upward in a smile. "And you'll always have mine, Elena." He lowered himself to the floor of the cave and stretched his legs. "Let's take our siesta now so we can be rested when we head out later this afternoon."

As he sprawled out on the ground and drifted off in slumber, José dreamt of his family and wondered if he would ever see them again.

44

Ryan cast an appraising eye at Karen as she strolled through the southside parking lot at Marina del Rey. Already half an hour late for their date, she was dressed sportily in a blue and white striped tank top tucked into white shorts. Strands of blonde hair spilled from beneath her Dodgers baseball cap and white tennis shoes adorned her long, bronzed legs.

He flashed a smile as she drew near him. "Glad you could make it today," he said drolly. "I was beginning to think you were going to stand me up."

She grinned sheepishly. "Sorry I'm late. I've never been to the marina before and it took me a while to find your dock." She moved her gaze across the colorful multi-story apartments, hotels and retailers that crowded the cobalt blue channels of the marina. "So what have you got planned for us today?"

Ryan held his hand out. "Close your eyes," he said softly. "It's a surprise."

Ryan led her down a long wooden walkway past a motley collection of vessel's ranging from resplendent yachts to rundown houseboats barely able to stay afloat. He stopped next to a modest sized catamaran tethered to a piling near the end of the walkway. "Okay, you can open your eyes now."

Karen looked the boat over and frowned. "Where am I supposed to sit? In the water?"

Ryan chuckled. "Don't be ridiculous. You can sit on one of the wing seats attached to the side of the hull."

Her gaze drifted apprehensively over the boat. "Mmmm . . . I don't know," she muttered. "What's to keep the sharks from chomping on me once we're out sailing on the sea?"

"You don't need to worry about sharks," he assured. "I'll be here to protect you."

"I'll try to remember that when they're using your leg for a tooth-pick," she said dryly.

"You'll be fine," he insisted. "I've been out hundreds of times and never had a problem with sharks."

"And with my luck, a whole school will show up on this trip to make up for lost time."

"There's nothing to be afraid of, Karen. I'm the best catamaran sailor west of the Mississippi River."

"And that's supposed to reassure me?" she quipped. "How many catamarans do you see sailing across the Great Plains?"

Ryan sighed. "Are you going to joke around all day or are we going out sailing?"

Unbeknownst to Ryan, Karen had an obsessive fear of the water. She glanced around anxiously, looking for a gracious way to bow out of today's outing without offending her date. Unfortunately, no quick solution sprang to mind. *Damn, it looks like I'm going to have to do this after all.*

Annoyance tinged Ryan's face. "Are you *coming*, Karen?"

"Yes!" she snapped. "But you better protect me if any sharks show up."

"I promise," Ryan replied, holding up his hand. "Now, can we get going?" He leaped gracefully from the walkway to the catamaran and held out his arm towards Karen. "Ready to come aboard?"

Karen extended her arm toward Ryan, and before she knew it, he whisked her aboard the boat as though she was weightless. He pulled a life vest from a compartment and handed it to Karen. "Before we head out, I'll give you a few pointers on sailing. Lesson one–*always* wear your life vest."

As Karen cinched the laces on her life vest, Ryan instructed her briefly on how to sail the catamaran. "You steer with the tiller. Push the tiller away from you to turn the cat into the wind and pull it towards you to turn away from the wind. Keep the movement of the tiller to a minimum, and try to . . ."

Karen's eyes glazed as Ryan continued his lecture. *I hope he's not expecting me to remember all this. If something were to happen to him while we're out on the ocean, I'm going to need God's help to bring us home safely.*

" . . . and that's about it," he concluded. He gestured towards the wing seats. "Make yourself comfy while I get us underway."

Several minutes later, Ryan undocked from the slip and began to tack his way through the channel. Karen kept occupied by watching boats drift through the marina, but she glanced down at the murky water every so often half expecting to see a great white shark in search of its next meal.

To relieve her unease, she turned her gaze towards Ryan as he piloted the boat through the marina. With his white Captain's hat tipped smartly atop of his head, and his well toned body straining under his green polo shirt and tan cargo shorts, it soon became difficult to concentrate on anything else.

He turned to meet her gaze. "Enjoying the view?" he asked drolly.

She felt the heat rise in her cheeks. "Uhhh . . . it's very–nice. Sailing is a lot more relaxing than I thought it'd be."

He nodded. "Yeah, as long as you don't notice those triangular shaped fins slashing across the water."

Karen whipped her head around. *"Where?"*

Ryan let out a short, hard laugh.

"What's so funny?" she barked.

"You. I've seen suspects fidget less under interrogation."

She folded her arms across her chest and pouted. "I can't help it. I've been afraid of the water all my life."

Puzzlement touched Ryan's face. "Why is that?"

"I don't know," she grumbled. "I can tolerate swimming pools and small ponds, but anything larger than that I avoid like the plague. I hate the ocean most of all because there's all kinds of nasty critters waiting to bite your ass."

"If you feel that way, then why'd you come out sailing today?"

Because I wanted to be with you, you schmuck. She looked out on the harbor and shrugged. "Maybe it's time I faced my fears."

"I don't want our date to be a test of your anxieties."

"Don't worry, Freud. Today's little trip will do more for me than a year's worth of sessions at some overpriced shrink." She looked up sharply. "Is there anything you're particularly afraid of?"

Ryan bit his cheek. *Yes—revealing how I feel towards you.* "I don't know," he replied casually. "I really haven't given it much thought."

"Come on," she teased. "There must be *something* that scares you."

He rubbed his chin. "Now that you mention it, women scare the hell out of me sometimes."

Karen's eyebrow twitched. *"Women?"* How could someone as big as you be–"

"I'm not *physically* afraid of women," he countered.

"Then what are you afraid of?"

He took a deep breath and exhaled. "Most of the women I've known make you tread across an emotional minefield that could explode at the slightest misunderstanding. I'd rather face a hail of bullets any day of the week than deal with a woman who's gotten her feathers ruffled."

She regarded him warily. "Is this how you feel about me?"

"No," he replied. "But I can see this discussion is already starting to tick you off."

"Not yet. But, I still don't see what you're afraid of."

"This is what I'm talking about. Women generally act on how they *feel*, while men usually act based on how they *reason*. And because of this, the dialogue between us sometimes becomes . . . strained."

"We're not that difficult to understand, Ryan. If you understood how we feel from the start, then your fear of women would disappear."

"But that's just it," he said. "We can't understand because you don't *tell* us how you feel."

Karen's eyes twinkled, clearly enjoying Ryan's discomfort. "Why do we need to tell you? If you really care about someone, you should already *know* how they feel."

He sighed. "Sometimes we need a little help, Karen. Men are different, after all."

A smile tugged at Karen's face. *And viva la difference.*

45

Leaning into the hallway, Calvin urged his dawdling son to get ready for the game at Dodger Stadium. "Hurry up, James," he shouted, "or we'll be late for batting practice."

Seconds later, James bounded from his room and screeched to a halt at the end of the hallway. Calvin looked over his son's Dodger uniform and frowned. "Why's your cap on backwards, James?" he asked. "Are you trying to be one of the gangstas?"

James flinched as his father twisted the cap around. "Awww, Dad– do I have to wear it this way? It's not cool."

"When you grow up and get out on your own," Calvin lectured, "you can wear your cap any way you please." He leaned down and straightened his jersey. "Where'd you put your glove?"

"It's in the closet," he said sheepishly.

"Go get it. I'll wait for you out in the kitchen."

Calvin plopped down at the kitchen table and looked around the room. Kati was at the counter marinating ribs for tomorrow's family get-together while Toni sat across from him hunched over her laptop.

James rushed into the kitchen, holding his glove overhead. "I found it, Dad!" His other arm shot into the air, clutching a small boy's bat. "And I'm bringing my bat so Tyler Lewis can sign it."

"Tyler Lewis may be too busy today to sign your bat, son." In reality, Calvin knew today's star athletes rarely signed autographs unless they were compensated. He preferred not to reveal this unfortunate truth so his son would not become disillusioned with the game.

"He'll sign my bat, Dad," James said. "I *know* he will."

Kati put down the tongs and turned to face them. "Who are you going to see today?"

James jumped into the air. "The Dodgers and the Indians!" he shrieked, a few decibels shy of rupturing their eardrums.

Toni looked up from her laptop, exasperation tinging her face. "We *heard* you, booger face!"

James stuck out his tongue. "*You're* the booger face!"

Calvin held up his hands. "Alright, kids. *Enough!*"

The room suddenly grew still, and Kati picked up the conversation where she left off. "Shouldn't the Indians be playing against the Cowboys instead of the Dodgers?" she asked.

James rolled his eyes. "Mom, the Indians can't play the Cowboys–they're a *football* team." He sighed. "Don't you know *anything* about sports?"

Kati bent down and wriggled his cap. "I bet you didn't know your Mom was a big sports star in college."

James eyes grew huge. "Really?"

She nodded. "I was one of the top runners on my college track team and just missed out on swimming at the '96 Olympics."

"Mom, running and swimming aren't sports," James stated.

She shot him a puzzled look. "They're not? Then, what are they?"

"They're games!"

Calvin shook his head and chuckled. "Well, you heard it, hon. Straight from the horse's mouth."

"Mmmm . . . sounds like it's straight from some other part of the horse's anatomy."

Calvin glanced at his watch. "Come on, James. We better get going if we want to catch batting practice."

"Will you be back in time for dinner?" Kati asked.

"We might," Calvin replied, "but we'll be so stuffed with Dodger Dogs and garlic fries that eating will be the last thing on our minds."

"Then would you mind swinging by the supermarket and picking up a few things on your way home?"

"Sure. What do you need?"

"A couple of cases of soft drinks for the women and kids to drink and half a keg of beer for the guys."

"Just half a keg?" he quipped.

"If we run out, one of you can make a beer run."

Calvin rose from his seat to leave. "Kati, I . . . I'm not sure this family get-together is such a good idea."

"Oh?" She tilted her head. "Why not?"

His gaze was steady. "Our families still aren't . . . comfortable . . . with our marriage."

Kati met his gaze but remained silent. But her message was unmistakably clear. *We'll discuss this later–when the kids aren't around.*

Calvin leaned over and pecked her cheek. "You're right, we can talk about this at another time." He reached down and grasped James' hand. "Let's get going, champ."

Their trip to the stadium was marked by silence as James entertained himself with a game on his iPod and Calvin listened to tunes on the local Jazz station. Once they arrived at the ballpark, Calvin purchased their tickets and took James to the concession stand to load up on snacks.

On the way towards their seats, they passed several maintenance personnel and a few scattered fans in the corridor. The scores of security guards posted at every entrance was a grim reminder of the tragedy in Seattle two years earlier.

Upon reaching their section of the stadium, they descended a stairway past rows of gold colored seats to a location behind the third base dugout. The smell of freshly mown grass cloyed the air, and Calvin recalled the times his father had brought him to Dodger stadium as a child. He looked up at the cloudless sky and smiled wistfully. *I think I know why you brought me here now, Pop. There's something timeless about this game that brings together a father and his son.*

The Cleveland Indians scrambled onto the field to practice several minutes later. A line soon formed at the batting cage as players waited to face the pitching machine's fury. Along the sidelines of the infield, several players limbered up by tossing the ball back and forth in a well-rehearsed routine.

Calvin watched with amusement as James scoured the field for Tyler Lewis. "The Indians will be warming up for a while, champ. Why don't we take a look at the program I gave you until Tyler Lewis comes out on the field?"

James rocked back and forth in his seat, a sour look on his face. "Where's Tyler Lewis?" he whined. "I want to see Tyler Lewis!"

Calvin looked at his son and exhaled. *Looks like it's going to be a long afternoon . . .*

Just when Calvin began to grow resigned to his fate, several Dodgers streamed out of the dugout to practice.

James perked up in his seat. "Look, Dad! It's the Dodgers!"

Calvin rose from his seat. "Let's go see if Tyler Lewis will autograph your bat."

James grabbed his bat, and Calvin prodded him towards the Dodgers' dugout. Near the edge of the infield, a growing number of fans waited by the railing to chat or have their collectibles signed by their favorite athlete.

As they neared the edge of the crowd, Calvin hoisted James upon his shoulders so he could get a better view of the field. "How's that, champ? Can you see everything now?"

James nodded his approval and smiled.

Calvin peered over the crowd and frowned. *There's no sign of Lewis anywhere. Maybe he was scratched from the lineup.*

As the minutes dragged by, Calvin grew discouraged by Lewis' absence. His heart stirred when a tall, broad shouldered ballplayer sporting the number twenty-six suddenly emerged from the dugout.

James leaned forward and threw his arms in the air. "There's Tyler Lewis, Dad! *There he is!*"

The crowd swarmed towards the Dodgers' star player. To Calvin's surprise, Lewis took a marker from his pocket and began signing autographs. After a ten minute wait in the jam-packed crowd, Calvin reached the railing and extended James' bat towards the slugger's meaty paw.

Lewis looked at Calvin and shot him a gap-toothed smile. "How you doin' today?" he asked gruffly.

James flailed atop his father's shoulders. *"Tyler Lewis! Tyler Lewis!"*

Calvin could barely restrain his son from flying off his perch. "Can't complain, Mister Lewis. Could you sign the bat 'To James–Keep on slugging–Tyler Lewis?'"

A grin tugged at Lewis' mocha hued face. "Whatever you want." He whipped his marker across the bat and handed it back to Calvin.

"Thank you," Calvin mouthed, but Lewis was already engaged with his next fan.

Beating a hasty retreat to their seats, Calvin lowered James into his chair and handed him the bat. His son rubbed his hand across the inscription several times, as if refusing to believe it was real.

Calvin sat down and draped his arm around James' shoulder. "Well James, it looks like Tyler Lewis signed your bat after all."

James looked up at him and smiled. "Thanks, Dad. I love you."

Calvin ruffled his hair and grinned. *I wouldn't trade this moment for all the millions Mister Lewis will make in his career.*

46

urning from the yacht's helm, Andrew strolled across the deck and stared expectantly in Candice's direction. *"Well?"* he asked.

Candice sat up in the lounge and placed the script in her lap. "It's really good, Andrew. A few more . . . tweaks . . . and it will be perfect."

Andrew chuckled. "I'm sure MacNeil will be *thrilled* to hear that." He settled into a wooden deck chair across from her and took a swig from his drink. "All right, what would you like to change?"

Riffling through the script, she pulled out page after page and set them in a neat stack on her lap. When she was finished, what remained of the original script was tossed on the table like yesterday's trash.

Andrew stared in disbelief at the mound of pages in her lap. *A few tweaks, Candice?*

She glanced at the top page from the stack and smiled. "Let's start with page four," she said. "The character I'm supposed to play is descended from old money. Correct?"

Andrew gulped down half of his drink and nodded.

Candice rose from her seat and began to pace around the deck. "The name Aileen doesn't have the panache associated with families from old money backgrounds. High heeled women from prestigious families usually have exotic or traditional names that reek of the fortunes that preceded them."

"And what would you suggest?" he asked.

"Callista and Daphne would be suitable exotic names or Catherine and Hope would fit the bill as a traditional choice." She looked over the page and frowned. "In any case, you must talk to MacNeil about changing the name before I agree to take on the part."

Andrew gave a dismissive wave of his hand. "What's next?"

She shuffled to the next page in the stack. "On page fourteen, Aileen first learns of her husband's philandering." She waved the script through the air and sighed. "The way this scene is currently written is so . . . so *clichéd* . . . that I usually know how the story will end before the second act is over."

"What's cliché about it, Candice? Men cheat on their wives all the friggin' time."

"It's not her husband's infidelity that's hard to believe," she replied. "It's the way he's so blatant about it. Most men use a little discretion when they are involved in an affair."

"Candice, this is a very powerful man. Men in his position generally do what they want–when they want–and they don't give a damn who they hurt in the process. Any woman who plans to enjoy the fruits from their labor should be willing to bite into a pit every now and then."

Her eyes narrowed. "In other words, my way or the highway, and don't let the door hit your ass on the way out?"

He shrugged. "That's another way to look at it."

She threw up her hands in exasperation. "I'm sorry, Andrew, but that's *bullshit*."

Andrew's face slackened. *"What?"*

"Aileen has the so-called *perfect life* until the rug gets yanked out from under her, is that correct?"

Andrew gave a slight nod. "That's the basic premise of the story."

Candice wandered to the edge of the deck and watched the sea for several moments. When she turned to face Andrew, her eyes were fierce. "When the world you love has been unexpectedly wrenched away from you, it takes an exceptional degree of perseverance to win it all back. Faith plays an important part as this story dramatizes, but you need more than *faith* to carry you through the hard times." Her gaze grew distant, unfocused. "I should know . . . I've been there."

Andrew was well aware of her past, and couldn't argue this point with her. It was one of the reasons he selected her for the role, though he tactfully chose to omit that small detail from her.

"Go on," he prodded. "I'm listening."

She snapped out of her reverie at the sound his voice. "If Aileen had the spirit to endure the hardships she encountered after her divorce, then she would have possessed this trait when she was married to her adulterous husband. A woman possessed with that strength of character would never tolerate her spouse's philandering without considering some form of retribution. Once she discovered his womanizing, he may very well wake up one morning and find a part of his anatomy missing." She gave a wry smile. "A very . . . *personal* . . . part."

Andrew winced. "Okay, I get your–point. I'll make some suggestions to MacNeil and see what he thinks."

Candice nodded her approval and continued to the next page in the script. "Let's move to page twenty. The divorce sequence could use . . ."

Andrew quaffed the rest of his drink and frowned. *This is going to take all fucking day.* He rose from his seat and headed towards the bar.

"Where are you going, Andrew?" Candice asked. "I'm not finished with the script–"

He held up his empty glass and smiled. "Just getting a refill, my dear. I need to be in the *proper* frame of mind to continue." *And just past comatose should do it,* he mused.

Andrew set his tumbler on the bar's countertop and massaged his temples. *Ahhh . . . why do actors always insist on changing the script? They're well paid, receive extraordinary benefits, but they still insist on 'improving' everything their characters think, do, and say.* He gripped the edge of the countertop and scowled. *Why can't they let the writers do the writing and leave well enough alone?*

He watched Candice peruse the script and filled his glass to the brim. *Are all her–tweaks–going to be a sign of things to come? The last thing I need is another project fraught with disaster after disaster.* He breathed deeply and downed half of his drink in a single gulp. *Once more unto the breach, dear friends, once more . . .*

Candice grinned as she watched Andrew stagger across the deck. "Are you in the proper frame of mind to continue?" she asked dryly.

He slumped into his seat and nodded. "I'm ready when you are."

"On page twenty of the script, just after she files for divorce, Aileen is out on the street without any visible means of support." She gave a headshake and chuckled. "What the hell was MacNeil smoking when he wrote this crap?"

Andrew thumbed through his copy of the screenplay, searching for the passage in question. But the words swam across the page in a blur, and he soon tossed the script on the table in frustration. "And how would *you* write it, Candice?" he groused.

"First off, hasn't MacNeil ever heard of a divorce lawyer?" she asked. "I would have cleaned this asshole's clock and left him standing in the street with his dick in his hand. There's no effin' way I'd be out on my ass scrounging for a meal ticket."

Andrew regarded her warily. *It's a good thing you never seriously considered marriage, Andrew. You might have wound up out on the street missing a body part–or two.* "Candice, there might have been a prenup that–"

She clucked her tongue. "Hello! I don't see anything about a *prenup* in the script. You can't always expect your audience to figure these things out."

Andrew nodded. *She's got me there. Most viewers could barely follow a plot, let alone one that had gaping holes in it.* "You're right, I'll have MacNeil fix it."

Candice smiled smugly, congratulating herself on her contribution. "Haven't you any ideas on how the script might be improved?"

Andrew struggled upright in his seat, trying to keep the anger from his voice. "I went over the script several times with MacNeil before I gave it to you. In my mind, it needed no further . . . improvements."

47

Ryan hung suspended over the water like a spider in a web, tugging furiously on the cables that controlled the catamaran's sail. "Wooo-eeeee!" he hollered. "We're *movin'* now!"

A stream of salty spray stung Karen's face as the boat slipped effortlessly across the sea on a single hull. She looked at the white-flecked foam flashing beneath her feet and shuddered. *Oh my God*, she thought anxiously. *We're gonna die for sure.*

Ryan looked in her direction and waved. "Do you want to want take a crack at it?"

Karen shot him a puzzled look. "What?" she shouted.

He cupped his hand over his mouth and yelled. "Do you want try sailing the boat?"

She watched apprehensively as Ryan leaned out from the hull, with absolutely nothing under him but air. "Ahhh . . . no thanks. I'm perfectly comfortable where I'm at."

Ryan chuckled. "Don't be such a fraidy cat. It's a piece of cake." He leveled the boat into the water and placed a cable in her hand. "All you have to do is pull on the line, and the wind will do the rest."

Hesitantly, Karen took the cable from his hand and followed his instruction. Within minutes, she grasped the rudimentary concepts of sailing and soon had the catamaran cruising across the waves at a moderate speed. Despite her fear of the sea, she sat back and enjoyed herself for the first time since their voyage began.

Ryan sat next to her on the wing seat and whispered in her ear. "It's not as hard as you thought, is it?"

She shook her head. "How am I doing so far?"

"Great. I was going take a nap since you seem to have things under control."

Her eyes widened. "Don't you dare! I'm not anywhere near ready to solo yet."

"Well, in that case, I'll just sit here and enjoy the view." He leaned back in his seat and looked her over.

Karen pretended to be embarrassed, but was secretly thrilled that Ryan showed some interest in her for the first time. "Does everything look *shipshape* to you?" she asked.

"Your keel looks pretty sleek and I must admit those are some of the nicest bulkheads I've ever laid eyes on."

She giggled. "Can't you ever give a *straight* answer?"

"Sure, but what fun is–" He whipped his head to the right. "*Look!* There's a bunch of fins heading straight for us."

"Oh, *please!* I'm not falling for that line again."

"I'm not kidding. Take a look behind you."

Karen turned her head, expecting to be the butt of Ryan's corny joke. Instead, she saw eight dorsal fins slashing through the water on a direct course towards them.

Startled, Karen released her grip on the lines, and the catamaran suddenly tilted out of the sea. She looked down breathlessly at the water as her seat rose higher into the air. *Oh my God–we're tipping over!* Her eyes widened with fear. *And the sharks are going to eat us! THE SHARKS ARE GOING TO EAT US!*

Ryan sprang from his seat and snatched the lines as they left Karen's hands. He tugged instinctively on the cables and the hull rocked back into the water with a loud splash. "*Whoa!*" he hissed. "Almost turtled it that time."

Karen searched the water for the fins. "Ryan, look! The fins are gone!"

"What do you expect?" he asked. "After watching your proficiency at the helm, they probably swam as far away as possible. I bet they're an ocean or two away by now."

"I'm sorry. I got scared and lost track of what I was doing."

"No harm done," he said softly. "Except for a few gray hairs I didn't have earlier." He glanced to his right. "Uh-oh, look who's back."

Karen followed his gaze out into the water. The fins tracked a parallel course with their boat.

"You said you've been out here hundreds of times and never had a problem with sharks." She jabbed a finger towards the water. "Explain that, *Captain* Rysinski."

He shrugged. "Like I said, I've never had a problem with sharks."

"Are you friggin' *blind?* There's a whole school of them out there."

Ryan's mouth curled upward in a grin. "Those aren't sharks. They're dolphins."

She shot him a puzzled look. *"Dolphins?"*

He burst out laughing. "You see them out here all the time. They like to race alongside the boat."

Her eyes narrowed. "You *knew* they were dolphins the whole time, didn't you?"

"Maybe," he replied, suppressing a smile. "But in my defense, I just *pointed* to the fins. Your own irrational fear did the rest."

Karen punched him on the shoulder. "Are you *crazy?* You could've gotten us killed."

"Can't you take a joke?" he asked, chuckling.

"Some *joke*," she groused. "You know I'm afraid of the ocean . . .

and sharks."

Ryan draped his arm around her shoulder. He could still feel her trembling. "I'm sorry. I guess I'm not making good on my promise to protect you, am I?"

Karen felt the strength of his embrace and suddenly felt more than adequately protected. She snuggled against his chest and let out a sigh of contentment. "This might make up for your . . . behavior."

For the next half hour they cruised in silence across the water, watching the dolphins frolic among the waves and growing comfortable in each other's arms. Upon rounding a rocky peninsula on the coast, Ryan cut the catamaran's speed and began a perpendicular tack towards the shoreline. "We'll be heading into the surf in a minute or so," he said. "Make sure you lock your feet into the trampoline–a really strong wave could knock you overboard."

Karen surveyed the roiling surf and frowned. *Mmmm . . . now the real fun begins.*

Guiding the boat in a zigzag course towards shore, Ryan studied the swells and timed his incursion to the surf's tempo. The first wave broke in front of the bow and soaked Karen's legs instantly. Moments later, another wave crashed behind them and drenched them with a fine spray. The next swell tipped the boat dangerously high, but Ryan regained control of the till, and the boat leveled back into the sea.

Several minutes later, the boat breached the surf line and Ryan jumped into the breakers to drag the catamaran ashore. "Man, I must be getting old," he said, as he dragged the boat onto the beach. "I used to haul this puppy around like it was nothing."

Karen chuckled. "Think it's time to break out the walker, gramps?"

"I think I still have few good years left, *whippersnapper.*"

They walked a short distance up the deserted beach and spread a blanket under a stand of palm trees. Ryan unfurled the umbrella while Karen opened a bottle of wine and unpacked assorted nibbles from the cooler. They stretched out under the shade of the umbrella and savored the cool breeze wafting off the ocean.

Ryan looked over the spread of food and smacked his lips. "So what kind of munchies did you bring us today?"

Karen poured the wine and handed Ryan a glass. "Some seasonal fruit, a round of smoked Cheddar cheese, and a tray of stone ground crackers."

"Looks delish." He sampled the wine and winced. "What is this stuff anyway?"

Karen examined the label on the bottle. "Selected Cellers Chardonnay from Napa Valley, California." Disappointment tinged her face. "Don't you like it?"

He took another swallow and tried not to grimace. "It's a little sweet for my taste. I guess I'm just a beer drinker at heart."

She reached into the cooler and handed a bottle to Ryan. "See if this hits the spot."

He looked at the label and chuckled. "Isn't this the same beer I had at Ráisons?"

She nodded. "Succinctly dry with a distinct hop bouquet."

He popped off the cap and took a swig. "And it tasted good, too."

"It better be *damn* good–I had to go to three different stores to find it. The restaurant's not licensed to sell beer to the public so they bottle their excess production and ship it off to the boutique markets." She shook her head and frowned. "Does that make any sense to you?"

"Does *anything* our government pokes its nose into make any sense?" he asked. "But what can you expect from a bunch of filthy rich fools with too much time on their hands?"

"They're not all fools, Ryan. I actually respect the opinions of several politicians I've met, although I must admit they're few and far between." She took a sip of wine and met his gaze. "Speaking of . . . politics, how do you feel about the Pangaea Festival coming up next week?"

He shrugged. "It's just another overhyped event to stroke the local politicos' egos."

"Then you may not be interested in what I have to say to you."

His face perked up. "What's that?"

"I'm been asked to co-anchor the event for my station with Martin Strothers. During the next several days, I'll be interviewing people across the Southland to get their viewpoint on the festival and how it's going to impact their lives."

"I certainly can't speak for them, but I could give you the opinion of a *cop* who's lived here all his life."

"I didn't bring my recorder with me today," she said drolly, "but I'd still like to hear what you have to say."

Ryan's expression sombered. "Maybe you . . . won't." He sipped from his beer and turned his gaze towards the sea. "As you know, this region has always had a large migratory population; a native Californian is about as rare as rain in July. Unfortunately, most of the immigrants that have settled in this area in the last generation or so have no intention of becoming citizens of this country. They are loath to adopt our language and culture, but expect our beliefs and ideologies to bend for them. They are the *hyphenated* Americans–choosing to identify with their country of origin and not with the land they chose to make their home."

"Can't there be room for everyone in this country to better their lives?" Karen asked.

He shook his head. "If you don't care to embrace our culture and traditions, to adopt our laws and our language, then get on the friggin' horse you rode in on and go back *home.*"

Sadness touched Karen's eyes. "Somehow, I expected a more tolerant view from you. As a migrant myself, I find the diversity of this area a welcome change from the life I knew back home. There, it's pretty much your typical white-bread community. Your typical–*boring*–white-bread community."

"It may be that way in your hometown now, but what is happening in our largest cities will soon spread across the nation like a plague. The Department of Homeland Security and the nation's police have put a brake on the illegal immigration onslaught, but hundreds of thousands still enter under the radar every year."

"Why do I get the . . . impression . . . that you don't support the multicultural theme of the festival?"

"Don't get me wrong," he said. "I'm not some card carrying member of the Ku Klux Klan advocating the return of white supremacy."

Karen gave a sour smile. "Gee–that's a relief."

"This country was built on the backs of immigrants, and I still believe everyone should have an opportunity to better their lives or to seek sanctuary from persecution."

"So you feel immigration is beneficial to our country's welfare?"

"Yes, but only if it's *controlled* immigration. America can no longer afford to be the dumping ground for the disadvantaged of the world."

"Why can't we still take in the tired, the poor, the huddled masses yearning to breathe free?"

"That might have the standard when Lady Liberty flashed her beacon over a century ago, but it's woefully out-of-date now."

Her eyebrow arched upward. "Why?"

"Simple economics," he replied. "This country simply can't afford to support every Juan, Chen and Parvani who wants to live here today. A hundred years ago, America needed the manpower to develop our industrial base, but machines can now do the job far more cheaply. Today, only those who can contribute to our nation's welfare should be allowed to become citizens."

"Those who support immigration argue that immigrants will do the jobs that no one else wants to do in this country."

"Perhaps they will, but where will that lead us–to a nation of workers who can't earn a living wage? Before you know it, we'll be back in the Middle Ages where feudal lords held sway over their kingdom of serfs." He gave a bitter laugh. "We may already be there *now*."

"A society of haves and have-nots?"

"That's right. The middle-class continues to disappear while most of us are a paycheck or two away from homelessness with no real safety net to catch us."

"Isn't there anything we can do to change things?"

Ryan paused to contemplate the question. "That's hard to say. You can't legislate change–true change must always come from within. I believe it's time to streamline the system so there's a more balanced synergy between the local, state and national governments. And after the system is overhauled, the citizens need to become more proactive in local and national affairs, rather than sit on their ass and bitch like they usually do."

"Back to a true government by the people, for the people?"

He nodded. "Like it was originally intended. I believe our founding fathers had the right idea, but over time their idealism has been undermined by corruption and greed. But one message has always rung clear–when people become angry enough with the status quo, change comes about quickly and violently."

"Do you see that happening soon?"

"I don't know. But anytime you mix a culturally divided society with an apathetic government, you're looking at the seeds for disaster."

Karen's eyes grew dour. "Now I see why you don't have any hope for the festival's success."

"Anything is possible," Ryan replied. "But if you think we'll all link hands and start singing *Kumbaya* . . ." He laughed softly. "It ain't gonna happen."

"No, I suppose not. But I still think we can attain the nationalism our founding father's dreamed of one day."

"Keep believing in your dreams, Karen. The dreamers of the world are never afraid to bring about change."

"What about you?" she asked. "Didn't you become a cop to change the world for the better?"

He took a deep breath and exhaled. "Yes, but that was a . . . long time ago. I know things *need* to change, but I've lost my optimism because I see the dark side of humanity everyday."

She reached out and grasped his hand. "Each of us makes the whole stronger."

He looked down at Karen's hand and smiled. "You know, there may be hope for me yet."

48

With one out in the bottom of the eighth, and a man stranded on second base, the Dodgers found themselves at the losing end of a 6-4 ballgame. Surprisingly, the fans had not made their customary exodus after the seventh inning stretch, preferring to see the drama unfold to the bitter end.

Calvin nudged James' shoulder. "Looks like the Dodgers are out of it today, son."

James looked up and nodded, his mouth packed with a Dodger Dog. "Mmmm," he mumbled.

Calvin's mouth curled upward in a smile. Today's outing would be treasured far into his golden years, continuing a tradition begun by his own father when he was a young boy.

A crack of the bat snapped Calvin from his reverie, and he turned back to the game as the ball soared deep into right field. The Indians' outfielder dashed to the warning track and easily flagged down the ball for the Dodgers second out. The runner on second broke for third base and was waved home when the outfielder's throw fell short to the second baseman. The Indians lead was now narrowed to a single run.

Joining the hometown crowd's support for their team, Calvin rose from his seat and cheered. *"Wow!"* he exclaimed. "It ain't over 'til the fat lady sings, Cleveland."

As he settled back into his seat, Calvin noticed three men sitting several rows behind him. Normally, they would have escaped his attention except all three sported colorful turbans wrapped around their heads. Two wore pastel colored sarongs in a nod to their culture, while one dressed conservatively in a western styled suit. Since he had not observed them earlier he assumed they migrated from another part of the stadium, attracted to the empty seats closer to the playing field. Although this practice was frowned on by stadium security, it was generally overlooked this late in the game if the seats remained unsold.

The crowd roared as Tyler Lewis strode towards the plate, his bat looking like an oversized toothpick in his burly paws. He tapped the dirt from his shoes and stepped confidently into the batter's box, daring the Cleveland pitcher to send the ball down the strike zone.

The pitcher rose to the challenge and hurled a fastball directly towards the plate. The ball cracked off Lewis' bat like a cannon shot, but veered towards left field for a foul.

The next pitch was wide and outside for a ball. Lewis stepped out of the batter's box and spit a healthy stream of tobacco juice on the field. He tugged on his batting gloves and glared defiantly at the pitcher for several seconds, sending the hometown fans into a frenzy.

Refusing to be intimidated, Cleveland's star southpaw fired another fastball towards the plate. The fans cheered loudly as Lewis swiped at the ball, but it barreled into the catcher's mitt for another strike.

Shaking off several signals from his catcher, the pitcher began his windup and launched the ball towards the plate. The ball careened towards the batter, then broke outside at the last moment for ball two.

The crowd began to chant Tyler's name in unison, and the stadium soon filled with the thunderous clamor of thirty thousand fans.

The pitcher ignored the crowd and stared fiercely at Lewis as he twirled the ball between his fingertips. After shaking off several signs from the catcher, he kicked into his windup and hurled the ball towards home plate.

At the last second, the ball swerved upward towards Lewis' head. He staggered out of the batter's box to avoid being beaned, and quickly regained his balance as the ball blew past the catcher and slammed into the backstop.

The crowd jeered, and Lewis pointed his bat menacingly at the pitcher. For several very long seconds, the slugger looked as though he would charge the mound, but he adjusted his helmet and stepped back into the box to resume play.

From behind, Calvin heard the faint strains of cheering over the taunts of the crowd. He turned, and saw the three turbaned men on their feet waving their arms through the air. *They must be from Cleveland,* he mused to himself.

With a full count on Lewis, the crowd was back on its feet anticipating an end to the showdown. The next pitch tumbled through the air, a white blur speeding sixty short feet towards its intended target. Lewis thrashed at the blur, connected with the sound of a thunderclap, and drove the ball hard down the left field line. At the last second, it curved into the stands for another foul.

Hysteria swept through the stadium, and Lewis stepped from the batter's box and pointed his bat towards center field in homage to Babe Ruth. He glared frighteningly at the pitcher for several moments, then took a couple of practice swings before he stepped back into the box to resume play.

Refusing to be cowered, the Indians' southpaw launched the ball directly towards the plate. Lewis studied the ivory sphere as it zoomed towards him, timing his swing perfectly. The ball exploded off his bat with a deafening crack and soared in an arc towards the centerfield wall.

The stadium gave a collective howl as the Cleveland fielder scrambled towards the warning track in centerfield. He snared the ball in a graceful leap near the edge of the fence, robbing Lewis of a home run and the Dodgers chances of tying the game.

The fans moaned their disappointment at the failed rally. No one was more discouraged than Lewis, who was rounding first base when his opportunity to be the hero was brought to an end.

The unfortunate turn of events knocked the wind out of Calvin, and he slumped back into his seat. From several rows back, he heard the turbaned trio break into a rambunctious cheer as the Indians squelched the Dodgers prospects for victory.

Suddenly, a derisive remark sent a chill up Calvin's spine. "Hey, you fuckin' *ragheads!* Whose *side* are you on anyway?"

Calvin whirled in his seat and saw five drunken louts glaring menacingly at the turbaned men. The turbaned men stared silently at their detractors, and even from twenty feet away Calvin could see the fear in their eyes.

A scraggly, pork-bellied man who looked like a card-carrying member of the Hell's Angels leaned over the chair in front of him and yelled, "Hey–didn't you *hear* what we said? Or don't you stupid ragheads understand *English?*"

A sallow skinned youth from the group climbed upon his seat and sneered. "If you camel jockeys don't wanna root for our team, then go back to your own country. Or at least back to *Cleveland!*"

Several fans laughed heartily at the jibe. James turned to watch the clash, and Calvin wanted to whisk him from the stadium so he would not have to witness a second sting of bigotry in the last several days. And yet, he remained seated, transfixed by the grim tableau as it unfolded before his eyes.

The turbaned men remained silent, trying to ignore the hateful remarks spewed in their direction. Calvin felt a strange kinship with the men as he recounted the hostile remarks he endured from his own troubled past. Then, as now, he could clearly recall each stinging barb as it tore away at his character.

The Hell's Angels' refugee approached the turbaned men until he stood ten feet away from their seats. "What are you *A-rabs* doing here anyway? Haven't you blown up enough stadiums in the name of *Allah?*"

No longer willing to ignore the group's insults, the tallest of the turbaned men faced the hooligans and pumped his fist angrily in the air. "We are *not* Arabs," he declared. "We are *Sikhs* from Sri Lanka!"

"Arabs, Sihks—what difference does it make?" the sallow skinned youth groused. "You fuckin' *foreigners* are all alike. When are you gonna get it through your thick *rag-heads* that we don't want you here?"

Watching the confrontation, Calvin had little doubt who had the thicker head between the two groups. He watched James listen intently to the altercation, and feared the discussion they had several days earlier was about to be questioned for its veracity.

The Sikhs glared at their persecutors but stood their ground. Calvin sensed the conflict had reached the point where it would subside peacefully or escalate to violence. He looked around the stands and wondered why security hadn't come to squelch the situation. His face suddenly slackened as he considered the unthinkable. *Maybe they don't want to stop it,* he thought. *Muslims—or anyone who looks Muslim—aren't winning any popularity contests right now.*

The turbaned men spoke briefly between themselves and decided any further confrontation would be futile. They moved silently down the aisle towards the exit. Several of the drunken men hurled cups in their direction, showering them with beer. As soon as the Sikhs cleared the archway leading from the stadium, the drunken louts let out a celebratory cheer.

Calvin stared at the drunken bigots and fumed. *Nice going, assholes. You just lowered our humanity down another notch.*

James tugged on his sleeve. "Why did they pick on the men, Dad? Was it because they were–different?"

As Calvin struggled to answer his question, the warning Kati spoke of several days earlier echoed hauntingly in his mind. *We can't always be there to protect him, Calvin. Sometimes the monsters are real.*

49

A portly man with a deeply seamed face stepped hesitantly towards José as he wakened from his siesta. "May I speak with you, señor?" he asked politely.

José rubbed the sleep from his eyes and regarded the man cautiously. "What do you want, amigo?"

The man removed his battered hat and held it to the side. His once thick thatch of coal colored hair had thinned to a scraggly patch of gray. "Miguel took off with six from our group and headed out into the desert."

"How long ago?"

The man shrugged. "Several hours ago."

José nodded. *He didn't waste any time. He must have had his supporters all lined up before he came over to harass us.* A fleeting smile swept across his face. *We'll see just how smart you are several days from now, Miguel.* "What about the others?" he asked.

"There are five of us who wish to continue with you, señor," he replied. "The rest are still bickering on what to do next."

José smiled wanly. "Thanks for your trust, amigo." He held his hand out. "I don't believe we've been introduced."

The man grasped his hand and smiled broadly. "I am Javier

Rodriguez." He glanced towards the back of the cave at a rosy-faced woman and a tall, gangly teen. "And this is my wife, Gabriela, and my son, Hector."

José nodded as they were introduced. Gabriela wore a too-tight blouse over her plump body. Her face was a beautiful circle marred by squirrelly eyes and buckteeth. Hector had the face of a fox, with long, straight hair combed loosely over his ears. Acne played a cruel game across his face.

Another man stepped towards José from the shadows of the cave. Square-faced, with wide-set eyes and a bulky build, his calm and affable manner made José take to him instantly. "I'm Manuel Trujillo, and this is my daughter Rosa."

A pale-faced girl just entering her teens shuffled towards the group wearing a pink t-shirt and a pair of faded jeans. She gave a shy wave of her hand but remained silent.

"What's our next move, señor?" Javier asked.

José studied the desert for several moments before he answered. "We'll keep heading north until we find . . . something." He turned and rested his gaze on each member of the group. "Are there any questions before we head out?"

"Do you *really* think we can make it out of here, señor?" Hector asked.

José gave a sour smile. "Yes–if luck is on our side." There was no need to state their fate if fortune failed to bless them otherwise; it weighed plainly on each of their faces. "Well, if there are no further questions, get your gear together and we'll head out."

A short while later the migrants slogged across the hostile land, following a path slashed by an ancient river many eons ago. Deprived of food and water for the last two days, the group moved slowly through the scorched environment as the sun dipped behind the mountains to the west. The first stars poked holes in the purpling sky and dusk soon settled over the desolate landscape.

After a five-hour trek under the star studded sky, the group flung their belongings to the ground and stopped to rest. The surroundings were combed for firewood, and within minutes the weary migrants stretched out comfortably before a blazing fire.

José pointed out the ghostly outline of a nearby ridge to Elena. "I'm going to hike to that hill over there and see if I can find some sign of civilization."

"Be careful, José," she said. "It can be dangerous out there in the dark."

José grinned. "You sound just like my wife, Elena. She's a real worrywart, too."

"Must I remind you that I'm a wife, José?" Elena asked. She lifted Angelina to her breast to feed. "And a mother, too?"

He blushed. "As much as I hate to admit it, there are some things that women can do better than men."

"More than you could possibly know." A look of concern tinged her face. "Be careful out there, José."

He nodded and took off towards the ridge. Within seconds, he was lost to the darkness.

50

Ryan hoisted Karen aboard the catamaran and dragged it into the surf, carefully inspecting the vessel for any damage before they made their way back to the marina. Satisfied that all was shipshape, he leaned across the hull and extended the lines to Karen. "Feel like taking her out?" he offered.

She held out her hand. "No thanks–I know my limitations."

He climbed aboard the craft and unfurled the sail. "Are you ready?"

She looked at the waves crashing along the shoreline and shrugged. "As ready as I'll ever be."

Ryan studied the surf and brought the catamaran perpendicular to the coastline. Starting on a starboard tack, he kept the bow above the wave front as the first swell hit the hull slightly off center. The catamaran crested the wave and he increased the vessel's speed, quickly moving the craft over the next swell before it broke. Continuing in the same manner, the catamaran quickly traversed the surf and soon entered the open sea.

Karen gave Ryan the thumbs-up. "That was some pretty smooth sailing there, Captain Rysinki."

Ryan tipped his hat and grinned. "What do you expect? I'm the best catamaran sailor–"

"Yeah, I know," Karen quipped, "west of the Mississippi. Don't get too cocky, Captain Crunch, we're still not back at the marina."

He gave a dismissive wave of his hand. "Ahhh, you worry too much. From here on out, it's a piece of cake." He slid into the chair next to her and squeezed her shoulder. "Did you have a good time today?" he asked softly.

She shrugged. "It was . . . okay."

"Okay?" His face slackened. "That's it?"

"Would you feel better if I said today was the most enjoyable day of my life?"

His brow furrowed. "Well . . . yeah."

She mulled it over for several seconds, clearly enjoying his discomfort. "Okay, today's date was without doubt the most enjoyable day of my life." She flashed him a smile. "Satisfied?"

"More than satisfied. But, you must lead a pretty sheltered life if our date makes the top of your list."

"You might be surprised. We Mid-Westerners can be pretty resourceful when it comes to finding contentment in life."

He shot her a puzzled look. "I'm not sure I follow you."

"I guess what I'm trying to say is we find joy in the simpler things of life. The relationships we have with our family and friends, the honoring of traditions and holidays, and the general feeling of being reasonably at peace with the world." She nibbled on her lip. "I've noticed that people look for personal gratification in . . . different ways here."

"Different?" Ryan asked. "How?"

"The pursuit of contentment is–for lack of a better word– manufactured. People seek pleasure at venues or activities instead of finding the joy of life within themselves. Take Disneyland for example, one the most visited vacation resorts in the world. Once one enters the park that Mickey built, they are now at the self-proclaimed *Happiest*

Place on Earth." She laughed softly. "I don't know about you, but if an hour long wait for a three-minute ride was Mister Disney's idea of happiness, then I'd sure hate to visit the *unhappiest* place on earth."

Ryan chuckled. "Been there, done that. But in all fairness, Disneyland is geared more for kids than it is for adults."

"You're right, but don't you see where this mind-set leads to? When you're indoctrinated into this way of thinking at a young age, it influences your perceptions on how to seek enjoyment later in life. Once you believe pleasure is found only through external stimuli, you lose that part of you that finds joy from the trappings of life itself. You never take the time to–if you'll forgive the cliché–stop and smell the roses."

Ryan rubbed his chin and frowned. "Strange–I never thought of contentment in those terms before. I just went out and had fun and never analyzed the meaning behind it."

"And children certainly don't, and yet they're exposed to television, video games, the Internet, and other mindless activities and are somehow expected to *entertain* themselves. I wonder how many parents have used these–devices–as a means of entertainment rather than spending time with the children themselves?"

"Quite a few, I'd imagine."

"It might explain why this last generation has had such a difficult time integrating into society. Their perception of life is primarily based on the manufactured realities presented on television, video games or the Internet. They've become acclimated to these artificial environments and lost part of their humanity in the process. And our culture further dehumanizes them by segregating them in an anonymous Web world devoid of true personal interaction. No amount of *friends* on Facebook or Twitter can ever substitute for the warmth of a live, intimate relationship."

"You may be on to something there," he noted. "From what I've seen on the streets, today's youth are disconnected from society–and none of the so-called experts seems to know why. I thought poor parenting might be to blame, but the parents are usually clueless when their kids get in trouble with the law. They usually pass the buck and point the finger at their kid's friends or some unknown factor in the environment. Maybe if they took a few hours out of their so-called busy lives, they'd find the cold, hard truth staring at them in the mirror." His expression suddenly grew dour. *People in glass houses,* he reflected, *shouldn't throw stones.*

Concern touched Karen's face. "Is something wrong, Ryan?"

He blinked. "Uh . . . no. I'm fine."

Karen studied him. *You can't fool me, Ryan. Something's bothering you.* She changed the subject. "How long before we get back to the marina?"

He scanned the shoreline for a moment. "Another thirty minutes or so, depending on the wind."

"How can you tell where we're at? The coast looks pretty much the same to me."

"That's why I'm the skipper of this boat, and you're my lowly first mate."

"Mmmm . . . just like Gilligan, huh?"

"You're definitely not a Gilligan," Ryan stated. "More like Mary Ann, I'd say."

She frowned. "Are you implying that I'm not pretty enough to be Ginger?"

"Not at all. If I had to make a choice between the two, I'd always pick Mary Ann."

"Really?" she asked. "Why?"

"She was more down to earth. More . . . real. If you really think about it, what kind of woman wears a formal gown on a three hour sightseeing cruise?"

"Maybe her casual clothes were at the cleaners that day."

"I don't think so." He shook his head and chuckled. "Only in Hollywood."

She snuggled against his shoulder. "Do you think you could spend a couple of years stranded on a deserted island with me?"

"Sure," he replied, grinning. "But I'd like it even more if Ginger and Mary Ann could join us."

51

"Candice, quit pacing around the deck," Andrew grumbled. "You're starting to make me dizzy."

She stopped mid-stride and looked him over. "Don't you think you've had enough to drink for today?"

Andrew took a swig from his glass and smiled. "Why don't you let me be the judge of that, my dear?" He snatched the script off the table and tried to focus on the page. "Now, where were we?"

"Forget about the script for now. Will you be able to take us back to the marina in your . . . condition?"

He shot her a crooked grin. "No problemo. And since you brought it up, I'll take us back to the marina right now."

"Now?" she asked, frowning. "Aren't we going to finish editing the script?"

Andrew ignored her query and staggered across the deck towards the ship's control room. Once inside the mahogany paneled chamber, his addled mind was quickly overwhelmed by the array of dials and switches adorning the instrument console. *Why do they have to make these things so friggin' complicated?* he groused to himself.

Checking the yacht's current position on the Global Positioning System, Andrew set a course back to the marina on the ship's autopilot system. A smile traced his face as he heard the yacht's engines roar to life. *I may not be able to take the ship back in my condition, Candice, but my fancy overpriced machinery will do it for me.*

After a brief stop at the bar to refresh his drink, Andrew stumbled back to his seat and picked up the script. "Now, where were we?"

"Act two, page forty-four," Candice prodded. "The scene where Aileen embraces her faith when her life takes a turn for the worse." She shook her head and frowned. "The way MacNeil has it written now, the whole scene just smacks of pious overkill."

Andrew's expression soured. *I've got to put a stop to this. Any changes to this act will destroy the story's integrity.*

She shot him a sideways glance. "So what do you think?"

"There's no need to make any changes to this act," he replied gruffly. "MacNeil's script paints a realistic portrayal of Aileen resolving her plight through faith."

"I disagree," Candice said tersely. "In today's world, no one would forgive their abuser's sins without some measure of retribution."

"And what if *Jesus* came to your door asking for help?" Andrew chided. "Would He be just another long haired *bum* looking for a handout?"

She sighed. "*Andrew* . . . you can't equate Aileen's path to redemption to the teachings of Christ. That's like comparing the light from a candle to the sun."

He slammed the script on the table. "Candice, up to now I've accommodated your suggestions because some have improved the script. But, I must draw the line *here*. Act two will remain as is—*without* any further changes."

Candice glared at Andrew for a moment before she hurled the script to the deck. Several pages were quickly borne by the wind and flung out to sea. "Didn't you want me for this role because it complemented my personality?" she asked.

"As it was originally written. But, your constant *tweaks* will change the character to such a degree that the entire storyline will become compromised." He leveled an intimidating glare in her direction. "And that–is something I can't allow to happen."

Tears drizzled from her eyes. "You know how I feel about hypocrisy, Andrew. It would be a mistake for me to take on a role I didn't truly believe in."

Andrew's eyes narrowed. "No, the mistake was mine," he contended. "For considering you for the role in the first place."

52

Ryan leaned over the catamaran's hull and pointed towards the coastline. "The marina is just beyond that peninsula," he said. "Keep the cat a healthy distance from shore because there's a rocky reef just beneath the water's surface."

Karen tugged gently on the tiller, and the craft swept around the peninsula in a wide arc. "How's that, skipper?"

"Not bad, mate. One of your ancestors must have had saltwater flowing through their veins."

"I doubt it," she said. "The closest anyone in my family has come to the ocean is buying a can of tuna at the market."

Ryan chuckled. "You could have fooled me." He swung down off the hull and slid next to her on the wing seat. "Want to try taking us into the marina?"

"Why not? How else will I ever become the skipper?"

Ryan removed his captain's hat and snugged it atop her head. "Consider yourself promoted."

As she guided the catamaran towards the marina, Karen faced an ever-growing number of ships vying for space on the ocean. Large ships and pleasure craft moved in procession between two lines of buoys on their way into the marina or out to sea.

Ryan pointed towards a group of buoys to the left of the catamaran. "Stay to the left of the red buoys and head straight into the marina."

Karen tapped the side of her cap. "As the ship's new skipper, I will give the orders on this vessel from now on."

Ryan snapped to attention and saluted. "Aye aye, sir—or should I say—madam?"

She extended her hand. "*Your majesty* will do."

He bent to kiss her hand. "M'lady."

She giggled. "As you were—Gilligan."

Karen scanned the harbor as she guided the catamaran to the left of the buoys. Several hundred yards away, she noticed a large, white yacht skimming across the waves in their direction. She pointed at the rapidly moving vessel and pinched her lip. "Isn't that ship getting a little too close for comfort?"

Ryan followed her gaze and shrugged. "I wouldn't worry about it. Sailboats have the right of way over powered boats in the harbor."

Karen nodded but kept a wary eye peeled in the yacht's direction.

"You need to bring the cat a little closer to the buoys," Ryan directed. "Decrease your speed and move the tiller to your left."

Karen yanked hard on the tiller, and the right hull suddenly became airborne. The cat's boom swung left and the sail deflated, leaving the catamaran stalled in the water.

Ryan started from his seat, but Karen waved him off. "I'll take care of it, Ryan."

He leaned back in his seat and grinned. "You're the skipper, *skipper.*"

Karen tried coaxing some wind into the sail as Ryan watched with amusement from the sidelines. Suddenly, a thunderous roar filled the air. Karen whipped her head towards the sound, her eyes widening as she watched the yacht skate across the sea in their direction. "Isn't anybody steering that thing?" she cried.

Ryan scanned the rapidly approaching ship and frowned. "It must be on autopilot, I don't see anyone at the helm." His face suddenly slackened. *And my boat doesn't have an on-board GPS transponder, so it's invisible to the yacht's auto-guidance systems.*

He leaped from his seat. "Come on—we gotta jump!"

Karen's eyes grew huge. "Jump?"

"Now!" He grabbed her around the waist, and they tumbled awkwardly into the sea.

The yacht rumbled ominously past the catamaran, missing the tiny craft by less than twenty feet. The resultant wake drove Ryan and Karen underwater, and they furiously paddled to stay afloat in the turbulent sea.

As Ryan broke to the surface, he noted the name inscribed on the bow of the rapidly departing vessel. He saw two people engaged in a heated discussion atop the rear deck, but the helm—from what he could see—was deserted.

He swam over to Karen, a look of concern etched upon his face. "Are you all right, Karen?"

She tugged the captain's hat upward, and a stream of water gushed down her face. "Are you *sure* you're the best catamaran sailor west of the Mississippi River?"

53

Kati looked up from the magazine she was reading as Calvin and James barged into the kitchen. "How was the game?" she asked. "Did the Dodgers beat the Indians?"

James rushed over to her side, waving the bat in his hand. "Look Mom! Tyler Lewis signed my bat!"

She took the bat from his grasp and read the inscription. "To James–Keep on slugging–Tyler Lewis."

"That's me, Mom!" he squealed. "Tyler Lewis wants me to keep on slugging!"

"He certainly does. But right now, it's time for a certain slugger to take his bath."

Revulsion crossed his face. "Awww Mom, do I have to?"

"I'm afraid so. Sluggers get dirty, too."

James took his bat and tramped loudly down the hall towards the bathroom.

Kati rose from her seat at the kitchen table and pecked Calvin's lips. "You're home later than I thought you'd be."

Calvin nodded. "Later than I thought, too." He set the soft drinks on the counter and pulled a beer from the refrigerator. "The game went into extra innings, and then we stopped off for some sundaes after our trip to the market."

"So how was the game? It looks like James had a good time."

Calvin sat down at the table and took a swig of his beer. "A real classic. The Dodgers tied the game in the ninth and went on to win in eleven on a long sacrifice fly." He flinched. "Sorry, hon. I keep forgetting you know nothing about baseball. I hope I'm not boring you."

"Not at all," she replied. "Just because I don't understand the rules doesn't mean I'm not interested in what happened while you were at the game."

"We arrived an hour early and James became a handful while we waited for the game to get underway. Fortunately, after Tyler Lewis stepped on the field, all he could focus on was getting his bat signed."

"So that's really his autograph?"

He nodded. "Frankly, I'm a little surprised. Most star athletes won't sign anything these days unless they're paid."

"Maybe you caught him on a good day," she said. "How'd the rest of the game go?"

Calvin gnawed on his lip. *Should I tell her about the quarrel between the fans?*

Kati cocked her head. "Calvin?"

"You know, it's . . . funny you should ask," he replied, keeping his voice light. "In the bottom of the eighth, there was a . . . an incident . . . between some of the fans."

"Incident?" she asked.

"It involved three turbaned men who sat behind us after the seventh inning stretch."

"Did they cause you any trouble?"

"Not unless you call rooting for the opposing team *trouble*."

She shot him a puzzled look. "What's wrong with that?"

Calvin chuckled. "Kati, in some cities, showing support for the opposing team might land you in the hospital."

She gave a disgusted look. "Why people find team sports so captivating is beyond me. So what happened after the turbaned men dissed the home team?"

"A group of drunken fans started shouting ethnic slurs–"

"You're *joking*. Right?"

He shook his head. "It's no . . . joke. The *ragheads* were asked in not too polite terms to get the hell out of Dodge."

"What did they do?"

"What *could* they do?" Calvin asked. "They were outnumbered, and they looked like–Muslims. And as you know, Muslims are virtual pariahs in our society right now."

"Still, they shouldn't have been singled out because of their appearance or because they chose to support the opposing team."

"I agree, but bigots and racists rarely need an excuse to express themselves when the opportunity arises." He took a draw from his bottle and frowned. "Especially when booze has loosened their lips."

"Was there anything you could have done to stop it?"

"Not really," he replied. "Even though I sympathized with their plight because of my own tortured childhood, I couldn't find a reason to come to their defense."

"But, they did nothing wrong. Wasn't that reason enough?"

"Maybe, but the risks weren't worth it." He took a deep breath and exhaled. "It's ironic in a sad sort of way, but maybe I should be grateful the Muslims are attracting the suspicion and anger that used to be reserved for my own race."

She blinked. "Are you serious?"

"For once in America's long, sorry history of ethnic integration, it's refreshing not to be viewed under the microscope. It's refreshing not be seen as another *nigger* hellbent on destroying America's communities."

"I know how you feel. Though my family has lived here for generations, I don't know how many times I've been treated like . . . a foreigner." Her expression grew dour. "Sometimes I feel like I'm a stranger in my own land."

"You may feel the occasional sting of persecution from time to time," Calvin said, "but Asians have never been enslaved or subjected to racist policies created solely to keep them under control."

"Have you forgotten about the Japanese internment camps of World War Two? Over a hundred thousand Japanese *citizens* were forcibly relocated because our government questioned their allegiance to this country."

Calvin rubbed his chin and nodded. "As if I *could* forget that sad chapter in America's history. Ignorance bred suspicion, which in turn bred . . . fear." He sipped from his beer and pinched his lower lip. "Americans are already suspicious of the Muslims in this country. How much longer before their suspicions turn to outright fear?"

"I'm afraid the handwriting's already on the wall," she replied. "But, it's a shame the actions of a few extremists have ruined the perception of the culture as a whole."

"I agree—one bad apple shouldn't spoil the whole crop. But, fear is an instinctive process, not a rational one. When you combine public opinion and nationalism, the balance tips for whatever cause is popular at any given time. Nazi Germany has already shown us that. Like the Jews and gypsies from that era, Muslims in this country are targeted by a society that disapproves of their actions. Tomorrow, another group may find themselves in the crosshairs if they fall from favor with the populist interests in this country."

"But one group of people isn't targeted by another without reason. Some kind of contemptible action must occur to antagonize one group against another."

"True," Calvin noted. "But the reasoning behind the action doesn't have to be rational—it can be driven by ignorance, suspicion, or fear. If you comb through humanity's troubled history, most conflicts have erupted due to one or any combination of the three."

"Not to change the subject, but how did James react to today's . . . incident?"

Calvin took a deep breath and exhaled. "I think he was a little confused, but after we left the stadium I tried to make it clear the turbaned men did the right thing by walking away. That's consistent with what I said to him earlier–that violence should only be used as a last resort to defend yourself."

"They're really impressionable at this age. A remark or action that might appear harmless on the surface could scar them psychologically for life. Do you think I should get involved?"

"I think the crisis has passed–for now. Just keep on loving him like you've done since he first came into our lives."

"Speaking of love and . . . family–are you ready for tomorrow's barbeque?"

He shrugged. "As ready as I'll ever be. But, I still don't think this get together is such a good idea."

She touched his hand. "Can't you let your resentment go?"

His face tightened. "Why should I? It's been *ten* years since we took our vows, and our families still haven't learned to accept us. For ten long years we've put up with excuses from the very people who should accept us unconditionally."

"People can change, honey. After ten years, maybe their prejudices have–disappeared."

"Ever the optimist, Kati." He shook his head and chuckled. "But you're right. If we ever hope to have a more tolerant society, we'll have to start building it one family at a time."

54

avier looked up sharply as José wandered like a wraith into the campfire's pale light. "Find anything out there, amigo?" he asked anxiously.

José gave a quick headshake. "Nothing but the glow from the stars."

The migrants turned their gaze upward at the swath of white pinpricks dotting the inky void. The Milky Way glimmered faintly in a billowy band against the sparkling sky.

"I don't think I've ever seen this many stars before," Hector said.

"Neither have I," José replied. "Though I live in the country west of Jiquilpan, the sky has never been as crisp as it appears right now."

The group marveled at Mother Nature's handiwork for several moments, each wondering if their final resting place would be beneath that same star spangled sky.

José clapped his hands to break the mood. "All right, get your gear together," he ordered. "It's time we move out."

They gathered up their possessions and trudged out into the night. Stands of sagebrush and cacti paraded past them in an endless loop, while gravel bit into their weary feet with each step across the desolate landscape.

Several hours before the sun rose above the blistered land, the migrants agreed to rest under an outcropping carved into the side of an ancient riverbed. Scores of dried branches were found along the gully's sandy basin, and within minutes a campfire punched a hole through the darkness.

While the women gathered around the fire to talk, José pointed out the murky outline of a ridge to Javier. "I'm going to head over towards that hill and see if there's something that might help us out." He gave a sour smile. "Maybe I'll get *lucky* this time."

A short time later, frustration scored José's face as he scanned the horizon for civilization from the top of the ridge. *Looks like I spoke too soon*, he grumbled. *Just where in hell are we, anyway?*

Suddenly, a scream from their camp pierced the night.

José's eyes widened. *Elena!*

Scrambling down the rocky incline, José ran breathlessly towards the campsite, using the glow from the fire to guide him. In the distance, he heard Elena wail loudly as though her soul was being wrenched from her body. *Dear God*, he wondered. *What's wrong?*

Elena stood near the fire as he stumbled into the camp, clutching Angelina in her arms. "It's Angelina, José!" she screeched. *"She's stopped breathing!"*

He rushed over to her side. "Let me take a look at her." Taking the infant from her hands, José placed Angelina gently on the ground and listened for any signs of respiration. *It's too late*, he thought glumly. *There's nothing I can do for her.*

Elena looked expectantly in his direction, tears streaming down her face. "Is she . . ?"

José met her gaze and shook his head.

Elena began to wail uncontrollably, and Gabriela and Rosa drew by her side to console her. She broke away from their grasp and reached out towards José. "I need to be with her, José," she rasped. "One . . . last

. . . time."

José placed the tiny bundle in Elena's arms and stepped away. An eerie silence drifted across the land as Elena parted the blanket and kissed Angelina gently on the forehead. "Goodbye, my sweet Angelina," she said as a tear drifted down her cheek. "I . . . I love you." She burst into a loud, wracking sob.

José snatched Hector's arm. "Look around here for two straight branches, Hector," he whispered, "while your father and I prepare a place for Angelina . . . to rest."

A short time later, a shallow hole was carved out of the graveled surface, and a makeshift cross was placed at the head of gravesite. José gestured for Gabriela and Rosa to bring Elena forward. The two women walked slowly towards the burial site, supporting the spiritless Elena between them.

José brushed the hair back from Elena's face and forced a smile. "She's with the Lord now, Elena." He took the baby from her arms and laid her gently into the grave. "Does anyone want to say a eulogy for Angelina?" he asked the group.

Everyone remained silent except for Elena, who began to moan hysterically.

Silhouetted against the flames of the campfire, the seven wayward travelers bowed their heads as José led them in prayer. "Our Father, who art in heaven . . ."

SUNDAY

55

asperelli hooked a thumb over his shoulder as he straggled past Ryan's desk at the precinct. "The Loo's lookin' for you, dude."

Ryan looked up from his computer and frowned. "Did he tell you why?"

"Do I look like your friggin' secretary?" Casperelli quipped. He plopped into the chair behind his desk and stuffed a doughnut into his mouth. "What's goin' on?" he asked between bites. "You workin' days now?"

"Only until Gleason gets off disability," Ryan replied. "It's going to be strange keeping the same schedule as the rest of the world after working nights for so long."

"You'll get used to it," Casperelli said. "Just think of it as another sacrifice for The Job."

Ryan rose from his chair and turned towards Lieutenant Cullen's office. "I know there's one thing I won't miss."

"What's that?"

"Looking at your ugly mug when I report in for work."

Moments later, Ryan poked his head into the lieutenant's office. "You wanted to see me, sir?"

Cullen waved him inside his office. "I've got a project that requires your attention, Rysinski."

Ryan's face perked up. "Some undercover work, sir?"

"Undercover work?" Cullen barked out a laugh. "I need you where you'll be the most effective, Rysinski, not out on the street doing lame ass undercover work."

Ryan's face slackened. "So what did you have in mind for me, sir?"

"Something that befits your . . . experience." He pulled a file from a lopsided stack of paperwork on his desk. "There's a recruit reporting for work today–"

Ryan groaned.

Cullen looked up sharply. "Was there something you wanted to say, Rysinski?"

Ryan gave a quick headshake and remained silent, resigned to his fate.

The lieutenant returned his gaze to the file. "The rookie you'll be partnered with is Patricia Ruiz. You're to familiarize her with departmental protocol for the next few weeks until she learns the ropes around the division."

"Sir, I'm . . . *flattered* . . . you chose me for this assignment, but there must be other officers who are more qualified to–"

Cullen held his hand up. "You volunteered to fill in for Gleason while he was out on disability. Since he was scheduled to orient all recruits to the precinct, the assignment now becomes your responsibility."

Ryan's jaw clenched. *Damn you, Gleason. If you weren't already out on disability I'd put you there myself.* "I understand, sir," he muttered. "What can you tell me about Ruiz's background?"

Cullen thumbed through the file. "According to the report, she graduated seventh in her class–with outstanding commendations from two of her instructors. She's bilingual, scored highly on diffusing conflict situations, and ranked in the top ten percent in marksmanship."

He leaned across the desk and handed Ryan the file. "Look it over when you get a chance."

"When is she expected to report for duty, sir?"

The lieutenant glanced at his watch. "Any minute now. I'll spend some time showing her around the precinct before I send her over to you."

Ryan nodded. "Anything else, sir?"

"That will be all, Rysinski."

Ryan trudged back to his seat and slammed the file down on his desk. *"Fuck!"*

Casperelli bolted upright in his seat. "*Whoa!* What's wrong, dude?"

"Ahhh . . . the Loo wants me to baby-sit some friggin' *rookie* out of the Academy. Gleason was supposed to do it, but now his shitload falls in my lap since I volunteered to take his place in the rotation."

"Man, that's rough," Casperelli said as he tossed half a doughnut into his mouth. "So who's got the . . . *privilege* . . . of workin' with ya?"

Ryan ignored his sarcasm. "Ruiz. *Patricia* Ruiz."

Casperelli choked on his donut. "A *broad?*" he sputtered out. "He's hooked you up with a . . . *a broad?*"

A look of disgust swept over Ryan's face. "Yeah. Can you fuckin' *believe* it?"

"Dude—you're *sooo* screwed." He let out a short, harsh laugh.

Ryan glared at him. "Your sympathy is greatly appreciated."

"Sorry, man," Casperelli replied, trying to suppress his laughter. "Is there a photo of her in the report?"

Ryan shook his head. "Just her results from the Academy."

"You know, I bet she's built like a linebacker," Casperelli ventured. "And probably has a face like one, too."

"God, I hope not," Ryan said, wincing. "Frankly, how she looks isn't as important as her ability to do the job. I don't want my ass on the line while she's touching up her makeup or painting her nails."

Casperelli slammed another doughnut down his throat. "When's she supposed to start?"

"Any minute now. Cullen's showing her around the precinct, and then she'll be my . . . responsibility."

Casperelli belched loudly. "I was about to leave for the day, but I think I'll stick around now just to see what you're up against."

"You don't need to stay on my account," Ryan groused.

"Someone's gotta watch your ass."

Ryan turned his attention back to the report. Despite her gender or appearance, Ruiz received respectable reviews from all her instructors at the Academy. Some marks, in fact, were higher than his own. *But then*, he mused, *the standards were much higher in my day.*

He looked up from the report and glanced anxiously around the department, hoping to glimpse the recruit with Cullen. When she failed to materialize, he thrummed his fingers on the desk and thought about yesterday's date with Karen. Despite their unexpected dip in the drink, it turned out to be one of the most enjoyable days of his life as well. *Which reminds me, I still have a loose end to attend to.*

Ryan logged into his computer and accessed the Department of Motor Vehicles database. A look of annoyance touched his face when the information he sought was not available. He turned and glanced at Casperelli. "Cap, do you know who handles maritime registrations for California?"

Casperelli looked up from his *Penthouse* magazine and shrugged.

Ryan called the Records and Identification Division and waited patiently until a gruff sounding voice came on the line. "Records, Sterling speaking."

"Hey, John–it's Ryan Rysinski from Wilshire."

The voice softened. "What's up, dog? I haven't heard from you in ages."

"Ahhh . . . you know," Ryan replied. "Same shit, different day. I was wondering if you could help me track down some information on a case I'm looking into."

"What do you need?"

"I'm trying to find the owner of a yacht that might have been involved in a crime. I couldn't find anything in the DMV database."

"The Coast Guard is in charge of registrations for that vessel class. Why not let them deal with it?"

"I wanted to . . . uhh . . . verify a few things before I got anyone else involved. Who do I contact to–"

"I'll take care of it," Sterling offered. "What's the name on the suspect's boat?"

Ryan's face tightened as he recalled the near collision in the harbor yesterday. The large, gold scripted words emblazoned across the yacht's bow were still seared into his mind. "No Regrets," he replied, keeping the anger from his voice.

"No Regrets," Sterling echoed. "An unusual name, wouldn't you say?"

"*Very* unusual. How long before you hear from The Guard?"

"A couple of hours or so. You want me to email you the information?"

"That'd be great. I'll send over a bottle of Mister Daniel's finest for your trouble."

"No problem, dog. Glad to be of help."

A feminine voice cooed over Ryan's shoulder as he hung up the phone. "Officer Rysinski?"

Ryan spun around in his chair, and his jaw dropped. Smoldering brown eyes, chiseled cheekbones, and full red lips framed a face usually found gracing the cover of fashion magazines. A lithe, busty body strained tightly against the standard issue uniform, and Ryan wondered if Cullen was setting him up by using a model dressed as a law enforcement officer.

Any doubt was quickly dispelled as she offered her hand. "Hi, I'm Patricia Ruiz," she purred. "Lieutenant Cullen said you'd be my training officer for the next several weeks."

Ryan shook her hand and nodded numbly.

She shot him a puzzled look. "Is everything all right?"

Before Ryan could reply, a loud crash erupted from behind him. He turned and found Casperelli sprawled on the floor next to his chair, a stunned expression on his face.

Casperelli scrambled to his feet and leaned next to Ryan's ear. "Forget about watchin' your ass," he whispered. "I'm gonna spend the rest of the day checkin' out *hers.*"

56

Sadness touched José's eyes as he brushed a strand of hair from Elena's slumbrous face. *She looks at peace now,* he thought glumly. *But inside, she must be going through a living hell with the loss of her daughter.*

Moments later, her eyes cracked open to greet the day. "Oh . . . it's you, José," she murmured. "How long have I been sleeping?"

He stroked her forehead and smiled. "Several hours now."

She flipped onto her back and stared at the rocky ledge overhead. "I had a dream about Angelina last night," she muttered. "But it was only . . . a dream."

"She's in a better place now, Elena."

Rage swept across her face. "*Anywhere* would be better than here," she hissed. "Angelina deserved more than an unmarked grave in the middle of Hell."

José touched her shoulder. "Elena," he said gently, "You mustn't torture yourself."

"It's *my* fault that she's gone. If I hadn't wanted something better for my life, none of this would have happened." She glared at him, tears streaming down her face. "Was it *worth* it, José? Was any of what we've gone through worth the life of my child?"

José took a deep breath and exhaled. "Nothing can atone for your loss," he replied. "But if you stayed in Mexico, what kind of life would you have?" He looked out at the waves of heat rippling across the desert and compressed his lips. "I don't know about you, but I'd die a thousand times in this shithole reaching for my dream than live a moment where I could not change my life at all." He paused. "America may not offer us everything, but we'll have a better chance at improving our lives than we'd ever find at home."

Elena's expression softened. "You're right, José. In my anger, I almost forgot *why* we made our journey." She met his gaze and sighed. "But must the price for a better life always be so . . . high?"

57

olding the phone close to his ear, Andrew gunned the Bentley's engine and snaked between two slow moving vehicles along the Pacific Coast Highway. "It looks like Candice won't be able to commit to this project after all," he groused to David Levin. "Yeah–the usual *creative differences.* I'll give you all the dirt when I meet you at Limoges in a half hour or so. Later."

The signal flashed red up ahead on the roadway, bringing traffic to a halt. While waiting in the shadow of a hulking SUV, Andrew looked out the window and frowned as he watched the turquoise tinged sea beckon him with its beauty. *A perfect day for the beach and I'm stuck in some downtown dive with a studio wonk.*

Twenty-five minutes later, Andrew cruised along Wilshire Boulevard searching for a place to park near the restaurant. He darted down several side streets, eventually finding a spot two blocks from his destination.

After he parked his car and fed the meter, Andrew strolled hastily towards the restaurant. He noticed numerous empty storefronts and the near absence of pedestrians along the usually teeming streets. A frown traced his face as he acknowledged the weak economy's impact on the business community. *I guess it's easy to ignore the troubles of the world when it passes in a blur past your window,* he mused.

As he approached a trash-strewn alleyway, Andrew winced at the stench wafting through the air. He started past the noxious smelling corridor when a large creature bounded out from behind a dumpster and suddenly blocked his path.

At first, Andrew thought it was a wayward bear foraging for food, but closer inspection revealed a large, scraggly looking man swathed in a hodgepodge of tattered clothes.

Stepping back, Andrew regarded the goliath with a watchful eye. "Wh–what do you want?" he asked cautiously.

The man-beast stared at him with half-crazed eyes but remained silent. His pustule rimmed mouth breathed rhythmically like a beached fish struggling to extract oxygen from the air.

The putrid stench oozing off the behemoth made Andrew's eyes water. "If you're here looking for a handout–you can just forgetaboutit. Quit leeching off the public and get a job like everyone else."

The stranger continued to stare but said nothing. Andrew glanced uneasily down the street, but the eerily quiet neighborhood was deserted. *I guess it's just me and Grizzly Adams locking horns in the urban wilderness,* he fretted.

Suddenly, the man-beast reached inside his grimy overcoat and withdrew a wicked looking knife. He looked intently at Andrew and smiled, revealing several blackened teeth in an otherwise vacant mouth.

Andrew watched the knife glint in the bright afternoon sun and frowned. *If this were a movie, the hero would subdue the brute with a quick punch to the face.* He took a step back and swallowed. *But, this is no movie.*

The giant lashed out towards Andrew. The blade slashed through his jacket sleeve and left a shallow gash on his arm. Andrew's eyes widened in horror. *Shit! This fucker means business!*

Fearing for his life, Andrew turned and dashed back the way he came. After several blocks blurred past his adrenalin surged body, he paused to glance back at his adversary. But the lumbering giant–to his amazement–had disappeared.

It's as though he'd never existed, Andrew mused. He peeled back his suit sleeve and looked at the shallow cut crazing his arm. *But, he was here–this gash is proof of it.*

Andrew took several moments to regain his composure and decided to risk a trip back towards the restaurant. As he neared the alleyway, he half-expected the behemoth to spring forth and finish off the job he started. But, the creature was nowhere to be found, seemingly swallowed into the depths of the city from whence he came.

Moving hastily towards his destination, Andrew breathed a sigh of relief when Limoges' maroon awning sprang into view. But his mood quickly soured when he noticed a police cruiser parked directly across the street from the restaurant.

Andrew looked at the black and white vehicle and fumed. *They're never around when you need them.* He stepped off the sidewalk and jaywalked across the street, ignoring the horns from several irate drivers as he made a beeline towards the cruiser.

Ryan watched Andrew cross the boulevard and climbed out of the cruiser to greet him. "Hello," he said amiably. "What can I do for you, sir?"

Andrew held his arm out. "I was *attacked,* officer."

Ryan examined Andrew's arm. A small amount of blood stained the edge of his torn suit sleeve, but the wound itself was little more than a scratch. "Will you require medical attention, sir?" he asked.

"I'll live," Andrew grumbled. "But, I need you to arrest the man that did this to me."

Ruiz stepped around the cruiser to join them. "Did you get a good look at him, sir?"

"He was huge," Andrew stated. "And smelled like rotting trash."

"And where did this alleged attack take place, sir?" Ryan asked.

"Alleged?" Andrew snorted. "This fucker tried to *kill* me!"

"Are you sure he was trying to kill you, sir?" Ruiz asked.

Andrew held up his sleeve. "What more *proof* do you need–*officer?*"

"There's quite a few mentally ill people on the street, sir," Ryan said. "He may have considered you a threat and tried to defend himself."

"Bullshit," Andrew scoffed. "This . . . thing . . . was a friggin' giant. How could I possibly pose any threat to him?"

"If this *giant* really wanted to kill you," Ruiz pointed out. "He probably would have had no problem doing so."

Andrew stared at Ruiz and frowned. "He should be taken off the streets before he attacks someone else."

"Did you see where he took off–?" Ryan asked.

"No!" Andrew growled. "Because I was too busy trying to save my life!" His gaze drifted across the motto emblazoned on the cruiser's door. "To Protect and To Serve," he mocked. "What a *joke.*"

Ryan shot Patricia a sideways glance. *What's this a-hole's problem?*

Ruiz caught his look and moved to defuse the situation. "Sir, there's no need to get hostile here," she said calmly.

Andrew's face went hot. "I'm not *hostile,*" he spat. "I just want that . . . that *monster* locked up before he hurts anyone else." A look of disgust crossed his face. "Is that too much to ask?"

"No, sir," Ryan replied. "After you provide my partner with some additional information, we'll do a block by block search of the immediate neighborhood to find the person who assaulted you. In the meantime, I'll contact the precinct and request some backup to help with the search."

Several minutes later, Ruiz joined Ryan in the cruiser after she took Andrew's statement. "Was it my imagination, or did the vic come on a little too . . . strong?"

Ryan chuckled. "Ya think? Just who was he anyway?"

Patricia scanned her report. "Andrew Landis. Claims he's one of

Tinseltown's most successful producers. He was scheduled to meet some bigwig at the restaurant across the street when the perp attacked him. It must be one helluva an important meeting because he dashed over there right after he gave his statement."

"Maybe Landis' brush with death will become the script for an exciting new movie," Ryan said drolly. He held his hands up, as if framing a picture. "I can almost see the title now—*The Bastard and the Beast.*"

Ruiz groaned. "Better not quit your day job, Rysinski. Cuz Cecil B. DeMille you ain't."

58

Peeking through the living room window, a frown soured Calvin's face as he watched his sister's car pull up in the driveway. "Looks like Cerise and Ronald are here," he muttered. "Better put on your flak jacket."

Kati chuckled. "Aren't you overreacting just a bit, hon?"

"Not unless you've *forgotten* what my sister could be like."

She stroked his shoulder and smiled. "Relax—everything's going to turn out fine."

Calvin took a deep breath and exhaled. "Yeah . . . I guess." His eyes darted nervously around the room. "Where are the kids?"

"In their rooms . . . getting into trouble."

He nodded absently. "Good. There's plenty of time for them to face the music later."

The doorbell echoed loudly throughout the house and Calvin stared glumly at the ceiling. *This is it. May heaven help us all.* As his hand reached out to grasp the doorknob, the dilemma faced by the princess' lover in *The Lady and the Tiger* raced through his agitated mind. *Frankly, I'd rather face the friggin' tiger right about now.*

When the door swung open, the snarling feline that Calvin wished for was replaced by his older sister Cerise and her malingering husband,

Tyrone. At first glance, his sister had changed little since they last met a year ago. Still grossly overweight, her gold frosted hair, pink tinted eye shadow, and inlaid lavender nails made her look more like a cheap street walking whore than a mid-level executive for one of the largest companies in the Southland. Standing demurely in her shadow, Tyrone stared forlornly in Calvin's direction like some wayward pet. Strands of gold chains hung from his scrawny neck and his feet sported a pair of platform shoes last seen on the set of *Saturday Night Fever*. Calvin looked over the garish couple and tried to suppress his laughter. *All Tyrone needs is a fedora and chinchilla frilled coat and he could pass himself off as my sister's pimp.*

A look of disgust crossed Cerise's face. "Aren't you goin' to invite us in?"

Calvin stepped away from the door and smiled. "Forgive me, sis," he said drolly. "Come in and make yourselves . . . at home."

She waddled into the house and looked disapprovingly at the interior. "I see nothin's really *changed* since my last time here."

Calvin ignored her snideness and extended his hand towards his brother-in-law. "How have you been, Tyrone?"

Tyrone smiled broadly, revealing a set of gold-capped teeth. He mumbled something unintelligible that Calvin took for a greeting.

Kati strolled into the foyer to welcome her guests. "Cerise, Tyrone— it's nice to see you again. We've got a lot to catch up on between our families."

Cerise's lips curled upward in a sneer. "I already know what's goin' on in *my* family."

Calvin flinched, but Kati took the snub in stride. "Good, I can't wait to catch up on all the latest news," she said.

A smile traced Calvin's face. *Good old, Kati. Hand her lemons and she'll give you lemonade.*

Making their way towards the living room, Calvin watched with amusement as Cerise cast a critical eye over every nook and cranny in the house. In contrast, Tyrone shuffled silently in his wife's shadow, almost oblivious to his surroundings. *I'd probably tune out the world too if I were married to Cerise for the last fifteen years,* he mused.

After the drinks and appetizers were served, the two couples drifted into casual conversation, or what could best pass as casual conversation between near strangers. Kati maintained the role of the gracious hostess even though her in-laws barely acknowledged her presence. "I heard you were promoted to Human Resources Director at Con Ed, Cerise," she remarked. "How's the job working out so far?"

Cerise looked disparagingly at Kati as she wolfed a finger sandwich down her throat. "It's worked out *fine* . . . so far," she said between bites. "But, Con Ed should have promoted me a long time ago, considerin' all the *sacrifices* I've made for them over the years."

Calvin looked at his sister and bit his cheek. *Cerise, you've never sacrificed anything in your life. Any second now, you'll start bitching about Con Ed treating you poorly because–*

"The only reason they didn't promote me earlier is because I'm *black*," Cerise grumbled. "Not that I'm *prejudiced* or anything, but white folks is always goin' out of their way to help each other out." She paused to scoop a handful of chips into her mouth. "The only time a *minority* gets noticed is when some civil rights group brings it to the public's attention. Then *whitey* can't fall over themselves fast enough to move a person of color up through the ranks."

"So what civil rights group came to your defense, Cerise?" Calvin asked dryly.

She stopped chewing and frowned. "No one came to my defense," she replied indignantly. "I was promoted strictly on *merit*. Con Ed recognized my value to the company and moved me up before I decided to move on to someplace else."

Calvin stifled a laugh. *Promoted on merit? If you had been employed at my company Cerise, you would have moved 'someplace else' a long time ago. Like to the unemployment line.* "So how does it feel to be on the other side of management issues after all your time at the company?" he asked.

"There's *no* difference," she hissed. "Because I don't treat the employees like dirt." She wolfed another finger sandwich down her throat. "Like the *rest* of the managers at the company."

Calvin's eyebrow twitched. *When did compassion become a part of your life, Cerise? Ever since I've known you, all you've ever cared about is yourself.*

Cerise settled back on the couch and belched. "And how are things goin' at your . . . *business,* little brother?"

Calvin's jaw clenched. His sister had always been critical of his company's success. "Things couldn't be *better,* sis. My *business* has just been selected to work on a very lucrative government project." *I may have temporarily fallen on hard times,* he groused to himself. *But I'll be damned if I'll let you gloat about it.*

Kati sensed the tension rising between the siblings and jumped into the conversation to defuse the situation. "When was the last time you saw your nephew and niece, Cerise? Toni's quite the young lady now and James is a spitting image of his father."

Cerise stared wide-eyed at Kati and Tyrone's normally taciturn face visibly snapped awake.

Calvin shot a nervous glance towards his wife. *Oh, shit! You've really stepped in it now, Kati.* He shifted his gaze to Cerise and could practically read her mind from the stunned expression on her face. *Are you crazy, bitch? How could a child of mixed race look anything like his father?*

A tomb-like silence fell over the room, and Calvin shifted anxiously in his seat wondering what to do next. *I knew I should have put my foot down on this family get together today. There's still too much resentment–*

still too much anger–for our families to ever reconcile.

The chime of the doorbell suddenly shattered the uneasy mood in the room.

Calvin blew out a breath of air and jumped to his feet. "I'll get it," he exclaimed.

Leaving the gloomy mood of the living room behind, Calvin made his way to the foyer and reached out to open the door. *Please Lord, let it be the tiger . . . please let it be the tiger . . .*

For the second time, a black and orange striped wildcat was not in Calvin's future. As he opened the door to the outside world, he was pleasantly surprised to see his mother and brother standing on the porch to greet him.

Calvin's mother was nearing seventy but her flawless caramel complexion and trim build made her look younger than her daughter Cerise. She was impeccably dressed in a dark green dress adorned with a stylish silver belt.

Curtis' dark piercing eyes were offset by a disarming smile. Slightly shorter than Calvin, his lanky frame sported a pair of khakis topped by a navy polo shirt.

He bent down to give his mother a hug. "Hi, Ma–glad you could make it today."

She looked him over and frowned. "You're looking a bit *thin*, Calvin. Is your wife feeding you enough?"

Calvin tugged on his pants. "That's strange," he replied, "I thought I needed to *lose* a few pounds." He held out his hand towards his younger brother. "How's it hangin', Curtis?" Unlike the relationship he shared with his sister, Calvin and his brother got together as often as their schedules permitted.

Curtis grabbed his hand and smiled. "Can't complain. And you?"

"Keeping my head above water." He took a step back and waved them inside. "Let's go join the others in the living room." He led them through the rambling ranch house towards the living room, hoping the mood had improved in the few short minutes since he was gone. *I hope so,* he mused. *Or it's gonna be a helluva long afternoon.*

Kati rose from the couch and hugged Calvin's mother. "Noreen, it's nice to see you again." She leaned up and kissed Curtis on the cheek. "And you too, Curtis."

Curtis gave Kati an affectionate squeeze and grinned. "It's nice to see you, too." His gaze drifted across the room where Cerise and Tyrone stared sullenly in his direction. "And how have you been, sis?"

"I'm doin' all right," she said brusquely. "How's life treatin' you at the big law firm?"

"Could be better, could be worse."

"Any talk of you makin' partner yet?"

He shook his head. "There are two other associates who will probably be promoted before me the way things stand now in the firm."

"Are these two other associates–white?"

Curtis shot her a puzzled look. "Huh? What's this all about, sis?"

Calvin clutched Curtis' arm. "Right before you arrived, Cerise claimed she was passed over for the director of Human Resources position because she's black."

Curtis shook his head and chuckled. "Cerise, you may find this hard to believe, but everything in life doesn't boil down to *race.* Did it ever cross your mind that you weren't promoted earlier because you lacked the qualifications to do the job?"

"No," she spat. "Because everyone knows the managers at Con Ed are a bunch of racist pricks."

"Do you have any *proof* to back up your statement?" Curtis asked.

"I don't need no proof. Just take my word for it."

"Listen to your sister, Curtis," Noreen said. "There were many times when your father couldn't find a job even though he was the most qualified person for the position. He knew they rejected his application because they didn't want any blacks working at their company."

Curtis exhaled loudly. "I wish you wouldn't take her side, Ma. You don't see Cal and I playing the race card every time something goes wrong in our lives. As a matter of fact, the world is filled with people who have risen above their so-called handicaps and gone on to lead successful lives. All you need is to believe in yourself and the desire to make it happen."

Cerise glared at her brother but remained silent. A strained silence settled through the room as everyone's spirits sombered.

Kati clapped her hands to break the melancholy mood. "Hey! Let's head out to the patio and get this barbeque on the road." She met Calvin's eyes and smiled wanly. "Can you fetch the kids and meet us out back, hon?"

Calvin was halfway to the kid's rooms when the doorbell rang again. He stood in the entryway with a frazzled expression on his face and stared at the doorknob for several moments. *The tiger would have ended things a whole lot quicker.*

Calvin greeted Kati's family as he swept open the door. "Hello, Mister and Missus Tanaka," he said warmly. "It's good to see you again." He nodded politely at Kati's brother. "And you too, Daniel."

George Tanaka was of average height and build with well-groomed hair and the puckered face of a Pekingese. His wife, Nadine, shared the same inquisitive eyes and porcelain skin as her daughter Kati. Her conservatively styled attire looked as if it was meticulously crafted with considerable thought. Daniel sported a spike haired crewcut and a budding goatee. His John Lennon glasses lent him a look of pensive intelligence.

Calvin stood back from the door and ushered them in. "Let me take you out back to meet the rest of the family."

Moments later, the Tanaka family strolled onto the patio and Kati rushed over to greet them. "Mom, Dad! I'm glad you made it. I was beginning to think that something might have happened to you today."

George Tanaka's mouth turned up in an impish grin. "It's your mother's fault we're late. She only had to try on seven outfits before she found something she liked."

Calvin chuckled. "Like mother, like daughter, eh?"

Kati squeezed Calvin's arm, hard. "And what's wrong with looking presentable when you go out? All guys ever want to wear is a t-shirt and jeans, regardless of the occasion."

"What do you want?" Calvin quipped. "That's the style these days."

"Calvin, that's been our style since the Sixties," Daniel contended. "But you do make a valid point. Why women make such a fuss about their appearance is still a mystery to me."

"Maybe that's why you're still single after all these years," Kati teased.

"And do you see me complaining, sis? I've got the freedom to do what I want—when I want. I don't have to tiptoe over my partner's feelings, worrying about what I do or say. No birthdays to remember, no frivolous anniversaries, no–"

"Okay, Daniel, I get your point," Kati said. "But someday, you'll meet that special someone who will change your life forever. And when that day comes, you'll be as happy as Calvin and I have been for the last ten years." She clutched his arm and smiled. "Right, honey?"

"Right," Calvin deadpanned. "Ten years of absolute *bliss*."

Kati giggled. "See how well I have him trained?" She led her family towards a large table in the backyard where Calvin's family was gathered. "Let me re-introduce you to Calvin's family. Don't you think it's time we all got along?"

59

Smiling wryly, Karen sprawled out across her bed and tapped a contact name on her phone's touchscreen.

A few moments later, a woman's voice answered. "Hello?"

Karen breathed heavily into the receiver, trying to suppress her laughter.

A pause. "Mister Clooney, is that you?

"No, it's not Mister Clooney," Karen replied in a masculine tone of voice.

"Really?" the caller replied. "Then *who* could it possibly be?"

"Ahhh . . . Jen, you knew it was me the whole time."

She chuckled. "Ever heard of Caller ID? It's the only way I can keep track of all my admirers." She paused. "Speaking of admirers, how did your date go with Mister Physique?"

"It was . . . interesting," she said coyly.

"Did you like–do it?"

A pause. "*No!* What kind of girl do you think I am anyway?"

Jennifer sighed. "You said it was *interesting.*"

"Do you want to hear what happened or not?" Karen groused.

"Why not?" she muttered. "I hardly get the chance to talk to any adults anymore."

"What about Robert? Doesn't he ever talk to you?"

"Sure, if you count the occasional grunt or groan as *meaningful* conversation." She paused for several moments. "He tries . . . I guess."

"Mmmm, am I beginning to detect some chinks in your marriage here?" Karen asked.

"It's not as bad as it sounds," Jennifer replied. "There's something to be said about the commitment two people make when they choose to share their lives. You'll understand someday–when you finally decide to walk down the aisle."

"Someday, Jen. When I find the man I can love–forever."

"Any chance of Ryan becoming that man?"

"Anything is possible," Karen replied. "As a matter of fact, I'm finding more to lo–*like* about him everyday."

"Correct me if I'm wrong, but wasn't he an obnoxious asshole the first time you met?"

"Yeah, but we've moved on since then."

"And has he made his move on you yet?"

"Not really," she confided.

"Nothing?"

"Nothing but some snuggling and a hug at the end of our date." She sighed. "What do you think is wrong?"

"I don't know. But, hugs and snugs smells like–friendship–to me."

"Somehow, I get the feeling that I'm more than just a friend."

"You know, there's another possibility . . ."

"What's that?"

"He's gay."

Karen snorted. "He's *not* gay."

"How do you know?"

Because a gay man wouldn't affect me this way. "I just know. Trust me–Ryan is the real deal."

"Then why hasn't he made his move yet?"

Karen mulled it over. "Did you ever consider that he might be a gentleman?"

Jennifer chuckled. "Are you kidding? Gentlemen are extinct."

"They're out there, Jen. All you have to do is–look."

"And *look* how that's worked for you," Jennifer quipped. "How long has it been since your last relationship?"

Karen bit her lip. "Too long," she said glumly. "Maybe if I weren't so . . . so *particular* . . . I would have settled down by now."

"You can't dwell on what might have been, Karen. Better to be alone and content than to spend the rest of your life with someone who makes you miserable."

"I suppose you're right. But, why can't one have the best of both worlds?"

"You can," Jennifer affirmed. "Despite what you've heard me say, Rob and I get along most of the time." She paused. "Just as long as he does what I say."

Karen giggled. "So that's the secret."

"You bet. And speaking of secrets–are you going to give me the dirt on your date or not?"

Karen took a breath and exhaled. "Jen, have you ever sailed on a catamaran?"

60

alvin felt his throat tighten as he rapped on the door to James' bedroom. *There's no getting around it, kids. It's time to face the music.*

James voice drifted through the doorway. "Who's there?"

"It's me, son." Calvin pushed open the door and entered a realm of alien invaders and malevolent spacecraft intent on our world's destruction. The sound of gunfire and explosions echoed loudly within the room as James dispatched the aggressors with a rapid flick of his wrist on the game system's wireless controller.

Calvin watched the carnage on the screen and shook his head. "Who's winning?"

James looked away from the screen and grinned. "Me," he declared. "I blew up twenty-two of their ships, and they only got six of mine."

"I guess that makes you the Supreme Ruler of the Universe."

James laughed. "Don't be silly, Dad. It's only a game."

A smile played across Calvin's face. *It's good to hear him laugh again. Maybe he's put the events of the last week behind him.* "Your relatives are waiting to see you, son."

James put down the controller and sulked. "Do I have to go out and meet them?"

Calvin's eyebrow arched upward. "What's wrong, son?"

"I don't like it when all the women . . . kiss me."

"You don't? Why?"

"It's kinda, you know . . . *creepy* . . . when girls kiss you."

Calvin suppressed a smile. "Creepy?"

He scrunched up his face and shuddered. "Yeah."

"Will you come out to meet them if I promise that there will be no kissing?"

James mulled over the question for a moment. "Okay," he grumbled. "But no kissing!"

Calvin hoisted him off the chair. "All right, now sit up straight and let me get a look at you."

After a brief struggle to make James presentable, Calvin strolled across the hallway to get Toni. He had to pound on the door several times to be heard above the music thundering from her room.

The sound inched down a notch and Toni let out a shout. "Go away, *butthead!*"

Calvin's face went hot. "Open the door, Toni! *Now!*"

The music ground to a halt and Toni yanked open the door with an innocent looking smile on her face. "Hey, Dad," she said cheerfully. "What's up?"

Calvin's eyes narrowed as he looked over her pastel colored room. "What's going on in here?"

"Nothing," she replied. "I was just texting Samantha on my laptop."

"Texting? That's all?"

"That's all." She shot him a look of puzzlement. "What did you think I was doing?"

He pinched his lower lip. "Sometimes I don't know *what* to think as far as you're concerned."

She sighed. "You've got nothing to worry about, Dad. It's not like I was doing anything illegal in here."

Not yet, he groused to himself. *God, what am I going to do when she's a full-fledged teen?* The mere thought sent a shiver down his spine. "Your relatives are here to see you. Are you ready?"

She glanced in the mirror and whisked her hair into a ponytail. "Did Aunt Cerise come today?"

Calvin nodded. "Didn't your Mom tell you the whole family would be here?"

"I'm just surprised she decided to show up."

He cocked his head. "Why?"

"I don't think she . . . likes . . . James and me."

"Has she ever told you that?"

She shook her head.

"Then why–?"

"It's the way she looks at us," she blurted out. "Like we're not . . . *good enough* or something."

Calvin's jaw clenched. *Looks like sis and me will need to have a little talk.* "I wouldn't worry about it, Toni," he assured. "You're probably seeing something that's not really there."

Her face clouded. "Yeah, I guess so."

Calvin's eyes grew dour as he watched his daughter dab some makeup on her face. *That's right, Calvin–tell her she's imagining things. Don't let on that her aunt is a narrow-minded bigot who cares only about herself.*

Several minutes later, Calvin led the kids to the backyard and was pleasantly surprised to see both families mingling together. Kati's parents were talking to his mother, while his wife and her brother were engaged in an animated conversation with his siblings.

Kati broke away from the group and joined Calvin and the children near the grill. "Toni, James, please bring out the rest of the food on the kitchen counter and put it on the picnic table."

The children exchanged scowls and tramped off towards the house to get the food.

Kati clutched Calvin's arm and trembled with glee. "See how well everyone's getting along today? I didn't need my flak jacket after all."

Calvin shrugged. "Okay, so I was wrong." He moved his eyes across the crowd, carefully watching their expressions as they conversed. "Everyone seems to be on their best behavior today. I don't remember it being like this on the day we were married."

Kati's smile faded. "Don't remind me. Though no one said anything to our face, you could literally see the disapproval roiling off our families' eyes."

"It was so bad," Calvin quipped, "that I nearly expected a riot to break out when the minister asked if anyone objected to our marriage."

"Mister Taylor, I thought the only thing you were concerned with that day was *me.*"

He smiled wryly. "Frankly, the only thing I was concerned about was what would happen that *night.*"

She giggled. "You're terrible. Is that all you men think about?"

He tossed a rack of ribs on the barbeque. "No, sometimes we think about food, too." He stepped back and inhaled the sweet scented smoke wafting off the grill. "Ahhh . . . I better not hear any bitchin' about my cooking today."

"And what are you going to do if someone pitches a fit, Calvin? Grill them to death?"

"You're just jealous because I'm a better cook than you are."

"Oh, yeah? Hand me that fork and I'll show you some *grillin'.*"

Calvin passed the fork to her waiting hand. "Time to put your money where your mouth is, Miz Tay–"

Suddenly, a loud squabble erupted behind Calvin. He spun around and saw his brother lunging towards Daniel. Leaping off the patio, he barreled his way between the two men and pushed them apart. "All right," he said, leveling his gaze in Daniel's direction. "What's going on here?"

"Nothing," Daniel said curtly. "Nothing at all."

Calvin turned to face his brother. "Is that right?"

Curtis shrugged. "Just a difference of opinion. That's all."

Kati rushed over and touched Daniel's shoulder. "It might help if you talk about it."

Daniel glared at her. "There's nothing to talk about. It's like Curtis said–a difference of opinion."

Calvin looked the two men over and frowned. "All right, what the *hell's* going on here?"

Daniel brushed away Kati's hand and stepped back. "Curtis and I disagree on Hideo Nakayama's pitching stats. I feel he's one of the best pitchers of the last decade and a certain shoo-in for Cooperstown." He cast a sideways glance towards Curtis and scowled. "Your brother–on the other hand–disagrees."

"And what's your side of the story, bro?" Calvin asked.

"Hideo is an overrated prima donna who wouldn't be getting any attention at all if he weren't *Asian*. Frankly, there are quite a few pitchers who are just as good, and aren't getting half the attention Hideo's receiving."

"So what's the big deal?" Calvin asked. "Can't you two just agree to disagree?"

Daniel stared at the ground for a moment. "Your brother didn't tell you . . . everything."

Calvin swept his gaze between the two men but remained silent.

Daniel broke the silence. "After Curtis and me . . . *disagreed* . . . about Hideo, he said there wasn't an Asian in professional sports today that could compete on the same level as an African-American athlete."

Calvin turned to face his brother. "Is that *true*, Curtis?"

"Sure, it's true. Other than baseball, name a sport where Asians are truly competitive. They're simply *inferior* and Daniel knows it."

Daniel's face flushed. "It's *not* true. I'll agree that Asians aren't represented proportionally in traditional American sports like football or basketball, which generally emphasize size and strength. But in sports that are dominated by speed and coordination, Asians are all over the map."

Curtis laughed derisively. "Yeah, if you count *Ping Pong* as a professional sport."

"Maybe you should consider this, Curtis," Daniel replied. "The professional sports you refer to primarily rely on brute strength. Very little . . . *brainpower* is involved at all. That's probably why blacks excel in these sports because everyone knows they're intellectually inferior."

Curtis' eyes narrowed to slits. "What are you trying to *say*, asshole?"

"Are you too *dumb*," Daniel sneered, "to figure it out?"

Curtis brought his fist back to strike Daniel, but Calvin reached out and pinned his brother's arm behind his back. He held his arm firmly in place and leaned in close to Curtis' ear. "Let it go, man!" he whispered. "Just let it—go."

Curtis looked back, eyes blazing. "I'm all right, Cal," he hissed. "Let me go."

Calvin released his grip and cast his gaze towards both men. Daniel bowed his head in shame, but his brother met his eyes with a defiant glare. "I was afraid something like this might happen today. Kati had hoped the differences between us had faded after all these years, but I *knew* you still couldn't accept our racially integrated family."

"That's hardly fair, Calvin," Daniel said. "I'm not prejudiced against your family. Today's . . . disagreement . . . simply got out of hand."

"You can't fool me, Daniel," Calvin replied. "Stereotypes die hard, whether there's any truth to them or not."

"It's a good thing your father wasn't around to see this," Noreen chided. "He always thought the mixing of races was wrong."

Calvin glared at his mother. "Ma, Pop was an angry man who

blamed whitey for all his problems, even though he brought most of them on himself."

She raised a finger towards Calvin. "Don't you *dare* speak of your father that way."

"Don't misunderstand me, Ma," Calvin said softly. "I loved Pop, and not a day goes by that I don't think about him. But, his views of the world were . . . obsolete. Times have changed, and today's battle for an equitable society must be won by proving how much we are alike, rather than emphasizing our differences."

"Why should we have to *prove* anything?" Curtis spat. "You'll never be able to convince everyone that we're all created equal–despite what is spelled out in our so called Declaration of Independence. The majority will always find reasons to deny the minorities in this country–whether the reasons are valid or not."

Calvin gave a reluctant nod. "It's never easy for people to change, especially when the traditions and beliefs they have known all their lives are almost as inviolate as law. But, all it takes is *one* person who's willing to view things differently–one individual who's willing to accept each person for who they *are*–rather than for what they *appear* to be." A look of sadness touched his eyes. "One such person did exist . . . over two thousand years ago. His belief in us was so strong that he was willing to make the ultimate sacrifice to save us."

"And was His sacrifice *worth* it?" Curtis asked bitterly. "Two thousand years later, things still haven't changed. People still go on hating–still go on killing each other."

"You don't understand, Curtis," Kati said. "Jesus was the just the spark–it's up to us to carry on the fire. If our own families can't learn to accept us, then how can we expect the rest of the world to ever get along?"

Calvin grasped Kati affectionately around the waist and moved his gaze slowly across the group. "Kati and I reached out to each other over ten years ago and never looked back. If you can't learn to accept that, then you can't accept–us."

Kati looked at her relatives with red-rimmed eyes. "I'm sorry," she said softly. "For *all* of us."

Calvin and Kati gathered their kids and trudged back towards the house without saying another word.

No sooner had it begun; the party was now over.

61

Ryan shot a furtive glance at his partner as he threaded the cruiser down the crowded lanes of Venice Boulevard. *I'm not too thrilled the Loo stuck me with Gleason's assignment,* he grumbled to himself. *But, things could be worse–Ruiz could have actually looked like a linebacker.*

Ruiz turned to face him, a look of disgust on her face. "Was there something you wanted to say, Rysinski?" she asked brusquely. "Or were you just going to give me the *eye* for the rest of the day?"

He snapped his gaze back to the street. "What are you talking about, Ruiz?" he asked innocently.

"Give me an effin' break, Rysinski. You've been checking out my body the whole damn day."

"Well, it is my duty to keep an eye out for you," Ryan said drolly.

She ignored his snide remark. "You know, you're no *different* from the rest of the men in the department. Even though I earned my right to be here through hard work and determination, the only *qualifications* anyone seems to care about are the size of my tits and ass."

"Don't you think you're making a mountain out of a molehill, Ruiz?" he asked.

"No, because every comment I've heard since joining the force is either a thinly disguised innuendo or out and out harassment." She shook her head and scowled. "Why does the department make it so hard for a woman to join the testosterone squad?"

"Maybe it's because the average guy can't figure out why someone as attractive as you would want to be on the force in the first place."

"If I can do the job as well as any man, then *how* I look shouldn't make any difference at all."

"I agree," Ryan said. "But the real world plays by a different set of rules."

She gave a bitter laugh. "A world whose rules and values have been defined by *men*."

"The world is what it is, Ruiz," Ryan said. "Take from it what you will." He drove in silence for several blocks before speaking again. "So, why'd you want to become a cop?"

She shot him an angry glare. "Does it matter?"

"Not really, but it might help me like you a little more."

Her expression softened. "I can be a real ass sometimes."

"I've seen worse," he replied. "But it's usually when I'm slapping the cuffs on someone."

She chuckled. "I'll try to be a good girl from now on."

"You don't need to be good, Ruiz—just be yourself." He shot her a sideways glance. "You still haven't answered my question."

She turned and stared out the window. "It's . . . personal."

"Sorry. I didn't mean to pry."

"You're not . . . prying," Ruiz replied. "I just never told anyone why I became a cop." She took a deep breath and exhaled. "Or, never told anyone . . . the truth."

Ryan steered the cruiser down the boulevard but remained silent.

"My little brother was a . . . gangbanger," she began, her voice barely above a whisper. "He was always getting into trouble, despite being raised in an upper class, nurturing family. My parents tried their best, but never could break his rebellious nature." She looked out the window and watched the neighborhood blur by while she gathered her thoughts. "One day, just two weeks shy of his nineteenth birthday, he was gunned down by some over eager cops who thought he was involved in a two-eleven at a nearby jewelry store. The police report said he was carrying, but I know better than that. Michael hated guns and wouldn't have anything to do with them."

Ryan's eyebrow rose. "A banger who never carried? I'm sorry for your loss, but I find that hard to believe."

"But, you didn't know my brother," she said bluntly. "When Michael was fourteen, he watched his best friend die during a drive-by that went horribly wrong. From that day on, he vowed to never use a gun again."

"So why'd he continue his self-destructive lifestyle instead of turning his pledge into something constructive for the community?"

"I don't know. He was a rebel by nature–maybe he couldn't change. But, I do know that any life lost without reason is nothing but a . . . waste."

Ryan nodded but remained silent. He had witnessed firsthand the lives destroyed through senseless gang warfare.

"After what they did to my brother, you might think I would have nothing but contempt for the police. And for a while . . . I did. But, my feelings eventually changed and I understood my rage would do nothing but make me an old, bitter woman. So I channeled my ill-will into something constructive, so no one would have to endure what my family experienced."

"It's strange how circumstances can give your life–purpose."

She nodded. "And if my becoming a cop can save *one* life from being lost, than my brother's death won't be in vain." She met his gaze and smiled wanly. "Now you know why I joined the force. What about you?"

"My reasons aren't as selfless as yours, but my commitment grew out of a desire to change our morally imbalanced world into something better."

"And have you made any *real* difference?"

Ryan shrugged. "It's a never ending battle. Sometimes the good guys win and . . . sometimes they don't."

"And sometimes," Ruiz grumbled, "it's not always clear just who the good guys are. Sometimes good guys do bad things–even if they believe their cause is justified."

"It's not a perfect world, Ruiz. You'll come to understand that the longer you're on the force."

A look of sadness touched Ruiz's eyes. "I think I *understood* the day my brother died."

The radio suddenly squawked to life. "All units in the vicinity respond. Two-eleven in progress, intersection of South La Brea Avenue and Washington Boulevard."

Ryan snapped the microphone from its cradle. "This is unit 7A52 responding Wilshire. ETA sixty seconds." He gunned the throttle and spun the cruiser in a wide arc into crossbound traffic. "Here's a chance to live up to your commitment, Ruiz. Just follow my lead and no one will get hurt."

The black and white dashed down La Brea Avenue and screeched to a halt in front of a light green convenience store streaked with graffiti. Rysinski and Ruiz stormed towards the storefront and nearly slammed into an obese, olive-skinned man rushing out of the building.

"Dey rob me!" the man shouted in heavily accented English. "Dey rob me!"

Ryan held up his hand. "How many did you see, sir?"

"Two of dem." He jabbed a finger down the street. "Dey get away!"

"Did you get a good look at them, sir?" Ruiz asked.

The merchant waved his arms in the air and frowned. "Why you wait?" he snarled. "Dey get away!"

Ryan looked the merchant over and exhaled. *This is getting us nowhere.* "Come on, Ruiz. We'll try to spot them from the cruiser."

The cruiser zoomed down Washington Boulevard, and Ryan soon spotted two young men dressed in baggy t-shirts and jeans trying not to draw attention to themselves. "There's our perps," he declared.

Ruiz studied the two men. "How do you figure? Is it because they look like gangbangers?"

"No, it's because they look *guilty.* Let's pull over and see what's up."

Ryan barreled the black and white upon the sidewalk, and the suspects bolted down the street in the opposite direction.

"Shit!" Ryan swore as he scrambled out of the cruiser. "Ruiz, take the one on the right, and I'll go after Mister Doo-rag."

Ryan's suspect sprinted down the street and darted into an alleyway. Ryan followed him into the trash-strewn corridor and was greeted by a salvo of gunfire. He dove headfirst behind a dumpster, and watched anxiously as the suspect dashed down the alleyway and disappeared around a corner.

When he deemed the coast to be clear, Ryan rose from behind the dumpster and moved cautiously down the alleyway. He peered watchfully around the corner and found the suspect clawing his way up a chain link fence blocking the end of the alleyway.

Ryan charged down the alleyway with his gun drawn. "All right, asshole," he growled. "Game's over."

The suspect looked over his shoulder and smiled slyly. Like a well-trained acrobat, he flipped over the top of fence and fired his gun in Ryan's direction as he tumbled towards the ground.

Ryan lunged towards the pavement as a bullet careened off a wall and ricocheted down the alleyway. The suspect turned and shot Ryan the single fingered salute as he dashed out of the alley and back to the streets.

Struggling to his feet, Ryan started for the fence when a sharp pain lanced through his leg. He pulled up his pant leg and watched with alarm as his ankle turned an angry shade of purple. Suddenly, the easy ascent over the fence looked as daunting as an excursion up the south slope of Mount Everest. He shook his head in disgust and tapped his shoulder microphone. "Ruiz, what's your situation?"

"I've got the suspect under wraps," she said breathlessly. "But, I need your assistance. *Now!*"

Ryan took a deep breath and exhaled. *Christ! What's wrong now?*

Hobbling back the way he came, Ryan found Ruiz surrounded by a hostile mob two blocks down the street. He withdrew his firearm as a precaution, but knew from experience its use would not be necessary. The crowd's bluster was merely a demonstration by the locals to show that they weren't going to be intimidated in their own neighborhood. Rarely did the dissent ever escalate to more than a shouting match.

Ryan waved his pistol through the air and pushed his way through the crowd. "All right now," he ordered. "Move back."

The crowd stared angrily in his direction. Several defiant individuals shouted taunts and gestured obscenely in disapproval of the situation.

Ryan met their scorn with a steely gaze. "Get the fuck back. *Now!*"

The mob inched backward, and Ryan moved quickly towards his partner. "Are you all right, Ruiz?"

She brushed the hair from her face and nodded. "The suspect struggled a bit until he tasted the pepper spray. What happened to Mister Doo-rag?"

Ryan's eyes dropped. "He . . . ummm . . . got away."

She chuckled. "Getting slow in your old age, Rysinski?"

"Not so *old* that I can't kick your ass, Ruiz."

She flinched. "Well, we bagged one of 'em anyway." Her eyes moved warily across the crowd. "I'm glad you got here when you did.

The natives were starting to get restless."

"Yeah, this shit happens every time you take down someone in the hood. Every Tom, Dick, and Harry crawls out of the woodwork to express their indignation against The Man." A look of disapproval swept over his face. "We risk *our* lives, cleaning up *their* neighborhood, and all we get is–shit."

"What happened to your idealism, Rysinski?" she asked drolly. "Aren't the good guys always supposed to beat the bad guys in the end?"

Ryan let his gaze drift across the ill-tempered crowd and smiled sourly. "Sometimes, I wonder if anyone knows the difference."

62

osé raised a sunburned arm against the sun's glare and scanned the desert for civilization. Weathered gray boulders and stunted green cacti stretched out as far as the eye could see. *We've traveled so far, but gotten–nowhere.* His expression grew dour. *How long before we all share Angelina's fate?*

Elena scampered up the sand dune to join him. "Anything?"

José shook his head. "It doesn't make any sense. We should have found some sign of civilization by now."

"We'll find something soon," she said cheerfully. "I know you're trying–"

"*Trying* isn't good enough, Elena. We must succeed . . . or else."

Elena wiped her forehead with the back of her hand. "How long do you think we can go on like this?"

"I don't know, but I've heard you can survive up to a week in the desert without water."

"*A week?*" She whistled. "I don't think I can last that long."

"Neither can I," José said. "That's why we need to find water soon." He dragged his boot across the parched surface of the dune, leaving a shallow furrow in the sand. "There has to be water out here–somewhere."

Javier trudged to the top of the dune and paused to catch his breath. "Did you say something . . . about water, José?" he wheezed out.

"Just wishful thinking, amigo," he replied. "There's no sign of water anywhere."

Javier bent over and gasped for air. "Damn. I would sell my soul . . . for one cold glass of water . . . right now."

Elena touched his shoulder. "Are you going to be all right, Javier?"

He nodded wearily. "Just out of breath . . . that's all."

José watched Javier for a moment. *He's not looking too good. The desert has taken its toll on all of us, but Javier's feeling it most because of his age and poor physical condition.*

Hector scampered up the slope and looked out over the barren landscape. "Are we going around in circles?" he griped. "Everything still looks the same to me."

Javier wrapped his arm around Hector's shoulder. "You mustn't give up hope, hijo."

"I haven't, papa." He turned towards José, a sour expression on his face. "Do you think we'll ever get out of here, señor?"

José nibbled his lip. "I don't know."

Manuel, Gabriella and Rosa tramped up the ridge of sand and joined the group at the summit.

"Hey!" Hector exclaimed. "You're just in time for the *par-tay!*"

Manuel shot him a fierce stare. "No offense, Hector, but your humor sucks." He wiped his face with a soiled bandanna and surveyed the bleak terrain. "It's nothing but Hell–as far as the eye can see."

"Bitching won't change things, Manuel," José asserted. "We need to keep moving if we want to get out of here."

Manuel turned from the inhospitable vista and scowled. "And *where* are we supposed to *go*, amigo?" He jabbed his finger to his left. "*There?*" Then to his right. "Or *there?*" He leveled a stony gaze in José's direction. "For all we know, we're back where the coyote's men dropped us off three days ago."

"That's not possible," José declared. "I've been using the sun and stars to guide us since we–"

"Then *why* haven't we found any signs of civilization, señor?" Hector argued.

"I don't know. The desert must be larger than I thought."

"Let's face it," Javier groused. "We're *lost*."

"We're *not* lost," José snapped.

"And what if you're wrong?" Manuel asked.

José shrugged. "Then I'm . . . wrong."

"Si," Hector said tersely. "And we're *dead.*"

"Stop it!" Elena hissed. "We need to quit all this *whining* and work together as a team."

"She's right," José said. "If any of you know a way out of here, now's the time to speak up."

Hector kicked self-consciously at the ground with his boot but remained silent. Javier pretended to study the desert, hoping to glean a clue that might lead them to safety. The others milled about uncomfortably, unable to offer anything constructive towards their salvation.

José studied their faces. *They are no different than Miguel–quick to complain, but offering no real solution to our problem.* He looked out across the desert and shook his head. "Come on," he grumbled. "Let's get the hell out of here."

The migrants gathered their possessions and slogged out across the wasteland. A short time later, they were halted by a forty-foot wide ravine that cut across their path.

Manuel peered over the edge of the gorge and frowned. "Do you think can make it across to the other side, José?"

José scanned the ragged slope and pointed to an eroded section of the ravine several hundred yards away. "Let's check out that area over there and see if there's a safe way to the bottom of the ravine."

The migrants hiked towards the spot José indicated and descended gingerly down the slope. About halfway down, the ground gave way under Gabriela's weight and she tumbled twenty feet to the bottom of the ravine.

Javier scurried down the steep walled canyon and rushed over to Gabriela's side. *"Cariño!"* he cried. "Are you hurt?"

Gabriella rolled over on her back and moaned. "What happened?"

Hector rushed over to his mother, a look of anxiety etched across his face. "You fell, Mamá."

She rubbed the top of her head and winced. "I feel like I just got kicked by a burro."

Javier helped her sit-up. "Do you think you can stand, querida?"

She nodded wearily. "I think so."

Javier and Hector pulled Gabriella to her feet. She took a hesitant step forward and screamed in pain. Hector clutched her around the waist and helped lower her to the ground.

José hurried towards the stricken family. "What's wrong?"

Gabriela grimaced. "My knee. I think it's broken."

Javier kneeled down and examined her leg. A spongy mass of mottled tissue surrounded her rapidly swelling knee.

"Well?" José asked.

"I'm no doctor," Javier muttered. "But, there's no way she'll be able to walk on her own."

A frown traced José's face. "You'll have to carry her until we can find a way to stabilize her leg." He turned and headed towards the opposite bank of the ravine.

Javier and Hector hoisted Gabriela on their shoulders and the migrants continued their journey, their progress significantly impeded by Gabriela's injury. After an exhausting three-hour trek, the migrants paused to rest and started a fire under the darkening sky. José, Elena,

Manuel and Rosa sat near the fire while the Javier and Hector tended to Gabriela at the edge of their campsite.

Manuel gripped José's shoulder. "We need to talk," he whispered. He pointed towards a stunted mesquite tree fifty feet away. "Alone."

The quartet rose and walked over to the tree.

"What is it, amigo?" José asked softly.

Manuel cast a furtive eye at the Rodriguez family. "Gabriela's injury will slow us down considerably, José," he murmured.

He met Manuel's gaze. "We're all in this together, Manuel. It's not Gabriela's fault her knee–"

"The rules must *change*," Manuel hissed. "To fit the situation." His eyes narrowed to slits. "We're talking about our *lives* here."

"What do you want us to do, Manuel?" Elena asked. "We just can't leave them here."

"Do you have a *better* idea?" Manuel asked.

Her eyes dropped. "No . . . I don't."

Manuel turned towards José. "What do you think?"

"We could take turns carrying her."

"Do you really think that will work?"

José sighed. "Probably not."

Elena snatched both men's arms. "*Quiet.* Javier's coming."

"How's Gabriela?" José asked, keeping his expression neutral.

"The same," Manual replied glumly. "She's said little since she hurt her knee. Doesn't want to be . . . a burden."

The others nodded but remained silent.

Javier took a deep breath and exhaled. "Look, I've been thinking about our . . . situation . . . and feel it's best if you continue on without us."

"Our odds are better if we stick together as a team," José asserted.

"I know, but I'd rather see some of us make it out alive than have all of us die together." His gaze was steady. "And don't try to change my mind. I've given it a lot of thought and feel this is the best

. . . solution."

Elena bit back tears. "Are you . . . sure?"

Javier nodded. "If nothing else, we'll be together as a family . . . at the end."

"Don't say that, señor," Manuel said. "You'll find some way to make it out of here."

Javier gave a wan smile. "Perhaps." He turned his gaze towards the sky. "I only pray God will look kindly on us when . . ."

A bitter taste filled José's mouth. *What kind of God would allow this misery to happen?* He stuck out his hand to Javier and forced a smile. "I wish you the best, amigo. Perhaps we will meet again . . . someday."

"Someday," Javier mused. "Perhaps we will."

Elena gave Javier a quick embrace. "Take care. Tell Gabriela and Hector I will never forget them."

"They will remember you always. As will I."

The four migrants quietly gathered up their belongings and headed out into the still desert night. A short while later, the glow from the campfire was nothing but a memory.

63

I n the darkened living room of a nondescript stuccoed house in Torrance, California, a frown crossed Mark Hildebrandt's face as he read a letter from the Veteran's Administration.

U.S. Department of Veterans Affairs
Federal Building, 11000 Wilshire Boulevard
Los Angeles, CA 90024

Colonel Hildebrandt:

Pursuant to new guidelines established under the Military Standardization Act, the disability on which you were medically discharged has been reclassified to Level Four status.

As a result of this reclassification, your monthly disability payment will be reduced by seventy-five percent to $453.69 effective October 1st. Hospital visits will be limited to twelve per year and your co-payment for any medication or medical hardware necessary to stabilize your condition will now be fifty-percent.

If you have any questions or wish to discuss this matter with a V.A. representative, please make an appointment at our main office Monday through Friday between the hours of 9:00 am - 5:00 pm.

Sincerely,
Thomas McKinnon
Medical Support Division
Southwest Region

Mark reread the letter, hoping it had been misaddressed or a mischievous prank played on him by one of his buds from the Army. But, the stationery appeared official, and his name at the top was all too real.

Sighing, he shoved the letter back into the envelope and pitched it on top of his desk. Tomorrow he would arrange to talk to a representative, but now he needed to take his prescribed regimen of medications so he could live to see another today.

Seizing the crutches from the side of his desk, Mark struggled to his feet and hobbled down the dimly lit hallway towards the bathroom. Once inside, he turned on a lamp above the medicine chest, wincing as the glare from the light stung his eyes.

He hardly recognized the man he saw staring back at him in the mirror. Two months past his thirty-eighth birthday, he looked like a senior citizen twice his age. His once flowing blond locks had been reduced to a sparse stubble of gray and dark circles smeared his piercing blue eyes. He had the gaunt, haggard look of a concentration camp survivor.

A look of revulsion swept over his wizened face. *I'm nothing but a shadow . . . of the man I used to be.*

But, he was not always the frail, hollow-cheeked man reflected in the mirror. Just seven short years ago, he commanded an elite Special Ops unit conducting counter-terrorism operations overseas. Comprised of specially trained soldiers and technicians, his unit was employed to infiltrate and surgically remove any threats to our country with plausible deniability. For five anxiety filled years his team had successfully carried out missions in every shithole across the world, until one fateful day, their luck had finally run out.

During a preemptive strike at an Al-Queda splinter cell in Indonesia, his life changed forever when a charge set to destroy a nerve gas cache prematurely exploded. The filter in his gas mask inexplicably malfunctioned, and a life-threatening dose of the toxic agent entered his unprotected lungs.

Rescued by his teammates, he spent the next six months recuperating in a Japanese hospital, where a barrage of experimental drugs barely kept him alive. After a grueling year of physical therapy he was eventually allowed to return to service, but the career he cherished in the field had abruptly drawn to a close.

Mark opened the medicine cabinet and shook some pills into his hand from several amber colored vials. Each had their purpose in keeping him alive, even if the life they sustained no longer seemed to have a purpose.

As he popped the pills into his mouth and swallowed, two other vials stared mutely at him from one of the cabinet's shelves. Untouched for the last two years, they were prescribed to combat the deteriorative aftereffects of the nerve gas on his mind.

A smile touched Mark's face as he scanned the labels on the vials. *Zeldox, 40 mg - take twice a day for schizophrenia. Zoloft, 50 mg - take once a day for depression.* He shook his head and chuckled. *Doctors. They think they can cure everything with a simple little pill.*

Shutting the cabinet door, he weaved his hands into his forearm crutches and ambled back into the hallway. Framed photos from his family's storied past hung on one wall of the gloomy corridor–haunting him. He removed the first picture off the wall and slanted it towards the fading evening light at the end of the hallway to get a better look.

It was a picture of his grandfather, taken at a Marianas Island airstrip during World War Two. A towheaded man barely out of his teens, he stood proudly near the fuselage of a B-29 bomber christened with the name *Pacific Belle*. Next to the aircraft's storied name, the image of dark haired vixen was splayed provocatively across the plane's battered nose; giving encouragement to the airmen on that distant isle to fight on another day.

Unfortunately, Mark never had the chance to meet his grandfather as he was shot down in a dogfight during the Korean War. His body was never recovered.

Mark returned the picture to the wall and pulled down a photo of his father. Sporting an easy smile and clear blue eyes, Samuel "Hawk" Hildebrandt was a crack pilot who earned the Silver Star and Distinguished Flying Cross during the Vietnam War. His flyboy days ended when a missile hit his fighter during a bombing run in the First Gulf War. His plane crashed in the desert and in a grim tribute to his father–his body was never recovered.

As Mark looked into his father's steely gaze, snapshots of his funeral flashed through his mind. The flag draped casket, the volleys of gunfire, the soulful sound of Taps echoing through the cemetery were all sad reminders of a celebrated career ended much too soon. He ran his hand reverently across his father's picture and returned it to its honored place upon the wall.

Directly beneath the photo of his father, his brother J.T. grinned maniacally near a camouflaged Humvee at a Marine outpost in Afghanistan. Tall and broad shouldered, his face had the hard, determined look of a man who had witnessed the brutality of a hundred lifetimes. Enlisting in the service right after 9/11, he was three years into his second tour of duty when a sniper's bullet pierced his heart in the hinterlands of eastern Afghanistan.

After J.T's funeral, the anguish in his mother's eyes made Mark consider early retirement after his next tour of duty was over. But he was unsure of what path to take, for he knew his father and brother would want him to uphold the values of a country his family had defended for three generations.

As fate would have it, the choice was made for him when he was medically discharged before his tour was over. Reunited with his mother after a two-year absence, her joy at his return was bittersweet, and within a year she passed away from a broken heart. The military had taken away all she loved, and in return had given her . . . nothing.

He placed his brother's picture back on the wall and stared at a stark black and white photo of himself taken nearly a decade ago in southern Uzbekistan. Flanked by several of his Special Ops buddies flashing the victory sign, his face held the promise and naivety that belied the years of disappointment and cynicism that lie ahead.

In a spasm of anger, Mark wrenched the picture off the wall and hurled it down the hallway. The frame shattered as it slammed against the wall, sending slivers of glass in a sparkling spray across the living room floor. He stared mutely as the smiling faces of his compatriots mocked him through the jagged shards of glass in the twisted picture frame.

Happier days. Simpler times.

Gone . . . forever.

MONDAY

64

Running forty-five minutes late for his shift, Ryan shot Ruiz a sheepish grin as he slid behind his desk at the precinct. "You're here early today, Ruiz," he said cheerfully.

Her eyebrow rose. "I don't think it's a matter of me being *early*, Mister Rysinski, but more a matter of you being *late*."

"Sorry," he muttered. "I had something personal to take care of this morning."

"Anything you want to talk about?" Ruiz asked.

He ignored her question and logged on to his computer.

"Well?" she repeated.

Ryan glared at her. "I just said it was *personal*." He turned his gaze back to the computer and bit his lip. *She doesn't need to know I was late because I was out shopping for Ashley's birthday present this morning.*

Her eyes dropped. "Okay, I know better than to stick my nose where it doesn't–"

"Look," Ryan said gently, "there's nothing wrong with showing a little concern for your partner's welfare."

"We're not *partners*," she said coolly. "I know you're only doing this because you volunteered to take Gleason's place in the rotation while he's out on disability."

Ryan took a deep breath and exhaled. "I have to admit I wasn't exactly thrilled to take on this assignment at first. Years of riding alone make it difficult to get used to a partner's needs—especially a *rookie* partner's needs. But you showed me something yesterday, Ruiz . . . you reminded me once again why I made law enforcement my career."

"If I can save one life from being lost . . ."

Ryan shot her a crooked grin. "I think you already have, Ruiz. And as long as we're going to be partners—even temporarily—I think it's time you called me by my first name."

Her mouth curled upward in a smile. "Okay—*Ryan*."

Turning his gaze back to the computer screen, Ryan noticed an email from the Department of Records in his mailbox. *Hmmm . . . it's the information I requested from John yesterday.*

> *Hey Dog:*
>
> *I'm forwarding the information I received from The Guard regarding your registration request. Hope you find what you're looking for.*
>
> *John*
>
> From: marshall.simons@uscg.mil.pacarea.gov
> To: jssterling@lapd.rid.org
> Re: REGISTRATION REQUEST
>
> *Per your request for registrant information on the maritime vessel "No Regrets"*
>
> **Registered Owner:** Andrew Landis
> **Address:** 24724 Malibu Road, Malibu, CA 90265
> **Hull ID Number:** 410067923XLS
> **Hailing Port:** CF14790 Marina del Rey CA
> **Coast Guard Vessel ID:** CAD3872098
> **Service Type:** Recreational/25-50 meters

Vessel Name: No Regrets

Flag: United States

Boat's Length: 135 Feet

Boat's Net Tons: 52

Ship Builder: Trident Yachts Limited

Propulsion: Gas Turbine

Purchase Price: $36,625,000.00 USD

Lein Holder: First National Bank of Malibu

Sincerely,

Marshall Simons
Administrative Supervisor
Department of Records & Registration
United States Coast Guard, 11th District
1001 S. Seaside Ave., Bldg. 20, San Pedro CA, 90731

The above information is confidential and subject to fines and/
or imprisonment not exceeding $100,000 or 10 years if used
unlawfully by unauthorized individuals pursuant to Section 10A of
the Maritime Registration Act.

Ryan's face tightened. *So now I have a name for the clown who almost killed us two days ago.* He rubbed his chin and frowned. *Andrew Landis . . . why does that name sound familiar?*

"Anything wrong, Ryan?" Patricia asked.

He gave a quick headshake. "Where are the statements you logged in from yesterday?"

"On the bottom of your inbox with the rest of the reports."

Ryan glanced at the wire basket on his desk and flinched. *Paperwork.* He riffled through the stack until he found what he was looking for. *Here it is. Andrew Landis was the vic assaulted by the unidentified assailant yesterday. A real self-centered prick.* He laid the report on his desk and stared at it for a moment.

"Find what you're looking for?" Patricia asked.

He picked up his coffee mug and held it out to Patricia. "Would you mind getting me some coffee?"

She shrugged. "How do you take it?"

"Black's fine."

Patricia took the mug and headed down the hallway. While she was away, Ryan folded the report into the shape of an airplane and sailed it into a trashcan six feet away.

He smiled wryly. *Case solved, asshole. No regrets.*

65

Stan paced hurriedly around his office, a vein threatening to pop in his temple as he screamed at some hapless soul on the phone. "And what makes you think you're right, asshole?" he growled. "Just cuz you graduated from *Harvard* don't make you any smarter than me."

Karen watched with amusement as her boss berated his caller with his usual tactful diplomacy. *He's in rare form today*, she mused. *This putz must be really pissing him off.*

While her supervisor continued his rant, Karen took some time to study his office. For the first time she noticed that there were no pictures, awards, or any personal effects tying him to friends or family. The sterility of the drab-looking room shocked her. *I guess I shouldn't be surprised*, she thought glumly. *He probably doesn't have any friends.* Despite her present feelings towards her supervisor, her heart sank as she pictured his lonely existence.

After several minutes of lambasting the caller with his usual finesse, Stan concluded the conversation by slamming the phone on his desk. "Man, can you *believe* that fuck?" He plopped into the chair behind his desk and smirked. "So how ya comin' with the Pangaea Festival assignments?"

"Today I'll be out interviewing the Mayor and some of the major entertainers scheduled for the event. And tomorrow I'll be heading out to several Southland communities to get the locals' perspective on how the Festival's theme of multiculturalism relates to them."

Stan ran a hand across his balding pate and nodded. "What's in the pipeline after that?"

"Don't worry, I've still got a few things up my sleeve."

Stan lighted a cigar, and within seconds the office was filled with the smell of cheap tobacco. He walked around his desk and faced Karen with a wolfish grin on his face. "If you need any help knockin' down doors, there's quite a few people in town that owe me favors."

Karen forced a smile. "Thanks, Stan. I'll keep your–offer–in mind." Growing uncomfortable with his closeness, she rose from her seat and turned towards the door.

"Wait!" Stan snapped. "Don't you have time to chat?" It came out more as an order than a request.

"I'd like to stay," she said graciously, "but my interview with the Mayor is less than an hour from now. And as you know, she doesn't like to be kept waiting."

Stan pulled on his cigar and unleashed a cloud of noxious fumes towards the ceiling. "How's your *relationship* with the cop goin'?" he said. "I'm still waiting to meet him."

Karen's eyes narrowed. "Don't worry, Stan. I'll bring Ryan around as soon as I can."

He took the cigar out of his mouth and frowned. "So that's your boyfriend's name–Ryan?"

"You got it." She stood in the doorway and smiled slyly. "And once you get the chance to meet him, you'll *never* forget his name." *Especially after I have him wipe that shit eating grin off your face.*

Just one small detail loomed large in her mind after she left his office. *Can I convince Ryan into helping me out?*

66

The lights brightened overhead in the screening room, flooding the cherry paneled theater with light. Ron and Andrew leaned back in their plushly upholstered seats and critiqued the dailies from Angela Carson's performance.

"Works for me," Ron said. "Angela nailed it on the very first take."

Andrew nodded. "It may turn out to be one of the best performances of her career. Her suggestion to change Corrine's part improved the final act considerably."

Ron lighted a cigarette and sent a jet of blue-gray smoke towards the ceiling. "Maybe we should toss out the rest of the script and let the actors improvise from now on."

"Frankly," Andrew said drolly, "improvisation would have been an *improvement* on some of the turkey's I've seen at the theater lately."

Ron chuckled. "There's no need to worry about that on this project. Thompson's screenplay is so well crafted that it practically directs itself."

Andrew looked at Ron and bit his cheek. *That's why I chose him to draft the script. Though in hindsight, I probably should have given more thought to my choice of director.* "When do you think the project will move into post?" he asked.

"A week, two at most."

Andrew's face tightened. *No need for you to be concerned–it's not your money we're talking about.* "Do you think you can bump it up to the beginning of next week? Some of the investors are getting a little–anxious."

Ron gave a dismissive wave of his hand. "You can't rush *art*, Andrew. Don't worry, I won't fritter your investor's stake away."

I sure hope you're right, asshole, Andrew fretted. He rose from his seat and started for the exit. "If you have nothing more to say, I've got a meeting to attend to."

"Speaking of meetings, how would you like to meet the President?"

Andrew shot him a puzzled look. "The president? Of what?"

Ron shot him a crooked grin. "The *President*–of the United States."

"You *know* the President of the United States."

Ron shrugged. "Let's just say we're old friends."

"And where will this little get together take place? At the White House?"

"I have a VIP invitation for the Pangaea Festival this week," Ron replied. "And I'm allowed to bring a guest." He took a drag on his cigarette and leaned back in his seat. "So how 'bout it? Are you game for a meeting with *The King* himself?"

Andrew stroked his chin and smiled. "Why not?"

67

Calvin sat quietly in his office, shuffling through a pile of unemployment forms and severance checks scattered across his desk. He took a swig from his coffee mug and winced. *Cold.*

Kevin extended his hand towards the mug. "You want a new cup, boss?"

Calvin shook his head and frowned. "I wish the coffee was the *only* thing leaving a bad taste in my mouth."

Kevin gave a sympathetic nod. "It's never easy letting people go."

"Why, Kevin?" he groused. "*Why?* Some of my staff are closer to me than my own family." He felt the sour taste return to his mouth as yesterday's family get-together flashed through his mind. "But now, they'll be out on the street through no fault of their own." He rubbed a hand across his face and scowled. "Just what does that say about me?"

"It says you care about the people who work for you," Kevin said softly. "And in today's world where jobs are outsourced or eliminated in the name of greed, you're truly a gem among stones."

Calvin rose from his chair and stared out the window. "If we had gotten the contract from Royce, none of this would be happening." His gaze grew distant as he watched a stand of eucalyptus trees sway gently in the breeze. "I keep wondering if there was something we could have done to change the outcome in our favor?"

Kevin placed his hand on Calvin's shoulder. "Who knows, boss. Maybe we didn't get the right person's . . . attention."

Calvin glanced over his shoulder. *"Bribery?"* He let out a short, harsh laugh. "I'd rather declare bankruptcy than ever compromise my integrity." A look of sadness tinged his face. "If that's what it takes to succeed in today's business world, then I'll always be destined to fail."

"For what it's worth, no one could ever be called a failure for sticking to their principles."

The clock on the wall loudly ticked off each second in the quiet room, prolonging the inevitable.

Calvin smiled wanly. "Somehow, Kevin, that doesn't make me feel any better."

68

M ark gave a look of disgust as he hobbled past rows of cubicles in search of his administrative officer at the Veterans Administration's office. *Christ,* he fumed. *This place is an even bigger clusterfuck than the Army.*

Several wrong turns later, he peered into a cramped space staffed by a pale, emaciated man sporting coke-bottle eyeglasses. "Mister Cheatham?" he asked politely.

The man looked up from his desk and shot him a skeletal smile. "You must be–" he glanced at a legal pad on his desk, "Colonel Hildebrandt. Please come in and make yourself comfortable."

Mark moved his crutches into the tightly confined space and extended his hand. "Thanks for seeing me on such short notice, Mister Cheatham."

"It's no problem, Colonel. We always have time for those who've given so much for our country."

Mark studied Cheatham's face before he released his grip. *He probably uses that line on everyone who comes in here.*

Slumping into a steel framed chair in front of the administrator's desk, Mark looked over Cheatham's sorry sliver of an office. Fashioned in dreary shades of gray, the well-worn furnishings were relics long before his birthdate. *I guess I shouldn't be surprised,* he reflected. *Uncle*

Sam has always treated us vets like cast-off furniture.

Cheatham folded his hands on his desk and stared lazily in his direction. "What can I do for you today, Colonel?"

Mark withdrew the letter he received and thrust it towards the slack faced administrator. "Why has the Army reduced my disability benefits?"

Cheatham glanced at the document and frowned. "Let's see what I can find in our system." He tapped several commands on his computer keyboard and looked at the screen. "It's just as I thought. Your disability status has been re-evaluated, and your benefits have been reduced accordingly."

Annoyance swept across Mark's face. "I already know that," he groused. "*Why* did the Army change my status?"

"It was all part of the Military Standardization Act passed by Congress six months ago. A clause in the legislation changed the medical and disability benefits for the vets."

"Didn't the veterans' advocacy groups have any say about this?" Mark asked.

"Yes, but veterans' groups don't have the clout they used to. The vet's needs were . . . downgraded . . . in the annual budgetary shuffle on Capitol Hill." He shook his head and sighed. "I'm afraid you're not a priority of this country anymore, Colonel."

Mark cocked his head. "Why not?"

Cheatham shrugged. "Our government–if I can be frank with you– is broke."

"*Broke?*" Mark exclaimed. "How can the *government* be broke?"

"Colonel, aren't you keeping up with current events? The government's debt level has scared our overseas investors to the point where they're cashing in their Treasury bonds. As a result, programs have been slashed or eliminated entirely as our leaders struggle to meet Uncle Sam's obligations to society. In the long overdue rush towards fiscal responsibility, veterans' benefits were just one of many programs to get the ax."

"Why take it out on us?"

"It's not personal, Colonel–it's *politics*. Cutting veterans' benefits just happened to be less politically suicidal than trimming the benefits from other programs. For example, if senior citizens found their Social Security benefits suddenly cut in half, the legislators would be hanged from every lamppost along the National Mall." Cheatham smiled briefly at the thought.

"So just like *that*–" Mark snapped his fingers, "–the government has ordained that I'm less disabled today than I was yesterday."

Cheatham nodded sympathetically. "I'm afraid so."

"Why aren't the vets–" Mark's face suddenly spasmed in pain.

Cheatham leaned forward in his seat. "Are you all right, Colonel?"

Mark clenched the side of his chair as a seizure short-circuited his brain. *No, not here . . . not now . . .*

Cheatham moved from behind his desk and grasped Mark's arm. "Do you need medical help, Colonel?"

Mark looked up at the administrator, his expression darkening. *So now you're concerned about my welfare, you smug prick?* "I think you've helped me *enough*, Mister Cheatham," he snarled.

Cheatham's face slackened. "Is anything wrong, Colonel?"

"*Wrong?*" Mark asked, eyes narrowing. "Why should anything be wrong?"

Cheatham moved back behind his desk and withdrew several documents from a file cabinet. "If you wish to appeal your case, there are some forms you can fill–"

"And how long will that take?" Mark snapped.

"With luck, the VA appellate court should get to your case within a year."

"*A year!*" Mark grabbed his crutches and struggled to his feet. "And how the *hell* am I supposed to get by in the meantime?"

"Colonel, there's no reason to–"

"No reason?" Mark growled. He slammed his crutch across the top of Cheatham's desk. "Does it look like I'm *fucking cured?"*

Cheatham's eyes widened. "I'm sure we can work something out–"

"There's nothing to *work out,* you bureaucratic bumbler. I've spent the better part of my life defending our country and all Uncle Sam can do now is fuck me in the ass."

The administrator backed against the wall of the cubicle, fearful for his safety. "Colonel, I'm going to have to call security if you–"

Mark leaned across the desk and scowled. "Go ahead, asshole–see if I care."

Cheatham searched Mark's eyes and found nothing but–darkness. Before he could respond, Mark snatched the documents from his hand and shredded them in a paroxysm of fury as he stormed out of the cubicle.

69

José studied the meandering trail left by the dried out river-bed across the landscape. Carved long before humanity took its first faltering steps across the ancient savannahs of Africa, it was now a powder dry trough leading towards nowhere. *Millions of years ago that river would have quenched the needs of an entire city. Now, it wouldn't relieve the thirst of a fly.*

As his eyes drifted across the harsh environment, he saw little to indicate that they had made any progress during the last three days. *Or is it four days now?* He wiped his face with the back of his hand and frowned. *It seems like I've been here since–forever.*

He wondered how Javier's family had fared since they had left them behind. *Did they try to continue on despite Gabriela's injury? Or did they realize their journey had finally reached . . . an end?* His expression grew dour. *And how will my journey finally end? Will I ever see my family–*

Elena touched him on the shoulder, snapping him from his reverie. "Sorry," she said softly. "I didn't mean to startle you."

He smiled wanly. "That's all right. My mind was . . . elsewhere."

She picked up a stone and tossed it into the dried out riverbed. A small cloud of dust roiled upward as it landed soundlessly in the parched basin. "I've noticed my own thoughts tend to drift out here. I don't know how many times I've tuned everything out and let my body continue mindlessly on with the journey."

"And where has that journey taken us?" he groused. "Why have we sacrificed *everything* to be here?"

Elena looked on but remained silent.

He pulled a sheaf of banknotes from his boot and held them towards her face. "Is the ultimate price—worth *this?*"

"I . . . I don't know, José."

"Do you think we made the right choice in coming here?"

"You said you'd die a thousand times in this shithole reaching for your dream than spend a moment where you could not change your life at all."

His eyebrow twitched. "I did?"

She nodded.

He sighed. "Must have been . . . a lifetime ago."

Manuel strolled over and sat down next to José. *"Hey!"* he quipped. "Is this a private party or is anyone welcome to join in?"

"If this is your idea of a *party,*" José replied sourly, "you can leave me off the invitation list next time." His expression softened. "Did we wake you?"

"Not really," Manuel replied. "I'm totally exhausted, but I can't get any sleep."

"I know how you feel," Elena said. "How's Rosa—is she still sleeping?"

"Rosa's not well, Elena." Concern touched Manuel's face as he watched his daughter curl into the overhang of their shelter. "When we stopped last night to rest, she complained of a fever. But she said not to worry—that she'll get better soon." Fear crept into his eyes. "But now, when I tried to wake her, all she did was groan and drift back to sleep. I am . . . afraid for her."

"This ledge will no longer shade us from the sun in an hour or so,"

José said. "Will Rosa be–?"

Manuel met his gaze. "I cannot go with you, José."

"We could carry her . . . " Elena suggested.

Manuel shook his head. "I will stay," he declared. "My place is with her." A smile traced his face as he looked over at his daughter. She slept soundly, unaware of the decision that sealed her fate.

José rose to his feet. "I will miss you, amigo. It's been a long, strange journey."

"And it's not over yet," Manuel said. "Good luck, my friend."

Manuel moved next to Rosa and began humming a cherished childhood tune to ease her pain. When he looked up at the end of the song, José and Elena were gone.

70

The black and white screeched to a halt in front of a beige stucco house south of Wilshire Boulevard. Patricia looked over the wilted grass and dying flowers on the postage stamp sized piece of property and wondered if the house had become another casualty to the wave of foreclosures sweeping across the Southland. "What's going on, Ryan?" she asked. "I didn't hear Dispatch send out a call to–"

"That's because there was no call from Dispatch," he replied curtly.

Patricia turned her gaze back towards the house. Still no sign of life. "Getting a little on the side?" she asked, a grin tracing her face.

He glared at her. "Has anyone ever said you *talk* too much?"

"I just want to know what's going on. Is that too much to ask?"

He took a deep breath and exhaled. "I don't have time to explain right now," he said. "Just wait here 'til I get back."

Before she could reply, Ryan scrambled out of the cruiser and retrieved a brightly wrapped package from the trunk. On his way up the stained concrete walkway, the doorway drew open to reveal a fashionably dressed blonde with striking blue blues.

"Ryan, what a *pleasant* surprise," Stephanie said coolly. "Are you here to bring your child support payments up-to-date?"

Ryan strode up to the porch and returned her icy stare. "You'll get your money, Stephanie," he declared. "I've never failed to meet my obligations to my daughter."

"*Our* daughter," she corrected. "Or have you *forgotten* who's putting in the time to raise her?"

Ryan bit his cheek. *Like you'd ever let me.* "No, I haven't forgotten. And despite our . . . differences, you've been doing a great job so far."

She sighed. "No thanks to you."

His eyes narrowed. "Are we going to have this discussion for the umpteenth time, or are you going to let me in to see *our* daughter?"

She stepped away from the door and Ryan crossed the threshold into the foyer. A quick peek through the house was revealing; his ex had discarded virtually everything from the relationship they had built a lifetime ago. *Including whatever feelings she had for me,* he thought glumly.

Stephanie crossed her arms and stared indignantly in his direction. "I don't have to let you see Ashley, you know. Your visitation rights only allow you to see her for family celebrations and on the weekend."

He nodded but said nothing, fully aware his ex loved watching him squirm.

"So why are you here?" she demanded.

Ryan held out a pink and green colored package and smiled. "I thought I'd bring Ashley her present today rather than wait until the following weekend."

Stephanie looked at the gift and frowned. "I haven't told Ashley that you won't be able to take her to Disneyland this weekend like you planned. She's already had enough . . . disappointment in her life."

His eyes dropped. "I know," he muttered. "But she'll understand why we can't go after I explain my situation to her."

"She'll *say* she understands, but after you're gone she'll do nothing but cry in her room for the rest of the day. And after you've left her behind with your empty promises—*I'm* the one that has to clean up your mess. *I'm* the one that has to explain why her Dad is too busy saving the world that he can't even take a day off to celebrate her birthday."

He looked up sharply. "That's not fair, Stephanie. You know *nothing's* more important to me than my daughter's welfare."

"Then why don't you *prove* it? Spend the day with your daughter instead of trying to win some idealistic crusade that can never be won."

"You don't understand . . ."

"I understand, Ryan," she said bitterly. "*More* than you'll ever know." She looked on with red-rimmed eyes and pointed down the hallway. "Ashley's in her room," she said softly. "Try to make her— understand."

Ryan hung his head as he trudged down the hallway. *That went fucking well.* When he reached his daughter's room, he mustered up his brightest smile and rapped on the door.

Ashley flung the door open with a look of surprise. *"Dad!"* she shouted gleefully. "What are you doing here?"

Ryan could see the glint of braces as she smiled. On her fair-haired, freckled face, it made her smile all the more beautiful. "Who says a Dad can't come over to surprise his daughter once and awhile?"

Her eyes twinkled. "I am *soooo* glad to see you. It's been such a boring day."

"Maybe it's time to head back to school if you've got nothing to do around here."

"Oh, no," she said emphatically, "it's never *that* boring."

Ryan sat on the edge of Ashley's poster bed and lifted her into his lap. "Have you been keeping out of trouble since the last time I was here or will I have to run you in?"

"Would you really put me in jail, Dad?"

"I might," he teased. "Just last week, the judge gave someone twenty years because they didn't eat their vegetables."

"You can't scare me with those stories anymore, Dad."

He cocked his head. "I can't?"

"I'm going to be eight in a couple of days," she declared. "I know you wouldn't really throw someone in jail just because they didn't eat their veggies."

His eyes widened. "You're going to be *eight* years old?"

She punched him in the arm. "Don't be silly. You promised to take me to Disneyland for my birthday, remember?"

Ryan fought to keep the smile on his face. "Of course I . . . remember."

Ashley met his gaze. "We *are* going to Disneyland for my birthday, aren't we Dad?"

"Princess, about your birthday . . ."

Her face slackened. "You *promised.*"

"I know honey, but something came up and I can't keep my . . . promise." He reached into his pocket and withdrew the package. "Here, I brought you something for your birthday."

Ashley took the bright colored package and began peeling away the wrapping.

"It's GirlTalk," Ryan said, trying to sound enthusiastic. "Your Mom says it's the in-thing right now."

She stared forlornly at the pink colored media player and smiled wanly. "It's very . . . nice."

"I'll make *sure* we see Mickey and his friends next weekend, honey. It's just with my job and all . . ."

Ashley nodded slowly. "That's all right, Dad. I . . . understand."

Ryan studied Ashley's face and bit back tears. All he wanted to do was make his daughter happy, but he was failing miserably. "How about giving your old man a hug before I go."

She reached out to embrace him. "I love you, Dad," she said, trying to keep the disappointment from her voice.

A tear grazed his cheek as he held her in his arms. "I love you too, sweetie." He wiped his cheek and leaned back to face her. "Next weekend, princess," he said cheerfully. "Promise."

Ashley forced a smile but remained silent.

Ryan left his daughter's bedroom quietly, half-expecting his ex to accost him on the way out. But she was nowhere in sight, so he slinked out of the house and made his way back to the cruiser without saying a word.

A grin played across Patricia's face as he stepped into the vehicle. "Who's the blonde, Ryan?" she asked dryly. "Are you *sure* we're not here on a booty call?"

Ignoring his partner's remark, Ryan clutched the steering wheel so tightly that his knuckles whitened.

Patricia reached over and pried one of his fingers away from the wheel. "Is something wrong?" she asked softly.

A vein throbbed in his temple. "Not really."

"Mmmm . . . it doesn't look that way to me."

"And how would *you* know?" he snapped.

"I'm just trying to help."

"Maybe I don't *want* your help."

She looked him over and nodded. "Maybe you don't."

He slammed his hand against the steering wheel. *"This fuckin' JOB!"*

Patricia flinched but remained silent.

He leaned his head against the steering wheel and closed his eyes. "Why can't I have a normal life like everyone else?"

"Do you feel like talking about it now?"

"You wouldn't understand."

She gave a wry smile. "Try me."

"Okay, *Doctor* Ruiz, here's the sad story in a nutshell. I can't take my daughter out for her birthday like I planned because of my friggin' job."

"That was your daughter at the door?"

Ryan snorted. "No, that was Stephanie—my ex-wife." His eyebrow rose. "How old do you think I am anyway?"

"Okay, let's not get touchy here, I'm only trying to help. What's your daughter's name?"

"Ashley," he muttered. "She'll be eight this Saturday, but she's already carrying the disappointment of an angst filled teen."

"Don't worry, Ryan. She'll get over it—eventually."

His eyes narrowed. "And what makes you so damn sure?"

"Let me tell you a story," she said. "About a girl I once—knew."

"I don't have time for *stories*."

"You might like this one," she whispered. "It's . . . true."

He turned and met her gaze. "I'm listening."

"Once upon a time, a little girl grew up in big, rambling house without knowing her father. He was never there for her birthdays, the holidays, or any other meaningful time in her life. Most of his time was spent overseas helping the poor in economically depressed countries get the medical care they needed. For month after lonely month, the only time she knew he was alive was through an occasional phone call or postcard. And yet, despite the heartache, and the endless disappointments, the little girl knew her father cared because the times they did spend together were all the more . . . memorable."

"Does this . . . story . . . have a happy ending?"

"If you want it to."

Ryan's face clouded. "I don't know. I've already let her down more times than I care to remember."

Patricia touched his shoulder. "As long as Ashley knows you love her, she'll be spared the greatest disappointment of all."

71

C alvin let out a groan as he pushed away from his desk. "Kevin, why do I feel like *I'm* the one who was fired today?"

"It's never easy letting people go," Kevin replied. "Especially when they did nothing to deserve it."

Calvin nodded wearily. "I'm glad I had your input on this. It made the task a little less . . . depressing."

"They all should be able to find work at another company—even in this economy. And your generous severance package should take some of the sting out of being unemployed for a while."

"Laqueesha will easily land a job with her administrative and computer skills. But the others?" He shook his head and frowned. "I'm not so . . . sure."

"You worry too much, boss. Carlos is a natural born grease monkey and will find work with any automotive firm in town." He leaned back in his chair and shot Calvin a crooked grin. "Let's face it. When was the last time you found a mechanic who could actually fix your car?"

Calvin chuckled. The numerous times his BMW had spent at the dealership had confirmed that fact. "Yeah, you're probably right. And Eric will be fine, too—his wife's in some high-powered law firm and pulls down more in a year than he makes in a decade. He'll probably kick back and work on that book he's wanted to write until he sorts things out." He folded his hands on his desk and met Kevin's gaze. "That leaves . . . Roger."

"He'll make out," Kevin assured.

"I don't know," Calvin replied. "His engineering skills can only be utilized by a few other companies in the country."

"Something will come along eventually."

"And what if it doesn't?"

"Technology's constantly changing, boss. If you don't keep up with the latest innovations you'll soon find yourself left behind."

"This isn't about technology or innovation, Kevin—we're talking about people's *lives* here. What happens to those who can't adapt to the demands of a constantly changing workforce?"

Kevin shrugged. "They retrain, reinvent themselves, become consultants."

Calvin snorted. "And how do they pay the bills while *retraining* or *reinventing* themselves?"

"I guess they get by . . . somehow."

"You *guess?* Have you ever been in this situation?"

Kevin's eyes dropped. "Thankfully, no. My skills have always been in demand."

"And though you're damn good at what you do, don't start thinking you're irreplaceable. The unemployment lines are filled with people who probably felt their skills would always be in demand." His expression grew dour. "Frankly, I wouldn't be surprised if machines took over all our jobs someday."

Kevin shuddered. "God, I hope not."

"Why?" Calvin asked.

"Because I could never get drunk with some damn *machine* after work."

Calvin barked out a laugh. "Let's get the hell out of here and show those machines how it's done."

"I'm with you, boss."

They left the office and headed down the hallway for the exit. A look of puzzlement crossed Calvin's face as they strolled past the doorway to the manufacturing section of the facility. "That's strange," he said. "Aren't the lights always supposed to be on in this section of the plant?"

Kevin nodded. "Ramon probably shut them off by mistake on his way out."

A gruff sounding voice suddenly boomed from the darkened room. "Why not ask *me* who turned out the lights?"

Although the intruder was shrouded in shadow, Calvin recognized the voice at once. "Roger?"

A short, bleary-eyed man emerged into the light, wielding a pistol in his hand. "Of course it's Roger, you son of a bitch. Who else were you expecting?"

The sickly-sweet smell of alcohol filled the hallway, making Calvin wince. "What can I do for you, Roger?" he asked softly.

His mouth turned upward in a sneer. "I think you've done *enough* for me today, fuck you very much."

Calvin took a step back. "If you want to talk about–"

"It's a little too late for *talk,* Mister Taylor."

"Calvin's right, Roger," Kevin said. "Why don't we head back to the office and–"

"Shut the fuck up!" he snarled, his eyes narrowing to slits. "When are you going to stop playing the good little *nigger,* Kevin, and tell your *boss* to fuck off?"

"Let's not get personal here, Roger," Calvin said calmly. "I'm sure Kevin only has your best interests at–"

"And how would he know what's in my best interests, Mister Taylor? Didn't I take the unproven technology behind the Frequency

Wave Module and turn it into an actual working prototype? Haven't I been nothing less than a model employee since I've worked here?"

Calvin nodded but remained silent.

"Then why am I out on the street?" he asked. "Is this how my *loyalty* is rewarded?"

"As we discussed earlier, you were let go because the contract from Royce fell through, not because of any performance issues on your part." He took a breath and exhaled. "I only wish things could have worked out . . . differently."

He bared his teeth with disgust. "Then why didn't you let Donna go? Is that worthless cunt more valuable to you than me?"

Calvin stood quietly and met his gaze. He understood the reasoning behind Roger's rage, but the character assassination of his employees was indefensible. "If it's *justice* you want–take it out on me. Just leave Kevin out–"

Kevin clutched his arm. *"Boss!"*

Roger raised the pistol towards Calvin's head. "I could have done so much for you," he said softly. "If I'd only been given . . . the chance."

Suddenly, a metallic sphere hurtled from the darkness, striking Roger in the head. The gun discharged with a thunderous roar, and Calvin flinched as the bullet whizzed over his head and slammed harmlessly into the ceiling.

Kevin's jaw dropped. "What the *fuck* was that?"

Calvin kneeled towards Roger's prostate body and plucked the Frequency Wave Module off the floor. "Not exactly what it was designed for," he said, "but the results are still the same." He flipped Roger over on his back and examined his eyes. "Looks like he'll be out for a while."

Ramon emerged from the shadows, a sheepish grin on his face.

"Ramon!" Kevin said. "What are you doing here?"

"I forget my wife's anniversary present, Señor Turner. I drive halfway home before I remember it."

"That was one hell of a pick-off, Ramon," Calvin said. "Where'd you learn to throw like that?"

Ramon stared shyly at the floor for several moments. "I was pitcher in Dominican Republic," he said haltingly. "But I not good enough for team–they cut me."

Calvin clasped his shoulder. "Well, Ramon, I'm glad you're part of *my* team. Why don't we head back to my office and give you something to make your anniversary a little more memorable."

72

nside his dimly lit living room, Mark mulled over his options after his ill-fated meeting at the VA office earlier in the day.

With the government's decreed cut in his benefits, he would be forced to sell the house. But in today's depressed real estate market, he'd realize little if nothing from the sale. With no family or savings to turn to, he would be out on the street by the end of the year.

But homelessness was the least of his worries. If Uncle Sam didn't subsidize the cost for his expensive medical therapy, he would be dead within weeks.

Government assistance was always a possibility, but the thought of going on welfare left a bitter taste in his mouth. *I'll eat my Glock,* he groused, *before I ever take a dime from charity.*

To take his mind off his troubles, he switched on the TV and surfed mindlessly through a variety of channels, eventually settling on a local broadcast of the evening news. He punched up the volume and watched as a stylishly dressed blonde reporter grilled a jowly-faced Latino man outside his east LA home.

"And why did you come to America, Mister Rodriguez?" the reporter asked.

The man listened intently for a moment and replied through a translator. "I was looking for a better life for my family. In my hometown in Mexico, it was very hard to find a job that pays a living wage."

Mark shook his head as the immigrant prattled on. *No habla Inglés, Señor Rodriquez? Why'd you even come to our country if you can't speak the language?* He glanced at the chyron at the bottom of the screen. *Karen Mitchell. Mmmm . . . just another pretty face in the drone coming from lamestream media.*

Karen listened courteously to the migrant's response and launched into her next question. "And what have you learned about this country since you arrived here?"

Rodriguez heard the translation, and then broke into a gap-toothed smile. "America has been very good to me. Your government has been kind enough to give me money and free health care until I find work. I can see why everyone wants to come here. America is truly a great country."

Mark's mouth opened in surprise. *Are you friggin' kidding me? Uncle Sam couldn't cough up the cash to pay for my disability, but he's able to support some third-world fuck from south of the border?* A look of disgust washed over his face. *And this is the country I fought to defend? A country that helps out immigrants and illegals before the needs of its citizens?*

Suddenly, another seizure wracked Mark's brain. He squeezed his head between his hands, trying to push the pain away. The torment increased steadily and Mark arched his back against the chair and screamed.

And as suddenly as it had begun, the pressure began to subside in his head. Mark slumped back in his seat and gasped for breath, anxiously wondering when the next seizure would reach out and grip his mind.

Refocusing his eyes on the screen, the bubbly blonde and fleshy-faced migrant were replaced by a local bureaucrat touting the benefits of a new water reclamation plant.

Mark switched off the set and struggled to his feet. He hobbled toward the front door and opened it to the world, feeling the sunlight jab at his eyes like thousands of tiny electrically charged needles.

Ignoring the pain, he stepped out on the porch and surveyed the neighborhood. A low-slung car breezed noisily down the street, its overcranked speakers pounding the strains of a hip hop tune through his still tortured mind. In a driveway two doors down, several teens tossed a basketball through a rusty hoop shorn of its netting. To his left, a young girl skated down the sidewalk under a row of jacaranda trees, arms swinging wildly outward to maintain her balance.

In another time, any of these scenes could have set the stage for a Norman Rockwell painting. But the Americana he depicted was on the verge of vanishing, the nationalism he treasured usurped by immigrants unwilling to assimilate into their adopted society. Somewhere along the way, the nation Mark fought for had changed for the worse, and for the first time in his life—he grew afraid.

This country can't continue its path towards self-destruction. It can't continue to remain divided by racial, economic, and political strife. We need to bring this nation together again, and return America to its position of reverence and grandeur.

As the sun melted into the distant hazy horizon, Mark contemplated his future and found his options wanting.

All but . . . one.

73

José watched with alarm as the ground crumbled beneath Elena's feet and she tumbled head first into a dried up gulch.

He scampered quickly down the slope and cradled her head in his hands. "Are you all right, Elena?"

Her eyes fluttered. "Ohhh . . . what happened, José?"

"The ground gave way and you fell into a gulch." Concern touched his face. "Do you think you can stand on your feet?"

She tried sitting up but a spasm wracked her body. "I can't . . . José." Her breath came in short, ragged gasps. "Tired. So very . . . tired."

"We'll rest for a while. Until you feel . . . better."

Elena smiled weakly. "It's too late for that."

"You'll be fine," José said, forcing a smile. "All you need is rest."

Elena tugged on a delicate gold chain that was draped around her neck. A small locket emerged from her tattered blouse, twinkling brightly in the waning sunlight. She sprang the gilded case open, revealing a small photo of her family. "Take this . . . to Eduardo, José."

He stroked her face with his hand. "You can take it to him yourself, Elena. After you get some . . . rest."

Her eyes clouded, as if remembering a cherished thought from her past. "Always the dreamer, José." She reached up and brushed a strand of hair from his face. "One day . . . I hope you find . . . your dream."

José's eyes widened. *"Elena!"* he wailed. *"Don't go!"* His voice softened to a whisper. "Please . . . don't go."

Sweeping her into his arms, José wept tearlessly as a series of gut wrenching sobs convulsed his body. *I'll make sure your wish is carried out, Elena. I swear it.*

After laying Elena to rest, José set out across the desert, the ground a dusky blur beneath his feet. As the sun dipped towards the mountains, he lifted a sunburned arm against the sky and noticed a swirling cloud of dust to the west. *What could that be?* he wondered. *A dust devil? Or something—more?*

His spirits lightened as the whirling vortex followed an unswerving course towards the mountains. *It must be a vehicle leaving a cloud of dust in its wake.* A shiver went up his spine. *It has to be.*

Buoyed by his discovery, José pushed off with renewed vigor towards the settling dust cloud. Several hard miles later, his strength faltered and he dropped to his knees, continuing to crawl in the direction where the whirlwind was last seen.

He shut out the world and pushed forward, ignoring the jagged pieces of gravel as it tore into his palms and knees. He put one exhausted hand in front of the other, until he trudged atop a black, crumbling highway several feet above the desert surface. Through eyes nearly swollen shut, he marveled at the ribbon of cracked asphalt as it stretched in a golden line toward the sun.

Reaching out towards the reddening ball of fire, a single word escaped Jose's parched lips before he collapsed by the side of the roadway.

"America."

74

Andrew took a swig from his cup of cappuccino and watched the early evening beachcombers parade past his balcony. A young couple jogged fluidly along the beach, a middle-aged man swept the sand with a metal detector, and a boy tried to coax a bat shaped kite into the sky.

Further up the coast, a flock of seagulls soared gracefully above the waves, and the silhouette of a yacht drifted lazily across the horizon against the setting sun.

Taking another sip from his drink, Andrew leaned against the railing and took stock of his life. Though the last several months had tested his resolve, he believed Fate must be finally smiling down on him. Despite the continuous delays and budget overruns, his current project was nearly completed and ready for its public debut. A group of investors looking more for a convenient tax shelter from Uncle Sam than creating a cinematic masterpiece for the screen had pledged financial support for his next project. Last, though far from least, the opportunity to meet with the President introduced an intriguing set of possibilities for his future.

Though he never took any real interest in politics other than casting the occasional vote, the President's network could allow him to build a media empire on par with the mega corporations dominating the industry.

The potential to improve his fortune was limitless, and Andrew planned to capitalize on his meeting with Jennings to the fullest extent.

A smile traced his face as he watched the sun brush its golden light on the shimmery sea. *Who would have dreamed that a person from a trailer trash background would one day have the opportunity to hobnob with the most powerful man on Earth?*

He shook his head and chuckled. *Only in America.*

75

Choking back tears, Kati embraced Calvin the moment he stepped inside the house. "Thank God, you weren't hurt," she cried. "I haven't stopped worrying since you called me from the office." She pulled him close, feeling the warmth of his body wash over her. "What's going to happen to Roger?"

"I don't know," Calvin muttered. "He was still unconscious when the paramedics took him to the hospital."

Concern touched Kati's face. "I hope he gets some help from a psychiatrist while he's there. In his state of mind, I don't think he realized what he was doing was wrong."

Calvin broke away from his wife's embrace and frowned. "Frankly, I don't know *what* to think anymore."

She met his gaze but remained silent.

"Someone I knew—or thought I knew—tried to kill me tonight. A part of me feels outraged by what happened and yet, another part of me feels . . . immeasurably sad." His eyes grew distant as he relived the confrontation in his mind. "I wonder, would I have reacted like Roger under similar circumstances?"

"It's not your fault, Calvin. Roger needed a focal point to direct his anger and you just happened to be the most convenient target."

"People get fired everyday and don't kill the messenger."

She shrugged. "We all have our limits, hon."

"I suppose," he grumbled. "But what finally caused him to snap?"

"We'll probably never know. People make poor choices when pushed to the edge."

"And what does that say about humanity when violence becomes the *first* choice in solving our problems?" Calvin asked.

"Sometimes violence is the *only* choice when all other options have been exhausted. Throughout history, countless people have used violence to get their beliefs recognized by society. Sometimes their convictions are justified, and sometimes . . . they're not. Ultimately, it's not the one with the power who wins the argument, but the one who believes the most in their cause."

"But if your cause isn't morally acceptable, than we really haven't evolved much at all since our ancestors first strode across the earth many millennia ago. Despite thousands of years of laws and traditions, we still tend to end our arguments at the end of a club."

"All the trappings of civilization can't change the fact that we're driven by primal needs and desires. Until we understand the reasoning behind our actions, we're destined for the same fate as the dinosaurs."

A look of sadness washed across Calvin's face. "You make it sound like humanity is doomed for destruction. And I always thought you were the optimistic one in the family."

"I am optimistic," she declared. "But I'm also a realist. My optimistic half believes in us–and in humanity as a whole. Sometimes we take a step back for every two forward, and sometimes we stumble and fall. But on the whole, we learn–and persevere. The optimist in me says we're going to make it, but the realist in me says it's going to take a long, long time." Her expression grew dour. "I only hope we find the right path before it's too late."

Calvin gave a sour smile. "It may already be . . . too late."

76

Karen surveyed the tattered vinyl booths and rusty chrome stools in the vacant diner and frowned. *Looks like I missed tonight's rush,* she mused. *Like this place could ever have a rush.* Wending her way through the faded Fifties décor, she slid into a booth across from Ryan and kept a wary eye out for cockroaches–or something worse.

"Is something bothering you?" Ryan asked.

"Not really," she replied. "Why do you ask?"

"You have this strange . . . look . . . on your face."

"I'll say this," she quipped, "you sure know how to show a girl a good time."

He glanced around the dimly lit diner and shrugged. "It does have its charm now, doesn't it?"

"*Charm* wasn't the first word that sprang to mind when I walked through the door tonight." Her hand touched something sticky on her seat and she shuddered. "So what's up? Do you have some inside scoop that will put me on track for the next Peabody Award?"

Ryan shook his head. "It's been a pretty slow day, I'm glad to say." He gestured towards the menu on the table. "Order whatever you want–I'm buying."

She picked up the grease stained menu and winced. "What would you recommend? That's . . . safe?"

"I don't know," Ryan said drolly. "They've hired on a new cook since the Health Department shut them down last month."

"And that's supposed to *help* me make a choice?" She peered into the dreary looking kitchen and watched a burly, hunchbacked man slam a sooty pot against the wall. *Mmmm . . . he was probably out in the alley hunting today's special a few hours ago.* "How's the coffee?" she asked. "Is that something I won't regret a few hours from now?"

Ryan took a gulp from his mug and smiled. "I think you'll like it. They roast and grind their own beans on the premises everyday."

"What kind of beans–pinto?"

"Look, I know the place looks a little shabby, but the food is to die for." He gave a wry smile. "No pun intended."

"You know, I'm really not that hungry after all."

Ryan raised his arm overhead and waved. "Let's see if Sarah can help you out."

Within moments, a haggard, middle-aged woman materialized in front of their table with a welcoming smile. "Is there somethin' I can get you, Mister Ryan?"

"My friend can't decide on what to order tonight. What do you recommend?"

Sarah flashed a smile shy several teeth. "Pierre make de best shrimp gumbo outside New O'leans."

Karen gave an eye roll. *Pierre–please.*

Ryan licked his lips. "Sounds good. Karen?"

"Sure," she said glumly. "What have I got to lose?" *Besides my life.*

Ryan handed Sarah the menus. "Thanks, Sarah. And bring the lady a cup of coffee while Pierre works his magic."

Sarah reappeared with the coffee a heartbeat later. "Here's your coffee, miss." She refreshed Ryan's mug and vanished back into the kitchen.

Karen sweetened her coffee and took a tentative sip. "Mmmm, it's really good. And not a hint of pinto to be found." She leaned forward in her seat and folded her hands on the table. "So what's up? You didn't invite me to the classiest joint in town just so I could taste Pierre's cuisine."

Ryan ran a hand over his face and frowned.

Karen's eyebrow rose. "What's wrong, Ryan?"

He took a deep breath and exhaled. "Ahhh . . . I've been feeling a little down today and needed someone to talk to."

"Something to do with work?"

He gave a bitter laugh. "It's got *everything* to do with work."

She reached out and touched his hand. "I'm all ears."

Before he could reply, Sarah arrived at their table with two steaming bowls of gumbo and a basket of red pepper cornbread. Even without tasting her meal, the tangy aroma wafting through the air made Karen's mouth water.

"Would dere be anything else, Mister Ryan?" Sarah asked.

"Not for me. Karen?"

She shook her head. "I'm fine."

"Enjoy your meal," Sarah said. She gave a fleeting smile and disappeared into the kitchen.

Ryan dipped a slice of cornbread into the gumbo. He savored the taste briefly, then turned his gaze back to Karen. "Although I enjoy what I do for a living, it can be a real pain in the ass sometimes."

Karen tasted her soup and nodded. "I can imagine."

"I don't know if you can. My job has always managed to come between me and those I care about."

Karen frowned. "Uhhh . . . this doesn't have anything to do with me, does it?"

Ryan snorted. "Of course not. This is about Stephanie, my ex-wife."

Her stomach gave a sudden lurch. "You were . . . married?" she asked, trying to keep the quaver from her voice.

"Once upon a time, but it didn't end happily ever after." He shot her a winsome smile. "Except for . . . Ashley."

"Ashley?"

He nodded. "My daughter."

Karen bit the side of her cheek. *Ex-wife, daughter? Are there any more–surprises–I should know about?* "I'm getting a little confused here, Ryan . . . "

Ryan sopped up some gumbo with another slab of bread and popped it into his mouth. "I guess I should explain," he said, between bites. "Ashley is turning eight this Thursday, and I promised to take her to Disneyland for her birthday. But now that the department has cancelled everyone's leave because of the Pangaea Festival, I had to let my daughter down . . . again."

"And this is why you're feeling blue?"

He gave a slight nod. "The look on her face . . . was more than I could bear."

"What's more important to you, Ryan," Karen asked, "your family or your career?"

His face clouded. "I . . . I don't know."

Karen's eyes widened. "How can your *job* be more important than your *family?*"

"Isn't your career important to you?"

"Yes," she replied. "But I'm not the one with the problem here."

"It's hard to explain why my career means so much to me. At least in terms you'd–understand."

"I'm a reporter, Ryan. I've spent my entire career learning how to understand."

Ryan leaned back in his seat and sighed. "Simply put, my career is a calling for me. Just as some feel the need to become an artist, a doctor, or a minister—I feel *compelled* to bring moral balance to this crazy world we live in."

"Have you ever thought about donning a bright colored costume to strike fear into the evildoers of the world?" she asked dryly.

His face slackened. "I *knew* you wouldn't understand."

"I'm not mocking you, Ryan. It's never wrong to trust your instincts—or to believe in what you know is right. Unfortunately, your dedication to career and your desire to improve your relationship with your daughter may be mutually exclusive goals."

He gave a reluctant nod. "I guess I'll have to work it out . . . somehow."

She squeezed his hand. "Tell me something about Ashley."

Ryan reached into his pocket and pulled a well-worn photo from his wallet. "A picture's worth a thousand words," he said, grinning.

Karen looked the snapshot over. A petite, pixie haired child sat atop a Shetland pony, beaming at the world through a gap-toothed smile. Her father stood proudly beside her, clad in jeans and a red flannel shirt. The photo bespoke of a happy and carefree time in their lives.

"Her hair is a lot longer now," Ryan said, "but she's just as cute as ever." His expression grew dour. "I just wish I could have been more a part of her life than I was."

"I'm sure you tried your best. It's never easy juggling the demands of family and career."

He looked up sharply. "I could have quit my job, Karen."

She met his gaze. "*Could* you?"

"I'll have to retire someday."

"And when that day comes, you'll have as much time to spend with her as you please."

He shook his head. "By then it will be too late. She'll be too wrapped up with her own life to care about me anymore."

"I don't know if you've noticed, but Ashley is wrapped up in her life *now*. Waiting until tomorrow to fix your relationship will only make you grow further apart."

He gave a sour smile. "We may have already grown too far apart."

"Only you can know the answer to that. But I'm betting Ashley isn't ready to throw in the towel yet."

"I don't want to lose her," he said softly.

"You won't," she quipped. "From what I recall, the guy in the fancy colored tights always gets the girl in the end."

He chuckled. "Are you always such a wise ass?"

"What can I say, you bring out the best in me."

He reached out and caressed her cheek. "Do you have any plans for tonight?"

"What did you have in mind?"

"We could cruise around town. Talk. Whatever."

Karen's eyes twinkled. *Whatever…mmmm.* "I'm game," she replied. "Are you ready to leave now?"

He rose from his seat and tossed a twenty on the table. "There's no time like the present, I always say."

They left the diner and stepped into the warm summer night. Ryan led Karen to the back of the restaurant where his cruiser was parked. "Ever ridden in a police car before?" he asked.

She looked the vehicle over. "Oh, sure," she lied. "Lots of times."

"Yeah, but how many times in the *front* seat?"

She giggled. "What are you going to do next? Frisk me?"

He shot her an impish grin. "Don't tempt me."

"In that case, I'll be your perfect law abiding citizen. A lady can't be too careful these days."

They settled into the vehicle, and Karen watched intently as Ryan scanned the incident logs on the mobile data terminal. Though his shift had ended several hours earlier, his dedication to his job kept him on duty twenty-four hours a day. *He seems so confident,* she reflected. *So unafraid to face whatever comes his way. And yet, there's a certain–vulnerability–about him that makes him human.* A smile traced her face. *I still have much to learn about Mister Ryan Rysinski.*

He turned off the display and glanced in her direction. "Ready to head out?"

"Where are we going?" she asked.

He shot her a wry smile. "Wherever the journey takes us."

"I like a man of mystery."

The car snaked out of the lot, heading towards the Santa Monica freeway. Traffic was typical for Los Angeles at this time–brutal.

"Do you know why I wanted to take my car tonight?" Ryan asked.

"No," Karen replied, puzzled. "Why?"

He flicked on the cruiser's lightbar and traffic scattered towards the side of the road like roaches scurrying away from a bright light.

Her eyes grew huge. "Isn't this against the law?"

Ryan grinned. "I *am* the law, remember?"

Karen watched with amazement as the cruiser darted through an ever-widening pathway in the road. "Do you think you can get a set of emergency lights for my car? It would cut my morning commute to the studio in half."

He laughed softly. "Now *that* would be breaking the law."

Twenty minutes later, Ryan angled the cruiser into a parking lot near the Santa Monica pier. They slipped off their shoes and strolled onto the beach, enjoying the coolness of the sand as it slid beneath their feet. Overhead, stars sparkled faintly in the hazy night while a sliver of a moon reflected brightly off the ebony sea. Most of the beachgoers had dispersed for the day, leaving them alone as they walked along the dimly lit coastline.

Karen reached out for Ryan's hand. "Is this where the journey takes us?"

He looked into her eyes and smiled. "If that's what your heart desires."

"Several days ago, we began our journey under less than desirable circumstances. And now, here we are . . . walking hand in hand . . . "

He stroked her face. "Life can be strange, sometimes."

Their lips met—and for a brief, joyous moment the past, present and future came together under a star streaked sky along the Santa Monica shoreline.

77

I n the back of a pickup hurtling down a desolate roadway, two migrant workers shared a bottle of tequila and laughed heartily in the hot summer night. The truck stumbled briefly over a rut in the pockmarked road, causing Alfonso to frantically juggle the bottle to keep it from tumbling overboard.

Pedro looked over at Alfonso and frowned. "Hey, pendéjo–watch the fuckin' tequila."

Alfonso took a draw from the bottle and grinned. "Don't worry, amigo. I'm as steady on my feet as *el yaguar*." To prove his point, he struggled upright in the lurching cargo bed and tried to maintain his balance.

Pedro looked at his friend's clumsy theatrics and laughed. "El yaguar?" he slurred. "More like *el hipopótamo* if you ask me." He watched his friend with wry amusement for several moments then turned his bleary eyes back to the road. The truck's feeble headlights barely illuminated the crumbling line of asphalt that cut through the Sonoran desert. On both sides of the abandoned roadway, the darkened sands of the desert stretched to the horizon, with only an occasional saguaro or yucca tree thrusting skyward to break the monotony.

Anxiety tinged Alfonso's face as he passed the half-empty bottle to

Pedro. "That's enough for me, amigo," he muttered. "Isabel is gonna kill me tonight for sure."

Pedro took a gulp of the amber colored liquid and shrugged. "What are you worried about, Alfonso? She has seen you drunk before."

"It's worse than that. I forgot to pick up the decorations for Teresa's Quinceañera while I was in town today."

Pedro chuckled. "Don't worry, amigo. She'll just use your *cojones* for the decorations instead."

"It's not funny," Alfonso replied. "You know how Isabel gets when– *Hey!* What's that?" He whipped his head around and pointed down the roadway. "Did you see it, Pedro?"

Pedro shook his head and laughed. "You've had too much to drink, padré."

Alfonso peered into the blackness. "No–I *saw* something." He rapped on the roof of the truck. "Stop the truck, Humberto," he shouted. "Now."

The vehicle rolled to a stop and Humberto leaned his head out the window. "What is it, Alfonso?"

"There's something by the side of the road. Let's check it out."

Humberto massaged the balky gearshift and the truck jerked into reverse. The taillights cast a reddish glow as the vehicle inched back along the broken surface of the roadway.

Alfonso jabbed at the darkness. "Over there! To the right!"

Pedro stared expectantly into the night. "It's just an old bundle of clothes . . . or a blanket someone threw away . . ."

Alfonso jumped off the truck and moved towards the shadowy shape at the edge of the roadway. He found José's unconscious face staring out at him in the dim crimson light. "It's . . . *a man!*" He kneeled down and touched the side of his neck, searching for a pulse. *"And he's alive!"*

Pedro and Humberto scrambled from the truck and rushed over to look at José's prostrate body.

"What's he doing out here in the middle of nowhere?" Pedro

wondered.

"Who knows?" Alfonso said. "Wherever he's from, he's a long way from home. Come, help me get him into the truck."

The men wrangled José's limp body into the cargo bed. Alfonso soaked his bandanna with water and wiped the grit from José's face.

"Have you ever seen him before?" Pedro asked.

Alfonso shook his head. "He's not from around here."

A faint groan escaped from José's lips. His eyes fluttered open, trying to focus on his surroundings.

Alfonso stroked José's feverish forehead and smiled. "Rest, amigo. You're among friends now."

José nodded and slipped back into unconsciousness.

Thirty minutes later, the truck stopped inside a migrant camp on the outskirts of Yuma, Arizona. The men wrestled José from the truck, and laid him on a bed inside Alfonso's single room dwelling while his wife looked disapprovingly on.

"Who's that, Alfonso?" Isabel grumbled. "Another one of your *drunken* friends wanting to spend the night?"

Alfonso brought a finger to his lips. "We'll talk about this outside, Isabel," he said softly.

Without saying a word, Isabel spun angrily around and stepped through the tattered carpet covering the doorway. Moments later, Alfonso trudged out of his home to join her, a look of concern gripping his face.

Isabel wagged her finger at Alfonso. "I thought we agreed your friends wouldn't-"

"He's *not* a friend," he cut in.

"Then who is he?"

Alfonso took a deep breath and exhaled. "I don't know."

"Then why'd you bring him here?" she hissed. "He must have family-"

"Did you *see* him, Isabel? We found him along the old, abandoned roadway leading from the desert–barely alive."

"Then who is he?" she asked. "And where is he from?"

Alfonso shrugged. "If you can believe the *documentos* we found inside his pocket, he goes by the name José Torres. But, it's almost impossible to know who he really is since most of the papers from Mexico are forged."

She gave a curt nod. "We'll let him rest here tonight, but tomorrow I want to know more about this José Torres."

While Alfonso and Isabel bickered outside their dilapidated home, José stirred to life and studied his surroundings. An old, brass lantern cast a faint glow from atop a heavily scarred table flanked by folding chairs. Work clothes and colorful dresses were draped over a rope strung across the room while the smell of disinfectant hung thickly in the air.

To his right, a teenage girl stared expectantly at him in the gloomy room. He raised his arm slightly and rasped out a greeting. "Hola, senorita."

The teen moved next to the bed and dabbed his forehead with a washcloth. "Don't be afraid, señor," she whispered. "You're safe now."

"Where am I?" he asked.

She brushed the oily hair from his face and smiled. "You must rest. We'll talk again in the morning."

José nodded wearily and soon drifted into an exhausted slumber.

TUESDAY

78

The florid faced salesman wheezed loudly as he led Mark towards a wheelchair at the back of the medical supply store. "And here's our top of the line model, sir. The UltraTrac 5000 is the most advanced powerchair you can find in America today."

Mark propped his walking canes against the side of the wheelchair and lowered himself into the seat. After a brief inspection of the ergonomics, he rocked side to side in the seat to check the wheelchair's stability.

"You won't be able to tip this baby over," the salesman affirmed. "The Five-Thousand has a sophisticated seat location system which provides proper weight distribution and virtually eliminates any problems with front-loading." He tapped the front wheels with his foot. "See these? The anti-tippers are dynamically fluid balanced so you can slide over any obstacles with no problem. Yes sir, the only way you're going to tip the Five-Thousand off-balance is by driving it off a cliff."

Mark gave a curt nod and leaned over the side of the wheelchair to examine the battery pack and motor unit.

Sensing a sale, the potbellied merchant moved in for the kill. "The Five-Thousand has a brushless servo motor that generates 400 watts of power. You won't be winning any stock car races, but you'll be able to bowl over your average pedestrian if they fail to get out of your way."

Mark continued with his inspection as the salesman prattled on. The wheelchair's capabilities mattered little to him as long as it fulfilled its final purpose. Glancing up at the greasy haired salesman, he was reminded of a day at the county fair, where hucksters dressed in cheap striped suits and straw hats peddled curiosities to the gullible crowds.

The salesman finished his spiel and wiped his forehead with a plaid handkerchief. "Do you have any questions, sir?" he politely asked.

Mark shook his head. "No, you've pretty much covered–everything. The Five-Thousand is just what my mother is looking for."

The salesman's brow furrowed. "Your . . . mother?"

"That's right," Mark replied. "My *mother*. She broke her hip and I thought a motorized wheelchair would make life a little easier while she's convalescing."

"Ahhh . . . the Five-Thousand would be perfect for her, sir. She'll have her independence back in no time."

Mark leveled his eyes at the merchant and gave a sinister smile. "Independence is like most things in life–you never really miss them until they're gone." He moved his gaze towards his legs and let it linger for several moments to increase the salesman's discomfort. "Is there anything in your life that you'd miss if it was suddenly taken away?"

The salesman's eyebrow arched upward. "Excuse me, sir?"

Mark looked up sharply. "It's a simple question," he said. "Would you miss your job, your home, or your family if they suddenly vanished from your life?"

The salesman rocked back on his heels and looked uneasily around the deserted store. "I never gave it much thought," he mumbled.

"Never gave it much thought?" Mark let out a short, harsh laugh. "Don't you value *anything* in your life? Or are you like most of the *sheeple* in this country who are afraid to take a stand for what they believe in?"

Puzzlement crept into the salesman's face. "I'm afraid I don't understand what you're talking about, sir."

Mark looked the salesman over and nodded. "No . . . I suppose not." *But one day you'll understand. They'll all understand.*

The salesman smiled broadly, hoping to move things along. "Is there anything else I can help you with today, sir?"

"That should be it. How soon can you deliver?"

"This afternoon if we have it in stock. And if you're dissatisfied with the UltraTrac 5000 for any reason, you can return it to our store within thirty days for a full refund."

"Should I be dissatisfied for any reason?" Mark asked.

"Of course not, sir. This is the UltraTrac 5000 we're talking about here."

Shut the fuck up already, you pompous windbag. "Say no more–I'll take it."

The salesman rubbed his hands together and flashed a wolfish grin. "And how do you wish to pay for your purchase, sir?"

Mark took a credit card from his wallet and passed it to the salesman's waiting hand. "I'll charge it."

As the vendor waddled towards the register to complete the transaction, Mark gave a sly smile. *Good luck collecting on the bill.*

79

alvin gave an easy smile as Kevin entered his office for a confidential meeting. "You're looking a bit relaxed this morning," he said drolly.

Kevin's eyebrow quivered. *"Relaxed?"* He took a seat across from Calvin's desk and chuckled. "Hell, I hardly slept a wink last night."

"Yeah, me either." Calvin muttered. "So what's the scoop on Roger?"

"He's conscious now, but they're keeping him in the hospital for another day to make sure there aren't any repercussions from the blow he took to the head." He shot Calvin a crooked grin. "I guess Ramon better take a little off his fastball next time."

"There better not *be* a next time," Calvin grumbled. "Is he going to jail after he leaves the hospital?"

"That depends. You *are* going to press charges, aren't you?" It sounded more like a demand than a question.

Calvin sighed. "Do I have any choice?"

Kevin's eyes widened. "Are you fuckin' kidding me, boss?" he groused. "He tried to kill us for Christ's sake!"

"Mmmm . . . I don't know. The more I think about it, the more I believe he was just looking for a way to rectify his situation."

"He wanted to *rectify* it all right. By making us a couple of chalk outlines on the hallway floor."

"Think about it, Kevin. If Roger really wanted to kill us, he could have done it right away. I'm sure he would have surrendered peaceably if we had given him time."

"Were we at the same place last night? The way I remember it, we were only seconds away from pushin' up daisies."

"So you feel that justice would be served by locking him up for the rest of his life?"

"Forget life—just stick in the needle and be done with it," Kevin replied. "Just one less *deviant* for society to deal with."

"Before last night, would you have characterized Roger as—deviant? The Roger I knew was always a perfect employee."

Kevin shrugged. "I guess we didn't know him as well as we thought."

"And how well do we really know anyone?" Calvin ventured. "Including ourselves?"

"Ahhh, let the freakin' lawyers sort it out. He needs to be punished for his actions."

"An eye for an eye, eh?"

"Works for me."

"And life goes on—as if nothing ever happened."

Kevin cocked his head. "What are you gettin' at, boss?"

"Have we really solved the problem by taking away someone's liberty or their life?" Calvin asked. "Kati and I discussed last night's incident and concluded that humanity hasn't made much progress since the caveman days. Despite our advances in technology, our adoption of laws and traditions, we still ultimately solve our conflicts at the end of a club."

Kevin snorted. "I guess some things will never change."

"Why?"

"Why *what*?"

"Why can't we change?"

"Because we are who we are."

"That's not an answer," Calvin chided.

"You want an *answer?*" Kevin snapped. "We're flawed, and every-thing we touch in this world is flawed as well."

"I'm not looking for *perfection*, Kevin. I just want some sign that society hasn't lost its sanity. Our culture has deteriorated to the point where lying, cheating, and thievery is condoned or in some cases–rewarded–without any fear of retribution at all." His expression grew dour. "Is this the legacy we want to leave for our children?"

"People have ranted about society's ills for generations, boss. It's not that bad from where I stand."

Calvin nodded. "In some ways–it is better. We live longer, and our quality of life is better than ever before. But, at what price? Apathy and self-loathing have gripped the nation and our so-called leaders can't find a way to turn things around."

Kevin held his hands out. "Don't look at me. I voted."

"So did I, but nothing really changes does it? We hear the same empty promises assuring peace and prosperity, but all we get is divisiveness and despair."

"And what can we mere mortals do to change things?" Kevin asked dryly.

"True change must come from within ourselves," Calvin affirmed. "It can't be legislated by authority. But before we head down the wrong path towards redemption, we must understand who we are and what gives our lives–meaning. Our forefathers didn't err in declaring certain rights inalienable–they erred in their assumption that a self-elected government would bring it to fruition. Our nation has strayed from the founders original design and we must rediscover what truly defines life, liberty, and the pursuit of happiness."

"Do you think we can ever reach that lofty goal?"

"I don't know. But, if we never understand what gives our lives purpose, then we're doomed to repeat yesterday's incident over and over again."

"It's not a perfect world, boss."

Sadness touched Calvin's eyes. "I know. But there's no reason why that can't change."

80

ndrew's face contorted with rage as traffic slowed to a crawl on the San Diego freeway. "What the hell's going on?" he groused. "Don't any of these friggin' idiots know how to drive?"

Exasperated, he punched a number on the automobile's phone system and rapped his fingers on the steering wheel while waiting to be connected.

"Thank you for calling Pacifica Productions," a voice trilled through the vehicle's speaker system. "How may we assist you today?"

"Good morning, Alicia, this is Andrew Landis. May I speak with Tom, please?"

"Certainly, Mister Landis. Please hold."

The gentle strains of Mozart filled the car's cabin, and Andrew amused himself by observing the drivers creeping forward on the freeway. On his left, a haggard mother scolded a pair of toddlers in an old, gray minivan. To his right, a jacked up executive argued on his phone with some faceless entity from the cozy interior of his Jaguar. Directly ahead, a smattering of faded bumper stickers shouted their slogans from the back of a rusty sport utility vehicle.

Andrew leaned forward and read the message on a blue and white sticker plastered across the rear door. PEOPLE WHO THINK THEY

KNOW IT ALL REALLY ANNOY THOSE OF US WHO DO. He shook his head and grinned. *Ain't that the fuckin' truth.*

A man's voice suddenly echoed though the interior, jolting him from his reverie. "Hi, Andrew. What's up?"

"Ahhh . . . the San Diego's a *bitch* today, Tom. Looks like I'm going to be a little late for our meeting."

"No problem. We'll start our presentation once you get here."

"Shouldn't be long, I'm just a few miles away."

"Just a few miles, eh? Maybe we should reschedule this meeting for tomorrow."

Andrew chuckled. "I hear you. I'll get off at the next exit and take surface streets to save some time."

"Sounds like a plan. Ciao."

Andrew shut off the phone and studied the congestion ahead of him. The closest exit was still a half-mile away. Normally, the Bentley's twelve-cylinder engine could have covered the distance in seconds, but today's snarl would easily add twenty minutes over the usual commute.

He leaned to his right and looked past the sports utility vehicle for a break in the traffic. When the hulking gas-guzzler moved far enough forward, Andrew edged the Bentley to his right and was promptly greeted with a prolonged blare from the suit in the Jaguar.

Andrew chortled as the strung out executive shot him the finger in his rear view mirror. *Blow it out your ass, putz.*

The Bentley crept forward for several hundred yards and Andrew looked frantically for another opportunity to move towards the exit. Suddenly, a gap opened up on his right when a driver failed to keep up with the flow of traffic.

Andrew grinned eagerly. *Here's my chance.* He throttled the Bentley towards the empty lane, only to find an old Ford Crown Vic bolting for the space at the same time.

His eyes widened with surprise. *What the–*

A heart-wrenching crunch reverberated through the Bentley's cabin as the rusted out vehicle slammed into his car. Andrew gripped the steering wheel and looked with dismay at the junker coupled to his quarter million dollar car. *Shit! Shit! SHIT!*

Andrew waved to the driver to move towards the shoulder. He couldn't discern the motorist through the sedan's heavily tinted windows, but a ghostly wave of the driver's hand showed he understood his intent.

Once both vehicles were safely parked on the side of the road, Andrew got out of his car to inspect the damage. His stomach lurched when he saw the dent creasing the right front fender.

Looking at the battered sedan parked directly in front of him, Andrew clenched his fists and fumed. *This moron better have insurance or I'm gonna beat the cost of fixing my car out of him personally.*

Moments later, a round-faced Latino man with a stubbly beard exited the sedan and strolled over to meet him. "Buenas días, señor," he said amiably.

Andrew's eyes narrowed. "What's *good* about it–señor? Your half-assed attempt at driving has totally fucked up my day."

A look of puzzlement crossed the Latino man's face.

Oh, great, Andrew seethed. *Fuckin' Pablo no habla Inglés.* He snatched the man's arm and dragged him towards the side of his car. "Look at what you did, asshole. It's going to cost a small fortune to have this fixed."

The man ran his hand along the crease in the fender and shook his head. "Lo siento, señor."

Andrew recalled the phrase from his limited Spanish vocabulary and scowled. "That's it?" he growled. "You're frickin' *sorry?*"

The man stared, too terrified to move.

"Do you have *insurance* to pay for this?"

The man shrugged.

Andrew glanced at his watch and frowned. *This is going nowhere fast.* "You know, Pablo, I don't have time to play games here. I'll just call up *immigracíon* and let them sort it out."

The man's eyes grew huge with fear.

"Ahhh," Andrew sneered. "Now there's a word you *do* understand." He pulled a phone from his pocket and dialed the operator. "I should have known you were here illegally right from the start."

As he waited to be connected, he noticed a doe-eyed girl clutching a tattered doll through the rear window of the man's sedan.

"Operator."

Andrew stared at the girl; her large brown eyes brimmed with tears. "Yes operator, connect me with the L.A. County immigration office, please."

"Please hold while I transfer you."

Andrew's face slackened as he watched a tear trickle down the girl's cheek. His thoughts drifted to a town from his childhood best left forgotten. *I was five at the time . . . and hadn't eaten in days. Mom had scrounged up a can of stew, and we huddled under an overpass to eat it when some zealous do-gooder threatened to turn us in.*

His face tightened as he replayed the memory in his mind. *She begged the stranger to leave us alone, but her pleas only angered him more. I can still hear his taunts echo off the rust stained concrete as he rocked her body over and over again with the back of his hand. "Where do you get off telling me what to do, you whore? There are good God fearing folk in this town—we don't want your kind here."*

I scrunched into a corner of the overpass as she screamed, clutching a small stuffed dog I named–

A woman's voice warbled over the phone. "Immigration and Customs Enforcement. May I help you?"

Andrew blinked. "Huh?"

"This is Immigration and Customs Enforcement, sir. Is there something I can do for you?"

Andrew's eyes focused on the girl. *I can't let it happen—again.* He clicked off the phone and looked at the stubbly-faced man. "Look, mister," he said softly. "I'm . . . uhhh . . . sorry about what I said to you earlier."

The man cocked his head in confusion.

Andrew withdrew a wad of bills from his wallet. "Take this," he said, slapping the money into the man's hand. "With my blessing."

The man looked at the money and smiled broadly, a hint of gold glinting from his mouth. "Gracias, señor," he said eagerly. *"Gracias."*

Andrew shot him a lopsided grin. "You're welcome."

The man clambered into the run-down Ford and inched back onto the freeway. Andrew watched as the girl brushed the tears from her eyes and flashed him a smile. He wiggled his fingers in her direction, a grin spreading across his face as he watched the vehicle disappear from view.

Strolling back to the Bentley, Andrew studied the dented fender and sighed. *Things can always be replaced,* he reflected. *But you can never restore a young child's innocence.*

81

A groan slipped past José's lips as he swam back towards consciousness. Gazing warily around the ramshackle dwelling, his eyes focused on the curious face of a teenage girl sitting by his bedside. Thin, with shoulder length brown hair and a broad featured face, she wore a baggy yellow tee over a pair of faded jeans and dingy tennis shoes. "I dreamed an angel visited me last night," he said softly. "It was you, wasn't it?"

A grin played across her olive-skinned face. "Si, señor. I was very worried when my pápa brought you here last night."

José nodded wearily. "The last I remember . . . I was watching the sun set on an old, crumbling roadway . . ."

She leaned forward in her seat, eyes animated. "Where are you from, señor?" she asked excitedly. "And what were you doing out in–"

The ragged piece of carpet covering the doorway was suddenly yanked away and a large, heavyset woman peered suspiciously into the room. "I thought I heard someone talking in here," Isabel said brusquely. She looked at José and frowned. "And how are you feeling today, señor? Better?"

"Si, señora." He glanced at the teenaged girl and smiled. "Thanks to your . . . angel."

Isabel shot her daughter a look of disapproval. "It's time for you to go, Teresa. The *caballero* needs his rest."

Teresa lowered her eyes. "Si, Madré." She rose from José's bedside and traipsed meekly towards the door. As she edged through the doorway, she turned and flashed José a smile out of view of her mother's watchful eye.

Isabel dropped a pair of jeans and a faded plaid shirt on top of the wooden table at the far side of the room. "My husband thought you might be able to use these, señor."

José sat up in the bed and smiled. "Gracias, señora."

"Last night, Alfonso and his friends found you along an old, abandoned road out in the desert." She put her hands on her hips and gave José a judgmental stare. "What were you doing out there alone, far from–"

"I was *not* alone," José interrupted. A look of sadness swept over his face as he recalled his journey through the desert. "At one time, there were twenty people in our group."

Her eyebrow rose with surprise. *"Twenty?"*

José took a deep breath and exhaled. "The coyote's men left us– kilometers from the nearest town. The desert slowly took each one of us . . . until I was the only one left."

Isabel lowered her eyes and traced the sign of the cross across her body. "May God rest their souls."

"I knew none of them in the beginning," José lamented, "but at the end, I was proud to call each . . . my friend."

Isabel bowed her head as she mourned his loss. Many of her friends and family had undertaken a similar route to America and did not live to finish their journey. "You must be starving, señor," she said affably. "At the edge of our village there's a place for you to freshen up. When you return, I will have something for you to eat."

"You have been most kind, señora. And please, call me José."

Her mouth curled upward in a smile. "I am Isabel," she said. "And you've already met my little *angel*, Teresa."

"She reminds me a lot of my own daughter, Esmeralda." His face tightened as he thought of his family back in Jiquilpan.

Isabel recognized the longing on his face, having seen it on every migrant's face many times before. "You'll see your family again, señor," she asserted. "God has willed it so."

José gave a fleeting smile but remained silent.

Isabel studied him for a moment before she turned to leave. "We'll talk more after you've freshened up. Welcome to America . . . José."

Her words fell on deaf ears as his thoughts were elsewhere. When he snapped from his reverie several minutes later, he noticed the room was empty. Rising from the bed, he ran a hand through his beard and matted hair, anticipating the simple luxury of a shower and a hot meal after his ordeal in the desert. After a brief inspection of his clothing and knapsack, he was relieved to find his documents and money were not missing. Though his rescuers lived a life of impoverishment, they were not thieves.

José stretched briefly and stripped the ragged shirt from his back. A flash of light caught his attention as an object fell from his shirt pocket and tumbled to the ground. He picked up the heart shaped keepsake, and the last moments he spent with Elena suddenly flashed through his mind. *Why, God?* he asked angrily. *Why did you let me live?*

He clutched the locket and began to weep uncontrollably, knowing his question would remain unanswered until another day.

82

eads snapped as Karen led Ryan past a row of cubicles in the KNBS newsroom. She pretended not to notice the wagging tongues and pointed fingers as they made their way towards the elevator to Stan's office. *Now you've really got something to talk about, you gossip mongering bitches,* she thought wryly.

Ryan glanced around the room and grinned. "Looks like we're the hot news around here today, Karen."

"Why don't we give them something to flap their gums about?" She wrapped her arm around his waist and pulled him close. "Half the people in this room have been spreading lies and innuendos about me for years."

They stepped inside the elevator, and Karen tapped the button for the third floor. "Thanks for stopping by during your lunch break today. I'm sure Stan will be more than surprised to meet you."

He tipped his hat and bowed gracefully. "Glad to be of service, ma'am. Besides, it's always nice to check out my competition."

"Just remember, I don't have any real proof to charge Stan with harassment. I just want to put a stop to this before it goes any further."

Ryan nodded. "Don't worry, I'll make sure he gets *the message.*"

"Don't do anything rash. I still want to hold on to my job after all this shit is over."

"There's no need to worry, Karen. After dealing with gangbangers and other low-lives on a daily basis, your boss will be a piece-of-cake."

"Let's go over the game plan one last time," Karen said. "Try to keep it friendly, but make sure he understands that he's not to bother me anymore. Capishe?"

Ryan pulled out his baton. "Can I use *this* to get my point across?"

She shot him an angry glare.

He shrugged. "Guess not," he said, feigning disappointment.

They stepped out of the elevator and strolled down the hallway until they reached Stan's office. Karen reached up and pressed her hand against Ryan's chest. "Wait here until I call you," she said softly.

Moments later, Karen sauntered into her supervisor's office and flashed a smile. "Hi, Stan," she said sweetly. "I brought someone by to meet you."

He swept his hand across a pile of paperwork on his desk and scowled. "Can't you see I'm busy here?"

She amped up her smile. "Don't worry, I won't take up much of your valuable time." She turned and poked her head out into the hallway. "Ryan, could you step inside, please?"

Ryan's six and half foot frame barged through the doorway and stood imposingly in front of Stan's desk. "It's a pleasure to meet you, Mister Roberts. I'm Karen's friend, Ryan."

Stan's jaw dropped. "It's . . . nice to meet you, too," he stuttered out. "I was beginning to think you were a figment of Karen's imagination."

"No, I'm the real deal," Ryan bragged. "A card-carrying member of L.A.'s finest."

"So what brings you in today?" Stan asked. "Slow crime day?"

Ryan chuckled. "Karen said you wanted to meet me. And after all she's said about *you,* I couldn't wait to meet you *personally.*"

"Well, you can't believe everything you hear. More times than not, the word on the street is nothing but bullshit."

"I know what you mean," Ryan replied. "I've seen so much shit during my years on the force that I've become a cynic for life. If I had a dime for every time a scumbag tried to shirk responsibility for their actions, I could retire for life." He leaned across the desk and met Stan's gaze. "But the *real* world doesn't work that way, does it, Mister Roberts? When you cross the line . . . when you step on the wrong person's toes . . . you better be prepared for *payback*." His voice hardened. "Do you *know* what I mean?"

Stan met Ryan's gaze and nodded dumbly.

Ryan's mouth curled upward in a smile. "I knew you'd understand. Karen said you were a good listener." He stepped back from the desk and glanced at his watch. "Well, would you look at that? It's time for me to protect and serve."

Stan fumbled in his pocket for a cigar. "Leaving so soon? We barely had time to chat."

Ryan turned towards the doorway. "We'll get together again soon," he affirmed. "Even *sooner* if I hear you're–bad."

Stan regarded him cautiously. "I'll try to stay off your shitlist from now on."

"Better to be on Santa's shitlist," Ryan said, "than *mine*." He gave a quick wink and bounded out of the office.

Karen looked at Stan's ashen face and suppressed a smile. "I've got to get going too, Stan. I hope you'll have no problem remembering Ryan's name from now on." She left her supervisor's office and caught up with Ryan by the elevator.

"So how'd I do today, boss?" Ryan asked.

She shot him a crooked grin. "I think he got the message."

Ryan caressed her cheek. "Are you free tonight?"

"*Maybe*. Do you have something special planned?"

"Whatever we do will be special because of you."

"How often have you used that hokey line on someone?"

He shrugged. "This week?"

She gave him a playful jab to the ribs. "Where are you off to next?"

"Just another routine patrol day," Ryan said as he pressed the button for the elevator. "Do you have time to see me out?"

She nodded. "My next interview isn't until three o'clock."

"What's it about?" he asked.

"I'm interviewing several generations of families to get their experiences on how each generation integrated into our society and what they've gained or lost in the transition."

"That's quite an assignment."

"And it all has to fit in a sixty-second news clip."

He whistled. "And I thought my job was a bitch."

The bell chimed overhead, announcing the elevator's arrival. They stepped inside, and Karen pushed the button for the first floor. "Do you ever get bored chasing down bad guys all day?" she asked.

"Not really. Sometimes a bad girl or two gets thrown in the mix to make things interesting."

She ran a finger up his chest. "Do you have something against bad girls, Ryan?"

"That depends. Are *you* bad?"

Her eyes twinkled. "Maybe you'll find out . . . someday."

Before Ryan could respond, the elevator door sprang open to the newsroom. They moved past two boarding employees and headed for the exit, once more ignoring the stares and whispers from the newsroom. A few moments later, they slipped out of the building and strolled towards the station's lushly landscaped parking lot.

Karen looked around the lot and chuckled. "Where's your cruiser?" she quipped. "Did someone make off with it while you were here?"

"My partner took it out on patrol while I handled the situation with your boss. She should be here any minute to pick me up."

"I thought you patrolled alone."

"I *do*," he grumbled. "But I've temporarily taken over the training schedule of another officer out on disability leave."

"So how's she doing so far?" Karen asked.

"Okay," he replied, shrugging. "So far."

"You mean, so far as a *female* is concerned?"

"I didn't say that."

"You didn't *say* it," Karen teased. "But you *meant* it."

He frowned. "That's not what I meant at all. Don't go putting words in my mouth."

"Then what did you mean?"

"Just what I *said*," he affirmed. "Up to now, she hasn't given me any reason to be critical of her performance. But at some point, she'll–"

A black and white car suddenly streaked through the parking lot and screeched to a stop directly in front of them.

Karen leaned up to kiss his cheek. "Thanks for helping me out today. I don't know what I would have done without you."

Ryan grinned. "All in a day's work." He pointed to his baton. "And if your boss gets out of line again, next time I'll use a little more– persuasion."

"That won't be necessary," she said. "Stan really is a good listener. Oh, I almost forgot–what should I wear for tonight?"

"Something casual. I'll call later and let you know what time–"

The horn blared, startling the both of them.

Ryan's brow furrowed. "I guess my partner's getting a little impatient." He whacked the side of his head with his hand. "Where are my freakin' *manners?* Let me introduce you to her."

He ambled over to the cruiser and stuck his head through the passenger side window. Seconds later, Patricia stepped from the vehicle and strode in Karen's direction.

Karen's eyes widened. *This is Ryan's new partner? She'd be at home on the cover of Playboy magazine.*

Ryan gestured towards his partner and smiled. "Karen, this is my partner, Patricia Ruiz," he said. "Patricia, this is my good friend, Karen Mitchell."

Patricia extended her hand. "Nice to meet you, Miss Mitchell."

Karen forced a smile as she shook Patricia's hand. "The pleasure is mine, officer Ruiz," she said curtly. "It's always good to see one of our own defending the territory."

"I've still got a lot to learn," Patricia confided. She reached up and squeezed Ryan's arm. "But Ryan is a very good teacher."

Karen's eyes narrowed. *Yeah, I'll just bet he is.*

83

Kati looked on with alarm as the spiky haired waitress carelessly plopped her lunch on the table. Her food slid precariously to the edge of the plate and barely missed falling into her lap.

Sweeping a vacant gaze across the table, the waitress popped her gum and said, "Will there be anything else?"

Kati pushed her plate forward. "Not for me." She glanced across the table at her brother. "Daniel?"

He looked ravenously at his burger and licked his lips. "I'm all set, thanks."

The waitress scooted off before the last syllable cleared his throat. Daniel watched her walk away and frowned. "Boy, I've gotten better service from an Indian call center," he said dryly.

"Maybe she's busy today," Kati said sympathetically.

Daniel scanned the umbrella topped tables on the virtually deserted patio and shook his head. "I don't think so," he groused. "And she didn't even notice how close you came to wearing your meal."

Kati noshed on her hot pastrami sandwich and shrugged. "No . . . harm . . . done," she squeezed out between bites. "It's probably her first day on the job."

"You're too forgiving, sis." He picked up his burger and wolfed half of it down in two bites. "Well, the service may suck, but there's nothing wrong with the food."

Kati slathered some ketchup on her fries and nodded. "I'll have to thank Amanda for recommending this place the next time I see her."

Daniel scarfed down the rest of his burger and belched loudly.

Kati winced. "Are you *ever* going to grow up?"

He grinned mischievously. "Why start now?"

She nibbled on a fry and gave a disapproving shake of her head. "Some things never change."

"Some things *have* changed, sis."

Her eyebrow rose. "What does that mean?"

"Why'd you ask me out to lunch today? It's not like we get together regularly and–"

"Then maybe we *should*," she snapped.

"Did Calvin put you up to this?"

"Calvin?" She blinked. "He'd freak out if he knew we were getting together today."

"Then *why* are we here?"

"To clear up any differences between us," she replied. "I still don't understand why last weekend's get-together was such a . . . disaster."

Daniel's eyes dropped. "It's my fault, sis. I shouldn't have let my emotions get the best of me." He took a deep breath and exhaled. "You're right, I've still got a lot of growing up to do."

"You're not entirely to blame, Daniel. I had hoped that the friction between our families might have disappeared after all these years."

"You've always viewed the world through a pair of rose colored glasses, Kati." He popped a fry into his mouth and chewed slowly. "I, on the other hand, have always looked at the world–if you'll forgive the expression–in terms of black and white."

Kati gave a sour smile. "They're really nice people, Daniel–if you take the time to know them."

"Even Cerise?" he asked dryly.

"There's a—pardon the pun—black sheep in every family."

Daniel chuckled. "I still don't understand why you married Calvin. There were other men you—"

Her eyes narrowed. "How often have we had this—discussion?"

He met her gaze. "Maybe we should have it . . . one more time."

Kati slumped into her seat and sighed. "I *love* him, Daniel—it's as simple as that. The color of his skin never made any difference to me; it's what he's like *underneath* that won my heart over in the end. Calvin's not perfect—no man is of course—but he's the perfect mate for me."

"I guess my glasses aren't as . . . color-blind . . . as yours."

"You can change," she said softly. "Isn't ten years long enough to put aside your anger . . . your prejudice—"

"I'm not *prejudiced*," he spat.

"We're *all* prejudiced, Daniel, whether we want to admit it or not. But, we need to face our fears head on and not stick our head in the sand and pretend the problems don't exist."

"Did you have any—fears—about marrying Calvin?"

"Of course. Did you think for a *moment* that our marriage would be the proverbial walk in the park?"

"I'm sure it hasn't been easy . . ."

"Easy?" She let out a short, harsh laugh. "Do you know how often we've been harassed or looked on disapprovingly by people who feel their *values* are beyond reproach?"

Daniel looked on but remained silent.

"Do you think it's *easy* watching your kids put up with derogatory remarks almost everyday? Do you think it's *easy* to turn the other cheek when your own family won't take the first step to accept you?"

Daniel looked uneasily around the patio. "Kati, people are beginning to stare . . ."

"I don't care!" she hissed. "Maybe they'll *learn* something."

Daniel reached across the table and touched her hand. "Kati," he said softly. "You've made your . . . point."

"Then are you going to stop asking me to *justify* my relationship with Calvin?"

He pinched his lip. "There's still so much I don't understand."

"Calvin's family is not much different from our own, Daniel," she said. "They share the same needs . . . the same dreams that every family wants from life."

"Where should I–start?" he asked.

"You can *start* by looking at the world as an ever changing mix of grays–rather than in black in white. You can *start* by embracing our differences, rather than ridiculing or fearing them." A smile touched her face. "And finally Daniel, you can *start* by keeping your mind open . . . along with your heart."

Daniel smiled wanly. "I'll try, sis," he muttered. "For you."

Kati grasped his hands. "No, Daniel," she declared. "You'll try–for *you*."

84

Feeling refreshed from a shower and his first meal in days, José took some time to wander around the migrant camp. He strolled down the rutted dirt path that served as the street, watching the women attend to chores and care for the children. As he drifted down the dusty road between the ramshackle dwellings, he was keenly aware that he was virtually the only adult male in the encampment. Most had left at the break of dawn and would not return until late in the day, their bodies beat down from a backbreaking day in the fields.

Originally no more than a few tattered tents strewn at the base of the Gila Mountains, the migrant encampment had grown exponentially during the last several years. A few budding entrepreneurs had set up a small general store and walk-in clinic in the transient community, even though the simple necessities of indoor plumbing and electricity remained a dream.

As he neared the outskirts of the encampment, José saw Teresa chatting with several friends under a copse of palo verde trees. He lifted his arm and shouted, "Hola, Teresa."

Teresa turned at his voice and smiled. "Hola!" She broke away from her friends and strolled over to meet him. "How are you feeling today, señor?" she asked amiably.

"Bueno," he replied. "Thanks to you."

She bowed her head shyly. "I'm glad I could help, señor."

"Please, Teresa–call me José."

Her mouth turned upward in a grin. "Will you be staying here long–José?"

José recalled his vow to Elena and shook his head. "I must go to Los Angeles," he replied. "There's a promise I have to keep."

"Have you found work there?"

"No, but I am–hopeful."

"I wish we could move there," she muttered. "I've heard that everyone lives in a great big house and drives a fancy car. They must all be very happy people."

José forced a smile. *Some day Teresa, you'll learn that money can't buy you happiness.* "I think you'll find the happiness you're looking for sooner than you think."

"Do you really think so? My pápa wants to go to a big city to find a better job, but he can never save enough money to take us with him."

"Where does he work now?"

"Wherever he can," she said. "Today he's out picking peppers in the fields." A look of sadness swept across her face. "He hates working in the fields. Every night he comes home and swears as mamá tries to massage the stiffness out of his back."

José nodded sympathetically. "Your father is trying his best, Teresa. You must never lose faith in him."

She nibbled on her lip and nodded. "I won't, José." Her expression suddenly brightened. "Oh! Will you be staying here tonight?"

"I think so. Why?"

"Tonight is my Quinceañera," she exclaimed. "I would like you to be there."

José understood the importance of the Quinceañera in Teresa's life. In a coming of age ceremony dating back to the Aztecs, she would leave the trappings of childhood behind and become–a woman. "I would be *honored*, señorita."

Teresa clapped gleefully. "I must go. My aunt is waiting to fit my dress." She ran a short distance down the dusty path and turned to wave. "I will see you tonight, José!"

José smiled, and for one brief moment, found himself . . . home.

85

The welding gun sliced through the tubular frame of the wheelchair, sending a spray of sparks across the floor of the dimly lit garage.

Mark snapped the rear support frame from the base of the wheelchair and chuckled. "So much for *the top of the line* UltraTrac Five-Thousand." He stacked the frame next to an ever-growing pile of parts on top of his workbench.

Using the workbench to steady himself, he pried the seat cushion from its moorings, revealing a tangle of wires to the wheelchair's servomechanisms. One by one, he probed each circuit with a multimeter and jotted some notes on a pad.

When his examination of the circuitry was complete, he gathered his crutches from the side of the workbench and hoisted himself to a standing position. He hobbled towards a small storage room at the rear of the garage while Jimi Hendrix wrenched unearthly sounds from his guitar on a local rock station.

Once inside the tightly confined room, Mark winced as he jostled a stack of large, crumbling cardboard boxes away from the wall. Several years ago, moving the boxes would have been an easy chore, but now even the most simple of tasks were an arduous endeavor.

Suddenly, one of the boxes ruptured and spewed its contents across the floor. A bright green plastic container rolled across the floor, and Mark knelt down to take a closer look.

Recognition dawned on his face as he looked the canister over. *I thought Mom threw this out a long time ago, while I was serving overseas.* He gripped the container and twisted off the lid, eagerly anticipating what he would find inside.

A maroon and chrome colored figurine tumbled into his hand, and Mark felt as though he was being reunited with a long lost friend from his childhood. And in a way, he was.

Growing up in the military, he rarely spent more than a year or two in one location before his father was transferred to another outpost. As a result, he made few lasting friends, and spent most of his free time pursuing solitary activities. One of those pastimes was creating complex imaginary worlds populated by characters produced by the various toy manufacturers. Most of his playthings had been given away or discarded long ago, but the figurine he held in his hand had somehow survived that tragic fate.

The Transformer known as Inferno stared mutely into his eyes, beckoning him to the make-believe world he had left behind. As if they had a mind of their own, his fingers manipulated the joints of the autobot and transformed him to his fire truck alter ego. He pulled several more figurines from the container, and soon Blaster, Shockwave, and Bonecrusher stood on the shelf next to Inferno to continue their battles from yore.

Mark stood back to admire his work for several moments, then turned his attention back to the task at hand. He shoved the remaining boxes to the other side of the room, revealing a large steel chest concealed in a cavity in the wall. Dropping to his knees, he pulled the chest from the recess and inserted a cylindrically shaped key into the hardened lock. The lock sprang open with a satisfying click, and Mark took a deep breath before flinging the heavy lid upward.

Inside the specially hardened container lay fifty kilograms of C-4 plastique explosive, still shrink-wrapped in their protective acrylic sleeves.

A smile traced Mark's face as his gaze drifted across the military grade explosive. *After all these years, the Army still doesn't know it's missing.*

After his rehabilitation in Japan made it clear that his Special Ops career was over, the Army transferred him to a less physically demanding job as Lieutenant Commander of the 73rd Ordnance Battalion at Fort Gordon. Though he enjoyed this new role at first, his satisfaction waned as the nerve gas took an increasing debilitating toll on his body. When the Army moved him to less responsible positions as a result of his affliction, he set on a course of retribution for the egregious treatment he and numerous others had received from the military through the years. *Uncle Sam never really cared about us,* he reflected. *We were only pawns in the politicians' endless grab for wealth and power.*

In his role as an ordnance-training officer, it was child's play to short the munitions from the training exercises and remove it from the camp by taping it to the small of his back. The Army had grown too complacent, or more likely–too arrogant–to suspect one of their own would steal from the base's stockpile.

Unsurprisingly, no one noticed or inquired about the missing ordnance. And here it remained, hidden from the eyes of nosy neighbors and government agencies for the last two years.

But, never let it be said that I'm a thief, Mark thought wryly. *Because I'm about to give every gram of it–back.*

86

Karen dug her mouth into a ball of cotton candy and giggled. "God, I haven't tasted this stuff in years," she said. "It sure brings back a lot of fond memories from my childhood."

Ryan took a bite out his corn dog and nodded. "Mine, too. For some reason, junk food always tastes better at the amusement park."

Karen moved her gaze across the colorfully lit rides and attractions lining the end of the Santa Monica Pier. "So why'd you invite me to Pacific Park tonight?"

"When I left you this afternoon, it looked like you could use a little cheering up. Are you still worried about your boss getting even for what happened at the office today?"

She pinched her cheek. *No, I'm worried about what you've been teaching your pretty little friend, Patricia.* "A little," she lied. "But, I'm more concerned about how I'll do at the Pangaea Festival. With my luck, I'll probably make a real horse's ass out of myself in front of a national audience."

Ryan draped his arm around her shoulder and smiled. "No way, José," he declared. "You're gonna knock 'em dead."

"Yeah, you're probably right." She sighed. "I wish I had your confidence, Ryan."

"Thanks for the compliment, but I wasn't always as confident as I appear to be." He looked up at the Ferris wheel, briefly enraptured by its gyrating display of light and color. "Hmmm . . . you're not afraid of heights, are you?"

Karen watched uneasily as the circular structure spun through space, its riders one thin restraining bar away from death. "Who, me?" she replied, trying to keep the tremor from her voice. "Besides, you'll be there to protect me if anything goes wrong." She clutched his waist. "Right?"

"You bet. Protect and serve is my middle name."

She smiled wanly. *Yeah, I get the protection, and your little rookie pin-up gets the service. What were you teaching her today–just how fast you can whip out your revolver?*

"Are you all right, Karen? You seem . . . distracted."

"Everything's cool," she muttered. "I was just thinking about something that happened earlier today."

Ryan cocked his head. "Oh? What's that?"

Before she could reply, the ride attendant ushered them into a seat on the Ferris wheel. Within seconds, they were soaring into the air, the city stretching before them in a matrix of twinkling lights.

Karen leaned over the railing, momentarily forgetting her fear of heights. "Isn't it beautiful? The lights of the city just seem to go on forever."

He wrapped his arm around her shoulder and nodded. "It's hard to believe such a beautiful city could bring so much pain into people's lives."

"It must be difficult to see the dark side of humanity everyday. How do you ever find the strength to carry on?"

"You learn to deal with it. Every job has its–drawbacks."

"How's . . . Patricia dealing with it so far?" she asked casually.

"Okay, I guess. I haven't heard any complaints so far."

"Why didn't you say anything about her to me earlier?"

He shrugged. "I don't know. It probably just slipped my mind."

She cast him an angry glare. *"Really?"*

His eyebrow twitched. "What's this all about, Karen?"

"You tell me," she asked curtly.

"Tell you *what?"* he asked. "There's nothing to tell."

"Then why didn't you say anything about your partner before today?"

Realization suddenly swept across Ryan's face. "Oh, now I'm beginning to understand. You're *jealous.*"

She crossed her arms and frowned. "I am *not* jealous."

He chuckled. "Sure you are. It's written all over your face like a bad case of acne."

"Give me *one* good reason why I should be jealous."

"I'll give you three . . . 38-24-36."

"So you *have* noticed," she said coolly.

"Of course I've noticed. As Ruiz's training officer, it's my responsibility to watch her every move."

Karen shrugged away his arm and scooted to the edge of the seat. *"Men!"* she hissed. "All you care about is your own personal gratification."

"Is that what you think?" Ryan said. "That I'm seeing Ruiz behind your back?" He took a deep breath and exhaled. "I'm disappointed in you, Karen. I thought we trusted each other."

Her expression softened. "I . . . trust you. But men have lied to me so often that I don't know what the truth is anymore."

"Then believe *this,*" he asserted. "I would *never* do anything to hurt you. And if you'll give me half a chance to explain, you'll see why Ruiz doesn't mean a thing to me."

She turned and met his gaze. "I'm . . . listening."

"Do you remember our conversation earlier today? You thought I was overly critical of Ruiz's performance because she's a woman."

"I was just teasing you."

"But there was some bias to your accusation, correct?

She shrugged. "A little."

"It doesn't matter. I wasn't passing judgment on Ruiz based on her gender, but on her time in the field. Any seasoned cop can tell you that rookies manage to eff-up at some point."

"Is this observation based on your own personal experience?"

Ryan lowered his eyes. "Yes." He turned and stared at the twinkling lights of the city while he gathered his thoughts. "I've never told this story to anyone so what you're about to hear is strictly off the record, understand?"

Karen nodded but remained silent.

"Around thirteen years ago, I was the rookie in training. Fresh out of the academy and hell-bent on changing the world, the division commander paired me with a respected veteran officer to continue my training. A respected *female* vet." His expression grew somber. "It all seems like . . . a lifetime ago."

"At first, it was strictly a professional relationship. Demanding–yet compassionate–she was a gifted mentor in every way. Under her guidance, I shed the immaturity of youth and took the next step in becoming . . . a man."

"Though we both tried to deny it at first, our relationship eventually turned personal. I don't know if it was her looks or her personality that first captured my heart, but one day I woke up and found myself in love with her."

"Is she still with the department?" Karen asked.

Ryan's face tightened. "She left . . . a long time ago." He said it so softly that Karen had to strain to hear the words.

"What happened to her?"

Ryan's eyes became distant, unfocused. "We responded to a domestic disturbance call just off Pico Boulevard. Nothing out of the routine–just some a-hole wailing on his girlfriend. We were the first to arrive on the scene, and Joanne–funny how hard it is to say her name now–was halfway to the house before I even got out of the car." He gave a sour smile. "She was like that . . . always giving a hundred and ten percent . . . in everything she did."

He took a deep breath and paused; unlocking long closed doors to his mind. "But, she never had a chance. Before she was halfway to the house, the perp shoved a shotgun out the window and cut her down." He tilted his head back and stared into the sky. "I can still see her . . . twisting through the air . . . her pistol sparkling in the sunlight as it flew from her outstretched hand."

"She hit the walkway . . . pleading for my help." He ran a hand across his face and bit back tears. "But I may as well have been on the other side of the planet for all I did for her that day."

"How did it . . . end?" Karen asked gently.

"From that point on, everything became a blur. Backup arrived . . . and after a fierce gunfight, the perp checked out by committing suicide." A tear drifted down his cheek. "But, not soon enough...to save Joanne."

Karen touched his arm. "I'm sorry, Ryan."

"Our relationship was a secret, so I put on the brave face and managed to soldier on. There was never time to mourn her loss, even though a part of me had died that day."

Karen lowered her eyes. "I've been a fool. There was never any reason to mistrust you." She swallowed and forced a smile. "Can you ever forgive me?"

"You didn't know, Karen," he replied. "But can you understand why I can't become involved with Ruiz? Though Joanne left me a long time ago, the pain from that day will never be forgotten."

"Do you miss her?"

Ryan nodded slowly and smiled. "She gave her life, so I might live."

87

Decked out in a full-length white dress festooned with gold embroidery, Teresa knelt at a makeshift alter to begin her Quinceañera while a bevy of *damas* and *chamberlans* looked on. Father Madera smiled warmly at the friends and family gathered for the ceremony, and then met Teresa's eyes to begin his invocation.

> *"Today I offer you, O Lord, my youth.*
> *Guide me in my actions,*
> *And call on me to live in the likeness of you forever.*
> *Grant me the grace to make this journey,*
> *and dedicate myself in the service of my brothers and sisters.*
> *I also offer myself to you, Mary, Mother of Jesus;*
> *Be my strength, and my guide so that I may learn what it is like*
> *to be a woman.*
> *Give me the power to change hearts, to live in unselfish ways,*
> *and to hear the word of God so that I may become a worthy*
> *daughter of yours in the eyes of our Lord."*

At the edge of the congregation, José brushed a tear from his eye as he watched the service unfold. *Will I be able to return to Jiquilpan two years from now to celebrate my own daughter's Quinceañera?*

A short time later, the ceremony drew to a close and the gathering moved towards a cluster of tables set up for the reception. A portable sound system was coaxed to life and Alfonso raised a glass of champagne to commemorate the occasion. "Today, my daughter Teresa has finally become a woman," he declared proudly. "Please join my family in celebrating this very important day."

The guests hoisted their glasses in a toast, and Teresa clutched her father's arm to begin the traditional first dance of the evening. "Thank you, Pápa," she said, "for making my Quinceañera a very special day."

He wrapped his arms around her and glided effortlessly across the ground. "It was my privilege, hija. You've brought nothing but joy into my life since the day you were born."

After several more dances with the chamberlan and family friends, Teresa wandered over to talk to José. "I'm glad you came to my Quinceañera today, José."

"It was a beautiful ceremony," he replied. "For a very beautiful–woman."

She smiled shyly. "You are most kind. Today will be the start of a very important journey for me."

"Treasure it always, for a woman's role is never to be taken lightly." He reached into his pocket and placed a small golden ring into her hand. "A gift . . . to celebrate your journey."

She slipped the band on her finger and smiled. "It's beautiful, José." Tears welled in her eyes. "I . . . I don't know how to thank you."

"My daughter gave it to me. She said it would bring me luck."

"Your daughter?" A frown traced her face. "You should keep this, José. I shouldn't take something that belongs–"

He took her hands and smiled. "I want you to have it, Teresa. The day I met your family was one of the luckiest days of my life."

Teresa admired the ring as it sparkled in the sun's waning light. "I will always think of you, José. Every time I look at it." Her expression suddenly grew dour. "How soon before you . . . leave?"

"Tomorrow morning," he replied. "One of your father's friends has business in Bakersfield and has offered to drop me off in Los Angeles along the way."

"I was hoping you'd stay, but I knew your destiny lay elsewhere."

José looked up in the cloudless sky and sighed. "Destiny," he muttered. "Can any of us truly know our destiny?"

"God has plans for you, José. As one day you'll come to see."

He gave a wry smile. "Mmmm . . . for one who has just entered womanhood, you have the wisdom of one far beyond your years."

She giggled. "Haven't you learned by now, José? We women are *born* wise."

88

"That's enough, Andrew," Clarise panted, "You've worn me out." She rolled over on her side and stared at him with a mischievous glint in her eyes. "I can be more than an occasional romp in the sack for you, Andrew," she purred, "Much, much more."

Andrew moved his gaze across her voluptuous body but remained silent. It had been years since Clarise Dumont had been a part of his life, and time had not treated her kindly. A perennial favorite on Tinseltown's 'famous for being famous' celebrity list, when the final chapter was written on her life, her antics would be the only remembrance of an otherwise lackluster career.

"Andrew, did you hear a word I said?" Clarise asked, frowning.

He blinked. "I . . . I heard you, Clarise."

"Then what do you think?" she asked. "Have you given any thought on what role I'll play in your next project?"

Andrew lay beside her in the bed and stared at the ceiling. Nearly a decade ago he gave Clarise a chance to star in one of his productions, capitalizing on her youth and naivety to the benefit of both their careers. She quickly became a rising star, but soon fell from the public's grace when the party life quashed her fledgling career. When she showed up at his table in one of L.A.'s poshest eateries the previous evening, he almost choked on his meal.

"Andrew, you still haven't answered me," she said, exasperation tinging her voice. "What part do you see me playing in your next project?"

"I don't know," he muttered. "But I'll make sure it's something suitable for your–talents."

Clarise wrapped her arms across her chest and squealed. "I knew I could count on you!" She ran a finger down his chest and smiled. "Won't it be *thrilling* to work together again after all these years?"

Andrew cast Clarise a sideways glance and compressed his lips. *Thrilling isn't the first word that popped into my mind, my dear.* Still, there was no reason why they couldn't work together again. Despite her tendency for flamboyance, her ample fan base could add considerably to his next project's bottom line if he played his cards right. *And hopefully,* he mused, *won't leave me the laughingstock of town.*

"I hope you have something dramatic in mind for me," she groused. "I'm tired of playing in comedic roles."

Andrew stifled a laugh. *Clarise, your entire life has been a comedic role.* "Don't worry, dear. With my help, your star will soar higher than ever before."

She sighed. "I hope you're right. You don't know how hard it's been for me lately." She moved her hand under the covers and giggled. "Or maybe you *do*."

Andrew grinned and returned his gaze towards the ceiling, momentarily distracted in thought. *For the first time in months, everything seems to be going my way. My current production is nearly in the can and the funding for my next two projects is all but secured. And in the next minute or so, I'll be making love again to one of the most beautiful starlets in town. I couldn't ask any more from life if I wrote the script myself.*

A wave of anxiety suddenly swept over his face. *Then why can't I shake this feeling of impending doom?*

89

Kati read the headline on the cover of her woman's magazine and yawned. *Mmmm, another boring article on how to improve your married life. Don't these psychologists have enough to do without screwing up everyone's lives?*

She thumbed to the inside of the magazine and squinted at the tiny photo of the author. Impeccably garbed in latest trendy fashion, she beamed from the page with a glowing smile. Upon closer inspection, Kati noticed the author had nary a wrinkle on her porcelain smooth complexion. *I'd probably look that good too if I visited a plastic surgeon regularly,* she mused.

Sighing, she placed the magazine in her lap and ran her fingers across her face. *I may not be as glamorous looking as the author, but she probably hasn't dropped two kids or done a lick of housework in her lifetime.* She studied the author's picture again and smiled wryly. *Photoshopped.*

Kati turned and watched Calvin snore blissfully beside her in the bed. *I bet he never worries about growing old,* she grumbled.

She traced her hand gently down his back as he slept. Though he'd gained some weight and lost some hair, there was no mistaking the man who awkwardly greeted her in the campus cafeteria twelve years ago.

Her face suddenly slackened. *Twelve years—was it really that long ago?*

She nudged his arm. "Calvin?" she said softly.

He uttered a grunt and twisted away from her.

She poked him in the ribs. "Honey—wake up."

Calvin opened a bleary eye towards the clock on the nightstand and moaned. *It's almost midnight,* he groused. *Doesn't she know I have to get up for work in the morning?*

"Honey," she cooed over his shoulder. "Do you still think I'm attractive?"

He clutched his pillow and winced. *Please, Lord. Please let me have the—right—answer.*

"Honey . . ." she repeated.

Calvin flipped over on his back, and was seized with dread when he saw the magazine in her lap. *Oh, shit—I'm screwed. Who knows what she's gleaned from the pages of that women's magazine?*

She looked on expectantly, awaiting his response.

"You've never been more beautiful," he ventured, "than you are right now."

Her mouth turned upward in a smile. "How do you feel about our marriage?" she asked. "Is there anything you'd . . . change?"

He flashed her a smile. "Not a thing, Kati," he said emphatically. "Not—*anything.*"

She held up the magazine. "Do you really feel that way, dear?" she asked. "Leticia Kellerman, a noted psychologist, wrote an article in this magazine on how—"

He pried the magazine from her hands and tossed it to the floor. "I don't need some *psychologist* to tell me how I should feel about you."

She giggled. "You're sweet."

He sat up in the bed and nuzzled her cheek. "There's a lot more . . . sweetness . . . where that came from."

Her eyes narrowed. "Don't you have to be up early for work?"

He shrugged. "I can always make time for—"

"Is that all I am to you, Mister Taylor? Your personal *sex* toy?"

"Not really. You're a pretty good cook and maid, too."

"Mmmm . . . it's nice to know I'm *appreciated* around her."

He patted the sheets and grinned roguishly. "Come over here Missus Taylor, and I'll show you some—appreciation."

WEDNESDAY

90

The battered pickup struck a pothole as it cruised down the street, sending a painful jolt through José's spine. He sat up and looked through the camper shell's crazed window, fighting back a wave of nausea from the exhaust fumes leaking into the interior.

Slumping against the back of the cargo bed, José fished Elena's locket from his knapsack. He watched it sparkle in the camper's gloomy interior, determined more than ever to live for those that died reaching for their dreams.

The wail of a siren suddenly pierced the camper's noisy interior. José peered out the back window and saw a police car drawing up ominously from the rear.

The pickup moved to the right and stopped beside the roadway. José looked at the cruiser's flashing lightbar and tried to remain calm, even though every instinct urged him to flee for the streets towards safety. *Have I come so far . . . sacrificed so much . . . only to have my journey end before I've reached my goal?*

José watched uneasily as a woman and a man exited the black and white vehicle and walked towards the truck. The woman was of medium height, slender, and very pretty. The other officer–a dark haired man much larger and more menacing in appearance–took a cursory glance under the truck and headed towards the driver.

José scrunched into a corner of the bed, hoping against hope that the *policia* would not search inside the back of the truck. Through the thin fiberglass wall of the camper shell, he listened as the dark haired man conversed with the driver.

"Hola," the officer said gruffly. "¿Puedo su licencia y registro de conductor por favor?"

José listened to the driver respond to the officer and then stiffened as the door of the camper shell suddenly tilted upward.

Patricia squinted as she peered into the camper's dimly lit interior. "Looks like we've got another one back here, Ryan."

"All right," he replied. "I'll be back to check things out after I finish with the driver."

Patricia watched José fidget and nodded. "Take your time. He's not going–anywhere." She leaned into the camper and flashed José a friendly smile. "There's no need to be afraid, señor," she said in Spanish. "Can I see your papers please?"

José shot her a puzzled look.

"Documentos?" she repeated.

His eyes brightened. "Si, señora." Reaching into his knapsack, he pulled the papers he had received from the coyote and placed them in Patricia's outstretched hand.

Patricia glanced at the documents and quickly realized they were counterfeit. She watched José squirm and wondered how far he had traveled for their paths to meet. *In another time, in another place,* she reflected, *it might have been me in the back of this truck.* For a moment, the fact that they shared a common culture bound them together. And though her mind said he should be deported, her heart told her otherwise. After several long seconds searching her conscience, she handed the documents back to José. "Gracias, señor. Have a nice day."

After his conversation with the driver was over, Ryan marched to the back of the truck and looked into the camper. "He check out?"

Patricia glanced at José and pinched her lip. "Yeah, he's . . . clean."

Ryan signaled to the driver to move back on the road. The truck edged forward and joined the traffic moving west on Venice Boulevard.

A giggle escaped Patricia's lips as the truck drove away.

"Mind letting me in on the joke?" Ryan asked, puzzled.

"It's your Spanish," she teased. "You sound just like a gringo."

"No one's ever complained before, *Miss Ruiz.*"

Her eyebrow lifted upward. "Uh, oh–looks like I touched a nerve here."

Ryan got into the cruiser and slammed the door. "At least I try to bridge the language barrier, Patricia," he grumbled. "Which is *more* than you can say for most of the immigrants here. All they're looking for is a fast buck or an easy way to scam the system. They don't give a damn about this country or the principles it was founded upon."

"They're not all like that, Ryan," she said gently. "It's not easy leaving your world behind and starting over in a strange land. And to make matters worse, the natives of your adopted country aren't exactly welcoming you with open arms. It shouldn't be any surprise that a newly displaced immigrant needs some vestiges of their homeland in order to survive."

"I agree–as far as first generation immigrants are concerned. But, second and third generation families from Latin America and Asia are increasingly reluctant to join mainstream American culture. They refuse to let go of their heritage and wall themselves off from society in their own clannish communities. All you need to do is drive through half the cities in the Southland to see what I'm talking about."

"If I didn't know better, Ryan, I'd swear you were a racist."

"Racist?" His face slackened. "Why would you think that?"

"Your contempt seems to be directed at *specific* ethnic groups who choose to make their home here."

"I'll admit to having some prejudices, but racism isn't one of them. I'm just concerned that our country's European heritage is slowly being overrun by the current wave of immigrants coming into this country. Their refusal to assimilate into our culture is a trend I find . . . disturbing."

"Are you saying there's no room for change in American culture?"

He shook his head. "Without change, a culture will stagnate and eventually die. But, any country must have certain ties to bind it together. And the most important of these bonds is a common language. If everyone in America chose to speak their native language, suspicion and distrust would soon be endemic across our nation."

"I see your point," she said. "But your tendency to cling to America's European roots still smells racist, even if you choose to wrap it in a nationalistic flag."

"Perhaps," he replied. "But, nationalism by definition tends to exclude those who do not accept its principles. You adopt the culture and customs of the country you choose to live in—or you don't. There is no middle ground."

"Why can't we—as Rodney King once said—just all get along?"

"Be careful what you wish for," he said dryly. "Or you'll be looking for another job."

She shot him a crooked grin. "You know, that's one career change I wouldn't mind making."

91

ndrew sipped on his cappuccino and scanned the shoreline from the comfort of his Malibu Beach home. *Just the usual cast of characters out for an early morning stroll,* he mused. *Joggers, sun worshippers, and the occasional bum looking for a handout.*

Out of the corner of his eye, he noticed a scraggly, middle-aged man try to make a pinch on a young couple along the beach. Seconds later an argument ensued, and the couple chased the scruffy looking man several hundred feet down the shoreline.

Andrew shook his head and chuckled. *Better luck next time, loser.*

Downing the rest of his drink, Andrew left the balcony and wandered over to a stack of mail parked on the kitchen countertop. He thumbed through the envelopes and packets and sorted it into three piles based on priority: answer immediately, no hurry and forgetaboutit. Unsurprisingly, most of the correspondence wound up in the last pile.

As he flipped the last envelope into the trash, a supermarket tabloid laying on the edge of the countertop caught his attention. *Mmmm . . . Clarise must have brought this in when she followed me home last night.* He looked over the splashy cover and grinned. *I wonder whose sorry ass is getting reamed this week?*

Riffling through the first several pages, Andrew saw nothing of interest until a single column article on page five made his stomach lurch.

Has the Golden Boy Lost His Touch?

by Rachel Phillips, RUMOR magazine staff

Known throughout the industry for his "Midas Touch," Andrew Landis' latest project may be destined for failure before its box office debut. Industry insiders have confirmed that *Dawn Rising* is thirty million over budget and far behind its shooting schedule. Director Ron Burgess and lead actress Angela Carson have shut down production several times due to creative differences over the script. Sources close to *Rumor* magazine have stated that Landis and his wunderkind director have contributed to the general turmoil by constantly bickering over the film's content and lack of direction on the set.

Andrew crumpled the tabloid and hurled it against the wall. "Damn it, Ron," he hissed. "You've fucked up for the last time." He fumbled the phone from his pocket and punched in his assistant's number.

Erin's voice trilled through the line several seconds later. "Good morning, Mister Landis. How are you–"

"I need to talk to Ron," Andrew said brusquely. *"Now."*

"He's not on the set, Mister Landis. He left with a crew early this morning to reshoot a scene in Ojai." She paused. "Should I page him?"

"Yes, it's urgent."

Andrew rapped his fingers on the countertop while he waited. *Why didn't Ron lock down the set to keep this from happening?* he fumed. *Just wait till I get my hands on–*

"He's not answering his phone, Mr. Landis. Would you like to leave a message?"

Yeah, he groused. *Ask him how far he'd like my foot up his ass.* "When is he scheduled to return?"

"Sometime around three."

"Okay, tell him to meet me at my office at four."

"You got it. Will there be anything else?"

"That's all," Andrew said. "Thanks, Erin."

"Have a nice day, Mister Landis."

A pair of hands wrapped around Andrew's eyes as he placed the phone on the countertop. "Guess who?" Clarise purred into his ear.

Andrew tugged her hands away and scowled. "I don't have time for games right now, Clarise."

"That's funny," she said coyly. "You had plenty of *time* for games last night, as I recall."

"That was *last* night, Clarise. In case you haven't noticed–today is a brand-new day." He rubbed his temples with his fingertips and sighed. "With a brand new set of . . . problems."

"Is something wrong, Andrew?" she asked, concerned.

He shook his head. "Just some loose ends I need to take care of."

"Is there some way I can help? I can be *very* persuasive."

"This problem can't be fixed with your kind of–persuasion."

"Are you sure?" she said, giggling. "It's always worked for me."

"Yeah, and look where it's gotten you."

She shot him a puzzled look. "What's that supposed to mean?"

"Have you taken a good look at yourself lately?"

She ran her hands down her body. "I can't see anything to complain about."

Andrew chortled. "You're a *joke,* Clarise. The laughingstock of town. And you know what's really funny? Everyone seems to be in on the joke but *you.*"

Sadness touched her eyes. "What kind of friend would–"

"*Friend?*" Andrew let out a short, harsh laugh. "There are no *friends* in this town, Clarise–only *users*. And you've been used–and abused–so many times that an entire industry has been built up around your antics." He shook his head and sneered. "You don't need a friend, Clarise–what you need is a psychiatrist."

Tears welled in her eyes. "Have you always . . . felt this way?"

"Do I even need to *answer* that?"

Her eyes narrowed. "I may be a laughingstock, Andrew, but there's one thing I have that you'll never possess in a million years."

"Oh? And what might that be, dear?"

She smiled wryly. *"Compassion."*

Before he could reply, Clarise stormed from the room towards the front door. "And you know what else you don't have, Andrew?" She held her fingers an inch apart. "You don't have what it takes to please a woman. You're a lousy fuck–you . . . *you fuck!"*

The door slammed with such force that Andrew felt a breeze ripple through the room. He stared at the door for several seconds and laughed softly.

Compassion, Clarise, only matters to people who care.

92

Karen stretched out on a bench and gazed at the quaint homes and verdant palms surrounding the lake at Echo Park. From the center of the indigo hued waters, three soaring fountains vied for attention with the glass walled towers of the nearby downtown skyline.

She watched a young mother with two small children throw bread crumbs towards a paddling of ducks and a pang of loneliness swept through her. *It's one of those picture perfect days,* she thought glumly. *I wish Ryan could be here to share it with me.* Sighing, she pulled out her phone and dialed Jennifer's number.

A few moments later, a breathless voice answered the phone. "Hello?"

"It's me, Jen. Are you free?"

"Are you kidding?" Jennifer quipped. "You're never free when you have a pair of rug rats look after."

Karen smiled wanly as the children tossed another handful of crumbs towards the ducks eager mouths. *They seem so innocent, so full of life, but can turn into hellions in the wink of an eye.* She took a deep breath and exhaled slowly. *Will I ever be ready for the responsibilities of motherhood?*

"Karen?" Jennifer asked. "Are you there?"

"I'm . . . here," she muttered. "I was just wondering what it would be like to have a child of my own."

"Don't even think about it!" Jennifer pleaded. "The next time you feel this way, rush to the nearest clinic and have your tubes tied."

Karen laughed. "But I thought you loved being a mother."

"I do. But that's before I realized it was a lifetime commitment."

"Funny how it works out that way, isn't it?"

"All in all, it's not that bad. And there's one thing I can look forward to in another twenty years or so."

"What's that?" Karen asked.

"They'll have kids of their own and then I'll have my revenge." She let out a short, hard laugh.

"Speaking of revenge, I think I've finally got Stan off my case."

"What did you do to change his mind? Pull a Lorena Bobbitt?"

"No, silly. I enlisted the services of a cop. A very *persuasive* cop."

"Ahhh . . . and how is mister tall, dark, and handsome anyway?"

"Fine," Karen said coyly. "Very fine, you might say."

"*Very fine?* What's going on, girl–I'm starting to get jealous."

"Nothing's *going on* yet, Jen. But, I see . . . possibilities."

"Possibilities?" Jennifer asked. "What the hell does that mean?"

"Let's just say I don't see any major roadblocks in the road ahead."

"Not even a pothole?"

Karen pinched her lip. "Well . . . "

"He's not married, is he?"

"Divorced."

"Does that matter?"

"And he has an eight-year old daughter, too."

Jennifer paused. "Do you think these *potholes* are going to detour your relationship?"

"I don't know. But it would have been nice if he revealed these things to me earlier."

"Well, now you know." She paused. "Do you think he's hiding anything else from you?"

Karen mulled over her question for several moments. *Last night, Ryan revealed one of the darkest secrets of his life to me. Is there anything else he could be hiding from me?* "I'm sure I'll learn something that will make me pause, but isn't that the chance you take when you let someone into your heart?"

"It can be the most thrilling–and most heartbreaking–ride of your life." The line was silent for several moments. "Are you up for it?"

"If you never take the time to find love," Karen reflected, "then love will never find you."

93

Safely concealed behind a military-grade encryption device to protect his identity, Mark hacked his way into the LAPD's computer database. He skimmed through the department's records and downloaded a folder marked *Security Operations: Pangaea Festival* to his laptop.

After logging offline, he breached the folder's password using a sophisticated decrypting program developed by the National Security Agency. Several minutes later, the information he was seeking was displayed on his screen.

A smile played across his face as he studied a diagram of Liberty Plaza's infrastructure system. *Mmmm . . . this looks interesting. Several large gas mains run under the stage where Jennings is scheduled to give his speech. If security fails to shut off the lines before the festival begins, I can shape the charge to detonate one of the pipelines and increase the wheelchair's destructive force many times over.*

He studied the rest of the files in the folder, making note of the security procedures and modifying his plans to defeat them. Once all the obstacles were overcome to his satisfaction, he gathered his crutches from beside the desk and hobbled towards his bedroom.

Retrieving a video camera from the bedroom closet, a frown traced his face when the camera failed to power on. *The battery must be dead,* he groused. *Well, what do you expect, it hasn't been used in years.*

Plugging in the AC adaptor, Mark powered up the camera once more. His eyes widened as a bittersweet scene unfurled in the camera's tiny view screen. *It's me. And J.T. Mom must have shot this several years ago. Before they . . . died.*

Amusement touched Mark's face as he watched a mock gunfight play out in the backyard between him and his brother. Dressed in battle fatigues and dodging behind trash cans and trees, the two exchanged a flurry of simulated fire until his brother clutched his chest and fell to the ground in an over-the-top death scene.

Watching his brother's simulated passing brought sadness to his eyes. *Just eight month's later, a sniper's bullet found J.T.'s heart for real,* he thought glumly. *Could he have known when we made this video that his fate was sealed?*

Several more snippets of their shenanigans advanced across the screen and then the viewfinder went dark. Mark switched off the camera and sighed. *I bought this for Mom so she would have something to remember us by.* His face tightened. *But there's no use worrying about that now.*

Mark limped back to the closet and pulled a tripod from the shelf. He attached it to the camera and focused the lens on a chair at the other side of the bedroom. He sat down in the chair and stared into the camera's cyclopean eye, exhaling loudly as he switched on the camera with the remote control.

"My name," he began in a clear, steady voice, "is not important. I am first and foremost—an American . . . hoping to preserve the values of a country I believe in."

"A proud country, once considered a beacon of hope to oppressed people everywhere. A country founded on the principle that all men are created equal, and are endowed by their Creator with the unalienable rights of life, liberty and the pursuit of happiness."

"Somewhere along the way, our country strayed from our founders ideals, and we began to condone immoral and illegal behavior as long as it didn't stand in the way of making a profit. The politicians and capitalists have auctioned off our future and caused misery in the name of power and greed. And because of their avarice, the America we knew and revered will become nothing but another failed dream."

He took a deep breath and exhaled. "Thomas Jefferson believed that a little rebellion now and then is a good thing, and as necessary in the political world as storms are in the physical world. He felt it was a necessary medicine for the sound health of government."

"The time that Jefferson spoke of is *now*. It's time our leaders listened to the people and renounced their corporate ties in the name of the common good. It's time we abandon our selfish materialism and once again become a nation that cares. It's time we leave behind our apathy and divisiveness and become a republic of the people, by the people, and for the people that shall never perish from the face of the earth."

"I am a simple man, with no pretensions of wealth or grandeur. My family has defended this country for three generations, each willing to make the ultimate sacrifice to protect the rights guaranteed under our Constitution. And if necessary, I will give my life gladly if others will be inspired to carry on my cause."

Mark stared resolutely into the camera lens. "Sometimes, we must make choices that many may consider . . . wrong. But, as the author of our Declaration of Independence once said–the tree of liberty must be replenished with the blood of tyrants and patriots from time to time in order to survive."

"In every cause, there is one who answers the call to battle. There is one who's willing to sacrifice all to make the world a better place. Tomorrow, I will be the first–but far from the last–to shed my blood in the name of America's next . . . revolution."

94

Concern crossed Kevin's face as he strolled into Calvin's office. "Anything wrong, boss? You're looking a bit down today."

Calvin looked up from the paperwork on his desk and rubbed his eyes. "I guess this week's events are finally catching up to me."

"Yeah, I know what you mean," Kevin quipped. "It's definitely been a week from Hell."

Calvin gave a sour smile. *You don't know the half of it, Kevin.* "How's morale holding up since the layoffs and the . . . incident with Roger?"

"About as well as can be expected, boss. Everyone knows how bad the economy is and they're thankful to have any job at all. I don't think anyone here blames you personally for the layoffs." He pinched his lip. "Except Roger, of course."

"I've decided to press charges," Calvin said. "I'm sure that will make your day."

"Good. One less asshole for society to deal with."

"I gave it a lot of thought and felt his actions couldn't go unpunished." Calvin's expression grew dour. "Still, it wasn't an easy decision to make."

"If it's any consolation, you made the right choice."

"Perhaps, but my decision will haunt him for the rest of his life."

"So?" Kevin said, a look of disgust crossing his face. "He didn't give a fuck about our lives, boss."

Calvin sighed. "No, I suppose not."

"You need put all this . . . this *shit* behind you. All work and no play makes Jack one fucked up dude."

Calvin's eyebrow twitched. "You seem to remember the proverb a little differently than I do."

"So sue me. You need to get the hell out of here. *Now.*"

"And what would you suggest–doctor?"

"I'm taking Ameenah to the Pangaea Festival tomorrow. Feel like tagging along?"

Calvin pulled on his chin. *I was hoping to kick back and watch the Dodgers game on TV tomorrow.* "Let me . . . uhh . . . think about it."

"Come on, boss. It'll take your mind off things for a while."

"All right, let me check with Kati first." Calvin smiled to himself. *She'll be my excuse to bow out gracefully.*

Kevin chuckled. "You need to get your *wife's* approval before you can decide on what to do?"

"Don't you?" Calvin asked.

Kevin's eyes dropped.

Calvin barked out a laugh. "I thought so."

Scooping the phone off the desk, Calvin dialed his wife's number. "Hi, hon. Kevin and I were just shooting the breeze, and he feels I need a break from all the . . . distractions of the past week. He suggested we join him and his wife at the Pangaea Festival tomorrow. What do you think?" He moved his hand under the desk and crossed his fingers. *Say no, Kati. Please say no.*

"He's right," she replied. "It's a wonderful idea."

Calvin's face slackened. *There goes the ball game.* "Are you sure?"

"You're always preaching how important tolerance is to the kids. The Pangaea Festival would let them see those values played out firsthand."

He bit his cheek. *Me and my big mouth.* "It's a go, then?"

"Yes," she insisted. "I haven't spoken with Ameenah in ages. It will be nice to see her again."

"Okay," he muttered. "I'll let Kevin know we're coming. Love you."

"Love you, too."

A grin tugged at Kevin's face. "So did the missus *approve?*"

Calvin smiled wanly. "She said it's a–wonderful–idea."

"It's going to be one of the most unforgettable days of your life, boss. I guarantee it." He rocked back on his heels and smiled broadly. "Besides, after the week you've had, how could things get any worse?"

95

José cast a wary eye along the street as he stood in front of Eduardo's drab green apartment building. A wizened man pushed a trash filled shopping cart up the sidewalk beneath the drooping limbs of a sycamore tree. On the stoop of a run-down house half a block away, several teens shared a joint and looked menacingly in his direction. In the vacant lot on his left, weeds poked through the rusted out frame of a black Chevrolet sedan. Up and down the tired old street, the scrawled graffiti and crumbling buildings were signs of a neighborhood long past its expiration date.

He studied the crumbling concrete stairway that separated him from his destination and frowned. *Just six small steps*, he thought glumly. *But each is far more difficult to make than the thousands I took through the desert.*

Trudging up the stairs, he entered the dimly lit lobby and scanned a row of tarnished brass mailboxes for Eduardo's name. *Here he is—in apartment 218.*

José slogged to the second floor and stood anxiously before Eduardo's doorway for several moments. *How do you tell someone the most precious things in their life are gone forever?* He took a deep breath and rapped on the door.

Several seconds later, a young man barely out of his teens peered cautiously through a crack in the doorway. "What is it, señor?" he asked, suspicion tinging his voice.

José forced a smile. "Hola. I am looking for Eduardo Sanchez."

The young man turned into the darkened apartment and shouted Eduardo's name. Moments later, a tall, wiry man with piercing black eyes came to the doorway and looked at José expectantly.

José recognized him at once from the photo in Elena's locket. "Buenas tardas, señor Sanchez."

Eduardo's eyebrow rose. "Do I know you, señor?"

Without saying a word, José withdrew Elena's locket and dangled it from his hand.

Eduardo's eyes widened. "It's Elena's," he cried. "Where did you find it?"

José met his gaze but remained silent.

"Did she come with you?" he pressed. "Is she here?"

"She . . ." José rasped out. "She won't be coming, señor."

Realization swept over Eduardo's face. "No." He clutched José's arm and wailed, "*Noooo . . .*"

José wrapped his arm around Eduardo's shoulder and choked back a sob. "I'm sorry. Our trip across the border did not go as . . . planned."

Eduardo slumped against the doorway and wept. "I must know, señor. Did they–suffer?"

José found himself back in the desert, listening to Elena's final words. "Her last thoughts . . . were of you and Angelina," he said softly.

Eduardo wiped his face and took the locket from José's hand. "Forgive me, señor," he muttered. "I never did get your name."

"I am José." He extended his hand. "José Torres."

Eduardo clasped his hand. "I wish we could have met under better circumstances, José."

José gave a wan smile. "I was lucky to have met her."

Eduardo nodded slowly. "As was I." He stepped away from the doorway. "Please–come inside. We have much to talk about."

José entered the sparsely furnished apartment and looked around. A threadbare brown sofa stood beneath a sliver of a window framed by wrought iron security bars. Two green plastic chairs and a salvaged red table lent the only color to the otherwise lackluster room.

Eduardo gestured towards the couch. "Would you like something to drink, amigo?"

"A cerveza, if it's no trouble, señor."

Eduardo brought him a beer and joined him on the couch. Prying open the locket, a tear trickled down his cheek as he stared longingly at the photo of his family. "Let's not dwell on how they died, José," he said, trying to keep the anguish from his voice. "But rather, let's treasure every moment that they lived."

96

From the comfort of Andrew's glass walled office, Ron scanned the article from *Rumor* magazine and scratched his head. "I don't know where they dug this shit up, Andrew," he said. "It certainly didn't come from me."

Andrew snatched the tabloid from his hands and scowled. "You expect me to believe that? As the director on this project, you're responsible for everything that happens on the set."

Ron met his gaze. "I don't care what you believe," he asserted. "I'm telling you the *truth*." He pulled on his beard and frowned. "You got any enemies who might want to do you in?"

Andrew shrugged. "No more than any other producer in town."

"Hmmm . . . I guess that narrows it down to almost everyone."

"Thanks for your *help*, Sherlock."

Ron chuckled. "Anytime." He snapped his fingers. "Wait! I know who might be responsible for this."

Andrew cocked his head. "Who?"

"Angela's always running her mouth off on the set, so there's no reason why she couldn't have blabbed her heart out to some sympathetic reporter looking for a story."

"But Angela's personal fortune is tied to the film's success," Andrew pointed out. "Why would she do anything to sabotage it?"

"Since when does Miss Carson need a reason to justify her behavior? She was probably in some uptown club getting soused when some hack overheard her rants and *repackaged* them for this article." He gave a wry smile. "You know how these rags operate–you say left and they print right."

Andrew nodded. "I suppose you're right."

"Damn right I'm right, Watson." He lighted a cigarette and blew a stream of blue-gray smoke towards the ceiling. "Speaking of left and right–are you still on for tomorrow's little bash at Liberty Plaza?"

"I'm actually looking forward to it."

"Great–I'll pick you up at your place around three." He took a drag on his cancer stick and exhaled. "By the way, did you vote for Jennings in the last election?"

"Does it matter?" Andrew asked drolly.

Ron laughed softly. "Not really. Most politicians are nothing but corporate shills anyway. Ten to one Jennings has his hands in half the–"

Andrew's phone trilled, interrupting their conversation. He glanced at the message on the screen and frowned. "I've got to run. My seven o'clock has been moved up an hour."

"All right," Ron said, "I'll see you tomorrow." He clapped Andrew across the back. "And don't worry about any more leaks from the set– I'll keep a tighter reign on Miss Carson from now on." He shot him a crooked grin. "I may want to direct another movie or two in this town and could use you as a reference."

Several minutes later, Andrew mused about meeting the President as he throttled his Mercedes down the narrow streets of the studio. With Jennings standing in his corner, there were no reasons why he couldn't make a name in the political arena. He had the business connections, the financial clout and the personal charisma to make it happen. Schmoozing with the pols would be a breeze after dealing with the backstabbing sharks of this town. If he played his cards right, he could be as politically renowned as others from the industry–perhaps one day sitting in the Oval Office itself.

Maybe it was always meant to be this way, Andrew reflected. *Maybe I was always destined for a life of prominence and grandeur.*

His mouth turned upward in a grin as he gunned his expensive German coupe past the studio's gates and out onto the highway.

Alea iacta est–the die has been cast.

97

APD deputy commander Mark Samuels stood before the assembled staff of the Wilshire Division and laid out the department's security plan for the Pangaea Festival. "Foothill, Harbor, and Rampart divisions will be responsible for the perimeter security of the Plaza extending out to Liberty Corridor and United Expressway." He slashed a line across the large screen behind him with his laser pointer. "Officers from these divisions will secure all visitors from the parking lots and the shuttles to the festival."

"Central, Northeast and Wilshire will be in charge of security within Liberty Plaza itself, performing secondary checks of suspicious visitors and maintaining order during the event. The Sheriff's department will coordinate with selected . . ."

Casperelli cast a sideways glance at Ryan and yawned. "Wake me when he's done, dude," he muttered. "I've heard this speech so many times I can recite it in my sleep."

Ryan nodded. "I guess the brass need a reason to justify their six figure salaries."

"You got that right," Casperelli replied. "You can bet Samuels won't be doin' any heavy liftin' at this event."

Patricia looked over her shoulder and frowned. "Keep it down, Cap.

Some of us are here to learn something."

Casperelli snorted. "*Sorry*, Miss Ruiz."

Patricia shot Casperelli a disgusted look and turned back towards the presentation.

Casperelli nudged Ryan's arm. "Dude, check this out," he whispered. He moved his hands close to Patricia's derriere and pretended to squeeze.

Ryan gave a fleeting smile, then lashed his fist into Casperelli's ribs with the speed of a cobra.

Casperelli grabbed his side and winced. "*Fuck!*" he whimpered. "What was that for?"

Ryan shot him a crooked grin. "For being . . . you."

"What's goin' on? You like her or somethin'?"

"Something like that."

The briefing ended twenty minutes later, and Ryan and Casperelli returned to their desks. Patricia pulled up a chair next to Ryan's desk and sat down. "What'd you think about Samuels' presentation today?" she asked.

Casperelli plopped his feet on the desk and stretched his arms. "If you ask me, Samuels coulda canned the speech and not wasted an hour of our precious time."

Patricia glared at him. "Don't you ever have anything *constructive* to say?"

Ryan held his hand up and sighed. "All right, you two. Save your strength for the Festival."

"So what do you think, Ryan?" Patricia asked.

"Overall, it's a well-thought out plan," he replied. "But no amount of preparation can guarantee complete success. A determined group or individual will always find a way to achieve their goals when a variable has failed to be anticipated. I think Cap is annoyed because our current tactics have prevented any further attacks since the Seattle Slaughter."

"Damn straight," Casperelli quipped. "Nothin' has happened since then and nothin's gonna happen tomorrow." He ran a hand across his face and yawned. "Like I said–it's a big waste of time."

"Can you be sure of that?" Patricia asked.

Casperelli's eyebrow twitched. "Huh? Sure of what?"

"How can you be sure that all our planning is foolproof? Terrorists are constantly looking for ways to exploit the weak link in the system. Nine-Eleven capitalized on the security flaws in the airline industry; the Seattle Slaughter succeeded because we placed too much emphasis on bio-metric detection; the terrorist group *New World Order* used our own health care system to–"

"All right, Ruiz," Casperelli groused. "I get your friggin' point. But, a terrorist would have to be crazy to–"

"Not crazy, Cap," Patricia interjected. "Only firm in their belief that their cause is justified."

"Just cuz you believe in somethin' don't make it right."

"I agree," she replied. "But millions have given their life throughout history to make sure their voice was heard. Including the founders of this country." She looked up sharply. "Would you call *them*–crazy?"

"Things were different then," Casperelli said. "Old King George ruled over the colonies with an iron fist."

Patricia gave a derisive laugh. "And where have you been the last ten years?"

"So what do you think we should do–Missus Jefferson?"

"I'm not proposing another revolution," she replied calmly. "But we're way overdue for a shake-up of the status-quo."

"And do you *really* think that will make a difference?" Casperelli mocked.

"Something has to be done. Our elected officials have lost touch with the citizens of this country."

"I believe that's been the consensus," Ryan said dryly, "since the ink was dry on the Constitution."

Casperelli chuckled. "Ain't that the truth. The rich get richer–"

"–and the poor keep taking it in the ass," Ryan concluded.

"The working class won't remain oppressed forever," Patricia pointed out. "When their options run out, they'll strike out at their oppressors like a cornered animal. And judging from the mood in this country lately, it's only a matter of time." Her face tightened. "Maybe as soon as–tomorrow."

"Not a chance, Ruiz," Casperelli said. "There's so much security at this event a fly won't get past our radar without bein' tagged."

"It only takes *one* person–" she warned.

He waved her off. "It ain't gonna happen, Ruiz. Not in a million years."

"Patricia's right, Cap," Ryan said. "No matter how confident we feel, we can't allow ourselves to become complacent. A terrorist only has to succeed once to achieve their objective. We have to be right one-hundred percent of the time."

"Which means sooner or later . . . " Patricia ventured.

Ryan gave a reluctant nod. "We'll be dealt a losing hand."

98

Mark leaned his crutches against the workbench and looked over his handiwork. Through hours of planning and perseverance, the UltraTrac 5000 had been transformed from a mundane motorized wheelchair into a sophisticated weapon of destruction. The tubular frame and seat cushions were filled with plastique explosive, ready to be detonated on command by a blasting cap wired into the wheelchair's joystick. Embedded in the plastique were thousands of hardened masonry nails that would cause death and mutilation when the wheelchair unleashed its fury in a blinding flash of light.

Mark ran his hand across the frame of his bastardized creation and smiled. *It's a modern day Trojan Horse; elegant in its stealth and simplicity.*

Snatching his crutches from the workbench, he hobbled into the living room and flipped on the TV. To his surprise, the blonde reporter he saw several days ago was engaged in an interview with the Mayor of Los Angeles. He punched up the volume and settled back in his chair to listen.

" . . . and what would you like to tell our viewers for tomorrow's Pangaea Festival, Mayor Santos?"

The Mayor faced the camera and smiled broadly. "Over the next four days, President Jennings and the top artists from the entertainment industry will pay tribute to the traditions and cultures that have defined the spirit of America. Countless individuals have worked tirelessly to make this event something to remember, so please come out to Liberty Plaza and celebrate the diversity that makes our city unique."

Karen tipped the microphone back to her face and nodded. "Thank you, Mayor. Join me and Mark Strothers tomorrow at two when KNBS begins its live coverage of the Pangaea Festival from Liberty Plaza. Back to you, Roger."

Mark turned down the volume and contemplated his strategy for tomorrow's event. Every aspect of his plan had been thoroughly analyzed and reevaluated to maximize his chances of success. All his years of Special Ops training would now be deployed in a consequential act to pursuade the citizens into reclaiming their country from the plutocracy.

He stretched back in his lounge chair and grinned. *I'm about to become the government's worst nightmare; the foe they have no true defense against.*

The enemy within.

99

oni moved the small pewter dog across the colorful squares of the Monopoly board, heading towards certain doom.

"Ha!" Calvin snorted. "Boardwalk–with a hotel. You owe me two grand, Toni."

Toni shuffled through her meager pile of money and frowned. "I don't have it, Dad. Can I give you some of my properties instead?"

Calvin leaned back in his chair and gloated. "Sorry. Cash only."

Pushing away from the table, she tossed her property cards and currency into the center of the board. *"Fine!"* she hissed. "It's a *stupid* game anyway!"

"Be thankful it's just a game," Calvin said. "Or you'd be spending tonight in a homeless shelter instead of your nice, warm bed."

Toni glared at her father for a moment, then stormed out of the room.

Kati looked at Calvin and frowned. "Don't you think you're taking this game a little too seriously, dear?"

"Huh? What are you talking about?"

"Think about it," she replied. "Every time we play you act as if real money and property are at stake."

He gave a dismissive wave of his hand. "Ahhh, you're imagining things, Kati."

"Was I *imagining things* when James left the table a half hour ago with tears in his eyes? And you just saw Toni's reaction to–"

"Toni always acts up when she doesn't get her way."

"Calvin, she's a nine-year old child–how do you *expect* her to act?"

He stared at the game board and pinched his lip. "Am I really that bad?"

She smiled. "Relentless."

"I guess I could be a little less . . . competitive."

"It is just a game after all."

He gave a slight nod. "Do you think the kids will still love me in the morning?"

"It will take a more than losing an old fashioned board game for the kids to hate you, dear. But, take away James' video games or Toni's laptop and you'll become *persona non grata* around here."

"Mmmm . . . it's always nice to know where I stand."

"A lot higher than you think. James practically worships you, and Toni . . ." She shrugged. "Toni may not always express her feelings for you openly lately, but she loves you more than you could possibly imagine."

"I've had my doubts about her lately. I always thought we had a perfect relationship."

"Toni was the apple of your eye, and the feeling was mutual."

"Then, what happened?" Calvin groused. "I feel like a wedge is being driven between us."

"Your little girl is growing up. She's nearly a young woman now."

"She's still a child, Kati. You just said so yourself a minute ago."

"In many ways, she is. But the stresses of today's world force kids to grow up a lot sooner than we did."

"That's what our parents said about us when we were growing up."

"And *their* parents probably felt the same way."

"When I was her age," Calvin said, "I didn't feel like an adult at all. Do you think things have really changed that much in the last generation?"

"In some ways. Kids certainly have more choices in life than ever before. And without the proper guidance to make those choices, they'll quickly lose their way into becoming responsible adults."

"And that's where we come in."

She nodded. "It's up to us to make sure they take the right path in life. A role we accepted on the day our first child was born."

Calvin sighed. "It never gets any easier, does it?"

She shook her head. "So cherish every moment with Toni and James because they're only going to be young once."

"I wish they didn't grow up so fast."

"I feel the same way sometimes," Kati replied. "And there are other times when I can't wait 'til they're out of the house."

100

Karen wended her way to the back of the movie line and kissed Ryan on the cheek. "Sorry I'm late–it's been one of those days."

He stroked her cheek and smiled. "Feel like talking about it?"

"Ever had a day start like shit and go rapidly downhill from there?"

"Are you kidding? Sounds like my *typical* day."

She chuckled. "Today began on a cheery note, but then I got stuck in the mother of all traffic jams on my way to work. By the time I got to the studio, Stan was ready to tear me a new one."

Ryan's eyes narrowed. "Did he cause you any more trouble?"

She pinched her lip. "Not this time. Unfortunately."

He shot her a puzzled look.

"If Stan was still interested in me, he might have cut me some slack for being late," she explained. "But my tardiness threw today's scheduled interviews for the Pangaea Festival totally out of whack." She shook her head and frowned. "Believe me, Stan was not a happy camper."

"Why didn't he just send another reporter out to cover things?"

"That's our standard operating procedure, but Stan wants me to be the station's representative for all the Pangaea publicity. It's what I signed on for when I agreed to co-anchor the festival."

"So what happened after that?"

"From there, the shit just kept hitting the fan," she said. "I was late for my interview at City Hall and had to kiss some ass to get back in the pol's graces. And because of more unexpected delays or technical problems, the rest of our interviews were pushed back or cancelled outright, leaving several of our intended interviewees more than a little miffed."

"They'll get over it."

"You're probably right, but it's not helping my station's credibility in the meantime." She sighed. "Or mine."

He kissed her forehead. "You've still got my support."

She smiled wanly. "I may not be out on the street dodging bullets everyday, but I'd like to feel that I'm contributing something positive to society." She looked at the line of people stretching towards the theater entrance and frowned. "So what's on the bill for tonight?"

"Before or after the movie?" Ryan asked, grinning.

Karen poked him in the ribs. "Better watch it or there won't *be* any after the movie."

He flinched. "In that case, I reserved us two tickets for *With Liberty and Justice for All.*"

"I saw some reviews on that. It's supposed to be some kind of Orwellian tale of our country's future."

He nodded. "The government uses propaganda and fear to instill order over a dystopian society."

"It sounds more like the world of *today* than tomorrow," she said drolly.

"I guess it depends on how you look at it."

She looked up sharply. "And how do you see it?"

"I've seen enough lying, thievery and butchery to last me a lifetime. It shouldn't be any surprise that I'd like to see more constraints on the citizens to protect the overall society."

"I have no problem with *some* constraints," she stated. "But where do you draw the line before our society becomes a bona fide police state?"

He shrugged. "I don't make the laws, Karen, I just make sure they're carried out."

"Mmmm . . . so you're just following orders like a good little Nazi?"

"What do you want me to say? It's my job to enforce the law."

"And at what point would *enforcing the law* start to affect you personally?"

"I'm not sure I understand your question."

"Let me state it clearly. If this country were placed under martial law, would you have any problems arresting or shooting the citizens of your own country?"

"If dissidents were threatening to disrupt or destroy the community, I wouldn't have any problem at all."

"Could you shoot me?" she asked. "Or . . . Ashley?"

His face clouded. "What you're proposing will never happen."

"How do you know?" she chided. "Aren't there plans in place to suppress the population of our country in the event of anarchy?"

"Yes, but they've never been put into practice."

"The fact such plans even exist imply our leaders expect it to happen."

"I suppose it's possible."

"Not just possible, Ryan–*probable*. Have you checked the mood of our country lately?"

"It's ugly," he affirmed. "But it's been ugly for years."

"How much longer do you think the citizens of our country will put up with the elitist attitudes of our elected officials before they decide to revolt?"

"I don't know," he said. "Do you feel oppressed enough to rebel?"

She shook her head. "Not yet. But Uncle Sam's trampled over our rights so much lately, I fear for what's going to happen next."

"Some information shouldn't be allowed to fall into the wrong hands. Surely you must agree with that."

"Of course. But, where do we draw the line on our right to privacy and free speech?"

"That's up to our elected officials to decide."

"And what if they decide to constrain those rights until the Constitution loses it legitimacy?" she asked.

"The Supreme Court will determine the validity of the laws and strike them down if necessary."

"That might work if the government preserves its current Constitutional framework. But, if the balance of power shifts from a democracy to an oligarchy–as is happening now–then the rights guaranteed to us under the Constitution may be lost forever."

"I think our judiciary system will err on the side of reason rather than repression."

"I disagree," Karen replied. "Since 9/11, our rights have been taken away from us in the name of national security. The Patriot and National Identification Acts have allowed Big Brother to intrude into our lives while increasing the fears and suspicions of our society as a whole. How long before our government's version of the Gestapo carries out a *Kristallnacht* against the imagined enemies of our country?"

"We have safeguards against that kind of persecution happening."

Disgust tinged Karen's face. "They had *safeguards* in Germany, too. Why not ask someone from Auschwitz how well that worked out?"

"It won't be allowed to happen again," Ryan affirmed.

"Let's assume it *could* happen. Would you be willing to carry out orders you find repulsive? Would you be willing to send me or Ashley off to some detention camp to *enforce* the laws of your superiors?"

Ryan pinched his lip. "I . . . don't know."

"Someday," she said softly. "You may have to make a choice."

He took a breath and exhaled. "Let's pray that day never comes."

101

"José, is that you?" The voice sounded very far away.

José looked out at the seedy neighborhood beyond Eduardo's apartment window and pressed the phone closer to his ear. "Si, Maria, it's me," he replied. "It's good to hear your voice again."

She let out a loud, wracking sob. "We were so worried about you, José," she choked out. "We've heard nothing from you in days." She paused. "Where are you?"

"America," he said softly. "I'm in . . . America."

"Then your journey was successful." She took a deep breath and exhaled. "Why did it take so long for you to call?"

José's face tightened. *Should I tell her what happened?* Images from the past week flashed like a series of snapshots through his mind. "I didn't mean to worry you, carino. I was . . . temporarily delayed at the border."

"What's wrong, José?" she pressed. "You sound–*different.*"

His eyebrow rose. *She doesn't believe me.* "I'm fine, Maria," he said in an attempt to assuage her fears. "I'm here in Los Angeles, staying with a friend."

"Los Angeles?" A pause. "What's it like there?"

"It is beyond words, bonita. The city stretches out as far as the eye can see."

"Are you going to remain there?"

"It's too soon to tell," he said. "But, my friend Eduardo knows of several places where I might find work." He paused. "Tomorrow we are going to a festival celebrating the many cultures of the world. It's called the Pangaea Festival."

"It sounds like your journey has gotten off on the right step."

If you only knew, he thought glumly. "Si," he muttered. "I've been . . . blessed."

"There's someone here who wants to talk to you."

The line was silent for several seconds. "Pápa?"

José's mouth curled upward in a grin. "*Esmeralda!*" he cried. "How are you?"

"Fine, Pápa." A pause. "I miss you."

"I miss you too, mieja."

"When are you coming home?"

"As soon as I can." He clutched the phone tightly and bit back tears. "Are you helping your mother around the farm while I'm gone?"

"Si, Pápa." She sighed. "Mamá gives me so much work that I have no time to spend with my friends anymore."

"Why don't you ask your brother for help?"

"Tomas?" She snorted. "All he does is *cause* problems."

"As his older sister, you must set an example for him."

"He is too *stupid* to learn, Pápa!"

José shook his head and smiled. *I see nothing's changed since I've left.* "You must have patience, mieja. Don't you remember what it was like when you were his age?"

"I was a lot smarter when I was his age."

And as I recall, José mused, *a bigger pain in my asno, too.* "Then you'll have to spend more time with him until he learns."

"Work, work, work!" she whined. "That's all I do around here!"

"It's time for you take on more responsibility, Esmeralda. In less than two years, you'll be celebrating your Quinceañera–"

"And then I will be a woman–an adult!" she declared. "And people won't be bossing me around like they do now."

José smiled wryly. *There will always be someone telling you what to do, my little querida.* "Be careful what you wish for. Once you become an adult, you're expected to take responsibility for your actions."

She gave a derisive laugh. "And you don't think I can do that? One day, I'll leave this boring little town behind and see all the places I've dreamed about."

"The world can be a very dangerous place, Esmeralda."

"I am not worried, Pápa. You'll always be there to protect me."

He looked out over the smoggy Southland basin and pinched his lip. *I'll always be there to protect you, mieja. But who will be there to protect me?*

THURSDAY

102

atricia yawned as the L.A. skyline whipped past the cruiser's window in a multicolored blur. "Not much traffic out on the road today," she said. "Looks like the highly touted Pangaea Festival is going to be a zillion dollar flop."

Ryan steered the black and white down the Santa Monica freeway and chuckled. "The gates don't open for another three hours, Patricia. Most of the working stiffs are probably taking the day off and sleeping in to avoid the crush from the festival."

Patricia yawned again. "I wish I could join them. I hardly slept at all last night."

"Hot date?" Ryan asked.

She rolled her eyes. "Yeah–*right*."

"Something wrong?"

She gave a slight headshake. "Not really."

Ryan guided the vehicle into the middle lane of the freeway but remained silent.

She took a deep breath and exhaled. "It's probably . . . nothing."

"Why not let me be the judge of that?"

"Last night," she said softly, "I had a . . . a premonition . . ."

A chill shot through Ryan's spine. "Premonition?"

"A feeling . . . that something was going to happen at the festival today." She shot him a sideways glance. "Something . . . bad."

"Do you have any evidence to back up your–feeling?"

"Nothing substantial." She nibbled on her lip. "Do you think I should report it?"

"Without any real proof, the department won't waste its time checking out your–feelings."

Her expression clouded. "Do you think I'm being paranoid?"

"Not at all. It's kind of a sixth sense that cops develop over time. Someday, a *feeling* may very well save your life."

"Is there anything on your radar?"

"Nothing like what you've experienced. But every time we have to police an event like today's festival, I always get a little anxious."

She cocked her head. "Why?"

"When you deal with large groups of people, you can never predict what will happen."

"But Cap said a fly won't get past security without–"

He waved her off. "Cap–if you haven't noticed–is full of shit. He's just as nervous as the rest of us, but wouldn't admit it in a million years."

"So there's a real possibility that something might happen today?"

He gave a reluctant nod.

"Is there anything I can do to increase the odds in our favor?"

"There are always things you can–and *should* do–but where does one draw the line between sensible judgment and paranoia? If you recall, the Department of Homeland Security had evidence that a large sporting event in Miami was targeted for attack by a group of Islamic sympathizers. It was just months after the Seattle Slaughter, and tensions were running high throughout the country at the time. Word went out to the local enforcement agencies to use ethnic profiling at the event, even though such tactics are generally frowned upon in today's politically correct world."

"It was a public relations nightmare for the Miami Police Department, if I recall correctly."

"That's an understatement," Ryan replied. "Once memos were leaked to the media about the ethnic profiling, the outrage from the Muslim and Hispanic communities was predictable. Miami's Chief of Police was forced to resign, and several high ranking officials from Homeland Security were publicly rebuked."

"Didn't the city of Miami have to pay out a settlement to the individuals involved?"

"Big time. Though in all fairness, the MPD could have used a little more . . . discretion . . . in carrying out their orders."

"Each of our actions is a reflection on the department as a whole," Patricia stated.

"And if any good came out of that debacle, it was an awareness that we shouldn't use ethnic or racial profiles to define a terrorist. A terrorist can be any gender, race, color or creed."

Patricia's face tightened. "If the LAPD had learned that lesson several years ago, my brother might still be alive today." She turned to gaze out the window. "Do you think there will come a time when prejudice isn't a determining factor in a person's guilt or innocence?"

Ryan gave a sour smile. "In a perfect world—yes." He drove several hundred feet down the freeway before speaking again. "But we don't live in a perfect world."

103

Calvin looked at the chocolate milk spattering James' shirt and frowned. "James!" he groused, "Can't you stay clean for one lousy minute?"

James looked at his shirt and grinned sheepishly. "Sorry, Dad."

Toni leaned across the kitchen table and giggled. "You're such a slob, James!"

Calvin glared at her. "Toni," he chided. "Keep your comments to yourself." He wiped his son's face with a paper towel and stripped the stained shirt off his body. "Can you get me a clean shirt from his room, Toni?"

She looked up from her magazine and sighed. "Why can't he get it himself?"

"Look, I don't have time for your *crap* this morning."

"It's not my fault he's a slob," she said.

"Just get me the shirt, princess." He flashed a smile. *"Please?"*

Toni scowled. "Oh, *alright!*" She slammed her magazine on the table and stomped out of the kitchen, disgust plainly etched across her face.

Calvin looked up at the ceiling and shook his head. *Why me, Lord? Why me?*

Moments later, his daughter tromped into the kitchen and hurled the shirt on the table. "Here's your stupid shirt, butthead."

Calvin snatched the shirt off the table and wagged his finger in Toni's direction. "You better start changing your attitude around here, young lady." He wrestled the shirt over his son's head and fastened the buttons. "Okay, James–try to keep clean the rest of the day," he grumbled. "Or at least until your Mom gets home."

"Yes, James," Toni mocked, "Try to keep clean until Mom gets home."

"*Toni,*" Calvin growled. "Grow up."

She slumped into a chair at the table and sulked. "Why do we have to go to this boring festival today?"

Calvin's eyebrow rose upward. "Boring?" he asked. "There'll be all kinds of things for you to do there."

She snorted. "Just give me one good reason why I should go."

Calvin's hands balled into fists. *Keep mouthing off and I'll give you a reason to go.* He studied the sullen expression on his daughter's face and smiled. *Maybe I can change her mind with a story from my childhood.* "Toni, when I was a boy . . ."

She gave an eye roll. "This isn't the 'I had to walk miles through blinding snow just to get to school' story again, is it?"

He blinked. *Mmmm . . . maybe I've told that story once too often.* "Uhhh . . . no. This story has nothing at all to do with school–"

"Good!" she cheered. "Because I'm still wondering why it snowed so much when you were a kid and now it doesn't snow at all anymore."

"Didn't you learn about global warming in school?" he asked dryly.

She shook her head and sighed.

Calvin sat at the table and lifted James into his lap. "Now, back to my . . . story. When I was a boy, your grandfather dragged your Aunt Cerise and me and to some dumb movie at the neighborhood theater. We whined and nearly drove your grandfather crazy, expecting to be bored out our minds for the next two hours." A fleeting smile crossed his face as he recalled the memory in his mind. "Imagine our surprise when the movie began and we entered the galactic world of Luke Skywalker and the evil Darth Vader."

"Is that why your closet is still full of Star Wars stuff even though Mom asked you to throw it out a long time ago?" James asked.

Calvin chuckled. "Just between us, son—you can *never* have too much Star Wars stuff."

"I don't see how can you compare a cool movie to some boring festival," Toni griped.

"You're missing the point, Toni," Calvin explained. "You can't always judge a book by its cover."

She shrugged. "It's still going to be a drag."

Calvin's face slackened. *Is there any way I can reach her?* "Look—I can't guarantee you'll have a good time, but you'll walk away from today's festival with something better. You'll learn firsthand that our differences are not something to be feared or ridiculed, but rather, important values to be explored or embraced." He shot her a lopsided grin. "So what do you say, princess? Are you willing to give it a try?"

Toni crossed her arms and frowned. "I guess," she muttered. "Anything's better than listening to one of your stories."

104

ndrew paused from his jog along the beach and scanned the coastline. A few hardy surfers braved the roiling waves a hundred yards up the coast, while further down the beach a teen flung a Frisbee towards his Collie's eager jaws. None of Malibu's rich and famous were out on the nearly vacant shoreline, apparently preferring the solitude of their walled off mansions to the soothing vistas offered by Mother Nature.

Stretching his aching calves, Andrew turned toward the sea and let the salty tinged spray wash over him. He closed his eyes, and the roar from the surf soon lulled his mind into a restful trance. *There's nothing like the ocean to refresh a man's soul,* he mused. *Though we aspire to greatness, our ancestors all sprang from the depths of the humble sea . . .*

The gentle strains of a whistled song snapped Andrew from his reverie. He turned and saw a scraggly, middle-aged man digging into the sand less than a hundred feet away.

That's strange, Andrew thought. *I could have sworn there was no one there a minute ago.* His brow furrowed. *At least I think it was a minute ago.*

He watched with amusement as the stranger used a long handled spoon to dig a shiny object from the sand. Delighted by his discovery, the man placed his new found treasure in a ragged looking satchel and walked up the beach in his direction.

A look of puzzlement touched Andrew's face. *Hmmm . . . he looks familiar. Where have I seen him before?*

As he pondered the question in his mind, the sun broke through the morning haze and cast a golden glow across the beachcomber's face. With his long matted hair and bristly beard, the stranger looked as though he hadn't showered in weeks. Andrew studied the bedraggled looking man and smiled wryly. *I wonder if he's related to that brute I met in the alleyway a few days ago?*

Any similarity to the goliath in the alley was quickly dispelled when the stranger opened his mouth to greet him. "Good morning," he said in a smooth, commanding bass. "Rather warm for July, wouldn't you say?"

Andrew stared at the stranger but remained silent. *Don't do anything to antagonize him—one knife attack this week is enough.* He gestured towards the satchel on the man's shoulder and gave an easy smile. "So how's pickings this morning?" he asked amiably. "Looks like you got lucky a minute ago."

The stranger shrugged. "Someone's lost trinket." He looked at the multi-million dollar homes lining the coastline and frowned. "You'd think this community would be a lot more . . . giving."

Andrew looked over the man's tattered clothing and pinched his cheek. *Giving? Mmmm . . . just as I thought—another bum looking for a handout.* "Don't kid yourself, mister. Most of the people in this town are a paycheck or two away from the street."

"Those who give have all things," the stranger said softly. "Those who withhold—have nothing."

"And how has that *philosophy* worked out for you?" Andrew asked dryly.

The man looked up sharply. "Far better than you could imagine."

Andrew nodded but maintained his silence. *This clown's definitely a few beers short of a six-pack.*

The stranger leveled his steely blue eyes at Andrew and smiled. "Perhaps I should . . . elaborate."

Andrew met the stranger's eyes and took a step back. The intensity of the man's gaze was unnerving. "Perhaps you should."

The disheveled man turned his attention back towards the homes ringing the beach. "Just a few short years ago, I owned one of the most successful businesses in town."

"You did?" Andrew asked increduously. "Wh–what did you do?"

The stranger turned, eyes blazing. "Does it matter?" He took a deep breath and exhaled. "But if you must know, I used to be a . . . consultant. Made billions for clueless investors and in the process became rich myself." He shook his head and smiled. "But money–as the saying goes–isn't everything."

"It may not be everything," Andrew replied, "but it's a helluva lot better than–"

The man waved him off. "Have you ever heard the expression 'shit happens?'"

Andrew nodded.

"That's what happened to me. I thought I was better than the system–but in the end–the system was better than me."

"You're taking it pretty well for a man who's lost everything."

The stranger shrugged. "Easy come, easy go. Life throws you lemons, you learn to make lemonade."

Andrew chortled. "Cute little witticisms won't change your life, my friend."

The stranger glared at him. "You really don't understand–do you?"

Andrew looked the man over and rocked uneasily on his feet. *I understand completely, Mister Loony Tune. You need to get back to your nice padded room as soon as possible.*

The stranger shielded his eyes from the glare of the sun and shifted his gaze towards the sea. "The world works in mysterious ways. We may believe we control our destiny, but the best–"

"Is all this leading to something?" Andrew groused. "Or are you going to waste my time with your *nonsense?*"

The stranger turned to face Andrew. "I am not here to waste your time, sir." A smile touched his face. "As if you had the time–*to* waste."

Andrew waved his hand through the air. "Get out of my way, fruit-cake, I've got a busy day ahead of me." He pushed past the stranger and began to jog down the beach.

The disheveled man called out from behind him. "Remember Andrew, the best laid plans of mice and men often go awry."

Andrew froze. *How did that crackpot know my name?*

And then, he remembered where he had seen the man before. *Just yesterday morning, I dismissed this man as a loser–another bum on the beach looking for a handout.*

But maybe it wasn't money he was after. Maybe he's here to deliver a message . . . and was snubbed by that couple on the beach like I ignored his rants just now.

Anxiety swept across his face. *What's he trying to tell me?*

Andrew turned.

The stranger was gone.

105

ark tilted back his head and breathed in the sweet floral fragrances wafting through the trees at the Los Angeles National Cemetery. A sultry breeze drifted across the freshly mown grass, hinting of the fierce Santa Ana winds that would rake the Southland later in the year.

Scanning the gently sloping hillsides, Mark noticed the cemetery was all but deserted at this early hour of the day. Though the inhabitants that rested beneath the lovingly manicured lawns had all eternity to wait for visitors, the time remaining to him was growing perilously short.

Cradling a cardboard box under his arm, Mark hobbled on a crutch past a maze of granite and limestone markers until he reached a secluded corner of the cemetery. There, beneath the upswept limbs of a gnarled oak tree, lay three gravestones inscribed with the names of his family.

Mark moved near his father's headstone and kneeled to the ground. He pulled a small wood-framed case from the box, and reverently regarded the medals from Samuel "Hawk" Hildebrandt's military career. Resting the case against his father's headstone, Mark bowed his head and began to pray.

"Hi, Dad," he said softly. "I hope you're listening, because I could really use your help right now. For what I'm about to do, does not come easily, when my actions will cause others . . . to die. You've often said the blood of innocents has been shed throughout history to right the wrongs of humanity. And when reason fails to sway your oppressors, sometimes the only recourse left is–force." He took a breath and exhaled. "Please Dad, give me a sign. Give me some signal that the course I'm about to take is . . . right."

Mark lifted his head and stared upward, looking for divine intervention. He saw nothing but a few wispy clouds brushed across a hazy blue sky.

With a sigh, Mark scooted towards the center marker and gazed at the inscription he had placed on his mother's headstone two short years ago.

EILEEN HILDEBRANDT
Loving Wife, Devoted Mother
A life that served as an inspiration to all

Could any dedication truly suffice in honoring the person who comforted him when he was troubled, who nursed him to health when he was sick, who asked for nothing in return but his unconditional love?

Perhaps one word says it best, he reflected. *Mother.*

He lifted a bouquet of roses from the box and placed them next to her headstone. "I . . . I miss you, Mom," he choked out. "I'll be seeing you again . . . soon."

Biting back tears, Mark wriggled across the closely cropped grass to his brother's grave and pulled the last item from his box. "I didn't forget you J.T.," he murmured. "Semper Fi."

Although the snapshot he placed at the base of his brother's marker was taken nearly two decades ago, to Mark the image was as fresh as if it happened yesterday. Two young boys, dressed in battle fatigues and sporting toy rifles, smiled naively at a world that had yet to color their minds. *Even at that early age,* he mused, *we wanted to follow in Dad's footsteps.*

Struggling to his feet, Mark bowed his head and paid homage to his family one last time.

Suddenly, a sharp pain knifed through Mark's head. He keeled over to the ground, and his body began to spasm uncontrollably. A wave of nausea overtook him, and he violently spewed the contents of his stomach on the ground. He lurched away from the vile smelling vomit and rolled over onto his back gasping for air. When the queasiness had passed, intense chills gripped his body, even though the early morning temperature had climbed well past ninety.

Curling into a fetal position, Mark waited for the chills and nausea to subside. When the worst of the biliousness was over, he reached out for his crutch and staggered to his feet.

As he started for the cemetery's exit, a golden blur flashed from the tree to his right. A red tailed hawk flew in a graceful arc over the cemetery, and then soared upward until it vanished in the sky.

Mark raised his hand and saluted. His father had answered his prayers at last.

106

José looked uneasily at the graffiti scrawled across the apartment's dimly lit lobby and frowned. "Eduardo, are you *sure* this is the right address?"

Eduardo studied the holes punched in the walls and ceiling of the rundown dwelling, the pipes underneath the crumbling plaster stripped out for the value of their copper a long time ago. "The Cipher is not your typical merchant, José," he replied. "He can't put a sign out on the street advertising his business." He kicked a small cardboard box across the trash-strewn floor and watched with amusement as a swarm of cockroaches scuttled across the floor. "Don't worry, amigo. We'll find him."

As they climbed the rickety stairway towards the second floor, José shuddered as he heard something scurry behind the walls. "If this is where he conducts his business, then he probably doesn't want to be found."

Eduardo peered over his shoulder and grinned. "It's important we find him. You won't be able to get a job in this country without the proper documentation."

"I have documentos," José replied, patting his shirt pocket. "The coyote gave them to me when he smuggled–"

"Your papers are no good here," Eduardo declared. "The CARD is the only legal form of documentation accepted by employers today, and it can only be obtained through certain government agencies. The Cipher can create a CARD for you that will pass nearly every security device in the country."

"Does the CARD let the Americano government monitor your every move?"

"Not yet," Eduardo answered. "But they're working on it. Anyone who looks out-of-place is always regarded suspiciously."

"And that includes . . . us?"

Eduardo gave a sour smile. "Though our Spanish ancestors settled this region many centuries ago, we are now considered–the outsiders."

They reached the second floor and glanced anxiously down the graffiti riddled hallway. Eduardo strode past several gutted apartments until he came to the last doorway.

He rapped sharply on the door and leaned in to listen. A minute passed with no response. "I guess no one's home today," he said dryly.

José gave a nervous laugh. "What a surprise."

Eduardo grinned. "He's probably on the next floor."

"Yeah," José said, nodding. "Let's hope so."

They ascended the stairs to the third floor and Eduardo pounded on the first door near the stairwell. Within seconds, a faint rustling sound was heard behind the closed door.

"Looks like we got lucky, José," Eduardo whispered.

"Who is it?" the voice growled harshly.

Eduardo leaned near the doorway. "I'm looking for the Cipher," he said softly. "Mario Fuentes sent me."

Eduardo and José stepped back from the door, wondering anxiously if the blast from a shotgun would be the last sound they heard in this lifetime.

Several suspenseful seconds later, the voice answered. "There's no one by that name here," it hissed. "Go away!"

They moved to the next apartment down the hallway. "Probably just some addict sleeping it off," Eduardo reasoned. He rapped on the door and was greeted with silence. The next two apartments were empty as well.

José gave a disgusted look. "Maybe your friend gave you the wrong address."

"We still have one floor to go, amigo. He'll probably be in the last apartment we check out."

"I hope it's sooner than that," José griped. "This place is creeping me out."

Several fruitless minutes later, they came to last apartment on the fourth floor. Eduardo reached out and rapped on the door. "This is it, José," he said. "If he's not here, we'll have to–"

A voice shot through the door, startling them. "Who's there?"

"I'm looking for the Cipher," Eduardo said. "I'm a friend of Mario Fuentes."

Silence.

Eduardo shrugged. "Looks like we struck out again, amigo."

The door opened a sliver, and a scruffy looking man stared at them with a wary eye. "What is it?" he growled.

Eduardo took a step forward. "Are you . . . the Cipher?"

The stranger's expression remained unchanged. "Mario sent you?"

Eduardo nodded.

The man opened the door. "Step inside, señor. It's unwise to be in the hallway without *protección*."

Eduardo and José crossed the threshold into the stranger's drearily appointed apartment. A mangy sofa and battered dinette sat atop a badly stained carpet on one side of the dingy room. In stark contrast, the other side of the room held an array of computers and sophisticated electronic equipment stacked neatly atop a pair of large folding tables.

The stranger beckoned Eduardo and José towards the couch. "Have a seat." It came out more a command than a gesture of politeness.

Eduardo settled on the couch and looked nervously in the stranger's direction. "Are you the–"

The stranger's eyes narrowed. "I am the one you seek." The Cipher was near forty, but looked older. His dark piercing eyes darted skittishly above a thick walrus style moustache. "What can I do for you, amigo?"

José leaned forward on the couch and smiled. "I need documentos, señor."

"Of course," the Cipher smirked. "Why else would you be here?"

José's gaze was steady. "Can you help me?"

"It depends on what you want. And how much you're willing . . . to pay."

José handed the documents he received from the coyote to the Cipher. "Will these be of any use to you, señor?"

The Cipher glanced at the papers and frowned. "Where did you get these from, amigo?"

"The coyote gave them to me before we came across the border."

The Cipher tossed the papers to the floor and laughed. "These are *mierda*. They wouldn't fool a blind man."

José looked at the documents and recalled his encounter with the female officer yesterday. *She looked at my papers and believed they were real.* His mouth turned upward in a smile. *Or did she?*

"I'm glad you find this amusing, amigo," the Cipher chided. "Perhaps the folks from immigracíon will be just as amused when you hand these papers to them."

"Don't mind him, señor," Eduardo said. "He's still learning his way around here. Do you think you can help him out?"

The Cipher combed his fingers through his moustache and smiled.

"One thousand dollars, amigo. American."

José's face slackened. "I don't have that kind of money."

The Cipher's gaze rested on Eduardo. "You are Mario's friend?"

Eduardo gave an affirmative nod.

A grin creased the Cipher's face. "Today's your lucky day, amigo. Business has been rather slow lately, so I'll make you a CARD for half my usual price."

José pinched his lip and nodded. He counted out the Cipher's fee and placed it in his waiting hand.

The Cipher pocketed the money and gestured towards the other side of the room. "Have a seat on the stool, and we will begin."

José sat down and the Cipher snugged a fiberglass helmet over his head. A metal visor was snapped down over his upper part of his face, and the Cipher adjusted a lens over his right eye.

"Do not be afraid, padré," the Cipher said softly. "A laser will be focused through the lens and be read by a retinal scanner. When I give you the signal, keep as still as possible."

The Cipher moved a small cylindrically shaped object attached to a flexible stalk near José's face. "You will feel a slight burning sensation in your eye for several moments, followed by a period of blindness. There is no need to be alarmed as your vision will return shortly after the scan is over." He focused the laser on the lens and tapped a series of commands into the computer. "Do not move," he ordered. "We will begin the scan—now."

A low level laser was directed into José's eye, causing him a moderate degree of discomfort. On a large monitor directly behind the Cipher, a computer mapped out a series of coordinates against the intricate pattern of capillaries on José's retina.

Several seconds later, the Cipher switched off the laser and removed the helmet from José's head. "That's it, amigo. It will take a minute or two for the computer to process the scan and convert it into a holographic image. In the meantime, I will encode your CARD with a registry number obtained from one of my . . . *associates* at the U.S. Immigration and Customs Enforcement office." He tapped several commands on the keyboard, and a series of sixteen digit numbers scrolled across the computer's screen. "What is your age, amigo?" the Cipher asked.

"Thirty-four."

The Cipher pecked several more commands on the keyboard and waited. One by one, the numbers vanished until only one filled the screen. "Congratulations, padré. From now on, your legal name is Paulo Gonzales, registry number 5700-7642-4652-8731." His voice hardened. "Don't forget it. Ever."

The Cipher removed a laminated card from a small black box and handed it to José. "What one man can create, another can copy," he declared. "Short of a Level Five scan, you are now an official citizen of the United States."

José turned the thin piece of plastic between his fingers, mesmerized by the hologram glinting off the surface of the card. *But will the price for my citizenship*, he wondered, *come at the cost of my soul?*

107

ooking out from the anchor desk high above Liberty Plaza, Martin Strothers waved furiously at the cameraman and scowled. "Move the camera a little more to the left, Bob," he groused, "I want to make sure my best side is seen by our viewers."

Karen glanced at Martin and stifled a laugh. *I didn't know you had a best side, Martin.* It was no secret that her co-anchor's arrogance and patronizing attitude made him a virtual pariah at the station.

Martin leaned back in his seat and shook his head. "You'd think with the ratings I bring into this station, they could at least spring for a comfortable chair." He adjusted a lever on the side of his seat and flinched. "Shit, and no lumbar support, either. My back will be freakin' killing me by the time this broadcast is over." He rose from his chair and slammed it against the desk. "How's your chair, Karen?"

She shrugged. "Seems fine to me."

Martin gave a disgusted look and sat on the edge of the desk. He lighted a cigarette and blew a stream of smoke towards the cloudless sky. "Well, there's one good thing about working outdoors today," he muttered, "I don't have to worry about the city's asinine smoking ban." He took another drag from his cigarette and looked out over the Plaza. "You certainly can't complain about the view from up here. We're high enough to see the entire plaza—yet we're close enough to the stage to see Jennings sweat."

Karen sat next to Martin and let her gaze drift across the plaza. Sixty feet below their news platform, the area where Jennings was scheduled to speak stretched across the north end of Liberty Plaza. Two eighty-feet high towers anchored each end of the stage, and a large aluminum framework containing the lights and audio equipment soared across the stage from the towers. A large video screen was perched atop each tower to provide intimate views of the stage to the crowd. With less than two hours to Liberty Plaza's public debut, a pack of technicians swarmed over the vast infrastructure to make sure all systems were fully operational before Jennings took the stage to speak.

Near the glass walled towers surrounding the plaza, Karen watched as security teams probed every nook and cranny for suspicious activity. She knew the Wilshire Division was charged with maintaining security near her location, but she saw no sign of Ryan—or his partner, Patricia—anywhere. *He's probably giving her a 'training lesson' behind one of the pavilions.* A frown traced her face. *Jealous, Karen?*

Martin placed his hand on her shoulder. "Are you all right, Karen?" he asked softly. "It looked like something was bothering you."

She smiled wanly. "Sorry. I must have drifted off for a second."

"We can't have that now, can we? How would our viewers react if you zoned out on the set?"

Karen looked up sharply. "Like they'd notice," she snapped. "Most of our audience has the attention span of a two-year old." She paused. "And about *half* the intelligence."

"Mmmm . . . in one of our cynical moods today?"

Her eyes narrowed. "Why should you care?"

He met her gaze and smiled. "You're too young to be so cynical about life, Karen."

"Really?" she groused. "I didn't realize you had to be a certain age to enter the world of disillusionment."

Martin chuckled. "When you get to be *my* age, you'll understand what cynicism is all about." He took a draw on his cigarette and looked out on the Plaza. "You know, I've covered quite a few of these events through the years. Most were unremarkable; nothing more than marketing drivel wrapped around some feel good cause."

"Like *today's* event?" she asked dryly.

He nodded. "Entertaining? Perhaps. But newsworthy?" He shook his head.

"The suits at the station might disagree with you."

"They might pay my salary, but they wouldn't know a newsworthy event if it bit them in the ass." He took another drag from his cigarette and gazed up into the sky. "Real news isn't staged or scripted by some corporate think tank or political spinmeister's agenda, they're visceral moments that seize your soul–*forever*. We all remember where we were when Kennedy was assassinated, when Armstrong stepped across the moon, when the Challenger exploded in a ball of fire, when the World Trade Center came tumbling down, and when Seattle's stadium disappeared in a blinding flash of light. Compared to those monumental events, today's festival is nothing but a blip on our collective consciousness."

"It's must have *some* significance," Karen pointed out, "or Jennings wouldn't take the time to be here."

Martin laughed softly. "Just your typical political grandstanding. Jennings' party has lost the last two elections in this state and can use all the help it can get. He'll dust off his same tired speech, throw in a multicultural metaphor or two, and hope that it appeals to our passions." He shook his head and chuckled. "God–would you *listen* to me? As long as I've been in the game, I should have known it's all been fixed from the start."

Karen looked on but remained silent. At the station, Martin was considered a dinosaur–a dying breed from television's golden age when news anchors were respected messengers of information.

But as the world entered the new millennium, the way news was delivered to the masses changed forever. The wikis, blogs, and social networking sites of the Attention Age transformed pundits into seers and distorted the news until it became senseless rhetoric. The politically euphemistic society Orwell feared in 1984 had been eclipsed by a world rife with corruption and deception.

Martin stood up and stretched his back. "We're pawns, you know. The *real* power is working behind the scenes–generating opinions and influencing decisions." He shook his head and sighed. "We're nothing more than glorified mouth pieces . . . delivering a message that no one wants to hear."

A shiver went through Karen's spire. *Haskell voiced the same fears to me several days ago at City Hall. Is there a possibility that he and Martin could be right?*

Martin lit another cigarette and trudged towards the edge of the platform. Once a trusted purveyor of information to the public, he had now become a victim to its progress. Though Karen had always loathed him for his arrogance, she now pitied him for not keeping up with the times.

Is this to be my destiny? she wondered. *My future? Will I be able to rise above the rhetoric, skirt the temptations of power, and still retain my dignity? Or will I crash and burn, just another sad victim searching for 'the truth'?*

108

Fifty feet from the main stage, Ryan swept a metal detector across an elderly man's chest to check for explosives. "Please extend your arms outward, sir," he said politely. "This will only take a minute or two."

A look of annoyance tinged the senior's deeply tanned face. "I don't understand, son. One of L.A.'s finest already asked me to walk through a metal detector when I entered the main gate."

Ryan flashed a smile. "We're doing random secondary checks to ensure everyone's safety, sir." He moved the wand down the visitor's torso. "Sorry for the inconvenience."

The man flinched as Ryan moved the wand near his groin. "Is all this necessary, officer? Do I look like a terrorist to you?"

"I don't know. What does a terrorist look like?"

The senior scratched his balding pate and frowned. "You got me there, son. I guess you can't take any chances."

Ryan finished his inspection and rose to his feet. He towered a foot above the stooped backed man's head. "Thanks for your cooperation, sir. Enjoy the festival."

The senior looked up at Ryan and smiled. "Thanks, son. Is there any sure fire way to identify a terrorist?"

"Not really," Ryan stated. "They could be–anyone."

"Sounds like you got a pretty tough job to do. Sorry I gave you such a hard time about it."

"Compared to some of my–customers–you were a pleasure, sir."

"I reckon you don't meet many nice people in your line of work."

Ryan chuckled. "There are some real characters out there."

The senior rubbed his chin and nodded. "Well, good luck, son." A frown suddenly puckered his face. "On second thought, maybe I shouldn't have said that."

Ryan looked the wizened septuagenarian over and suppressed a laugh. "Have a good day, sir." *Speaking of characters* . . .

As the elderly man faded into the crowd, Ryan scanned Liberty Plaza for any suspicious activity. The turnout was still on the light side, but he expected attendance to peak in several more hours when Jennings took the stage.

Moving his gaze across the southeast quadrant of the Plaza, he focused on a group of four teens near a taqueria. From the owner's animated gestures, he could tell that things were about to take a turn for the worse.

He hustled towards the red, white, and green colored food stand, hoping to quash any problems before they materialized. "What seems to be the problem, sir?" he asked the proprietor.

The proprietor–a short, flabby man with slicked back hair and a beaked nose–pointed towards the teens and scowled. "No pay for food," he bellowed in Spanish tinged English.

Ryan turned and surveyed the teens. *Just your run of the mill bangers,* he mused. *Shaved heads, baggy clothes, too many tattoos.* He stepped forward and snatched the tallest teen's arm. "Is that true?"

The teen took a bite from his taco and sneered. "No way, man. The old bendejo's loco."

The other three teens quickly chimed in. "Loco!"

Ryan pulled out his baton and motioned towards the back of the food stand. "I think we need to have a little–*talk."*

The teens glanced at each other, around the plaza, and then back at Ryan.

Ryan's face tightened. *Okay, boys. Make your move.*

The tall teen shrugged and moved towards the rear of the taqueria. The other three followed with surly expressions on their face.

Ryan pointed towards the wall. "You know the routine."

The tall teen glared at him. "Why you hasslin' us, man?"

Ryan shot the banger a crooked grin. "Because it's my job–man." He pointed towards the wall. "Assume the position. *Now!"*

A voice called out from behind Ryan. "Need any help, officer?"

Ryan glanced over his shoulder and frowned. *Shit–it's Patricia.* "Everything's under control here, officer," he said curtly. "You can just . . . move along."

Ignoring his request, Patricia strolled behind the bangers and stopped behind the tallest teen. "Mmmm, what have we got here?" She leaned close and spoke several words of Spanish into the banger's ear.

The teen glanced over his shoulder at Patricia and spat. "Vete a la mierda, *puta!"*

Patricia stepped away from the teen but remained silent. With a quick, one-handed motion, she whipped out her baton and rammed it between the banger's legs. "Sorry," she said gently. "I didn't hear what you said. Would you mind *repeating* it?"

The teen groaned. "I'm sorry, señorita. I didn't mean to disrespect you."

She pushed the baton further into his groin. "You don't sound very sincere, *maricón."*

He gasped. "I swear, señorita. I will not disrespect you–again."

Patricia leaned close and whispered something into the teen's ear. The teen nodded, and she released her grip from the baton. "Make sure

I never see your face around here again," she ordered.

The teen gave her a harsh stare but said nothing. He motioned to his compadres, and they slinked off into the crowd.

Ryan shot her a puzzled look. "What was that all about?"

"Just a small misunderstanding. But I cleared it up."

"How?" Ryan asked. "By slamming your baton into his balls?"

She gave a slight shrug. "Sometimes they need a little *sweet-talk* to understand."

A frown tugged at Ryan's face. "And why'd you let them go? I wasn't done talking with–"

"Come on, Ryan, were you really going to bust them over a taco?" She shook her head and chuckled. "You should be thankful I helped you out–just think of all the paperwork I saved you."

"That's not the point, Patricia. They crossed a line and needed to be punished."

She gave a wry smile. "Don't worry. They were."

"What are you talking about?"

"You've lived here your entire life, but you *still* don't understand our culture. Their leader was just humiliated by a woman–which is far worse punishment than he would ever receive from our overworked judicial system. Believe me, it will be a long time before he regains the respect of his homies again."

"That's not the way we do things around here, Ruiz."

"Let it go, Ryan," she said softly. "Someone will come around to take their place."

He gave a sour smile. "You're right about that," he groused. "There will *always* be someone to take their place."

109

Eight short miles from Liberty Plaza, James uttered four words every parent fears. "Are we there yet?" he screeched.

Calvin gripped the van's steering wheel and cringed. *Right on schedule.*

"Are we there yet?" he howled again, insistent.

Kati pulled out a well-worn DVD binder, looking for an activity to occupy his mind. She held up a disc up for approval. "How about *Pokemon*, James?"

James gave a disgusted look. "Pokemon *sucks,* Mom!"

While Kati searched for another selection, Calvin watched Kevin and Ameenah fidget in the van's rear view mirror. "You still thinking about starting a family, Ameenah?" he asked dryly.

"We're trying," she said. "But haven't been blessed yet."

Calvin's eyebrow twitched. "I don't know if *blessed* is the—" He caught Kati's glare on his right and paused. "You don't know what you're missing. Raising a family can be one of the most *rewarding* experiences of your life." *Right above a root canal,* he mused.

Kati held up another disc. "What about *Major League Baseball,* James?"

He clapped his hands. "That's my favorite!"

"Is that all right with you, Toni?" Kati asked.

She pried the headphones from her ears and scowled. "Anything to shut him up."

Kati popped the DVD into the player, and Calvin relaxed as tranquility swept through the van's interior again. He looked back to Ameenah and found her dark, mysterious eyes returning his gaze in the rearview mirror. "So how did Kevin persuade you into going to the Festival today, Ameenah?" he asked.

"I'm afraid I'm the one that had to do a little–persuading."

Kevin slipped his arm around her shoulder and smiled slyly. "Let's just say she made me an offer I couldn't refuse, boss."

Calvin gave a wry smile. *Mmmm, I bet she did.* "So why did you want to go?"

"I was curious to see if the Festival could live up to all its hype. Any event promoting cultural harmony is always worth exploring."

"If you're expecting some sort of nirvana to sweep through the Southland after the Festival, you're going to come away disappointed. There's no way any event can fulfill the needs of a diverse group of people, even for a single day."

"I know," she concurred. "But anything that begins to bridge our differences can prove beneficial in the long run. If more of us learned to overlook our differences, I wouldn't need to live like a recluse in the land I've called home for the last ten years."

"It hasn't been easy for her, boss," Kevin grumbled. "After the attack in Seattle two year ago, every Muslim in America has been living with a target on their back."

"Has it really gotten that bad?" Kati asked.

Ameenah nodded. "I used to wear the *jilbab*–the traditional Muslim dress–but after the World Series tragedy I've been forced to wear Western style fashions because of the slurs I've received in public. Because of what my religion symbolizes, I'm under constant scrutiny from every so-called *patriot* in this country." Her expression grew dour. "As a result, my liberties–and my life–have been taken away from me."

Sadness touched Calvin's eyes as he recalled the Sikhs ordeal at Dodger Stadium several days ago. "It's easy to become bitter when your culture is placed under a microscope," he stated. "Believe me, I should know. But you need to look beyond the judgment of a few narrow minded individuals and try to change the thinking of society as a whole."

"That's easier said than done, boss," Kevin groused. "Just how does one change feelings of animosity to amity?"

"Complete harmony will never be achieved, regardless of how hard you try. There will always be ignorant fools in every society that won't be swayed by any amount of compassion or diplomacy. Fortunately, most of the folks I've known will make the effort to reach out and reconcile any differences between them." He extended his arm and grasped Kati's hand to assert his point. "Kati never would have become my wife if she didn't choose to disregard our differences and take the next step forward in our relationship."

She looked at Calvin and smiled. "It's a choice I've never regretted, despite all the hardships we've been through."

"Hardships are a given in *any* relationship," Kevin said, "let alone one constrained by racial, religious, or cultural differences. Ameenah and I learned long ago to build on our differences, rather than let them be a wedge between us."

"If we are blessed today," Ameenah reflected. "Some may learn in a single day at the festival what has taken us a lifetime to understand."

Kati nodded. "It's never too late to realize our differences are less than we make them out to be."

Kevin gave his wife an affectionate squeeze. "See honey–there may be hope for us yet."

Calvin's mouth turned upward in a smile as he steered the van towards the exit ramp to Liberty Plaza. *Four down—another seven billion to go.*

110

on Burgess swung his BMW Seven Series into the left lane of the San Diego freeway and zipped past a lumbering cargo truck. "If the traffic keeps up like this, Andrew, we should be at the festival in no time. Hopefully, the local pols won't take up too much of Jennings time so we can–*Hey!* Did you hear a word I said?"

Andrew stared listlessly at the blur of pastel colored buildings and palm trees passing by his window. Ever since his meeting with the stranger on the beach this morning, his feelings of apprehensiveness had returned.

Ron nudged his shoulder. "Something wrong, Andrew?"

He blinked. "Huh?"

"Is something bothering you? You look out of it."

A frown touched Andrew's face as another Spanish-styled community zipped past the Bimmer's window in womb like silence. "Do you think we can control our destiny?" he blurted out.

Ron's eyebrow rose. "What?"

"Do you think we have the power to change our fate? Or has every detail of our lives already been predetermined until we die?"

"Like in . . . predestination?" Ron exhaled loudly. "I'm not sure if I can answer that."

"It's a simple question."

"It's *not* a simple question," Ron declared. "Predestination is a concept that philosophers and scholars have debated over since religion began. To believe we have the choice of free will would be a renouncement of your faith–an admission that your God is not truly omnipotent."

"Forget the theological implications for a minute. What do *you* think?"

"Personally, I'm a great believer of free will. I refuse to put my fate in the hands of an entity who has not rationally been proven to exist."

"Then you don't believe in religion at all?" Andrew asked.

"I'm more a . . . spiritualist," Ron replied. "There are things in this world that have no rational explanation, but the idea of an omniscient being controlling our lives doesn't really appeal to me." He paused. "I respect those who make faith a part of their lives, but I can't embrace the obligations that come with organized religion."

"So you do believe we can change our destiny?"

Ron nodded. "Maybe not as easily as editing a movie, but we have the capacity to choose–and through that power–ultimately set the course of our lives." A look of concern tinged his face. "Why the sudden interest in your future? Did a black cat cross your path today?"

Not a cat, Andrew reflected. *Someone, or . . . some thing.* "No, nothing like that," he muttered. "Just doing a little–thinking."

"A *little* thinking?" Ron said, chuckling. "Do me a favor, let me know when you find the answer."

Andrew shifted anxiously in his seat and watched the city race past his window. *I don't know if I want to find . . . the answer.*

111

Mark finished editing the video camera footage on his computer, and then burned the contents to a disk. He hoped his message would inspire the citizenry to change the course of our nation.

Somehow, he reflected, *John F. Kennedy knew it would come to this. He predicted that 'Those who make peaceful revolution impossible will make violent revolution inevitable.'*

Once the transfer of data was complete, Mark placed the disk and a handwritten manifesto in a packet addressed to the FBI's Los Angeles field office.

A spasm furrowed his brow. *Wait! Why should I make it easy for them?* He pulled the disk and manifesto from the mailer and placed them on top of his laptop. *That's better. Even the fumbling Feds should be able to find it here.*

And they would find it—eventually. The Department of Homeland Security would use every resource at their disposal to root out the perpetrator of the heinous act. The digicam footage from Liberty Plaza would be enhanced frame by frame until the images became nothing more than a mosaic of brightly colored pixels. The remains of the UltraTrac 5000 would be microscopically scoured and traced to a sale at a medical supply store. Once the purchaser's identity was revealed through his credit card transaction, the Feds would link his address within seconds.

But in the end, Mark mused, *all the government's vaunted resources will be put to shame by a local cop called to check on my disappearance by one of my nosy neighbors.*

He shook his head and chuckled. After years of serving in the military, he was keenly aware that Homeland Security suffered from the same inefficiencies that all bureaucracies do; their ability to work together as a cohesive unit only existed on a departmental organizational chart.

Gathering his crutches from beside the desk, Mark hobbled into the garage to admire his handiwork one last time. To the average eye, it was a routine conveyance designed to transport a handicapped individual to their destination. Few could suspect under its humble skin lay the potential for widespread destruction.

He ran his hand along the cold tubular frame and frowned. *Something's missing.*

Moving his gaze across the garage, his eyes rested on the perfect complement for his modern day Trojan Horse. He limped over to his workbench and pulled a small American flag off the shelf. The red, white, and blue symbol of freedom was respectfully unfurled and secured to the back of the wheelchair.

Mark looked the wheelchair over and pinched his lip. *It's still needs–something.*

He combed the garage once more, hoping for the hand of divinity to guide his vision. As if in answer to his wish, a finger of light streamed through the grimy garage window and settled on a small purple figurine in the utility room.

Mark hobbled across the garage and snatched his childhood friend from the shelf. *Perfect.*

Pulling a roll of duct tape off the workbench, Mark fastened the aptly named Shockwave to the wheelchair's joystick. When the propitious moment arrived in Liberty Plaza, the figurine would disintegrate into a million fragments as it transformed for the final time.

A horn's blare suddenly startled Mark from his reverie. He glanced at his watch. *It's the shuttle for Liberty Plaza. It's here to pick me up.*

He sat down in the wheelchair and took one last look around the garage. *It's not too late. You can still turn back . . .*

The horn honked again, insistent.

Mark snugged his Delta Force beret over his head and opened the door to the garage. He slipped on his sunglasses and focused his gaze forward as the bright afternoon sun swept through the darkened room.

The shuttle driver leaned once more on the horn; a clarion cry to battle.

A grin tugged a corner of Mark's face as he powered the wheelchair down the driveway towards his destiny.

Showtime.

112

ifteen miles away from Mark's date with destiny, Karen grappled with her own debut in the heart of Liberty Plaza. " . . . and in approximately two hours," she said to the eye of the camera, "President Jennings is scheduled to address the nation. Meanwhile, let's check in with Celena Reyes for an update on today's entertainment at the European pavilion. Celena?"

The light on the camera winked off, and Karen slumped back in her seat with a sigh. "How do you make this look so easy, Martin? My tongue feels like it's going to trip over every other word that pops out of my mouth."

"Is that how it looks to you?" He chuckled. "To tell you the truth, I'm scared shitless every time I sit out here."

Karen's eyebrow quivered. "Come on—with *your* experience?"

"Experience can actually be a detriment in this profession. After years of repeating the same tired drivel to your viewers, you reach a point where you no longer . . . care."

"Has that happened with you?"

He shrugged.

"When did you lose your . . . passion?"

"When today's news began to sound suspiciously like *yesterday's* news." He turned and looked out across the plaza. "In some ways, I envy you, Karen. Your youth and lack of seasoning give you the power to communicate the news in a refreshing manner." His expression grew dour. "Unlike an old dinosaur like me."

She blinked.

"Don't look so surprised, Karen. I've known for years how I'm viewed at the station. The only reason I'm allowed to stay on is because I can still bring the Boomers' discretionary income to our greedy advertisers' pockets." He gave a short, bitter laugh. "It's *always* about the money, isn't it?"

"Don't sell yourself short, Martin. You still have a few good years left ahead of you."

He shook his head and frowned. "I don't think so. My contract comes up for renewal in a few months, and I've heard nada from the station." His eyes dropped. "Maybe it's time for this . . . dinosaur . . . to move on."

"Retirement?"

He pinched his lip and nodded. "There's a kind of *finality* to that word–don't you think?

She forced a smile. "You've still got a lot to look forward to."

"Perhaps," he muttered. "I suppose the missus and me might finally get out and see the world, but we're no longer . . . close." A look of sadness washed over his face. "I'm not sure if I *can* retire. But someday . . . the choice will be made for me."

The set manager waved his arm. "You're on in ten, Karen."

Karen's face clouded as she watched the clock countdown to airtime. *Will I eventually share Martin's fate?* she wondered. *Will I become just another embittered broadcaster doubting the integrity of my career?*

Staring into the dark eye of the lens to address her audience, the future she envisioned for herself began to slip inexorably away.

113

itting in the rear of a Metro bus bound for the Festival, José examined his CARD and frowned. "You know, Eduardo," he said. "There's something strange going on here."

Eduardo cocked his head. "Strange? What do you mean, amigo?"

"Yesterday, the Cipher said the documents I received from the coyote weren't worth the paper they were printed on."

"Wouldn't have fooled a blind man he claimed."

"Then why did the policia allow me to remain in this country after they checked out my papers?"

"That *is* strange," he replied. "Did you bribe anyone, amigo?"

José shook his head. "A young Latina officer looked over my papers and let me go."

"She did?" He rubbed his chin. "Maybe she . . . pitied you, José."

"No, I do not think so. But as she looked over my papers, something passed between us, a . . . a *connection* of some kind."

Eduardo shrugged. "There are many things in this world that can't be explained. Just count your blessings and move on." He paused. "Are you still planning to leave for Stockton tomorrow?"

José nodded. "My cousin said the poultry factory near his home is looking for help." He gave a wry smile. "Gutting chickens."

Eduardo pulled a business card from his wallet and handed it to José. "If the job in Stockton doesn't work out, you might be able to find work here."

José glanced at the card and handed it back towards Eduardo. "Thanks, but my cousin said there–"

Eduardo held up his hand. "Keep it, my friend. You may find a use for it someday."

José slipped the card into his pocket and looked out through the soot-smeared window at the city. A week ago, he rode a Border Patrol bus back to his homeland steeped in despair. Now, for the first time since his journey began, he was buoyed with hope.

114

Kevin stopped under the shadow of the Asian Pavilion's giant red pagodas and hooked a thumb over his shoulder. "Hey boss, would you mind if Ameenah and I took some time to explore the festival on our own?"

Calvin looked at his wife. "I don't mind. Kati?"

"Not at all. When do you want to get together again?"

Kevin shrugged. "How 'bout we meet up by the entrance after Jennings finishes his speech?"

"Sounds like a plan," Calvin said. "Have a good time–*exploring*."

A look of puzzlement tinged Kati's face as the Turner's melted into the crowd. "Do you think it was something we said?"

Calvin glanced suspiciously at his kids. "Maybe it's better if we didn't know." He wrapped his arms his family and smiled. "All right– what do you want to do next?"

Toni pointed to a small blue and gold booth tucked behind the spires of the North American Pavilion. "How about that place over there?" she asked.

Calvin looked in the direction she was pointing. A fat, greasy haired huckster regaled the crowds under a bright red sign that said MILK BOTTLE TOSS - $5.00 A THROW. He looked over at Kati and grinned. "What do you think, hon?"

She studied the barker and frowned. "Are you kidding?"

Calvin nuzzled her cheek. "Let's check it out. It'll be . . . *fun.*"

Kati sighed. "Come on, kids. Your Dad wants to relive his childhood again."

As they strolled up to the modest sized booth, Calvin noticed his wife's quip was not far off the mark. The bright colored bunting, shelves of kitschy prizes, and baseballs on the countertop made him feel like a ten-year boy again. In a world of interactive videos and online games, the carnival attractions of his youth had all but disappeared.

The huckster gave Calvin the once over and sneered. "Think ya got what it takes, Mac?"

Calvin drew up next to the counter and surveyed the pitching arena. Six metal bottles were stacked atop a gold painted barrel roughly thirty feet away. *Hmmm . . . when I pitched for my Cal State team, I used to throw over twice that distance to the plate.* A grin tugged at his face. *This will be like taking candy from a baby.*

The barker leaned across the counter until he was inches from Calvin's face. His breath reeked of alcohol. "What's the matter, Mac? Chickenin' out?"

Calvin hefted a baseball from the countertop and tossed it in the air. He had heard the carnies had weighted the balls to give the advantage to the house. *Nothing wrong here,* he thought. *It appears to be your standard issue baseball.* He met the hawker's gaze. "House rules?"

A smug smile played across the carnie's face. "It's easy, Mac. Knock down all the bottles, you wins yourself a prize." He rocked back on his heels and smirked. "So whaddaya say, Mac? Think you're *man* enough to try it?"

Calvin ignored the pitchman's sarcasm and looked at his daughter. "See anything you like, Toni?"

She looked over the barker's tawdry goods and pointed towards a small pink item perched on the middle shelf. "That."

"What is . . . that?" Calvin asked, puzzled.

"It's GirlTalk." She shook her head and giggled. "Like, where have you been, Dad?"

Calvin handed a twenty to the hawker and picked up the first ball. "All right, Toni," he declared. "If GirlTalk is what you want–then GirlTalk is what you'll have."

As he began his windup, Calvin's thoughts drifted back to his Cal State pitching career. In those days, his prowess led his team to two division championships, and if not for a season ending injury, a crack at a major league career. His fingers caressed the baseball's stitching, and he could almost hear the crowd cheering him on again. *Like taking candy from a baby . . .*

The first ball soared through the air and missed its intended target by three feet. It slammed into the backstop with a sickening thump.

The pitchman snorted. "Nice *throw*, Mac."

Calvin glared at the barker but remained silent. He plucked the second ball off the counter and studied the stack of bottles thirty feet away. *You just need to shake off the rust, Cal. Your next pitch will–*

"Come on, Dad!" James squealed. "Knock 'em down!"

Calvin turned and tousled James' hair. "Don't worry, son. When I pitched for my Cal State team, I could have knocked these bottles over in my sleep."

Toni looked at her father and rolled her eyes. "Is this going to be another one of your *stories?*"

Calvin frowned. "Ask your mother if you don't believe me."

"As I recall," Kati said dryly, "your father had problems getting past first base."

The hawker rapped his cane on the countertop. "Come on, Mac. I haven't got all day."

Calvin turned his attention back to his target. *Thirty feet, Calvin.*

Child's play . . .

The second ball hurtled through the air and grazed the top bottle on the stack. It wobbled briefly–defying gravity–and then tumbled to the ground.

Calvin pumped his fist in the air, believing the magic from his youth had returned.

The huckster shook his head and snickered. "You haveta knock *all* the bottles down–Mac."

Unruffled, Calvin snatched another ball from the counter while the pitchman replaced the bottle on the stack. "I'm just getting warmed up, kids," he assured. "This time those bottles are going *down!*"

Toni looked up at her father, hope brimming in her eyes. "You can do it–Dad."

Her support gave him the confidence he needed. He focused on the bottles, pitching once more in the game of his life. *It's the bottom of the ninth, full count, and one last pitch separates me from victory . . .*

The third ball whistled through the air; a fast moving sphere of matter and energy. The Taylor family watched anxiously as the ivory colored blur hurtled towards its target.

The ball pierced the heart of the pyramid, and Calvin watched proudly as the six bottles clattered to the ground. He turned towards the barker and grinned. "How 'bout that–*Mac?*"

The pitchman gave Calvin his prize and he placed it in Toni's hands. "Here's your reward, princess," he said softly. "Thanks for believing in me."

Toni wrapped her arms around him and smiled. "I've *always* believed in you, Dad."

It was the first sign of affection he had seen from his daughter in weeks. She had won a popular child's toy that day, but for him, the prize was infinitely more gratifying.

He had won . . . her heart.

115

A look of disgust crossed Mark's face as he guided his wheelchair through the throngs of Liberty Plaza. *Whoever's in charge of security today ought to be shot. There's no way any of my men would have passed someone through the gates with nothing more than a token glance at their driver's license.*

Several minutes later, the stage where Jenning's was scheduled to speak came into Mark's view. The large turnout he had anticipated had yet to materialize, giving him the opportunity for a ringside seat directly in front of the podium.

His mouth turned upward in a grin. *Well, there's a lucky break. I guess Jennings' popularity has slid even more than I thought.*

Nudging the joystick forward, he moved in a beeline towards the stage when a tall, dark haired police officer suddenly veered into his path.

Mark slowed the wheelchair and looked the policeman over. *Is he on to me?* He wrapped his finger around the detonator button and watched anxiously as the officer towered over him several feet away.

Ryan looked at Mark and flashed a smile. "Good afternoon, sir. How are you doing today?"

Mark inched his hand from the detonator button. *Good, he suspects nothing.* "Fine, officer," he replied amiably. "Is anything wrong?"

"Not at all, sir. I'm just conducting random security checks through-out the plaza." He held up his security wand and grinned. "Do you mind? It will only take a minute or so."

Remember your training, Mark thought to himself. *Don't do anything to arouse his suspicions.* He removed his sunglasses and held his arms out. "Go ahead, officer. Do your duty."

"I wish everyone felt the same as you, sir. You wouldn't believe some of the–"

Mark held up his hand. "No need to preach to the choir, officer. Or maybe you haven't *noticed* what I'm wearing today."

Ryan glanced at his beret. "Hard *not* to notice. Rangers?"

"Close–Delta Force." He shot Ryan a lopsided grin. "You've seen some military action too, if I'm not mistaken."

"I did a stint with the Marines a while back, but it was nothing compared to what you've probably experienced." He laughed softly. "I bet you have some stories to tell."

"I'd tell you," Mark quipped, "but then I'd have to kill you."

"And you probably know over a hundred ways to do it," Ryan replied, chuckling. "Look–you've got better things to do than listen to me ramble on all day. I'll get this over with as quickly as possible so you can be on your way." He looked the wheelchair over and frowned. "Since you're . . . uhh . . . physically challenged–"

Mark barked out a laugh. "There's no need to use any of that *politically correct* horseshit with me, officer. I'm as sure as the Pope is Catholic that we've heard far worse coming from our commanding officers' mouths."

"You got that right," Ryan affirmed. "My CO could string a line of obscenities so well that he advanced profanity into an art form." He clipped the metal detector to his belt and kneeled next to Mark's wheelchair. "Well, since my wand won't be of much use in this situation,

I'll have to search you the old fashioned way."

Mark stiffened. *Careful now, this one could ruin everything.* "Be my guest. I've got nothing to hide."

Ryan started patting down Mark's arms and worked his way down his body. As his hands moved over his legs, he paused for a moment.

A fleeting smile crossed Mark's face. *Now's my chance to distract him.* "I sense your . . . unease, my friend. Are you wondering how I became—*a cripple?*"

Ryan stopped his search and looked into Mark's eyes. "Was it . . . in the line of duty?"

Mark's expression grew dour. "That's what one might think. But it wasn't a sniper's bullet—or an IED—that cost me the use of my legs. No, the real reason was much more . . . *mundane* than that." The resignation left his face, and was quickly displaced by rage. "Some *bitch*, talking on her cell phone, ran me over in her SUV less than a block from my home." He gave a bitter laugh. "It's hard to believe, isn't it? Sometimes . . . I can hardly believe it myself."

Ryan forced a smile. "There's nothing I can say—or do—that will change things. But we sincerely appreciate the sacrifices you've made to make our nation a safer place."

A tear welled in Mark's eye. "Thank you, officer. That means more to me than you'll ever know."

"It's people like you who should be up on stage today," Ryan said. "You're the *real* heroes of our country." He rose to his feet and placed his hand on Mark's shoulder. "Well, everything checks out, soldier. Enjoy the rest of your day."

Mark gave him a cursory salute. "You never know when it might be your last."

Sadness touched Mark's face as he wheeled away from Ryan and headed towards the stage. *I wish I didn't have to distract him with that pathetic little story. He seemed a decent sort of guy—and in another time, in another place—we might have traded war stories over a beer or two.*

Mark maneuvered the UltraTrac 5000 in front of the stage and bowed his head. When the final curtain came crashing down, he hoped the officer was away from the blast zone.

116

I n a sequestered area behind the stage, Andrew looked over the horde of VIPs swarming around the President and shook his head. "Doesn't the Mayor ever come up for air?" he groused. "She's been kissing Jennings' ass for half an hour now."

Ron shrugged. "You know how these politicians are. They'll brown nose anyone with a pulse to further their careers."

"Well, I hope she shuts her yap soon. Jennings is scheduled to speak less than an hour from now."

"Scheduled to speak and actually speaking are two different things, Andrew. When you're the President of the United States, everyone's schedule pretty much revolves around you."

Andrew exhaled loudly. "At the rate he's sucking up to the pols, that means we'll be here all friggin' day."

Ron placed a hand on Andrew's shoulder. "Take it easy, man," he said gently. "I'm sure Jennings will spend as much time–"

A voice boomed over Ron's shoulder. "Is this a private tête-à-tête, or can anyone join in?"

Ron turned and clapped Jennings on the shoulder. "*Uncle Cameron*– it's good to see you again." He shot him a sideways grin. "Dad sends you his regards."

Jennings chuckled. "How is the old SOB doing these days?"

"Same as always–still fighting for the rights of the oppressed everywhere. I don't think he ever forgave you for leaving the firm to seek out a political career."

"I'm still fighting for the little guy, Ronny. The only difference now is I want to be paid for doing it. Doing pro bono work might enrich your life, but frankly, it can never make you rich." He looked over at Andrew and smiled. "Who's your guest, Ron? Someone willing to contribute generously to my next election campaign, I hope?"

Ron clutched Andrew's arm. "This is Andrew Landis. He's the producer of the movie I'm currently working on."

"A pleasure to meet you, Mister Landis," Jennings said, extending his hand. "So how did my nephew persuade you into hiring him for your project? Did he hold a gun to your head?"

Andrew shook his hand and grinned. "Nothing so crass as that, Mister President. He was simply . . . the best man for the job."

Jennings smirked. On his beady-eyed, porcine face, it looked more like an expression of evil. "Mmmm . . . if you say so." He pulled a cigar from his pocket and lighted it. "I hear you're quite a mover and shaker in this town, Mister Landis. But, for a man of your wealth and power, I've never seen you at any of the usual shindigs in town. Are you affiliated with any political group?"

"When it comes to politics, Mister President, I'm usually stuck out in center field."

Jennings barked out a laugh. "Spoken like a true politician. But one does not achieve success by straddling both sides of the fence. I'm sure you've grabbed a few balls now and then when you wanted to get things done."

"I can vouch for that," Ron said dryly.

"You can't move forward by standing still, I always say," Andrew stated. "I didn't get where I am today by playing by the rules."

"I agree," Jennings said. "I'm a damn the torpedoes, full speed ahead kinda guy myself. Contrary to what the Bible says, the meek shall not inherit the earth."

"The meek will only inherit the world's *problems*." Andrew declared. "Only the strong-willed and courageous among us will ever truly survive."

Jennings blew a stream of smoke towards the sky and grinned roguishly. "We're a lot alike, Mister Landis. We share similar goals . . . and ideals. Let's get together after the festival, and see how we might benefit each other in the future."

"I'm generally not a man of consensus, Mister President," Andrew said wryly. "But for *you*, I'll make an exception."

117

José stood near the fountains at the center of plaza and spun slowly around to take in the grandeur of the festival. Nearly a quarter square mile in diameter, Liberty Plaza was a lushly landscaped circular park surrounded by twelve silver skinned high rises east of downtown Los Angeles. To mark its public debut for the Pangaea Festival, seven internationally themed pavilions were interspersed through the plaza, each representing a continent of the Earth. And along the plaza's stone walkway perimeter, 192 giant flags rippled in tribute to the world's countries.

Eduardo moved his gaze across the crowd and whistled. "Wow!" he exclaimed. "Impressive, isn't it, amigo?"

José nodded. "I've never seen anything like it. The Americanos sure know how to throw a party."

"All this excitement is making me hungry. Feel like getting something to eat?"

"Just point the way, padre."

They ordered some burritos, sopes, and two glasses of aguas frescas from a nearby taqueria and sat at a small metal table to enjoy their meal.

Eduardo sunk his teeth into the burrito and smacked his lips.

"Mmmm, not bad. What do you think, José?"

José dug into his sope and sponged the excess salsa from his chin. "Bueno," he affirmed. "But, something seems to be—missing."

"What's that, amigo?"

"It just doesn't taste like . . . home." Sadness washed across José's face. "Do you ever miss it?"

Eduardo put down his burrito and wiped his lips. "Sometimes." He turned and swept his arm across the plaza. "But this is my home now."

"It's not the same."

"I know," Eduardo replied. "But in the land I once called home, there was no way to make a *living*." He took a bite from his burrito and looked out on the Plaza. "Besides, it's not so much different here. There are lots of places you can go and still feel like you're in Mexico."

José shook his head and frowned. "I do not think so, my friend. Our culture may have moved here, but what we call *home* has been lost in the transition."

"I do not understand, José."

"We're not wanted here, Eduardo. Home is where your neighbor accepts you without judgment or prejudice."

He shrugged. "I am here now. And here's where I'll make my life."

"But you're not welcome here, regardless of how hard you try to fit in," José stated. "Does that not matter to you?"

Eduardo's face tightened. "I have lost my family, José. What could *matter* after that?"

118

Two hours into her broadcast from Liberty Plaza, Karen watched Martin deliver the commentary with his usual aplomb. Despite his confession earlier, she saw no sign that he had lost one iota of passion for his profession. *He's either lying to himself,* she reflected. *Or he's one of the most consummate actors I've ever seen. Will I have even half his fervor when I enter the twilight of my career?*

With a sigh, Karen rose from the desk and looked for solace among the throngs attending today's festival. She searched for one particular individual in the crowd, hoping his warm embrace and confident manner could dispel the doubts she had about her future. *Where are you, Ryan?* she wondered. *I could use someone to protect me right about now.*

The mere thought of Ryan's brawny arms entwined around her body made her pulse quicken. *I wonder how he'd look as a modern day superhero,* she mused. *Clad in a skintight costume that emphasized all his–masculine–features.* A smile played across her face. *I bet he'd be a real man of steel once the costume came off . . .*

The set manager nudged her arm. "Mind letting me in on the joke, Karen?"

Her eyes fluttered. "Huh?"

"What's so funny? You had this cute little smile on your face."

She felt the heat rise in her cheeks. "Ummm . . . some things are better kept to oneself."

"Jennings' handlers have given us the word that he's about to make his speech," he said. "Get ready to make the announcement once we return from break."

Karen returned to the anchor desk and slid into her seat. "Martin, I just got word that our fearless leader is ready to give his speech."

"Jennings?" Martin snorted. "He couldn't lead the Pope in a prayer session."

"You too?" she quipped. "Doesn't anyone support him?"

"He must have gotten *someone's* vote," Martin grumbled, "or he wouldn't be living it large at 1600 Pennsylvania Avenue."

"Maybe the taxpayers should charge him rent since he was elected by the smallest plurality in history."

"It's a sad day when our leader isn't elected by most of the people in this country." He shook his head and frowned. "We can do better than that."

"Unfortunately, with our country divided as it is, no candidate can address today's issues and still receive a lion's share of the vote. One person's panacea will certainly be another's poison."

"You mean they still do that?" Martin asked.

Karen shot him a puzzled look. "Do what?"

"Address the issues. I thought our elected officials didn't give a rat's ass about anyone but themselves."

"Hasn't it always been that way?" Karen asked. "Since the first Continental Congress took office?"

"No, it wasn't always that way," he declared. "You're too young to remember, but this country used to be governed by people who actually *cared.* Even though partisan bickering still ruled the day, America progressed steadily and became the most admired nation on Earth."

"Ahhh, the good old days. Why did things–change?"

"I don't know," Martin muttered. "Greed and incompetence have always been endemic within our government, but an arrogance has crept into our leaders that I find disturbing. Their reckless attitude and deceit would never have been tolerated by the voters just a few generations ago."

Karen gave a disgusted look. "What's the hell's wrong with us, anyway? How much longer are we going to let our country go to shit?"

"Your guess is as good as mine. But, if someone doesn't step up and change things soon, we may never find our way back."

The set manager waved his arm. "You're on in ten, Karen."

"It's time for Jennings to give his speech," Karen said. "For better or worse, he's all we've got right now."

Martin took a breath and exhaled. "May heaven help us all."

Karen looked towards the camera and summoned up her thousand-watt smile. "This is Karen Mitchell, continuing our coverage of the Pangaea Festival from Liberty Plaza. Please join us as Cameron Jennings–the President of the United States–delivers a message of hope to our nation."

119

President Jennings strode confidently across the stage, greeted by a mixture of polite applause and derisive jeers from the audience. With his current approval ratings dropping like a rock, the Pangaea Festival gave him a desperately needed opportunity to bolster his souring reputation with America.

Leaning stiffly against the podium, Jennings looked out across the crowd and smiled broadly. "My fellow Americans, today we are riding on a wave of discovery—a journey begun over two centuries ago in the City of Brotherly Love . . ."

Directly below the podium, Mark smirked as he listened to Jennings words of inspiration. To his combat trained senses, the President appeared exhausted; his delivery, stale. Moving his gaze across the spectators in the crowd, the bored expressions and vicious stares confirmed his suspicions that the President's message was failing to connect with its intended target.

Mark settled back in his seat and yawned. *Looks like it's going to be a long afternoon,* he mused. *A lot longer than anyone ever imagined.*

• • •

Twenty feet behind the podium in an area reserved for the local VIPs, Andrew squirmed uncomfortably in his seat. He could ignore the call to nature no longer.

He looked anxiously offstage for a portable latrine and frowned. *The promoters of this event must have some kind of facility close by,* he fretted. *Surely they didn't expect Jennings to take a shit with the riffraff.*

He tried to ignore the pressure in his bladder, but was soon forced to rise from his seat. Threading his way past a row of dignitaries, he squeaked out his apologies and scurried hastily offstage.

No sooner had he moved off the stage than a pair of Secret Service agents bounded into his path. "May we help you, sir?" one of the agents asked.

Andrew looked the men over and suppressed a smile. Their dour expressions, cheap sunglasses and poorly tailored suits gave credence to every bad stereotype he had seen on the silver screen. "Is there a latrine around here?" he asked politely.

The agents stared intently in his direction but remained silent.

Andrew's eyes narrowed. "Come on, guys. I'm *desperate.*"

One of the men nodded curtly to his left. "Through that door, sir."

Barging through the door, Andrew scowled when a latrine failed to materialize before his eyes. *What the—is this their idea of a joke?*

Before he took another step, two more agents swarmed into his path. The taller of the two stepped towards Andrew and smiled. "Is something wrong, sir?"

Andrew's bladder was about to burst. *"Where's the freakin' can?"*

The agent gestured towards a doorway to his right. "Through that door, sir."

Sprinting through the doorway, Andrew found three olive-colored Porta-Potty's standing in a row. He let out a chuckle when he noticed the largest latrine had the Presidential seal emblazoned across the door. *I guess rank still has its privileges,* he mused.

• • •

Ryan snapped the metal detector into his duty belt and smiled at the bespectacled matron. "Everything checks out, ma'am," he said amiably. "Enjoy the Festival."

Patricia surged through the crowd and drew up by Ryan's side. "How's it going so far?"

"Just your usual miscreants and malcontents," he quipped. "What about you?"

"All quiet on the Western front." She pinched her lip. "So far."

Ryan nodded. "Let's hope it stays that way." *Maybe her premonition will turn out to be nothing more than just a bad dream.* He turned towards the stage and listened to Jennings jawbone for several seconds. "Mmmm . . . judging from the expression on everyone's faces today, Jennings has lost his credibility with the crowd."

"What do you expect?" she replied. "The working class and minorities aren't exactly Jennings' base. The only reason he bothered to show up was to lift his lousy approval ratings out of the toilet."

"If the crowd's reaction is any indication of his success, maybe he should start looking for another speechwriter."

"In case you haven't noticed," Patricia said, "his spiel is the usual tired tribute to truth, justice, and the American way. He's dusted off that speech so many times Lincoln must be spinning in his grave."

"You know, maybe that's what we need right now," Ryan ventured.

Patricia's eyebrow twitched. "What?"

"Maybe that's what this country needs right now—another Lincoln." He watched Jennings leer at the audience and shook his head. "Abe would be outraged that the republic he fought to save is being destroyed by a bunch of self-serving clowns."

"You got that right," she said. "Is it too late for us to change things?"

"It's *never* too late. When the citizens of this country demand more from their leaders, they'll get off their ass and do something about it."

Patricia pumped her fist in the air and smiled. "Viva la revolucion."

. . .

Jostling their way through the jam-packed crowd, Eduardo and José secured a spot near the stage to listen to Jennings' speech.

José craned his neck over the mob and frowned. "Do you know what's he's saying, Eduardo?"

"My English is not so good, José," he replied. "But I will try." He cocked his head towards the stage and listened. "The same empty words . . . the same empty promises . . . assuring us a better future." He snorted. "We've heard the same lies come from our own Presidenté's mouth, José. The only difference here is the language has changed."

"That's not true," José stated. "One *can* dream of a better life here."

"Perhaps . . ." Eduardo muttered. "If your *dreams* don't cost you—your life."

"And what would you rather have, Eduardo? A country where we are welcome, but unable to make a living—or a country that allows us to work, but treats us as criminals?"

"You already know the answer to that, or you wouldn't be here. Sometimes José, you have to make a choice, and sometimes . . . the choice is made for you."

José looked up sharply. "Do you think you made the right choice in coming here, Eduardo?"

His eyes dropped. "I thought so. But now . . . I am not so sure."

. . .

Eighty feet from the stage, Calvin watched with feigned interest as Jennings delivered his message to the crowd. *What does Kati see in this loser, anyway?*

Though they disagreed about little in their marriage, when it came to politics, they sat on opposite sides of the fence. His wife had conservative leanings, while he was a dyed in the wool liberal. After ten years of marriage they agreed to disagree, but certain issues occasionally got the tempers roiling between them.

President Jennings and his administration's policies had turned up the heat between them more than once. Kati felt Jennings was one of the best Presidents of modern times while he generally took an opposing view of his exploits. During today's event, he resolved to keep his opinions to himself to preserve peace within the family.

While Jennings droned on with his speech, Calvin took some time to study the crowd. To his eyes, the spectators appeared bored if not borderline hostile to the rhetoric spewing from the stage. As his eyes drifted over their faces, he wished he could reach inside their minds and make their thoughts his own.

What is the little old lady in the green paisley dress gleaning from Jennings' speech? he wondered. *Is she worried about her shrinking Social Security benefits or the lack of affordable health care in her life? And what about the young man dressed in blue jeans and a Metallica t-shirt? Is he concerned about losing his job or whether his standard of living will ever rise again? And what about the man in the wheelchair near the front of the stage? What exactly is he thinking?*

Calvin looked out across the sea of faces and compressed his lips. *Billions of people—each with their own unique destiny—all inextricably linked in this game we call humanity.*

He turned his gaze towards his children. They had no concept of Jennings' agenda, and yet the policies of his administration would impact their lives for many years to come. *Will we leave our children with a better world—or will they be burdened with debt and despair? If our past is any testament to their future, their lives will be a mixed blessing at best.*

James tugged on his pantleg and grinned. A spot of vanilla ice cream smeared his cocoa-tinted face.

"What is it, son?" Calvin asked.

"I can't see, Dad."

It's only fitting that he see his future, Calvin mused. He hoisted James on top of his shoulders and smiled. "There you go, champ. The best seat in the house!"

• • •

Glancing at the clock on her laptop's screen, Karen counted the seconds until airtime and sighed. *Just two more hours and the opening festivities of the Pangaea Festival will draw to a close.*

The remainder of today's duties would be limited to celebrity interviews and the ubiquitous commercial breaks. In a hundred and twenty short minutes from now, her national newscast debut would come to an enjoyable but rather unremarkable end.

And would the career she had hoped for come to an end as well? Martin's pending retirement made clear her goal of becoming a network anchor was becoming irrelevant in the digital age. The news anchors and reporters of today would soon be replaced by the citizen watchdogs and pundits of tomorrow as information spread across the globe in an era of open communications. In just a few short years, *she* would become the dinosaur.

But where can I go from here? she wondered. One thing was certain; she needed affirmation that her education and insight would lead to some greater purpose. Years of honing her craft would be meaningless if the world could not benefit in some way.

A shiver suddenly shot through her spine. *That's it! I need to be a voice for the people; a beacon of light for the citizens of our nation. Martin fears our country has lost its way and needs someone to step up the plate to encourage change. Maybe it's time I leave my corporate sponsored career behind and fight to save our nation.*

The idea sounded farfetched—a random thought that would be considered ludicrous an hour from now. But in her heart, she would never be satisfied until the world was left a better place than how she found it.

Unlike Martin, she had not lost hope for her country.

Yet.

120

gnoring the derogatory signs hoisted by detractors in the audience, Jennings plowed on with his speech. "We must never forget the selfless dedication of those who defend us from the enemies of freedom . . ."

Directly below the podium, Mark sneered at Jenning's hollow declarations. "*You're* the one who's forgotten, you hypocritical bastard. *You're* the one who's sold us out us in our time of need."

Jennings looked out across the audience and smiled. "For only when we stand together and embrace the needs of our citizens, will America fulfill its destiny as the greatest nation the world has ever known."

A smattering of applause erupted from the audience. Jennings smirked briefly and focused his attention on a man sitting in a wheelchair several feet away. "A nation founded on brotherhood, nurtured by freedom and opportunity, and dedicated to the principle that defines us as . . . Americans."

Mark's eyes blazed with contempt as he met the President's gaze. "American?" he snarled. "You don't know the *meaning* of the word." He gave a short, derisive laugh and squeezed the button to the detonator.

• • •

The shockwave from the explosion reverberated through the plaza, shattering windows in the nearby glass towers and sending a roiling orange fireball into the air. As the UltraTrac 5000 disintegrated in a blinding flash of light, a hail of hardened nails mowed through the crowd, shredding those closest to the explosion into hamburger.

Scant seconds later, the underground gas mains ruptured in a paroxysm of fury, rocking the high-rises and sending several of the pavilions up in flames. Thousands began a dash for the exits, trampling the injured and infirm in the mad rush for survival.

In just a few short moments, a celebration praising the virtues of humanity had suddenly become a journey into Hell.

• • •

The shockwave slammed Andrew to the stage as he stepped from the latrine, momentarily stunning him. "Ahhh . . ." he groaned. "Where am I?"

Shaking the cobwebs from his head, he looked up at the sky and frowned. The aluminum framework spanning the stage had sheared away from one of the towers and tilted ominously over his head. Cables swung from the structure like an angry nest of snakes, spitting a shower of sparks across the stage.

He saw dark clouds of smoke billowing across the stage and tried to struggle to his feet. "What the–" he hissed. "Why can't I get up?"

Turning to his left, he found his arm pinned under one of the portable latrines. He tried wrenching it free when a second wave of explosions shook the plaza.

A look of anxiety washed over his face. *What the hell's going on? Are we under attack?*

The aluminum framework over his head shuddered briefly, then plunged several more feet towards the stage.

His face slackened. *Shit! I've got to get out of here. Now!* He yanked on his arm and flinched as pain shot through his shoulder. "It's no use," he groused. *"I'm stuck!"*

Twisting his head around, Andrew tried to survey his surroundings. The spectacle unfolding from his vantage point was unnerving: flames licked the edge of the stage, screams echoed from the plaza and a thick, acrid pall hung in the air like death.

He took a deep breath and stretched out against the stage, almost thankful he could not see the horrors transpiring just beyond his view.

• • •

Karen jerked back to consciousness in a topsy-turvy world. The desk she sat at moments earlier was splintered and singed, and the platform beneath her feet was tilted upward at a frightening angle. *What happened?* she wondered. *I was picking up a sheet of paper I dropped on the floor when . . .*

She rubbed the back of her head and moaned. *Man–talk about your mother of all headaches . . .*

Looking around in the murky light, Karen tried to get her bearings. An acidic stench filled the air, and clouds of thick, black smoke swirling up from the plaza burned her eyes. She peered into the inky void and saw that Martin, and the rest of the crew, had simply vanished.

Her brow furrowed. *Where'd everyone go?*

Using the desk for support, Karen tried to prop herself upright when a sharp pain lanced through her side. She looked down at her blouse and saw a streak of scarlet staining her side.

"Shit!" she hissed. *"I'm wounded!"*

Curling up against the battered desk, Karen listened fearfully as cries of anguish echoed throughout the plaza. Her world was now a darker place and she was very much alone.

• • •

The moment the blast sundered the air, Ryan plunged to the ground to avoid injury. His military training proved correct as shrapnel whizzed overhead like an angry swarm of bees.

He lay on the ground and waited, anticipating another attack.

Moments later, a second wave of explosions rumbled through the plaza, sending several of the high rises and the pavilions into flames.

Rolling on his side, Ryan scanned the plaza for the source of the attack. His eyes widened as he focused on the stage. *Jennings–and the VIPs–gone!* He looked to the right of the stage for Karen and the KNBS platform, but thick clouds of smoke obscured the west side of the plaza.

For the moment, checking on Karen's welfare would have to wait. As the ranking officer in this section of the plaza, it was his responsibility to mobilize the other officers in the area.

Ryan slammed his hand down on his shoulder mike. "This is Rysinski–Squadron Four. All available officers assemble at the entrance to the North American pavilion." He released the transmitter button on his microphone and got nothing but static. Switching channels, he tried again with the same results.

Scrambling to his feet, he searched the area for Patricia. He found her sprawled fifty feet away, a pool of blood spreading from her head. For a brief, heart-wrenching moment, he found himself reliving Joanne's death again.

"Please, God," he muttered as he rushed to her side. "Please don't let it happen again."

He turned Patricia over and gasped. A piece of shrapnel had carved a path of destruction across her face. Reacting instinctively, he ripped the sleeve off his shirt and thrust it against the wound.

Less than a minute later, blood began seeping through the makeshift bandage. *It's no good,* Ryan thought glumly. *She needs to get to a hospital. Stat.*

He tapped his mike again. Bupkis. *What's the snafu with the radio?* he groused. *The department invested millions in a new communications network and I can't get shit.*

Moving his gaze across the plaza, Ryan looked for a safe haven to take Patricia while he waited for backup. He didn't want to leave her behind, but others in the plaza needed his assistance even more critically than she did. It was imperative to bring order to the situation before any more people perished.

In the shadow of the North American pavilion, Ryan spotted a lone vendor defending his food stand with a baseball bat. He scooped Patricia off the pavement and scurried towards the relative safety of the red, white and blue colored kiosk.

The vendor watched Ryan scamper towards him and breathed a sigh of relief. "Man, am I glad to see you, officer. It's fuckin' crazy out–"

"I've no time for chit chat," Ryan growled. "Have you got a place where I can set her down?"

The foxy-faced man hooked a thumb over his shoulder. "There's a table in the back. She'll be safe there."

Barging into the back of the food stand, Ryan laid Patricia down on a stainless steel table in a cramped storage room. "Do you have any medical supplies around here?" he asked gruffly.

The vendor pointed to the wall. "Just what's in that first aid kit over there."

Ryan pawed through the contents and frowned. "Anything else?"

The man shook his head.

Ryan scanned the interior for something to staunch Patricia's bleeding. *Canned goods, condiments, paper supplies–Wait! That might work.*

He pulled several terrycloth towels off a shelf and held them against his partner's face. The hemorrhaging appeared to have diminished, but she still looked much too pale for comfort. His jaw clenched as the image of Joanne's blood streaked face filled his thoughts again. *I can't–I won't–let it happen again.*

Ryan unclipped Patricia's shoulder microphone and slapped it into the shopkeeper's hand. "Take this," he instructed. "Call out that an officer is down. Before you know it, half the cops in L.A. will be beating a path to your door."

The merchant took the microphone and smiled. "I'll keep an eye out for her, officer."

Ryan grasped his arm. "Thanks," he said softly. "She means a lot to me." He turned and raced out of the room towards the plaza.

It was time to earn his pay.

• • •

Several minutes after the second wave of explosions tore through the plaza, José massaged the back of his neck and struggled to his feet. "Ohhh . . ." he moaned. "My head feels like it's been kicked by a burro."

Clouds of viscous, burning smoke swirled across the plaza grounds, making him cough violently. When the fumes began to dissipate, he shook his head with disbelief at the tragedy before his eyes.

"Mierda," he muttered. "Nothing but death as far as the eye can see." His expression saddened as he looked over the mangled bodies and smoking debris that littered the plaza. "Who would do such a thing?"

Looking around, he found Eduardo trapped beneath the mutilated carcass of an obese woman several feet away. He rushed over and kneeled next to his friend, a look of concern on his face. "Eduardo," he cried over the roar of the fires. "Can you hear me?"

When his friend failed to respond, José pushed the butchered woman off his body and dragged him to the edge the plaza. He propped him against one of the flagpoles and watched uneasily as his head listed limply against his body.

José studied Eduardo's face and frowned. *He's hurt worse than I thought.* He rose to his feet and looked out across the smoke filled plaza, hoping against hope that help would soon be on its way.

And that's when he noticed the dark red stain leading towards Eduardo's body.

• • •

Calvin let out a groan as he rolled over onto his back. "Man, what the hell happened?" he grumbled. "One second, I'm listening to Jennings rant about our future–and the next . . . I wake up with the worst freakin' headache in my life."

Smoke savaged his nostrils and he instantly wrenched awake. He sat upright and blinked, trying to make sense of the grim tableau that unfolded before his eyes. *This is no dream, Calvin . . . what you're seeing is all too horribly real.*

His eyes suddenly grew huge. *Kati!* He glanced behind him, and seeing his wife's limp body sprawled against the cold, unfeeling concrete slammed him back to reality. Adrenaline surged through his body as he crawled the few short steps to her side. *Please, Lord,* he fretted. *Please let her be all right . . .*

He lifted her shoulders off the pavement and cradled her in his arms. "Kati, it's Calvin," he shouted. "Are you all right?"

She lay in his arms, unmoving.

"Kati," he urged. "Wake up."

Her eyelids fluttered. "Mmmm . . . where am I?"

Calvin forced a smile. "You're going to be all right. We'll get–"

She saw the fear in his eyes and jolted alert. "What's wrong, Cal?"

His face tightened. "I . . . don't know. An explosion of some kind."

She shook free from his grasp and looked out across the plaza. "*Oh, my God!*" she cried. "This can't be happening!" Panic swept across her face. "Where are the *kids*, Calvin?"

His mouth slackened. *How could I have forgotten the kids?* He whipped his head around, dreading the worst. "There's Toni!" he yelled, pointing to his left. "And over there–James!"

"I'll check on Toni," Kati said. "See if James is all right."

He rushed towards James lifeless body and flinched. A large spike bulged out from his skull, directly above his right eye.

"How is he?" Kati asked.

Calvin examined James' face and bit his lip. "He's hurt. But I don't know how–"

James coughed ferociously, spraying Calvin's face with blood.

Kati's eyes widened in horror. "He's bleeding, Cal!" she screeched. *"Do something!"*

Calvin wiped the blood from his face and frowned. *I'm no doctor– what the hell can I do?* He looked over his son's motionless body and weighed his options. *Seek medical help. And pray, Calvin–don't forget to pray.* He lifted James off the ground and tried to bite back tears. *I've never noticed how small he is before–how . . . frail. For the first time, I'm keenly aware of his vulnerability, and how I failed to protect him when he needed me most.*

Calvin turned and watched Kati coax Toni to her feet. They stood uneasily for a moment in the smoke filled plaza, looking to him for hope in a suddenly chaotic world.

He knew no mere words could undo the evil that occurred that day. The safe, sensible life they had known had changed forever.

Meeting their gaze, he mustered up a smile to console them. "Stay together," he said gently. "And no matter what happens–just remember I love you."

121

ndrew slammed his arm against the stage and howled in frustration. He was pinned like some oversized insect on an entomologist's mounting board. *And if I don't get free from here soon,* he thought anxiously, *I'll be just as dead.*

Just beyond his view, Liberty Plaza erupted in a cacophony of sound. Cries of anguish pierced the roar of the fires and the intermittent blast of windows shattering from the heat. On the periphery of his hearing, the continual wail of sirens teased him with the possibility of rescue.

Andrew closed his eyes, trying to block out a world beyond reason. *This is probably nothing more than some form of mass hysteria. If I relax and concentrate, I'll find myself back in my seat listening to Jennings—*

Seconds later, reality came crashing hard as one of the giant video screens slammed into the stage and wracked every bone in his body. A high pitched shriek pierced the air, and the framework over his head sheared away from one of the support towers and plunged towards the stage.

Andrew tried scrambling out of the way of the falling structure, but his body was stuck to the stage like a fly on flypaper. The framework plummeted several more feet, and then stopped its descent as if Fate stuck out her hand to stop it.

Andrew took a deep breath and exhaled. *Shit! That was too damn close.* He raised his head and screamed, hoping that someone in the plaza would hear his plea for help. But his cries were lost in the tumult, and he soon slumped against the stage in resignation. "Ahhh . . . what's the use?" he muttered. "Even if someone could hear me over the noise coming from the plaza, they've probably got enough problems of their own before they'll come to rescue me."

A few moments later, the stage began to rumble, and he heard something large crash behind his head. Several deep vibrations resonated through the air, as though the strings from a giant bass were being plucked one by one.

Once again, the framework over his head slid downward and Andrew twisted his body in an attempt to save his life. And then, the structure came to an abrupt halt a mere six feet over his head.

Andrew clenched his teeth and hissed. *Are you playing some kind of fucking game with me, God?*

The structure now spanned Andrew's entire field of view, and he took the time to carefully scrutinize every inch of its surface. The charred metal struts that formed the skeletal structure; the ragged cables that weaved through the framework like arteries; the tattered patriotic bunting that festooned the surface like skin—inanimate materials that bore no malice or feeling, yet were fully capable of changing his life forever.

As he committed the structure to memory, his mind worked feverishly for a way out. He quickly crossed each possibility off his list, until all that remained was one last, desperate gamble.

There was enough space between the struts of the structure for him to safely fit, but only if he timed its descent to the precise second. Any miscalculation, any wrong move, and he would be squashed like the proverbial bug. He blinked the sweat from his eyes and steeled himself for what was to become the most important decision of his life. *You only got one shot at this, Andrew, so you better not fuck it up.*

He tuned out the mayhem and horror erupting through the plaza and concentrated on the structure overhead. He sensitized his body to every tremor in the stage, readying himself to move the instant the structure fell earthward.

Suddenly, the framework moaned loudly–as if its very soul were being wrenched from its body. The stage spasmed, and the aluminum structure twisted against the soot-clogged sky. Then, with a loud shriek that made Andrew wince, the structure sheared free from the last of its moorings and began plummeting towards the stage.

This is it, Andrew thought anxiously. He twisted his body leftward, eyes widening as the structure fell quicker than he anticipated. *It's moving too fast,* he fretted. *No time to–*

The structure crashed onto the stage, crushing Andrew just above the waist. Pain shot through his body like a lightning bolt, and he arched his body upward and screamed. As waves of agony seared upward through his spine, he breathed in short measured bursts in an effort to maintain consciousness. Excruciating seconds ticked into tortuous minutes, and soon the distant roar from the fire lulled him into a state of semiconsciousness. As he slipped in and out of his dreamlike trance, the prophecy augured from the stranger on the beach stirred disturbingly in his mind.

"The best laid plans of mice and men," Andrew rasped, "often go awry."

He chuckled, amused by the irony of his situation. *The stranger tried to warn me about hubris, but I was too absorbed with my own trifling ambitions to listen. Now all that I've strived for . . . everything I've fought to accomplish . . . will be snatched away from me by the remorseless hand of Fate.*

He looked up through the gloom and focused on a beam of sunlight piercing the sky, its golden glow beckoning him towards salvation.

The glimmering light caressed his face, and Andrew dreamed of white sandy beaches kissed by warm azure seas. He felt the pain leave his body and stretched out serenely against the stage. *Perhaps now*, he mused, *I will find . . . the answer.*

He closed his eyes and let the light wash over him. A few moments later, there was only–darkness.

122

Ryan sprang from the foodstand and found himself cast in a scene out of chaos. Fires raged through the lower floors of the high rises along the west side of Plaza's perimeter, and the Asian and South American pavilions were fully engulfed in flames. Hundreds of people raced haphazardly towards the exits, trampling the injured underfoot in their dash towards safety.

Rushing into the surging crowd, Ryan held up his arms in an attempt to restore order, but pandemonium ruled the day. He looked at the frenzied hordes hurtling past him and shook his head in frustration. *It's no use,* he groused. *It's like trying to hold back a tsunami with a sieve.*

A hundred feet from his location, Ryan spotted a heavily armed SWAT team jostling through the crowd towards the stage. He decided to abandon his post and tag behind the group so he could learn of Karen's fate.

The closer he drew towards the stage, the less likely he deemed her odds of survival. Shredded bodies and severed limbs lay in scattered heaps across the blood soaked ground. At the center of the scarlet tinted mass, a geyser of flames from a ruptured gas main soared thirty feet into the sky like Satan's little campfire from Hell.

Ryan looked up through the smoky gloom at the remains of the KNBS broadcast platform. Most of the struts coupling the platform to the tower had buckled, causing it to slope at a severe angle. The battered anchor desk teetered perilously off the edge of the platform, ready to plummet earthward at any moment.

Moving closer to the tower to get a better look, he found several fractured bodies beneath the platform, but Karen was nowhere to be found. A quick reconnoiter of the area proved fruitless as well.

Ryan looked around the Plaza and scowled. *She can't be dead,* he seethed. *She can't!*

Gripped by an uncontrollable rage, he screamed her name skyward, hoping against hope that she would hear him one last time.

123

José probed the cause of Eduardo's bleeding and felt something sharp prick his finger. He pulled away quickly and flinched when he saw his blood soaked hand. *Eduardo's hurt*, he thought anxiously. *Bad.*

He lifted the back of Eduardo's scarlet stained shirt and gasped. A piece of shrapnel protruded from his back just above his shoulder blade. He studied the seeping wound for several moments and shook his head. *There's nothing I can do for him here. He needs to see a médico as soon—*

Eduardo's voice jolted him from his concerns. "José," he said hoarsely. "What happened?"

José looked into Eduardo's eyes, trying to keep the anxiety from his face. "Something exploded near the stage," he said calmly. "Many people died."

Eduardo nodded wearily. "We must leave. The policia will be here soon." He tried rising to his feet, but fell back to the ground when a sharp pain lanced through his body.

José placed his hand on his shoulder. "You must rest, Eduardo. Help will be here soon."

"No time for that. We must . . . leave." He tried to stand again and groaned.

"Rest," José pleaded.

Eduardo slumped against the flagpole and nodded. "Si," he muttered. "Must . . . rest."

José looked his friend over and pinched his lip. *If he doesn't get help soon, he'll–*

Eduardo's head snapped back, as if struck.

José grabbed his hand. "What's wrong, padre?"

Eduardo's teeth clenched. "*Pain,*" he hissed. "Hurt . . . bad . . ."

José tightened the grip on his hand. "You'll be fine, amigo," he said, forcing a smile. "All you need is . . . a little rest." He paused. "Why don't we check out that company on the business card you gave me and see if I they have a job?"

"Then you have changed your mind about leaving?"

José shot him a lopsided grin. "Gutting chickens never really appealed to me."

Eduardo smiled weakly. "Bueno. Tomorrow we'll talk to the–" A spasm suddenly wracked his body.

José clasped his Eduardo's hand. "Hang in there, Eduardo. Help will be here soon."

A look of serenity passed over Eduardo's face. "I think you're going to have to make that interview on your own, amigo."

Tears welled in José's eyes. "No. We'll go *together,* Eduardo."

A smile traced Eduardo's face, as if recalling a pleasant memory from his past. "I'm not going anywhere," he muttered. "But home . . . to my family."

José began to sob as Eduardo's grip slackened in his hand. *Why, God?* he asked angrily. He looked up at the smoke streaked sky and scowled. *Why did you let me–live?*

There was no reply but the angry howl from the fires sweeping across the plaza. No answer in a land José had chosen to adopt, but could never truly call his home.

124

Karen's voice was faint against the roar of the fire. "Ryan?" she cried. "Is that you?"

Ryan cocked his head skyward. "Karen?" He swept his gaze around the plaza and frowned. "It can't be her," he muttered. "I must be imagining things . . ."

"Ryan?" she repeated.

He looked up towards the platform, eyes widening. *"You're alive!"* He took a deep breath and exhaled, almost unable to believe his fortune. "Are you hurt?"

She glanced at the spreading crimson bloom on her blouse and bit her lip. "Not too bad."

He moved towards the tower. "Wait there," he ordered. "I'll come up and get you."

She nodded and slumped against the anchor desk. *My hero.*

Ryan ran to the rear of the tower and frowned. The lower half of the stairwell had been sheared away in the blast, leaving the closest step twenty-five feet above his head. He grasped the closest strut and began the arduous climb up the tower.

A short time later, he reached the platform and found Karen clinging anxiously to the side of the desk. "Are you the party that ordered the large pepperoni pizza?" he asked drolly.

She shot him an angry glare. "Are you going to get me down from here or what?"

Ryan grinned. "Piece of cake." He lay down on his belly and slid out across the platform.

The platform shuddered ominously.

Karen's eyes grew huge. "What's happening?"

Ryan inched back towards the tower and bit his lip. "The platform can't support my weight without collapsing. I'll have to find another way to get you down."

"Didn't you bring a rope with you?"

He snorted. "Do I look like the *Lone Ranger* to you?" He bent down and studied the bracing under the platform. "I've got an idea."

"What's that?" Karen asked.

"I'm going to climb above the platform and hang down from one of the struts on the tower. When I reach out, grab my hand and I'll pull you to safety."

Her eyebrow rose. "Any other ideas?"

"Yeah, you could jump."

She peered nervously at the ground and winced. "On second thought, your plan sounds pretty good after all."

"I thought so," Ryan said, smiling.

He climbed up the tower and hung upside down from one of the struts. Karen braced her legs against the desk and reached out towards Ryan's hand. Twelve inches separated their outstretched fingers.

"Damn," Ryan carped. "So close."

"What about plan B?" Karen asked.

"I don't *have* a plan B."

The platform creaked loudly.

Karen trembled. "You know, I'm game for *anything* right now. Plan C, D, E—you name it."

"I've got another idea," he ventured. "But you're not gonna like it."

"*Try me.*"

He looked over the deck and gnawed his lip. "We're only going to get one shot at this . . ."

The platform groaned and began to tilt upward.

"*Ryan!*" she snapped. "We're running out of time here."

"On the count of three, I want you to shove off from the desk and grab my hand. We're not much more than a foot apart, but we gotta get it right on the first try. The platform will probably collapse once the weight shifts."

Karen met his gaze. "Is this going to be another one of your *pieces of cake?*"

A grin tugged at his face. "I think this time we're talkin' the whole friggin' bakery."

She gaped at Ryan's outstretched arm and swallowed. *Twelve inches. Might as well be twelve miles.*

"Well?" Ryan asked, impatience tinging his voice.

"I'm *thinking.*"

A loud crack shot through the air as a brace snapped. The platform shook violently and began to break away from the tower.

Ryan stretched out his hand. "*Move!*" he hissed. "One–two–"

Karen pushed away from the desk as the platform vanished beneath her feet. "*Ryan!*" she screamed.

Ryan reached out and snagged her wrist in midair. "*Gotcha!*" A sharp pain lanced through his shoulder. "But I can't hold on to you for long. Try to hook your leg around one of the struts on the tower."

Karen kicked her leg outward. Her side screamed in protest, and her foot fell short of its intended goal.

Ryan gritted his teeth. "Try it again."

Karen shot her leg out, trying to ignore the pain. Her foot caught the bottom of the strut and slid off. "I can't do it," she whined. "It's too high."

"You *can* do it," he urged. "I know you can."

She looked up sharply. "What do you really know about me?"

"I know you're not a quitter."

Karen pinched her cheek. *Damn, I hate when he's right . . .*

Tuning out the pain in her side, she focused on her goal and kicked upward. Her leg wrapped around the strut and she gave a triumphant shout. "I did it!"

Ryan felt the pain leave his shoulder and exhaled. *About time.*

Karen managed to wrap both legs around the strut and hung upside down until Ryan plucked her to safety. He braced her against the side of the tower and stroked her face gently with his hand. "I thought I'd lost you forever," he said softly.

She laid a gentle kiss on his lips and smiled. "Not a chance. Someone's got to keep you in line."

He looked down at her blood-streaked blouse and frowned. "You're bleeding."

She shrugged. "It's . . . nothing."

Ryan pulled her arm away and saw the spike protruding from her blouse. "You need medical help. Pronto." He looked over the edge of tower and studied the distance to the ground. "Think you can make it?"

She peered through the framework and nodded. "Piece of cake."

With Ryan's help, they reached the base of the tower several minutes later. Karen found Martin's battered body near the remains of the splintered platform and bit back tears.

"He didn't deserve this," she muttered.

Ryan looked out at the mangled corpses littering the plaza and grunted. "None of them did."

"It's strange, but just a few hours ago Martin was worried about his future. He wasn't quite ready to retire, but knew he would be forced into it someday."

"Maybe he looked ahead and didn't like what he saw. For Martin—maybe this was the way it was supposed to end."

Karen turned away from Martin and surveyed the carnage. "Oh, shit! It's even worse than I thought." She looked at the smoldering section of stage where the podium once stood and gasped. "Jennings?"

Ryan shook his head.

Her face slackened. "*Jesus!* What happens now?"

"The usual horseshit," Ryan groused. "And after all the finger-pointing is said and done, maybe we'll stop it from happening again." A scowl slashed across his face. "*Maybe.*" He wrapped his arm around Karen's shoulder and led her towards a line of rescue vehicles gathered at the edge of the plaza. "Come on, let's get you checked out. It looks like I'm gonna be pretty damn busy for a while."

125

As he herded his family towards the exit, Calvin's face swelled with disgust as he watched the last pretenses of civility crumble before his eyes. On his left, two men battled with an EMS worker over who would be treated first for their injuries. To his right, a petite woman clawed at a woman twice her size so she could put her child on the next available ambulance. Directly ahead, a Muslim family fought with several police officers to leave the plaza. In every direction, in every expression, courtesy and compassion were abandoned in the name of survival.

Calvin's jaw clenched as the calamity stretched the crowd's resolve to the breaking point. *They should have anticipated something like this happening today. Now, because of their poor planning and lax security, hundreds of people will die.* He looked down at James lifeless body and scowled. *But, I'll be damned if my son is going to be one of them.*

Barreling his way through the crowd, Calvin made his way towards a harried group of physicians and EMT workers assisting the crowd. He stood in line and watched anxiously as a middle-aged doctor sutured a gash on an obese woman's arm. *Come on, let's get moving,* he fretted. *Every second you take could cost James his life.*

The doctor finished dressing the woman's wound and motioned

Calvin forward. Tall and bespectacled, his warm brown eyes projected an air of confidence. "What seems to be the problem, sir?" he asked amiably.

"It's my son," Calvin replied. "He's got a piece of shrapnel stuck in his head."

The doctor pointed towards a gurney to his right. "Lay your son down and I'll take a look at him." He leaned over James and examined the spike embedded in his skull. "Is this the extent of his injuries?"

"He's been coughing up blood, too," Kati said, concern etched on her face.

The doctor's brow furrowed. He snapped a stethoscope to his ears and listened to James' chest.

"How is he?" Calvin asked softly.

The doctor met Calvin's eyes. "Without more tests, I–"

"Will he *live*, doctor?"

"I . . . I don't know. His head wound appears superficial, but he may have sustained internal injuries from the blast." His face tightened. "I'd say he has an even chance to make it."

Calvin's shoulders slumped. *An even chance.* He looked at Kati and choked back a sob. "He'll be all right, honey. I *know* he will."

The doctor put his hand on Calvin's shoulder. "I'll put your son on the next available ambulance," he said. "Does anyone else in your family require my attention?"

Calvin shook his head. "My wife and I received a few bumps and bruises, but nothing I'd call serious."

The doctor glanced at Toni. "And your daughter?"

"She was knocked out for a while," Kati replied, "but seems to be fine now."

The doctor smiled. "Why not let me be the judge of that?" He kneeled down and looked Toni in the eye. "Hello, young lady. How are you today?"

She shrugged. "Okay . . . I guess."

He pulled out a scope and examined her eyes. "Any blurriness in your vision?"

"No," she said meekly.

"Dizziness?"

She shook her head.

"How about the rest of your body? Does anything hurt?"

She hesitantly extended her arm.

The doctor moved her arm up and down. "Does this hurt?"

She winced. "A little."

He twisted her arm to the right. "How 'bout this?"

She yelped.

The doctor released her arm and stood.

"Is it serious?" Kati asked.

"A simple sprain," the physician said, smiling. "She'll be fine in a day or two."

Two paramedics rushed over to the gurney and began to wheel it towards a nearby ambulance.

The doctor shot Calvin a crooked grin. "Looks like your ride is here." He reached out and clasped Calvin's arm. "God bless."

Calvin started to thank him, but the doctor had moved on to the next patient.

The EMTs lifted James into the ambulance and attached an array of sensors to his body. Calvin started to climb through the rear door, but one of the techs stopped him with his hand. "Only authorized personnel are allowed to ride in this vehicle, sir. You can see your son at Pacific Crest hospital."

"But we need to be with him," Calvin asserted.

He met Calvin's eyes. "I'm sorry, sir."

"Isn't there any way . . ." Kati pleaded.

The tech exhaled loudly. "I'll probably lose my job over this . . ."

"I'll make sure you get a commendation," Calvin said.

"Okay, but there's only room for one of you. We're stretched thin enough as it is."

Calvin stroked his wife's cheek. "Go."

"Are you sure?"

He nodded. "Get going–every second counts."

She clambered into the ambulance. "Don't worry honey, everything will turn out fine." The paramedic reached past her to close the door. "See if you can find the Turners. I'll meet you at the hospital."

Calvin waved. "I love you."

She returned his wave and smiled. "I love you, too." The doors snapped closed with a sense of finality, and the ambulance rumbled away from the smoke choked plaza.

A tear trickled down Calvin's cheek as he watched the vehicle vanish into the murky gloom. *Please don't take him Lord, he still has a lot to give.* He reached down and grasped Toni's hand. "Come on, princess. Let's head back to the entrance and see if the Turners are there."

He turned and looked back on Liberty Plaza one last time. Sadness tinged his eyes as flames licked at the giant flags surrounding the plaza. But there was only one flag that held any meaning for him. Its fifty stars and thirteen stripes gave hope to the oppressed and offered opportunity to those who wished to realize their dreams. And though its leaders occasionally lost their way, Old Glory symbolized that freedom would never die.

Toni squeezed his hand. "I hope he's all right."

Calvin snapped out of his reverie. "What, hon?"

"James. I hope he's all right."

His eyebrow rose. "But all you two do is fight."

"James can be a real butthead sometimes. But he's still *my* little brother."

A smile traced Calvin's face. In her own roundabout way, Toni was trying to say she loved him.

We'd all be better off if we took a lesson from her playbook. It's time we resolved our differences and learned to live together as one. If a child is willing to take that first step, there's no reason why we adults can't follow.

He recalled a verse from the Bible that brought him comfort during the lonely years of his own tortured childhood. A collection of words written many generations ago, but all the more relevant in a world teetering on the edge of destruction.

> *The wolf also shall dwell with the lamb,*
> *and the leopard shall lie down with the kid;*
> *and the calf and the young lion and the fatling together;*
> *and a little child shall lead them.*

He looked down at his daughter and smiled. *It will all come to pass someday. All we need to do is . . . try.*

About the Author

An unconventional thinker and political enthusiast, Michael Wheary has lived in nearly every region of America, from the snow swept vistas of Alaska to the sun kissed beaches of Florida.

Through his travels across the nation over the past five decades, he has met people from all walks of life that served as the inspiration for this book.

He envisaged this novel because serious sociopolitical issues threaten this nation and it's time people put aside their differences and forge the society intended by our founders.

Currently residing in Florida, Michael works as a freelance artist and writer while continuing his quest for . . . the answer.